NEW GUINEA

ru
s.C.
lsche

Solomon Islands

ENDEAVOUR STRAITS

TORRES STRAITS

Louisiade Is.

Route of Dutch Vessel. England via Capetown

New Hebrides

LAND

A)

New Caledonia

Route of Escape from Botany Bay

Botany Bay

Route of the Convict Ship from England

Van Diemen's Land (TASMANIA)

d

7918

7918

K

FIC
NOR
BOT

FIC
NOR
BOT

Nordhoff & Hall

Botany Bay

Dec 5	4236	Apr 3	7574
Dec 12	1980	Apr 21	323+
	Wickman	May 6	Sidney

This book may be kept

FOURTEEN DAYS

A fine will be charged for each day the book is kept overtime.

BOTANY BAY

By
CHARLES NORDHOFF
and
JAMES NORMAN HALL

AN ATLANTIC MONTHLY PRESS
BOOK

BOSTON
LITTLE, BROWN AND COMPANY
1941

Published November 1941
Reprinted November 1941 (twice)

7918

ATLANTIC—LITTLE, BROWN BOOKS
ARE PUBLISHED BY
LITTLE, BROWN AND COMPANY
IN ASSOCIATION WITH
THE ATLANTIC MONTHLY PRESS

PRINTED IN THE UNITED STATES OF AMERICA

Dedication

GEORGE MACKANESS, ESQ., M.A., LITT.D., JAMES
COUTTS SCHOLAR, UNIVERSITY OF SYDNEY, RE-
SEARCH SCHOLAR, UNIVERSITY OF MELBOURNE,
SYDNEY, AUSTRALIA.

DEAR DR. MACKANESS: —

Permit us to dedicate this book to you as a small
acknowledgment of the pleasure and profit we have
derived from your researches in the field of early
Australian history.

As you will see, our story is what might be called
a romance of the First Fleet, in which, for dramatic
effect, we have been obliged to take certain liberties
in the matter of dates, incidents, and the like; but
our purpose throughout has been to keep close to
fact with respect to First Fleet events.

We hope that you may find some entertainment
in following this furrow over an almost untilled field
in the realm of historical fiction.

Sincerely yours,

J. N. H.   C. N.

SAUSALITO, CALIFORNIA,
April 22nd, 1941

CONTENTS

I	Tom Oakley	3
II	At Garth's Farm	19
III	Newgate Prison	34
IV	Transportation for Life	50
V	Mortimer Thynne	59
VI	Phoebe and Doris	73
VII	The First Fleet	88
VIII	Aboard the *Charlotte*	102
IX	Botany Bay	122
X	The Felon Pioneers	136
XI	Sentenced to Pinchgut	149
XII	Goodwin's Homecoming	166
XIII	The Upper Hawkesbury	186
XIV	Sally	200
XV	The Second Fleet	212
XVI	Garth's Vengeance	228
XVII	The Riot at the Guardhouse	239
XVIII	The American Brig	254
XIX	Escape	271
XX	A Thousand Leagues	282
XXI	The Parting at Snapeness	296

CONTENTS

XXII	At Tower Hill Gardens	311
XXIII	"To Be Hung on Monday"	327
XXIV	The Hanging Chapel	340
XXV	Newgate Street	358
	Epilogue	367

BOTANY BAY

I

TOM OAKLEY

IT has been a glorious day of Australian spring, without a cloud in the sky; the air cool enough to be bracing, yet warm enough in the afternoon to permit taking my ease, here in the shade of my favourite tree. The long, narrow lagoon is just below me, where I can watch the black swan and other water-fowl moving about the wind-flawed surface, and Arthur's cattle approaching in groups to quench their thirst, or to stand knee-deep in the cool water they seem reluctant to quit. The sun is halfway down; toward the west, the green, gently rolling downs stretch away as far as the eye can reach.

For many miles in that direction the land is my son's. His house stands on a knoll overlooking the still water and timbered bottom land. It is a dwelling of the pioneer sort, such as my ancestors erected two hundred years ago in Maryland. Rude the house is, but solid and comfortable, with flower beds in front and a fine kitchen garden at the back which my daughter-in-law has laid out with her own hands. Smoke is rising from the chimney, for she and Sally are busy at their baking. The corn stands tall and green in the fenced field below the house. This red soil, blessed in normal years with an abundant rainfall, grows wheat as bountifully as the best land on the Potomac, and when left untilled to produce its native grasses it will support three hundred and fifty sheep to the square mile. With limitless tracts of such land, the future of New South Wales seems bright indeed, yet only forty-three years since there was not a white man on the Australian Continent.

I can recollect, as though it had happened yesterday, how the convicts were disembarked in Sydney Cove, and how a village of tents sprang up on both shores of the little bay. Sydney is a thriving town in these days, with busy streets, shops and warehouses of stone, and a forest of masts along the waterfront. It is strange to reflect that I was one of the first boatload of Englishmen to set foot on the shores of the cove. It has been my misfortune, or good fortune perhaps, to live in an era of mighty changes: the war which freed the American Colonies from British rule, the revolution in France, the efforts of Napoleon Bonaparte to make himself master of Europe, and the end of Spain's empire in the New World. Though unimportant by comparison, the greatest event in which I have played a part has been the settlement of New South Wales.

Australia has a character of its own and is beginning to breed a race of men upon whom that character is stamped indelibly. Though first settled by convicts, it is by nature a land of freedom, of bright sunlight and vast plains and mountain ranges. Yet it is a harsh land, where only the strong can thrive. Our vegetation, inured to storm and drought, is the hardiest in the world, and men must share this hardihood. The sons of Australia are wanderers, adventurers, and pioneers.

My own children are widely scattered. One of my younger sons is a sea captain and the other a farmer in Tasmania. My daughter, Sarah, is married to the son of Tom Oakley and lives in Sydney, where her husband is a partner in the prosperous firm of Thynne and Oakley, printers, engravers, and stationers. My oldest boy, Arthur Phillip Tallant, named for the Governor whose memory all Australians revere, lives here at Beaumont Downs, already spoken of as one of the most promising stations in the Colony.

It is strange to contrast the life here with that I knew as a boy, on the Potomac. Like the estates of the American planters, Arthur's home is self-sufficing, though in a simpler and ruder way. Beef and mutton are in abundance, and wild game; bread is baked from corn grown on my son's land. Potatoes, onions, and cabbages flourish on the bottom land; good cheer and hearty appetites make up for what we lack of the more refined table, and polished manners, of Maryland. In place of Negro slaves, my son's farmhands are assigned convicts and a few young men from our local tribe of blackfellows.

Like his men, Arthur spends half of his life in the saddle, mustering his cattle at the proper seasons, and waging warfare on those inveterate fanciers of mutton, the dingoes. He contrives to keep order among his somewhat turbulent men because he is the best of the lot. It is remarkable to see what he has done for some of his assigned convicts: what with firm but humane treatment, hard exercise in the open air, and an abundance of wholesome food, their self-respect, if they have ever possessed that quality, returns to them. Some become fine horsemen, skilled at handling the stock; hearty, jovial fellows, from whose faces the hangdog expression is banished, who look forward to the day when they shall be free to farm, or to breed sheep or cattle for themselves. You must recollect that many of these men have been transported for the most trivial offenses, under the savage laws which are a disgrace to England. Men have been transported to New South Wales — some of them boys of fourteen or fifteen — for stealing a gamecock, two pounds of sugar, or a pair of stockings. To treat such offenders as hardened criminals and to consider them incapable of response to just and humane treatment are crimes in themselves. If I speak for the convicts, and lay claim to some understanding of their thoughts and character, it is because I myself have been one of them.

The tutor Arthur has had assigned to instruct his four young children is a case in point. He is an Irishman and a scholar, a witty, agreeable fellow, whom every member of the family loves. For what offense he was transported I have never inquired, nor do I wish to know. He may have fought a duel and killed his man, or, like so many of his countrymen, have become involved in seditious practices. Yet my grandchildren will live to look back upon their mentor with deep gratitude. It is strange that this scholar should love Beaumont Downs as I do. He knows every bird and beast of the countryside, and the name of every tree and wildflower; when we take the dogs out to hunt kangaroo, no man joins more wholeheartedly in the chase. And Sally and I, in spite of our years, still love to follow the hounds.

More than a month has passed since we drove out from the Hawkesbury, over the remarkable road constructed by Surveyor Evans. We traversed the region which baffled successive exploring parties until 1813, when Blaxland, Lawson, and Wentworth crossed the Nepean River and ascended the Dividing Range. On attaining the summit, they gazed with astonishment and delight at the distant Fish River, and the wide, green Bathurst Plains. They had discovered an Empire.

My son Arthur, then twenty years of age, was of their party and resolved upon the spot to establish himself in this rich pastoral region as soon as it should be opened to settlement. During the eighteen years which have passed since that day, Arthur has proved that the pioneer strain in our blood is far from extinct; he has made for himself, in what was a wilderness, the home he now wishes his mother and me to share.

I have discussed the matter with Sally, my wife, and we shall comply with Arthur's wishes. We have already chosen a site for the small house we shall build, here beneath this great tree, on the high bank overlooking the lagoon. It may seem odd that a man of seventy should be planning a new home, but my back is still straight and I may be good for another twenty years. As for my Sally, she might be forty, instead of sixty-one. The truth is that we are weary of our farm and shall abandon it to an overseer. The country thereabouts is becoming as tame as England; we feel hemmed in by our neighbours and cannot breathe as freely as in these incomparable solitudes.

Sally was reared among the lakes and forests of Canada, and I in tidewater Maryland, yet we love Beaumont Downs as though born and bred here, and hope that men of our name may live on the land for generations to come. With our descendants in mind, wishing that they may know something of their ancestry and of the early history of New South Wales, in which my wife and I played humble parts, I have decided to set down what I can recollect of my life, and of the beginnings of the settlement at Sydney Cove. What I shall write will be of interest to my children, at least, and the ransacking of memory will serve as a pastime for an idle old man. Of the events which led to my transportation to New South Wales, I shall write as briefly as possible.

* * * * *

The founder of our family in America, for whom I was christened, was Hugh Tallant, from Bedfordshire, where the name has long been extinct. In 1639 he crossed the Atlantic to settle in the newly founded colony of Maryland, a vast domain granted to Cecilius Calvert, Lord Baltimore, by King Charles the First. Baltimore's brother, Leonard Calvert, had entered the Potomac River five years before, with two ships, the *Ark* and the *Dove*, — Maryland's First Fleet, — and founded the town of St. Mary's, at the head of an extensive inlet on the north shore of the river, close to where it debouches into Chesapeake Bay.

Some fifteen miles inland from St. Mary's, a second large inlet, or estuary, opens on the north shore. This is Bretton Bay, and on its east side, on a considerable estate which was granted to him, together with manorial rights, our ancestor established himself with his young wife and the bondsmen he had fetched out from England. Here, close to the water's edge, and commanding a fine prospect of the long, wooded peninsula of Beggar's Neck and the shores of St. Clement's Bay beyond, Hugh Tallant erected his first dwelling of logs. Nearly a century later, on the same site, his grandson built the house called Beaumont Manor, where I was born. I was twenty years old, and it was clear at last that England had lost the American War, when our house was sacked and burned to the ground by a mob, some of whose members I had known since childhood. They did their work thoroughly and murdered those of our servants who strove against them.

I have often thought that civil war, for all its cruelty, may have a part to play in the universal design. The men of the losing side, their estates forfeit and their lives in peril, have no choice but to uproot themselves and emigrate to foreign lands, where they may prove vastly useful in trade or manufacturing, as did the Huguenots in England after the revocation of the Edict of Nantes, or become pioneers in the wilderness as did the same Huguenots in Capetown and the Loyalists in Canada.

The American War was a civil conflict as cruel as any in history, making enemies of neighbours and brothers, and on the Potomac, at least, uprooting families who had lived on their estates for nearly a century and a half. Nothing could have been more shortsighted than England's treatment of the Colonies; none of our neighbours was more keenly aware of English injustice than my father, but when it was no longer possible to remain neutral, he took up arms for the King. Both he and my elder brother paid for their loyalty with their lives: they were killed early in the war. When I was seventeen I was received into my father's regiment with the rank of cornet, promoted lieutenant two years later, and severely wounded in one of the last battles of the war. Some time after our house was burned and our estate confiscated, my mother and I were fortunate enough to make our way to one of the English vessels anchored near the mouth of the Potomac, and to reach New York by sea, with Mr. Robert Fleming, an old neighbour, my father's lawyer and closest friend.

New York was already crowded with Loyalists, uprooted folk, bewildered, penniless in many cases, and still mourning their dead. Some planned to sail direct for England, where they would present their claims for compensation from the Crown; others were going to Canada, to settle on the land promised them there. My uncle, whose estate adjoined ours on Bretton Bay, was for Canada, and we decided to accompany him. On Mr. Fleming's advice, we pooled what we could spare from the few hundred pounds remaining to the three families, signed the necessary petitions and powers-of-attorney, and delegated him to go to London to lay our claims before the committee appointed by Parliament. My mother and I asked for ten thousand pounds, less than a quarter of what our estate was worth.

Mr. Fleming was detained in New York until the city was evacuated and General Washington's forces moved in to replace the King's troops. My mother and I, with her brother and his family, had embarked several months earlier for Nova Scotia, where we hoped to establish ourselves. I shall not describe the hardships of our first winter. Though accustomed to a gracious life in the genial climate of the Chesapeake, my mother displayed great cheerfulness and fortitude in the Northern wilderness. In summertime, and even in spring and autumn, Nova Scotia was a pleasant land enough, with abundant game in the woods and trout and salmon swarming in the streams. But the winters were of almost arctic severity, the soil was poor, and the labour of clearing and planting our fields, singlehanded, was more than disheartening. Nevertheless I might be in Nova Scotia to-day had not a letter from Mr. Fleming reached us in the fall of 1784 urging me to come to London as soon as possible.

I still have that old letter — it lies beside me as I write — and it is strange to think that so perishable a reminder of past days should have survived the vicissitudes of nearly half a century: —

New England Coffee House
Threadneedle Street
London, *November* 12*th*, 1784

My dear Mrs. Tallant and Hugh:

You will be eager to learn what I can tell you of our fortunes on this side of the water. I regret to say that they are in no forward state at the moment, and many here are beginning to despair of the Loyalist claims ever being met by His Majesty's Government. I am more hopeful. Parliamentary committees, particularly those concerned with money affairs, work with painful slowness, but I am convinced that England is mindful of us, and that, in the end, this business will be carried through. But every claim is scrutinized and verified by the Committee with minute care and thoroughness, which accounts, in part, for the little action taken thus far. The Tallant claims will, I feel certain, be allowed, and the more readily because they are so modest in comparison with the actual losses you have suffered.

Meanwhile, let me speak of a matter of great importance and promise in connection with the Loyalists. The New England Coffee House, where this letter is being written, has become headquarters for the Loyalists here to press their claims. A few days ago I attended a meeting here, under the auspices of the President of the Royal Society, Sir Joseph Banks. He had with him a Mr. James Matra, who laid before us the heads of a most interesting plan. You may recollect that on one of Captain Cook's voyages, he skirted the eastern coast of New Holland, and dropped anchor in a harbour he named Botany Bay. This was in 1770, and both Sir Joseph and Mr. Matra were with Captain Cook at the time. After giving us some account of the climate, which resembles that of Southern France, and of the country, said to be of immense extent and great promise, Sir Joseph introduced Mr. Matra, as the originator of a plan which might prove of interest to the American Loyalists.

Mr. Matra then explained briefly what he had in mind. There were at present a great number of Americans in England, whose loyalty to the King had cost them everything they had possessed. They deserved well of England; they were of the best English stock, many of them skilled in pastoral and agricultural pursuits, and descended from men and women who had been pioneers in the New World. It would be a great pity if their country could not make use of these folk, at the same time offering them some compensation for what they had lost in the American War. Mr. Matra proposed, therefore, that such of the Loyalists as desired to emigrate might be sent out to Botany Bay at government expense, granted large tracts of land, and provided with food, clothing, implements, and live-stock to tide them over until the new colony should be self-support-ing. The Ministry had been appraised of the plan, and it was understood that it might be considered favourably if enough of the Loyalists would signify their desire to settle in Botany Bay.

When the speaker sat down, Sir Joseph assured us that, if we so desired, he would exert his influence to further the idea. I hasten to write of this matter because I believe that it may offer a splendid opportunity, particularly to young men like Hugh. Botany Bay may prove another Maryland, and its settlers may prosper as our an-cestors did. But Mr. Matra's plan needs the hearty support of all who desire to emigrate, and for this reason I advise Hugh, if money can be found for his passage, to come to London as soon as possible, that he may acquaint himself with the details at first hand, and be prepared to enroll when the time comes.

I scarcely need to say that Mr. Fleming's letter stirred my imagination and set me longing to be off. My mother gave me every encouragement, saying that I should go to England, and that if all turned out as we hoped, she would remain with her brother until I wrote her to join me in Botany Bay. We had settled accounts with my father's agent in London, and the balance he forwarded made us considerably better off than when we had left New York. I parted from my mother with mingled anticipation and regret, but I had her blessing, and funds enough to keep me in England for a year or more.

*   *   *   *   *

Reaching London in the spring of 1785, I took lodgings with Mr. Fleming and was introduced to the Loyalists who met at the New England Coffee House. A few of the claims for compensation had been settled, but so tedious was the process and so long the delay in considering each case that many despaired of the business ever reaching a final settlement. We discussed the Matra plan frequently, read Captain Cook's account of Botany Bay, and learned the little we could of New Holland, or New South Wales, as the eastern half of Australia was then beginning to be called. Sir Joseph Banks, whom I had the honour of meeting on several occasions, was enthusiastic about the proposed colony, and informed us that he hoped the Government would give favourable consideration to the project. We were even asked to submit estimates of what each settler would require, and the tonnage of shipping that would be needed to transport us to Botany Bay, in order that the total expense of our establishment might be made known to the Chancellor of the Exchequer. But our hopes, which had seemed so bright at first, were tarnished by interminable delays. The summer passed, and the autumn; when the new year began, our ten thousand pounds' compensation and my prospects of emigration to Botany Bay seemed as remote as on the day of my arrival in England.

Waiting is the hardest of all tasks for a young man. I lived in a constant state of suspense, watching my small hoard of shillings dwindle at an alarming rate, and hoping from one day to the next that the Government might act on Mr. Matra's proposal, or that our petition for compensation might be granted. Of London, I had long since had enough, for no young man can enjoy life, however rich and varied, as a mere spectator. Mr. Fleming was different; he had visited London many times in the past, and loved his cozy lodgings, the evenings with his cronies at the Coffee House, and the noise and bustle of the streets. As bad luck would have it, I was the one to stop and he to go, for he informed me, early in the summer of the new year, that he was obliged to join one of his nephews in Canada, where he would remain until his compensation had been granted.

Some little time after my old friend's departure, I learned to my great regret and disappointment that Mr. Matra's plan had been set aside. No explanation was given, but we were told that our hopes of emigration to Botany Bay must be abandoned. Had I possessed the means of paying my passage to Nova Scotia at this time, I would have returned at once, but my money was nearly gone, and idle seamen so numerous about the docks that it was impossible to work my passage. So many ships had been paid off at the conclusion of peace, and so many regiments disbanded, that hundreds of seamen and soldiers were begging on the streets.

In comparing England with the various nations of Europe, I had often heard it stated that no industrious Englishman could starve. Nothing could have been further from the truth. The Enclosure Acts, which had begun to depopulate the countryside as far back as the reign of Queen Elizabeth, were now culminating in a state of affairs shocking to every true Englishman. They had made homeless, and driven to London, thousands of men, women, and children of the sturdy country stock which has ever been the backbone of the nation. Most of these unfortunates asked nothing more than the chance to earn an honest livelihood, however hard the work or scanty the wage. Yet for a large proportion the chances of this were slight indeed. It was well known that there were more than twenty thousand homeless in the great city: folk forced to live like animals, or worse, with no shelter from the weather, and no caves or hedgerows into which they might crawl at night. And for each of the homeless there were certainly ten other poor wretches, able to obtain only the miserable daily pittance required for a bed in some crowded and filthy doss house. Begging, theft, robbery, and prostitution would at least lift a man or woman out of the ranks of the homeless, and these occupations were followed by many thousands of London's inhabitants. Of beggars alone, there were more than fifteen thousand at this time, and it was said that they lived better than honest men. If I write with some assurance of London's poor, it is because I have lived and worked among them, been confined with them in gaol, and know them better than any other class of English folk.

There was nothing I could do but seek employment, and attempt to save enough to pay my passage back to Canada. Without influence, it was useless to hope for dignified or well-paid work. There were scores of applicants for every place of this kind, whether in the countinghouses of the City, the East India Company, or in Government employ. I tried my hand at a dozen humble occupations and lost employment time after time because I could not learn to swallow my pride. The poor man who wishes to pick up a living in London must above all be obsequious; the bow, the servile smile, the hat in the hand, the "Yes, my lady," and "Your Honour's too kind" — these are the touchstones which transmute copper pennies into silver sixpences. I held horses, swept crossings, frequented the courtyards of inns in hopes of earning a few coppers as a porter, carried a sedan chair, and worked as a lumper, unloading the cargoes of ships at anchor in the river. In this latter occupation I might have enjoyed a modest prosperity had I been willing to steal, as did my fellow workers, almost without exception, every day of their lives. At last, by a stroke of good luck, I obtained steady work, at a wage which enabled me to save a few shillings a month.

During my first summer in England, Mr. Fleming and I had often visited the Black Swan, in Holborn, whence the York coaches left three times each week. The landlord was a pleasant, jovial fellow, for whom we both felt a hearty liking. One day in the late autumn, when I had pawned every-

thing I could spare and was nearly at my wit's end, I decided
to renew my acquaintance with the man I had known in
better days. He proved a friend indeed, questioning me in a
manner so kindly that I opened my heart to him, and was
soon installed as a night hostler, with a warm bed in the straw
and a bellyful of good food twice each day.

It was here that I met Tom Oakley. He was a horse dealer,
as I supposed, and since, like all Maryland men, I love a fine
horse, we were drawn together by my admiration of his mare,
Rosamond. Oakley came frequently to the Black Swan; when
our acquaintance had ripened into friendship, he often invited me to his room upstairs, to talk of horses and share a
bowl of punch or a bottle of claret. Tom was a strong-made,
smallish man of twenty-five, with a weatherbeaten, ruddy
face and bright blue eyes; he went plainly dressed, in breeches
and a long, square-cut coat, but his waistcoats were of satin
and there was always fine lace at his throat and wrists. I put
him down as the son of a wealthy yeoman farmer, or even of
some squire in a distant county.

I was thinking of Tom as I trudged homeward one wintry
afternoon. It was my custom to inquire at the New England
Coffee House for letters from Nova Scotia. On this occasion
I found a letter from my uncle, informing me that my mother
had fallen ill of a wasting consumption, and was not likely
to live through the winter. He urged me to sail for Nova
Scotia at once, since my mother longed to see me once more
before she died. The news placed me in a cruel position. Ships
bound for Canada were few; the cheapest passage I had been
offered cost thirty pounds, which might as well have been
three hundred, and of working my way there was still not
the slightest hope. Mr. Fleming was gone, and I knew no one
from whom I might borrow more than a few shillings. Tom
Oakley was my only hope. I doubted that I could bring myself to borrow from him, but hoped that he might be at the
Black Swan on my return. The landlord had been so kind to

me that I would as soon have spat in his face as asked him to lend me thirty pounds.

I found the pair of them in the court of the inn. Oakley was showing the landlord a strong sorrel gelding he had fetched from the country. I took Rosamond from one of the other hostlers, rubbed her down well, blanketed her, and walked her for a time before I led her inside. Oakley came into the stall where I was stroking the mare's neck as she munched her oats.

"How fares it, Hugh?" he asked. "Come, dine with me; I've a leash of wild duck and two bottles of the best."

It had been a lonely and depressing day; I was glad to join Oakley in his cozy chamber upstairs. He was in a gay mood and began to entertain me with droll stories of his trading in horseflesh, and the trickery and subterfuge employed by the horse copers of Southern England. Presently he broke off and glanced at me keenly.

"Ye've a face to curdle milk," he said. "What ails ye? Come, out with it!"

"I'm in the dumps," I admitted, with a wry smile; "but naught's so bad it can't be mended."

"True enough, but there's times when a friend comes in handy. Ye're in trouble, that's clear. Make a clean breast of it; two heads are better than one."

His glance was so friendly, and his interest so genuine, that I found myself explaining my sorry situation and the events that had led up to it, while he put in a question now and then. I said nothing of my mother or her illness, but made it clear that my uncle required me in Nova Scotia, and that I had no means of getting there. When I had finished, he sat silent for a time.

"Ye've had a rough hard time of it," said he. "So ye fought for the King in the American War? There's aplenty here in England would say ye chose the wrong side. Where's all the redcoats and jack-tars now? Begging in the streets and sleeping in hedgerows! England's no place for a man of spirit these days. No . . . It's every man for himself, by fair means or foul!"

I nodded, somewhat glumly, for he had done no more than put my own thoughts into words.

"We were small farmers in the North of England," he went on; "my father, and grandfather, and his father before him. Our village and its common lands went back to Norman times. We was poor, but we lacked naught needful, and we was free men, by God! Then Parliament passed another Enclosure Act, and the land we'd ploughed and planted for seven hundred years went into pasture for His Grace's sheep. My father had hopes for me, before we was enclosed. He gave me more schooling than our station warranted. What for? And what's one deserted village, out of a thousand, when ye come to think of it? The others crawled away to take service, or beg, or walk the streets of London, if they was females, and young. But not Tom Oakley!"

He took a long pull at his glass and grinned at me suddenly. "Enough o' that! One Friday face'll do the pair of us. . . . See here, Hugh — England owes 'ee a debt, there's no question of that. Why not take the collectin' of it into yer own hands?"

"What do you mean?" I asked.

He looked at me shrewdly. "What I say — no more and no less."

He rose, glanced up and down the passageway, and closed the door again. After a moment of striding back and forth in thought, he went on, lowering his voice: "I've not known ye long," he said, "but I know a man I can trust when I see him. How far would ye go for a double fistful of guineas? I've jobs now and again, too risky to tackle singlehanded. Would ye join forces with me, for to see how ye'll thrive at my trade? 'Tis a good one, I promise."

His eyes met mine in a clear, straightforward glance. "Ye

don't take my meaning? Damme, I'll out with it! I'm a highwayman. And what of that? I'm only getting my own back, and I've the right, by God! The fact is I'm a kind of chirurgeon for your lords and ladies, and purse-proud citizens. I slit their purses and save 'em from a congestion of gold."

"More power to you!" said I.

"Think it over. There's risks in my work, but well worth the taking. I just saw my cruiser. There's a horse load of guineas comin' our way! It's as sure as rain at a review, or ladies at a rape trial! But think it over. I'll not press ye for aye or nay on the dot."

Before I left Oakley, I had agreed to become a highwayman. And although the admission may seem strange, coming from a man brought up as I had been, I can affirm that I did not then, and do not now, feel shame at having turned to such desperate work. I was destined to feel bitter regret, when it was too late to mend matters, but nothing more. Oakley directed me how to find the farm of a certain Mrs. Nellie Garth, northwest of London, where his horses were kept, and when I spoke to the landlord of the Black Swan, next day, he tipped me a wink that was like a nudge in the ribs as he informed me that he knew of another man who would take my place.

II

AT GARTH'S FARM

THERE had been a heavy frost during the night, and the sun shone in a pale-blue wintry sky. It was bitter cold, but I walked briskly through the squalor and misery of St. Giles, along Oxford Street to the frozen stillness of Hyde Park, where patches of snow lay on the grass, and the trees stood gaunt and half-dead in the grip of the frost. The long, narrow lake, ice-covered, glittered in the sunlight; the waterfowl had taken refuge in their little ornamental houses, and sat with feet tucked under them on beds of straw. Leaving London behind, I followed the Uxbridge Road, through Ealing, and came at last to Southall, where Oakley had directed me to turn north.

A narrow lane, deep-rutted and hard as iron under the frost, led me through the village of Northolt, and I was tempted to stop for dinner at the inn where several carriers' wagons were drawn up. Since all the folk were indoors and no one had noticed me, it seemed best to continue on to Wood End, a village of no more than half a dozen houses, where I was to turn west and make my way across country to Mrs. Garth's place. The lane I now followed, bordered by hedges of thorn, was scarcely more than a cart track, so narrow that two wagons could not have passed. I followed it for half a mile without passing a single house, and the sun was in my eyes when I came to the gateway Oakley had described, between two fir trees that gleamed with ice crystals in the level light.

The farm was as small as it was lonely, and I could see that it was an orderly, well-kept place. A hundred paces back from the lane was a stone cottage with a low, thatched roof, and the farm buildings beyond looked as neat and substantial as the dwelling.

I knocked, and waited for some little time before the door was opened by a woman who stood in the entryway eyeing me coldly. She might have been in her late twenties, or early thirties. Her eyes were dark blue, under level brows, her colour fresh and glowing, and her figure, considerably above the average height, would have served as a model for a statuary.

"Mrs. Garth?" I asked, raising my hat.

"Aye," said she, regarding me with the same frosty look. "What d'ye wish?"

"I was directed to you by Tom Oakley. He asked me to meet him here."

"I know no Tom Oakley."

"But he told me to come to your house," I replied.

"What he may have told ye is your affair, and his. It's none of mine," said she.

She stepped back, ready to close the door, eyeing me in the same hostile manner. There was nothing for it but retreat.

"Then I wish you good evening," I said.

Her only reply was to shut the door and slide the bolt.

The moon, round, yellow, and at the full, was rising as I retraced my steps in the narrow lane. I had a couple of shillings in my pocket, but it would be a weary walk back to Northolt, where I planned to spend the night. If Oakley were hereabout, he would guess, perhaps, where necessity had taken me. I was puzzled by the woman at the farmhouse and wondered if I could have mistaken the name given me by Oakley. What an Amazon, I thought, as suspicious as she was strong and handsome.

I had gone no great distance when I heard the sound of a

horse's frost nails ringing on the frozen road. It was Oakley's mare, coming on at a fast easy canter. He pulled up at sight of me.

"What the devil!" he said. "Where bound, Hugh?"

"Where bound? From Mrs. Garth's, to be sure! She's never heard of you. She looked ready to set the dog on me!"

Tom laughed heartily. "Staunch old Nellie! Cautious is the word with her. Ye might have been a constable for aught she knew. About-face, lad! Ye look half-froze."

He dismounted stiffly and walked at my side, leading the mare. When we turned in at the gate, Mrs. Garth gave the pair of us a welcome as warm as mine had been cold half an hour before.

"Tom," said she, "when ye wish to meet friends at my house, I'll thank ye for word in advance."

"I thought to be here before him, Nellie. Would there be a bite of supper for a pair of starved travelers?"

"There might," said Garth, with a smile. She ushered us into her warm kitchen, and a quarter of an hour later we tucked into a hearty meal, a cold joint with bread and cheese and home-brewed ale to go with it. I felt more at home in this place than I had since leaving America. It was just such a kitchen as one finds among the farmers and small planters of Maryland: clean, cozy, glowing with comfort and good cheer. The great spit in the fireplace, on which fifty pounds weight of beef might have turned, the spotless floor, the shining pots and pans, the hams, sides of bacon, and strings of onions hanging from the beams, all showed the well-managed farm and household where thrift and simple abundance were matters of course.

While we were at table the door opened, and the lad who had taken Oakley's mare came in. He looked at me with shy wondering eyes as he went to the fireplace to warm his hands.

"Ye've rubbed her down well, Nat?" asked Tom.

The boy nodded.

"And put the heavy blanket on her?"

"Aye."

"Ye can trust him with the horses," said Garth. "They know him as well as yourself."

Nat was a waif of fourteen, whom Garth had found starving in Covent Garden Market, some years before. A widow, with no child of her own, she centred all the love of her generous heart upon this boy, who, though not precisely simple-minded, had the trustful, confiding nature of a child of five. When Mrs. Garth rescued him from the London streets, Nat had been cuffed from pillar to post for as long as he could remember, but under her cherishing care he had forgotten that evil existed in the world. He worshiped his foster mother, followed her about with his soft brown eyes, and would spring to do her bidding almost before her wish was expressed.

Not a word was said during the evening of the purpose of my coming here. Presently Mrs. Garth went to her own chamber; Oakley lighted a candle and led the way up a steep flight of stairs, to a garret under the thatch. There were two narrow beds in the place, some articles of clothing hanging on pegs, and a chest of drawers. Oakley seated himself on one of the beds.

"Well, Hugh, how do ye like my countryseat?" he asked.

"A snug spot," I replied. "Do you come here often?"

"Whenever I'm working this side of London." He gave me a steady searching look. "Now that ye've had time to sleep on the matter, how does it strike ye? There's no call for haste, if ye wish to weigh it further. . . ?"

"I made my decision at the Black Swan. I'm your man, if you'll have me."

"Have 'ee? That I will!" he replied heartily. "Call it settled, then." He paused. "Here's what I've in mind: ye've heard, maybe, of a young Mr. Baxter, him that won the ten thousand pounds in a night, at Brooks's."

"I can't say I have."

"No matter for that. He's at Bath at this present moment, taking the waters by day, and all the rhino in the place by night. My scout tells me he's like to leave for London around this day week. So far he's won a bag of guineas would break a horse's back. If his luck holds, we'll ease him of it as sure as my name's Oakley."

"How'll we know when he's to leave Bath?"

"Trust my cruiser for that. I'll have word, with all the particulars, well in advance." He drew out a handsome watch, in a gold hunting case, and wound it slowly. "Now, lad, I'm for bed. I've ridden a good thirty miles since morning." He pressed the stem of the watch, and it sounded ten soft, clear chimes. "Have a look, Hugh. I took that, with a bonus of fifty guineas, from the biggest thief in the Kingdom."

"A thief?"

"Aye," said Oakley with a grin. "But he robs by law, from inside the Admiralty Victualing Board. How the rogue hated to part with his watch!"

"You don't fear to carry it?"

"Not now. I've had it christened. Look!"

I glanced at the maker's name: "Ducour Frères, Paris."

"It strikes the French chimes now," Tom remarked. "But Basset & Harvey made it. Their name's off as clean as ye wipe a slate. . . . Well, lad, I'm for bed," and a moment later he was fast asleep.

*　　*　　*　　*　　*

After my wretched hand-to-mouth existence in London, the peace and homely comfort of Garth's farm made the place a haven indeed to me. Oakley was away a good part of the week, and I returned to the life of a countryman with a keenness of interest and pleasure that won me Mrs. Garth's friendship from the first day. I took over the outside chores, milking the cow, feeding the pigs, cutting fire-

wood and the like, and ate Garth's excellent meals with
the appetite of a harvest hand. She was no woman to pour
out her history to a stranger, but I learned a good deal
about her life during the days that followed. She came of
farming folk in the West of England, and had lived there
until the time of her marriage. Since her husband's death,
some years before, she had managed this farm herself, going
twice a week with her horse and cart to carry produce to
Covent Garden Market. She asked nothing of her neighbours
save to be left in peace, and I gathered that she had but one
close friend in this part of the country, a Mrs. Windle who
lived half a mile distant, and whom I once saw for a moment.
It was plain that she had a hearty liking for Mrs. Windle,
as warmly returned by her neighbour. For the most part,
Nat was her only companion. The relationship between the
boy and his foster mother was something to touch the heart
of a looker-on. Few words passed between them in the course
of a day: they seemed to have no need for much speaking.
To be together was all either needed for that content which
is something deeper than happiness.

One evening when Oakley was absent and Nat had gone
to bed, Nellie opened her mind to me freely about Tom.
He had first come to her place two years before, she said,
with three horses he wished to put out to grass.

"I struck a bargain with him, Tallant, for I was willing
enough to put by a bit of extra money. I boarded and cared
for the horses, and let him the garret at five shillings a week,
for the times he said he'd be coming this way on his business.
He'd be in and out of the place, sometimes a day or two in the
week, and again we'd not see him for a fortnight; but it came
to be a kind of home to him in the end. We took to him,
Nat and me, straight off, and looked forrard to his coming.
I never doubted he was a dealer in fine horses, for they was
the main part of his talk and I could see the love he had for
'em, but one day he says to me: 'Nellie, ye're an honest law-

abiding woman, and I can't abide to carry false colours in this house. Ye'd best know the truth about me. I'm a highwayman, and I think shame to myself for not having spoke before. Say the word and I'll take my nags and clear out.'

" 'I esteem ye none the less for that,' said I, 'but if I'd known when ye first came here, I'd not have harboured ye for so much as a day.'

" 'Then ye wish me to go?' said he.

" 'I haven't said it yet,' I told him. 'I'll think about it and let ye know for certain when ye next come.'

"And so I did, and the more I thought, the less I liked the notion of sendin' him about his business. Nat thought the world and all of him; I knew the lad would miss him sore, and so would I, for the matter of that. Afore I was married I'd lost a brother as like Tom as two men could be, not of the same blood. Well, I thought and I pondered, and the end of it was that, when he came again, I said: 'Tom, bide here and welcome as long as ye please, but Nat's never to know the trade ye're in, and I wish to know no more of it than ye've told me already.' And that's how it's been since. There's times I've been worried and anxious, as though he was my own kin, for fear he was catched; and I've worried more for Nat's sake, for if Tom was took, they'd have me up for harbouring, and where would the lad be then?"

I had thought of the same thing more than once. Though I knew that Mrs. Garth received nothing from Oakley save the money for rent and pasturage and feed, I had little doubt as to how she would stand in the eyes of the law.

She regarded me with a grim, anxious smile. "And now I've a pair of ye to harbour! And what'll come of it, in the end . . . Tallant, I don't doubt but ye'll make the best of companions for Tom; he needs just such a man as yerself to stand back to back with him. But mind what ye do! Ye don't belong in that trade, and Tom knows it as well as myself. Whatever have ye took to it for?"

"It's not one I mean to follow for long," I replied, and then I told her something of my life up to this time, of my miserable existence in London, and of my plans for a return to Canada as soon as I had money enough for a passage. "That's understood between us," I added. "Tom has taken me in, not so much because he needs me, but to help me over a bad stretch of road."

"Mind it's not the end of the road, young man! I wish ye was well beyond it, on the kind of road ye should be traveling."

"Never fear. I shall be, before many weeks."

"And ye're for America again? Sometimes I've teased myself with the notion of going there. What like of a country will it be where ye came from — all wilderness and savage Indians?"

"Far from it," I replied. "You'd see fine settled valleys, the land cleared long since, with fat cattle and sheep grazing in the pastures, and arable land richer than could be found in the whole of England. You could buy a farm five times the size of yours for a fifth of what would be paid for this. I'd like well to coax Tom to come, for he'd thrive there, on his own fine acres, as a breeder of horses. There's no great towns and no miserable starved creatures such as you see everywhere in England. The black slaves fare better than the half of London."

"I'd like well to go there," said Garth, musingly, "and who knows? Mebbe I will, some day. But egg Tom into it if ye can. 'Twould be a heavy load from the heart to know him safe, and settled into an honest life. If he stays in England, I see the end as plain as I see his mare yonder in the pasture."

Tom came back on the Saturday noon with the news we'd been waiting for. Mr. Baxter was London bound from Bath and had spent the previous night at Reading. He was not traveling by post chaise but in his own carriage, with his own horses, and making a leisurely journey of it. Oakley had learned from his cruiser that Baxter would leave Reading about two o'clock this same afternoon.

"Reading is forty miles from London," he said, "and I know exactly how he means to come. We'll be off, Hugh, when we've polished off Nellie's dinner, comfortable-like, and jog south-along to Heston. It's thereabout we'll meet him, and, by the Lord, he'll be well worth waiting for!"

"His luck's held, then?" I asked.

"No, but ours has, or call me out. This I know: He dropped all but three hundred guineas before he left Bath, and he'll drop what's left afore ever his horses' hoofs touch pavement. My cruiser has spied out his company. There'll be none but himself inside, with the coachman and a third on the box beside him. Hugh, if ye're set for Canada, ye can go to London to-morrow to take passage, though I'll be the last to urge haste upon ye."

The winter afternoon was half spent when Oakley and I set out. He rode his favourite mare, Rosamond, and my mount was a spirited sorrel. It was a delight to be on a horse's back once more. Garth stood in the doorway, looking glumly after us as we cantered down the lane leading to the highway. Little I dreamed, then, where that road was to take us. It was the first leg of a journey of better than fourteen thousand miles, that was to fetch us up at Botany Bay.

I felt no prickings of conscience, no misgivings, as we rode on at a smart pace through the gathering winter dusk. I was reminded of raids I had made, with Loyalist comrades, into enemy territory during the American War: there was the same heightened sense of expectancy, of adventure with risk attached, the same quickening of the blood. As for Tom, I could see how keenly he relished the prospect of the work before us: it was like food and drink to a man of his spirit.

Night had fallen by the time we reached the place where we were to wait: a small thicket thirty paces from the highroad, two miles to the west of Heston. The air was crisp and bracing and the winter stars sparkled in a cloudless sky. Here we dismounted, looked to the priming of our pistols, and fastened handkerchiefs over the lower part of our faces.

"Lad, how's the pulse?" asked Tom.

"Steady," said I, "but racing a bit."

"And that's just as it should be," said Tom. "There's times when I relish the waiting, with action just to come, as the best part of it — if the waiting's not too long," he added, with a grin.

"They couldn't have passed?" I said.

"Never ye fret for that; we're in good time. . . . Now, Hugh, all's clear?"

"Yes. I'm to handle the coachman and anyone with him on the box."

"Right. And I'll attend to Mr. Baxter and the company inside, if he has company. Mind ye this! We must be prepared for what we find. The best of cruisers may be wrong in the advance tips. There's three we know of to come, but Baxter may have changed his companions on the way."

We had waited about twenty minutes when we heard the clatter of a heavy coach which had just breasted the rise, a quarter of a mile distant.

"By God! Here they are!" said Tom, gleefully. "Mark ye, Hugh! Spare to shoot if ye can, but take no chances. It's us or them."

We mounted and stood fast. The coach was coming on at a brisk eight-mile clip, but it was drawn by four horses instead of the two expected, and we made out a postboy riding the off horse of the leading pair.

"Now!" said Tom, and we spurred for the road.

"Stand for your lives!" Tom called, and there was no nonsense in the quality of that clear hard voice. We were alongside in five seconds. The coachman stood and hauled back with all his strength on the reins. The postboy was a lad of fourteen or thereabout. I seized him by the collar and yanked him from his horse, covering the coachman at the same time. The boy cowered on the ground, without an ounce of spirit in him; no more had the coachman, for he yelled, "Never shoot, sir! I yield!" Meanwhile Tom was at the window of the coach. "One here, lad," he called to me. "Hold fast as ye are, and it's done in three minutes!"

We had not looked for such luck as this. In a wink, Tom had the one fellow inside standing in the road with his arms raised. Meanwhile, I had the coachman and the post boy standing beside him, covering the three whilst Tom sprang into the coach. He leaped out a moment later with a heavy bag of soft leather which he quickly attached to Rosamond's saddle. "Look sharp! Watch the road!" he called whilst he was at this work. By this time I was convinced that the fellow from inside was not Baxter, but his servant, perhaps, for the man put up not even a show of resistance. What neither of us knew, then, was that Baxter, with a friend, had hired saddle horses in Reading for the last part of the journey. They had halted briefly somewhere on the way, but came galloping up just as Tom was ready to mount. In the exchange of shots that followed, I downed Baxter's horse, and he was thrown headlong, but the half-ounce ball from his companion's pistol caught me full in the left shoulder and all but unseated me. Tom saw I was hit and was alongside in three seconds, steadying me in the saddle as he turned and fired at Baxter's companion. Then it was a hard gallop for home, and with Baxter wanting a mount, his friend made no attempt to follow us. We rode fast for a matter of three miles, going by a roundabout way, and at last halted in a thicket of firs where Tom bound up my wound and staunched the flow of blood as best he could. The ball had missed the bone, but had torn loose the muscles under my left arm. We reached Garth's place in the small hours, and while she washed and dressed the wound, Oakley spilled out young Baxter's winnings on the bed and counted it back into a canvas bag.

We had taken three hundred and twenty-two guineas, in gold coin. Tom hid the bag under his shirts in the wardrobe, and, as we had not been followed, and were a good twelve miles from the scene of the holdup, we slept soundly.

Garth kept her misgivings to herself, but I could see that she was more than uneasy during the week that followed. Young Baxter came of a notable family; furthermore, he was a proud determined fellow, and the fact that two men had gotten the better of his party of five rankled with him. A hue and cry was raised and a reward of five hundred pounds offered for the capture of the highwaymen. After lying low for three days, Tom was bound to go to London for news. He returned early in the evening, and he and Nellie came up to the attic where I lay.

"How goes it, Hugh?" he asked. "No fever, eh?"

"None," I replied. "Nellie is the best of nurses, but she won't let me go downstairs."

"Ye'll rest where ye are, young man, till I give the word," she said. "Now, Tom, what have ye heard?"

"We've slit a hot haggis, as the Sawneys say," Tom replied. "Young Baxter swears he'll not touch cards again till the pair of us are stretched. He's out with a party of his own raising, and there's handbills posted in all the taverns. Hugh, d'ye wish to hear what fashion of man ye are?"

He drew one of the bills from his pocket and read: " 'Tall, wide-shouldered fellow, probably in his early twenties. Would weigh around fourteen stone. Almost certainly wounded as he was seen to reel in the saddle when Mr. Baxter's pistol was fired. Riding a sorrel horse with four white stockings.' "

"What of yourself?" I asked.

" 'Smallish, strong-made man, with a North Country accent, quick and active in his movements. Might be thirty years old. Riding a handsome bay mare.' "

Oakley smiled as he put the bill back in his pocket.

"Save for the wound, there's men by the dozen, by the score, will answer both descriptions. No, we're safe enough. 'Twas the devil's own luck that Baxter winged ye, but the price is small to pay for the taking. Better than three hundred guineas for five minutes' work! Beats groomin' nags, don't it?"

"Ye's best find a safer place to hide it in than the wardrobe," said Garth.

"Pooh, Nellie! Where's the need? We're as safe here as in a church. Baxter's men are chasing their noses through the country in every direction but this. Some say we're in town; some think we've a hideout down Wiltshire way. Trust my cruiser. He'll know in good time if ever they get on the scent."

One morning, when my wound was nearly healed, I rose to find Tom saddling one of his horses to ride in for a day with some of his cronies who gathered at the Black Swan. Nellie had left at dawn for Covent Garden Market with two hundredweight of potatoes and a fat hog to sell.

The day was warm and fine; when I had eaten my breakfast, which Nellie had set out on the kitchen table, I went about the chores. I opened the fowl house and sprinkled corn for the birds in the barnyard. The ducks made for the horse pond, trotting in single file, increasing their pace comically as they neared the water. The turkey cock lowered his wings, strutted for a moment while they trailed the ground, and gobbled defiantly. The sound carried me back to the forests of Maryland, where I had stalked many a wild gobbler.

The chores finished, I went for a walk, returning just as Garth and Nat drove in, an hour before noon. She handed me the *Morning Herald* I had asked her to buy, and I went to the kitchen to read it. Nat was leading old Davy away for his bait of oats when his mother called to him.

"Come into the house, Nat, when ye've fed Davy; I'll

have ye take a basket of eggs down to the inn. Tell Mr. Judd I want a shilling's worth of salt."

The lad set off a few moments later, and a fateful errand it was for the members of the Garth household. I will now speak of what happened at the Wood End Inn, asking leave to describe an event I did not witness, but learned of, later, from Nellie and poot Nat, who played, in all innocence, a most tragic part.

Arriving at the inn, Nat went into the taproom where the landlord's assistant was drawing ale for half a dozen travelers whose horses stood outside. They were dressed like countrymen, but all were armed with pistols, under their coats. Their leader, a man of about twenty-five, paid the score, and, on second thought, ordered the pots to be filled again. Nat set down his basket and stood looking on. His small figure caught the young man's eye.

"Come here, lad," he said.

Nat went to him readily.

"You live hereabouts?"

"Yes, sir. My mother's farm is just up the lane."

"What's your name?"

"Nat, sir, Nat Garth."

"And a fine lad you are, Nat. Now then, maybe you can help me. Come, think hard: have you heard no one speak of a wounded man here in the countryside?"

"Oh yes, sir," said Nat, eagerly, happy to be of service. "Mr. Tallant was hurt. He's lying at our cottage."

"You don't tell me! And who's Mr. Tallant?"

"He's a friend of Tom Oakley's, sir."

"Well, now, think of that! And what like of a man is Mr. Tallant — a big, tall, strapping fellow?"

Nat nodded, vigorously. "He's that tall he has to duck his head to come in at the door."

"There! I'll be bound he's the man I'm looking for, Nat. I've the best of news for him. Mr. Tallant will call it lucky that I found you. He's at your mother's house, you say?"

"Yes, sir. He was in the kitchen readin' the paper when I left the house."

"Then here's a shilling for you, to show us the way there."

Meanwhile, at Garth's house I had taken my newspaper and climbed the stairs to our attic room, now warmed a little by the midday sun. Lying on my bed, I glanced idly through the news. Presently I laid the paper aside and fell into a doze.

*   *   *   *   *

I was awakened from my nap by the sound of loud voices and of a violent struggle in the room below. For a moment I lay bewildered; then I heard heavy footsteps coming up the stairs at a run. I started up, still half asleep, as the door burst open and three men rushed into the room, pistols in their hands. One of them, I felt pretty sure, was Baxter.

"Surrender, in the King's name!" he ordered.

One of his companions seized my useless arm and gave it such a wrench that, heedless of the pistols, I swung about and gave him a heavy blow on the jaw. He went down with a crash; the pistol flew out of his hand and was discharged as it struck the floor. At the same instant I received such a blow on the head, from behind, that I was knocked senseless; when I came round I was lying on my bed, bound hand and foot. The sunlight of midafternoon streamed into the small window. Baxter was sitting on Tom's bed, a pistol in his hand, his bag of guineas beside him, and two of his men stood in the doorway.

"Headache, Tallant?" he asked. "They'll cure that for you in Newgate."

III

NEWGATE PRISON

TOM was caught all too neatly in the trap set for him when he rode home at dusk, and we were held at Garth's house till late on the following afternoon. A long day it was for me, for I was alone in my upstairs room, with the guard at the door outside. His companions were below, and I could hear their voices and the coming and going of men on horseback in the stable yard and the lane beyond. For all the loneliness of Garth's farm, the news of our arrest had spread and by midday there was a crowd of farmers and farm labourers gathered outside in the hope of seeing the highwaymen. Among others who came early in the day was Nellie's friend and neighbour, Mrs. Windle. I have no doubt that she knew all about Oakley and that Nellie harboured him with a full knowledge of his profession; but, like most humble folk, whether living in towns or the open country, she had no love for officers of the law. I heard her lashing out shrilly at our guards for taking a poor hard-working woman into custody, and "two honest gentlemen, as anyone could see," who chanced to be stopping at her house for the good of the country air. She remained at the house throughout the day and took charge of the kitchen in our behalf. Food for the guards was brought from the inn on the main road, but there was none for us, and it was thanks to Mrs. Windle that we did not set out for London with empty stomachs.

The winter afternoon was drawing to a close when I was ordered down to the kitchen. There was Nellie on a settle by

the wall, with young Nat beside her, a look of terror and bewilderment on his face as he gazed at his foster mother. The
lad, in his simplicity, had betrayed us, but Nellie's reproaches
were, as I knew, all for herself. Her face was hard set and
there was a great bluish bruise on one cheek, received in her
struggle with the constables. She gave me a quick glance as
I came down the stairway, but said nothing. Mrs. Windle stood
by the fireplace, her fists on her hips, glaring defiance at the
constables. A moment later Oakley was brought in from
the stable where they had kept him overnight. He had a horse
blanket over his shoulders, and from his condition I could
picture the fight they had had to subdue him. His jacket
and waistcoat were gone and he had only the half of a shirt
to his body. One arm was covered with dried blood and
there was a welt on his forehead the size of a hen's egg. One
of the guards had an eye swelled shut and the head of another
was bound round with a dirty napkin. Three of these fellows
had rolled on the stable floor in subduing Oakley, but they
had had time to clean themselves whilst Tom had been left as
he was when the struggle ended. He was at his lowest at such
a moment, for if ever there was a man who loved cleanliness
and something approaching splendour in his dress, it was
Tom. Nellie's eyes blazed as she saw him in this bedraggled
condition. She turned to the fellow in charge of the guards.

"Ye've left the man, the day long, in such a state as this?"
said she.

"No matter for that. He'll have time and to spare to wash
himself at the pump in Newgate," said the guard.

"Was ye brought up in a pigsty?" said Garth. "There's
none of us leaves this house till he's made decent."

She spoke with so determined an air that the man gave a
surly consent. Oakley was taken to the wash house at one
side of the yard, where he enjoyed a complete scrub. Meanwhile, Mrs. Windle, at Garth's direction, had fetched him
clean clothing, and when he reappeared he had put on with

it his old assured and carefree manner. He was now dressed in a suit of blue broadcloth with silver buttons, white silk stockings, and black shoes, and this transformation had its immediate effect upon the guards, who were more civil to him.

I had wondered at the long delay at Garth's house; the reason was that the men who had taken us were not of the regular constabulary, but had been hired privately to search for us. When they had found us, or at least men answering to the description of those wanted, warrants had to be procured for our proper arrest. This had now been done and the sun was just setting when an old country coach drawn by two horses was brought to carry us to London. Nat was in despair and clung desperately to his mother, who tried to console him.

"There, Nat," said she. "Never fret, laddie; it's all right. I'll be home within the week — see if I don't, and till then you're to stay with Mrs. Windle."

"To be sure he is!" said Mrs. Windle. "Why, Nat, where's your spirit? Hush, now! Mercy me! A boy of fourteen and crying the like of this!"

"You'll look out for the place, Mrs. Windle?" Garth asked.

"Trust me for that," the latter replied. "I've daughters and sons to spare, Nellie, and with Nat here to help, we'll keep all shipshape, won't we, Nat?"

The boy nodded, miserably, and a moment later we were led out of the house, through the crowd of gaping, staring countrymen, to the coach. The guards mounted their horses, and with two in front and four riding behind, we proceeded toward London.

I shall try to recollect what I can of the young man I then was, and what he felt and thought as he sat bound in a lumbering old country coach on the way to Newgate prison. For the feelings, there was no shame — none: not a shred or an atom, except for being caught, and that was chance and no fault of ours. I had tried every honest means of earning a living open to a young man without friends, in a strange country, and when I was in desperate need I took the chance Oakley offered without two thoughts about the right or the wrong of it. Beside this, my heart was sore at the way the Loyalists had been used by Government, and I'd lost all hope of the promised compensation ever coming to anything. After three years of waiting not one penny had we received. I was none too happy, of course, about the future. I had not lived in England this while without having seen the bodies of highwaymen swinging in chains from gibbets at lonely crossroads, and I well knew that these were but a small part of the number who met their end at Newgate. For all that, I was in no mood of despair, for I had a power of life in me, and it is next to impossible for a young man to imagine the worst that can happen. What worried me most was that young Nat, in his innocence, had betrayed my name to the men who caught us. At first, I was minded to deny stoutly that my name was Tallant, but they had found it written in a pocketbook I carried, and since they had this double confirmation, I decided to let matters take their course. My mother would never know, and the only other person I cared deeply for was Mr. Fleming, and he was still in Canada. As for the other Loyalists, I had dropped all connection with them long since, and it was far from likely that they would ever learn what had become of me.

I was blessed in my companions in misery, but I didn't know then how great was my fortune in having such friends, nor how events to come were to draw us together. Garth said little as the coach rolled and jolted over the uneven road. She was worried about Nat, for the lad was as dependent upon her as a babe in arms; she loved him the more because of his simple mind and his need for her. She wondered how he'd fare with Mrs. Windle, who was a good woman but sharp of temper and likely to hurt the boy without meaning to. Tom distracted her thoughts by singing songs all the way along, for there was never such a man to face a dark prospect with a blithe spirit. As I write these lines I hear the fine tenor voice he was so proud of ringing out as clearly as I heard it then. You would have thought that he had not a care in the world and that we were bound for London on a pleasure jaunt. Presently he broke off and said: "Hugh, have ye ever been to Newgate?"

"Never," said I, "but I've passed the place a time or two."

"Then I'd best prepare ye," said Tom, "for if a man is to be chucked into a laystall, the shock will be the less for knowing it before he finds himself there. It'll be worst for you, Nellie."

"Never ye fret about me," said Garth. "I'll fend for myself."

"Aye, you're a woman of courage; I grant that, and yon's the place ye'll need the whole of it."

"I've seen the inside," said Garth.

"What! Newgate?"

" 'Twas before ever I knew ye, Tom — five years back. My husband — as honest a man as ever lived — was took for stealing some fowls at Covent Garden Market. The wretch that did it was caught later and my man was cleared when it was too late. He died of the gaol fever the week I got him home. Four Sabbaths I spent with him in Newgate before that happened. Sabbaths in hell ye might well say."

"Nellie, ye never told me this!"

"And why should I? But I know the place."

"There's a hundredweight lifted off my mind on your account," said Oakley, in a relieved voice. "Knowing the worst afore it comes is half the bearing of it."

"And what is the worst?" I asked.

"The whole of it, but there's shades of worst, even in Newgate, and the Felons' Common Side, as they call it, is the bottom of the black. With only ten shillings amongst us, it's to the Common Side we'll have to go. We'll be for it at the start, till I can reach some of my friends outside, but that'll be soon, I promise."

He then went on to speak of the different wards in that home of misery and of the hierarchies of felons who lived there. The lowest was the Common Side, one ward for men and one for women, where those convicted or awaiting trial, and having neither friends nor money, were kept. Next above this was that part called the Masters' Side where those with money could buy themselves in and away from the misery of the Common Side.

"And how much is needed?" I asked.

"Thirteen-and-six a head for the entering," said Tom, "with half a crown a week more for a bed and bedding. Then there's ten shillings' garnish collected by the steward for coals, candles, plates, knives and forks, and the like. And beyond all this is the food ye must buy, for ye get no victuals in Newgate save a penny loaf a day and pump water to wash it down with."

But the best accommodation was on the State Side, open to all who could pay, no matter what their crimes. Here the fee for admission was three guineas, and ten-and-sixpence a week more was charged for the rent of a single bed. Prisoners who could afford it sometimes paid for the extra beds and so secured for themselves the luxury of a private room.

"And to the State Side we'll go," Oakley went on, "the minute I can get word to my friends outside. And Nellie shall have her own good quarters near by, trust me for that. We'll do far from bad once we're settled in the place. But for a night or two we must take the luck of beggars."

"You speak with a wide knowledge of the place, Tom," said I.

"And why not? I've had friends in the cursed hole, and I've done for them what they'll do for me, for the three of us, now. If ever a man wants friends, it's there. Shall we fight for our coats, lad?"

"Fight for them? Why?"

"There's the matter of garnish, or footing, demanded by the felons of the Common Side of every newcomer the instant he comes in: It'll be pay or strip for the three of us."

"Speak for yourself," said Nellie, grimly. "They'll take naught of mine, I promise ye."

"No, Nellie, it's best to pay; the garnish is but two-and-six. That's seven-and-six for the three: we'll have half a crown to spare."

"Ye'll pay naught for me," said Garth. "I won't have it."

"God bless ye, Nellie! Ye've a fist like the Rock of Ages and the weight of a draught horse to drive it with. But mind this! They'll be twenty to one against ye — aye, fifty to one. Ye'll be lucky to get off with your shift."

"Never ye mind."

"Ye'll be alone amongst the harridans in the women's part. Hugh and I will be wards away."

"I want no help."

"Ye mean to fight, then?"

"I do if needful," Garth replied, with the same confident grimness.

"There, Hugh," said Oakley; "Nellie's decided all for us. We'll not be shamed by a woman."

"What are ye saying?" said Garth. "Will ye have Hugh fight with but the one arm and the flesh already torn apart a second time?"

"God's truth!" said Oakley. "I'd clean forgot his wound."

"I'll not have you held up on my account," said I. "I can favour the wound and my right arm's as good as ever. You mind the old saying? 'A good brawl cheers all.' We'll be the better for it."

"So we would, but it can't be," said Tom. "Ye'd lame yourself for months to come. No, we'll pay, and so will Nellie, if she'll take counsel."

"I pay *naught*," said she, with such emphasis that Tom

shook his head with a give-it-up expression. "Well, Mrs. Garth," he said with a grin, "more power to ye! We'll see who's naked the morn."

London was now at hand; we passed the scattered houses of the outskirts and from the open road to the cobbled streets, the coach and our guards on horseback making a great clatter over the uneven stones. The clocks were striking eight as we came along Holborn in a thin wintry fog that blurred the scant lights and made going slow. The air was harsh and raw; it was a night for indoors by a snug fire and none were abroad save the homeless. A few hackney coachmen stood at the corners, by lampposts or in entryways, and their poor nags, with their heads hanging low, looked the very picture of outdoor misery. We were miserable enough, ourselves, and all but perished with cold when we drew up before the gloomy front of Newgate prison.

Of all the horrors of Newgate, the smell of the place was, I think, the worst. I was no squeamish fellow; in my wanderings about London, I had walked the filthiest courts and alleys of St. Giles, Spitalfields, Lock's Fields, and elsewhere, but in these places the air was abroad: in Newgate it was the confined stench of ages that had simmered and thickened and slimed the walls since the place was a gaol, long before the time of Henry the Third. As the ponderous iron-and-oaken door was pushed ajar to admit us, the cold smell of human misery and hopelessness struck me like a blow in the face, or, better, in the pit of the stomach. I gasped and glanced at Tom, and for all that he knew what to expect, he was as hard hit for the moment as myself. He gave me a sickly grin and said, "Draw it in and be done with it, for it'll never be done with you. There's no other way: ye must conquer or be conquered by it." Garth's courage in meeting it was a help. If a woman used to clean sweet country air could suffer the change without wincing, it was not for us to quail before it.

We had not been shackled for the journey to London for the reason that no shackles were to be had. In lieu of them we had been roped together by the leg, with our hands tied behind us, but the guards had had the decency to leave my left arm free because of my wound. We were now unbound and a blessed relief it was to have the cords removed. They gave us a minute or two to stamp our feet and to beat our numbed arms across our breasts to start the blood flowing once more; then we were marshaled down a passageway that looked like an entrance to the infernal regions, — as it was, in fact, — and into a room to the right, down a flight of steps. It was a place about a dozen feet square, furnished with a table, some shelves for prison records, and two settles on either side of the fireplace. The smell here was no different from that in the passageway except for the warmth from the fire which seemed to stir and liven it. Three as mean-looking rogues as ever I'd set eyes on occupied one of the settles. An honest constable mindful of his duty, if you can imagine so great a rarity, meeting them in the street would have taken them up at once, on suspicion. They were turnkeys of the prison, and none but rogues can be found to accept such a position. These three eyed us up and down; they reminded me of so many mongrel dogs sniffing up from afar the knowledge of how to behave toward strangers. Oakley paid no attention to them, but Garth turned and stared them out of countenance. Their smiles and winks seemed to indicate that they expected a rich harvest from our coming. I was decently dressed, and Oakley's costume was only a little this side of elegance. Garth, in her stout shoes, grey flannel petticoat, shawl and bonnet, made a handsome picture of a decent countrywoman who had gotten into the place by mistake.

The man seated at the table pushed aside the candlestick and peered at us over a pair of spectacles with an air of benevolent interest, as though he had been a superannuated schoolmaster welcoming new scholars to his establishment. There's no place like London for queer specimens of humanity, and this strange little fellow took the eye at once. His name was Tillot, as I afterward learned, and he had been keeper of the records at Newgate for close to fifty years. His complexion was like that of a resurrected mummy and he couldn't have weighed above six stone. He was nothing but skin and bones, with a head so large that you wondered how he managed to support it. And within that massive head, completely tabulated and ready for instant reference, were records of crime and human misery that dated back over a half-century.

Tillot booked us with an air of quiet satisfaction, as though he were a merchant setting down items in a valuable bill of goods. Newgate was home to him, and he must have thought that the wretches who were brought there regarded it in the same light. Beginning with Oakley, he wrote into his great ledger our names, ages, occupations, places of residence, and in the column to the right he set down the charge — highway robbery. Garth was booked as an accessory.

An assistant keeper who had received us from the guards at the door now returned and took us in charge. He was a greasy wretch with a nose like a beetroot, and small piglike eyes under bushy brows. All the grime of Newgate seemed to cling to his person like mildew, and his oily smile was meant, perhaps, to be ingratiating. He had guessed, from our decent appearance, that we were well provided with money. He went before us like the landlord of some low tavern prepared to show distinguished guests his best accommodations. One of the turnkeys followed. We were led, first, along the main passageway to a room bare of furnishings save for two candles burning in an iron sconce fixed to the wall. Heavy locked doors opened from this in three directions. The keeper halted here.

"And now," said he, "we come to the parting of the ways."
He turned to Oakley. "Ye and your friends will be wishing
the best we have to offer, sir?" he asked.

Oakley looked at him in silence.

"What do ye mean by that?" said Garth.

"Ye've never been here before, ma'am, that's plain," said
he. "There's degrees of comfort in this inn, and ye must pay
for the best or be lodged with the sluts."

"We've no money," said Garth, shortly.

The fawning smile vanished at once. "No money?" said
the keeper, as though not sure he heard aright.

"No," said Garth, "and I'll thank ye to show me at once
to the females' apartments. The worst slut in the place, I'll
warrant, would be too good for the likes of yourself."

The fellow gave her a black look.

"Ye'll gain nothing by that, mistress, I promise ye," he
said.

"Pah!" said Garth. "Keep yer threats for them that fears
'em. I'd scorn to wipe my feet on such a thing as you be."

She waited with her arms folded while the man unlocked
the door to the passage leading to the women's quarters;
then, with a curt nod to us, she followed him out and the
door was closed behind her. We were left with the other
turnkey, and whatever bully and tyrant he may have been
with scared and humble prisoners, he seemed to be at a loss for
the line to take with us. Neither of us paid the slightest attention as he fumbled with his keys and unlocked the door
to the passage we were to take. We stood looking through
the barred door that had closed behind Nellie.

"Yon's a grand woman, Hugh," said Tom. "It makes me
fair sick to think it's us that brought her here."

"You've seen the quarters she'll be sent to?" I asked.

Tom nodded glumly. Suddenly he turned his head toward
the turnkey who was waiting by the other door. "See here,
corny-face," he called.

"Ye'd best come along now," said the fellow, sullenly. "Ye'll have me in trouble, else."

"Ye've a thirsty look," said Tom, "and we're not as stony as we said just now." He took some coins from his pocket and jingled them in one hand, eyeing the wardsman appraisingly. "Would two shillings wet down such a gullet as yours?"

"Aye, it might," said the fellow, perking up. "What do ye wish?"

"Have ye the keys to the women's court?" Oakley asked. The man shook his head.

"Then can ye take us where we can see the place?"

"Aye," said the man. "There's a room that looks into it from above the wall. I could take ye there, but not for long, mind!"

"Lead on," said Oakley, "for there's to be the battle of the ages directly."

"If it's your friend you're thinking of, there's naught ye can do to help her," said the wardsman. "She'd best pay her garnish else they'll not leave a rag to her back."

"That's as it falls out," said Oakley. "Make haste now, for we wish to be there at the start."

It was the custom at Newgate to lock the felons into their wards at nightfall, and from then on until day there were no keepers amongst them. The man led us through a maze of passages and up a stairway to a miserable room about eight by ten feet with a wooden barrack bed against the wall. This was one of the supposedly luxurious apartments reserved to female prisoners with money, but the place was empty now. In one wall was a barred window looking directly into the women's court, a stone-paved area as dank and dismal as some underground dungeon. It was the common court for the lowest, poorest class of women, and was lighted by a few candles stuck into blackened niches in the walls. Leading off from it were passages to their sleeping quarters if ever sleep could be possible in so frightful a place. For all that it was now past nine o'clock, the din that rose from the court was worse than Bartholomew Fair, and it was given back redoubled in volume from the walls. As my eyes became accustomed to the dim light I saw children, like the offspring of famine, amongst the adults, and slatterns with infants in their arms sitting against the walls. Many of the women were barefoot, and others were shod in rags they had tied about their feet. Here and there I saw groups huddled together for warmth, for they had no fires. Nothing I had seen in the most wretched quarters of London had prepared me for the sight of the women's court at Newgate. Here, surely, was the "bottom of the black," as Oakley had called it.

Then we spied Garth. She was standing with her back to the gate she had been let in by, and in front of her was at least a score of the vilest creatures in the place all yelling "Garnish! Garnish!"

"God help her!" said Oakley with a groan. "Nellie, Nellie! Pay and be done with it!"

He said that not for Garth's hearing but as a kind of prayerful entreaty; indeed, Garth could scarcely have heard him had he shouted at the top of his voice. "She's a grand woman," he added. "I see how it is with her; she wishes to be roused; there'll be no bearing the place unless her blood is up."

A striking figure she made in that dismal setting, her shadow towering behind her on the wall. Mrs. Garth was just under six feet and weighed better than twelve stone, and there was that in her bearing to make any woman think twice about attacking her. The harridans that ringed her on three sides kept their distance at first; then one made a rush in an attempt to snatch her bonnet. Garth met her with a powerful open-handed slap that sent the woman sprawling.

Yells of delight followed this resolute action, for, in that pitiful hopeless place where the women had nothing to do from day's end to day's end, they became desperate for some diversion, some bit of excitement to make them forget their miserable lot. There was a rush to the side of the court where Garth stood, and those who had been baiting her now crowded closer, reviling her in terms so foul that I must omit them here. They were out to conquer her now; they could see that she was a decent woman, and they may have thought to subdue her with abuse alone, for none of them ventured to step forward to receive what she had given the first of their number. A semblance of quiet followed as Garth untied the strings of her bonnet. She held it for a moment, then tossed it amongst them. "That ye may have," she announced. A score of hands clutched wildly at it, and in their greed they tore it to bits. Whilst this was happening a huge woman appeared from the rear of the court and shoved the others aside till she stood before Garth. She glared right and left at her companions.

"What are ye about, ye bitches!" said she. "Do ye fight and send no word to me?"

"The fine lady is only just come, Moll," said one, "and she'll pay no garnish."

"Won't she so?" said the other. She turned to Garth and gave her a mock courtsey. "Well, me handsome duchess! Do ye think to buy us off with the bunnit? Stand against us, would ye?" In half a minute she had worked herself into such an appalling tantrum that she had to pause for breath. "We'll have every rag to yer body, ye milk-fed trollop, and yer blood with it! Strip!"

This woman was a horror to see. Her name was Moll Cudlip and she was the bully of the female side. She had a hoarse voice, and had she been dressed as a man you would never have guessed her sex. Her hair was cropped short, making the egg-shaped head appear small and out of place on shoulders which were as broad as those of a Thames barge-man. Her only garment was a quilted petticoat black with age and grime, reaching to her knees. Her arms, legs, and feet were bare, but she seemed indifferent to the cold.

"Stand back!" she said to her companions. "I'll handle her!"

The others made room amid cries of, "Go it, Moll! Christen her! Paint her red! We'll show her who's mistress here!"

Oakley gripped my shoulder in his anxiety. "Nellie, Nellie, if only ye'd listened to me!" he groaned, in a low voice. I was as worried as himself, for this Cudlip would have weighed a good two stone above Garth. But Nellie stood her ground, her eye fixed upon her opponent as she quietly unpinned the brooch that held her shawl in place. She then folded the garment as neatly as though she were about to lay it in the drawer of her wardrobe at home. Cudlip watched her with an air of triumph, but instead of passing over the shawl, Nellie thrust it quickly into the bosom of her dress. Then she stepped back until she was braced against the gate.

Cudlip had not expected this. With a bellow she rushed at Garth, who raised her foot and shoved it with terrific force full into Cudlip's stomach. The latter doubled up and fell in a heap, gasping for breath. Garth leaped upon her and, seizing her by the ears, bashed her head again and again against the stone floor. The others might have overpowered her then by sheer weight of numbers, but they were so taken by surprise that instead of rushing her they fell back. Now Garth's blood was up. She seemed to have been gifted with the strength of all the furies, and with her eyes alight and her strong fists clenched, she laid into those nearest with rights and lefts straight to eyes and noses, using her feet at the same time. I've seen battles now and again, but never one so hopeless-seeming at the start that ended so quickly. With their leader conquered, Cudlip's followers showed the craven spirit that was native to them, and within three minutes Garth was mistress of the ward. There must have been well over a hundred women in the place but not above a dozen had taken an active part against her. At the end she stood in the midst of the yard, scarce breathed by the encounter and looking as though she could have battled the night through had there been any with the courage to meet her. Then her eye fell upon a woman crouched by the wall with a sickly half-naked child huddled in her arms for warmth. Garth stepped over to her; we could not hear what was said, but she drew forth her warm shawl and wrapped it about the child as gently as though it had been her own.

"There," said Tom, "Nellie's paid her garnish in the only way she'd ever consent to pay it. God bless her! They'll meddle with her no more, that's certain."

Cudlip lay where she had fallen, but a moment later she lifted herself slowly to a sitting position and stared about her. At our last glimpse she was still here, with such an ache, I'll warrant, in that egg-shaped head as had knocked the conceit out of her for days to come.

IV

TRANSPORTATION FOR LIFE

Tom and I were taken to the men's Common Side, which was worse, if possible, than the dismal hole for the women. We paid our garnish and then were double-ironed and triple-ironed. Our decent clothing stood us in bad stead here, for we were judged to be men with money, or who would have money later, when we could send to friends outside. And so we were loaded with three sets of shackles to our feet so that we could be forced to buy easement of irons when, and if, our funds came in. It was past midnight when we were shown into a cell room that was no more than a corridor eight feet wide and three times as long, filled to suffocation with sleeping men. The door and two small barred windows high in the wall offered all the ventilation there was. A whale-oil lamp burned in this place, and by its light I could dimly see the inmates, old men, young men, and mere boys, huddled on a wooden platform raised about six inches from the stone floor. This was the common bed with nothing but the bare boards to sleep on. Some had pieces of filthy canvas for covering, but most of them only the clothes they lay in. Along the narrow passage at the foot stood the slop tubs.

At first Oakley and I stood by the wall, resolved to wear out the night in that position. It required something beyond mere fortitude to stretch out in that huddle of human beings. Nevertheless, we were forced to it in the end. There was no place else to go and we couldn't sleep on our feet. So we shoved our way into the mass of snoring, groaning, cursing prisoners, and before day came we slept as soundly as the others.

We spent three days in the men's Common Side, and hour by hour Tom became more restless and impatient for news from outside. On the first morning he had sent word to one Nick Sabb, who, Tom said, was his fence. Sabb was a man of great influence, not only in the underworld of London, but among the police as well. He had been in and out of prison a dozen times, but never for long. He was, ostensibly, a pawn-broker, with a shop in Cloak Lane, off the Poultry, but this was merely the front behind which he carried on his various activities. Aside from his business as a receiver of stolen goods, he was a great vender of counterfeit money, the real source of his wealth. Sabb was far too astute to coin on his own, for the penalty, on conviction, was certain death. But by one of the many inconsistencies of criminal law, the buy-ing and selling of base money was ranked only as a mis-demeanour and the punishment for it light. Sabb, said Oakley, was the most prosperous merchant in this line in the whole of London.

"Nick never fails a friend," Oakley was saying as we paced the court on the afternoon of our third day. "I love the old rogue like a father; there never was a man with a kinder heart, and why the devil I've not heard from him afore this . . . My note's not reached him, that's sure. The cursed wardsman has pocketed my shilling and spared himself the trouble of sending it out."

I was as much in the dumps over this miscarriage of plan as Oakley himself, for I do not believe there is a human situation more truly miserable than that of men without money in Newgate prison. Heaven be thanked, we did not have to suffer it for long. It was getting on for dusk that same afternoon when a turnkey, the fellow who had first brought us here, came into the court and bustled up the moment he spied us.

"I'm to fetch ye out o' this, masters," he said with a grin.

"Why couldn't ye a told me in the first place ye're friends o'
Nick Sabb's? He's here, in quod himself."

"What!" said Tom.

"Aye," said the man; "on the State Side. Ye're to come
with me directly ye've had easement of irons, for he's paid for
that in advance."

With that the turnkey gave him a note scribbled on a bit
of grimy paper. Tom read it eagerly; then passed it to me: —

TOM:

The note went to Cloak Lane and back here. I've had it only this
minute. Welcome to Newgate. You and your friend are to lodge
next to Ned Inching and me.

"All's well now," said Oakley, "but what Ned Inching's
doing in Newgate is more than I can guess."

"Who is he?" I asked.

"The cleverest pickpocket in the Kingdom, bar none. He's
been at that game since babyhood, ye might say, but I've
never known of his being in quod before."

"Now, gents, if ye'll step along," said the turnkey.

Hard stepping it was with three sets of irons to our legs,
but the two extra sets were struck off in a little room close
by; we then followed the turnkey through a labyrinth of
passages leading to the State Side. As the man was unlocking
a door, Oakley regarded me with a faint smile, and I could
detect a glint of anxiety in his eye.

"Has it come home to ye, this place?" he asked.

"It's beginning to," I replied; "all but the irons."

Tom nodded. "They're a cursed nuisance and no mistake,
but there's no buying easement of the one pair. We'll be
obliged to wear 'em to the end, whichever way it goes with
us. We've an anxious time to come, but never lose heart.
We're not turned off yet. But what I would say is this: here
we are, two honest highwaymen, set down amongst thieves,

pickpockets, forgers, coiners, housebreakers, and the Lord knows what all. Can ye take 'em as they come?"

"Of course. Why not?" I replied.

Oakley gave me a hearty slap on the back. "Forgive me, lad, I might ha' known ye're not the man to sit on a high horse. And I want ye to take to Sabb. As he stands, I'd choose him for a friend above many that sits in the seats of Parliament."

The turnkey opened a last door leading to the State Side Court. Compared with the place we had left, it seemed to embody the height of comfort and luxurious ease. Money, as I was to learn, could do anything at Newgate, save open the door to freedom or banish the cold prison stench. It was now the shank of the evening for Newgate's nobility and gentry. The court was thronged with them, some as well dressed as respectable citizens on 'Change. There were candles and spermaceti lamps a-plenty: the brisk stir and bustle, the laughter and loud talk, the running about of waiters with trays of ale, grog, and hot food brought in from the cook-shops outside, put me in mind of some London tavern when the evening coaches come in, and the passengers, after their long journeys, are in the best of spirits, thinking of the good cheer at hand.

I would not go so far as to say that the State Side at Newgate resembled any of the London inns for homely comfort. Far from it. The place was mean and dingy; but there were fires going in the various rooms off the court, beds to sleep on, and some, at least, of the comforts and conveniences of life. We looked into rooms where men were sitting at cards; in others they were making merry over bowls of hot punch, for prisoners with money could send out for what they pleased in the way of food, ale, or spirits. Only the occasional clank of fetters reminded me that these men were felons.

We crossed the court and entered the room which Nicholas

Sabb shared with his friend Inching. Sabb waved his hand at sight of Oakley.

"What cheer, Tom?" he called. "Here's a stout heart! He lets himself get nabbed to keep an old friend company!"

Sabb was a man of middle age, and his belly alone would have made three Ned Inchings. His round, high-coloured face gleamed in the lamplight, and he wore his own hair, an untidy shock that stood out in all directions. Inching looked to be around fifty. His face was the colour of old untanned leather and seamed with a thousand wrinkles, and his ears stood out from his head like the handles of an urn. His hands were no larger than those of a boy. There was a third man present, Mr. Mortimer Thynne, and he looked strangely out of place in a prison. He was a little under middle height, slender of build, with a pale face of considerable refinement. His expression changed from moment to moment according to his mood, but for the most part, gayety shone from his grey eyes as though it came from an inexhaustible fund within.

There was no mistaking the sincerity of Sabb's welcome, and he received me with the same cordiality. The introductions over, places were made for us at the table. There was a good fire burning at one end of the room, and on the opposite side were two beds furnished with comfortable mattresses, pillows, and coverlets. A wash-hand stand stood by the wall with a small mirror over it. On the table itself were two bottles of Canary wine, and Sabb immediately ordered in two more for our benefit.

"Lads, sluice your gobs," he said, heartily. "We'll sup directly, but now's the hour for a whet. Wonders will never cease! Here's a merry party of friends and to-be-friends to meet up in the shade of the Old Bailey!"

"Is it not, Nick?" said Thynne. "Mr. Oakley, Mr. Tallant, here's to our better acquaintance."

The conversation that followed was kept going at a lively

pace by Sabb and Thynne, with Oakley putting in a word now and again. Inching's comments comprised a series of grunts, and squeaks like the rasping of a saw or file, and an occasional shrill chortle that always seemed to be cut off in the middle with a sharp "ik!" Not a word was said as to why any of us was in Newgate, nor was the least curiosity shown in the matter (though we learned later that Sabb, for all his wealth and influence, and for all his cleverness in keeping clear of the harder clutches of the law, had at last run afoul of it in such a manner that he had been tried and convicted as a receiver of stolen goods and sentenced to seven years' transportation). We might have been a group sitting in a coffee-house, as free of the law as so many respectable citizens. The talk was mostly of places, people, and events I knew nothing about, but I pricked up my ears when Thynne referred to his wife, who was with him in Newgate. He spoke of her with great respect, in a frank easy manner, as though it were perfectly natural and in the course of events that she too should be an inmate of Newgate. Presently he rose.

"Nick, my thanks and compliments. Better Purl Royal I've never tasted. And now I must be going."

"But why not stop with us?" said Sabb. "There's a hamper of vittles on the way; enough for a half a dozen."

Thynne smiled. "Another time, Nick. Mrs. Thynne and I are dining *en famille*. As you know, I cultivate the domestic virtues. Gentlemen, good evening, and *bon appétit!*"

Sabb had said no more than the truth about the coming supper. A waiter, himself a needy prisoner in Sabb's hire, brought it. He laid out the tableware and then set before us dishes of sliced turkey's gizzard, pickled oysters, cold pickled tongue with West Indian potargo, veal-and-ham pies, an excellent joint of beef, a bean tansey piping hot, in a huge earthenware dish, and another dish of boiled, creamed onions. And there was ale in plenty to wash all down. Tom and I needed no urging to do full justice to the meal, for we were

all but starved after the miserable pickings of the penniless
on the Common Side.

When the meal was over, Inching left us to join the crowd
in the court, and Tom then spoke of Nellie Garth. He was
telling Sabb who she was and what she was, and where she
was now lodged, when Nick halted him.

"Say no more," he said. "I'll have the good woman out of
that before the hour strikes."

He sent his lackey to fetch the wardsman, and in five
minutes' time he had arranged that Mrs. Garth was to have
a room to herself, — the one we had looked out from when
we watched her battle, — with coals, candles, bedding, food,
and everything needful for her comfort.

"God bless ye, Nick," said Oakley. "Ye've never served a
better turn to a better woman."

"And why shouldn't I?" said Sabb. "But Tom, how come's
it ye're as stony as all this?"

Tom then related our story, explaining my part in it, and
how we had been taken by Baxter's men. "And the worst of
it was, Nick," he added, "that they got the whole of the
money, save for a couple of guineas spent, and the fault for
this is mine. Worse still, there was French and Spanish pieces
amongst the English guineas, the same young Baxter had won
at Bath."

"There's no great danger in that," said Sabb, "for there
might well be foreign coins in any bag of guineas." He was
silent for some little time; then he added, "But that's evidence, of course, and there's this beside: the pistol wound of
your friend, here; your mare and Tallant's recognized, or
thought to be recognized. . . . What else? They can't swear
to your faces?"

"They was covered," said Tom.

"Was anything took off ye to tell against ye?"

"Aye, my striking-watch, mebbe," said Tom. "Ye've seen
it, but that was christened."

Sabb was again silent, and at last Oakley said: "Well, Nick, out with it. How do we stand, think ye?"

"Not bad, mebbe . . . and none so good, neither. Have ye a weatherproof story to account for Tallant's shoulder?"

"Aye, that's ready," said Tom.

"Ye was a fool to keep the watch," said Sabb. "Christened or not, it may do ye harm, for there's none cleverer than watchmakers for knowing their own handiwork. If they do, there's a piece of circumstantial evidence that'll tell. . . . Well, Tom, ye're far from being hung. But I'll say this: I'd sooner have my head on Tallant's neck than yours."

Sabb was no comforter; he had too much good sense to play that role. Late that night, a good two hours after Oakley and I had gone to bed in the adjoining room, Tom called, "Hugh, are ye sleeping?" and I knew that he was thinking as soberly as myself.

*　　*　　*　　*　　*

We had been some days in Newgate when the Governor himself came into court one morning, and inquired for Oakley and me by name. He was a tall, lean, middle-aged man, with a face that glowed like a sea-coal fire, noted for having a thirstier gullet than any of his pensioners, and for his favours to some of the younger, more personable female prisoners, several of whom were always employed as servants in his bachelor establishment. A turnkey followed with a bundle of clothing, and another fellow with a hammer and chisel. The Governor glanced at us incuriously when we had answered to our names. Our irons were then struck off and we were ordered to dress in our boots and riding clothes, fetched for the purpose from Garth's place. Presently we were handcuffed and led by two guards to the street in front of the prison. I was surprised to find that Tom and I held the centre of the stage for the crowd gathered there; furthermore, Tom's mare and the sorrel I had ridden on the night of the robbery were awaiting us. Oakley forgot the crowd when he saw Rosamond, and the mare laid her head on his shoulder, fondling him with her lips.

We were ordered to mount, and then the horses were led back and forth in front of the gate while the crowd looked us over. Notice had been printed in the papers and elsewhere that the two highwaymen, suspected of having robbed the coach of Reginald Baxter, Esq., on the Bath Road on the night of December eighth, would be exhibited before the main gate at Newgate, and that any gentlemen having been robbed in recent months were requested to be present to view these men.

It was a trying ordeal, and I all but sweat blood lest I should chance to be seen by some of my Loyalist acquaintances. However, nothing of the sort happened, and when we had been viewed by a crowd of, I dare say, five hundred people, from first to last, we were ordered to dismount and led back into the prison.

And now, if anyone wishes to hear the whole story of the trial and conviction of Messrs. Hugh Tallant and Thomas Oakley, he can whistle for it, so far as I am concerned, or go to the records, for the year 1787, kept at the Old Bailey Sessions House. We were tried at the January assizes — tried, convicted, and condemned to death, and the weeks that followed I have spent forty-five years of my life trying to forget. Oakley and I both had reason to thank God for that quality in our race which forbids an Englishman, not wholly sure of his ground, to swear away the life of another man. Nevertheless, the evidence pointed so strongly to our guilt that a verdict was found against us, but with it went a recommendation of clemency. It was not until early in March that we learned that our sentences had been commuted by His Majesty's Privy Council to transportation for life. Poor Nellie Garth was given seven years' transportation for being an accessory.

V

MORTIMER THYNNE

It was late in December, 1786, when Mrs. Garth, Oakley, and I entered Newgate prison. On the fifth of May in the year following, we left the forbidding place as convicted felons bound for Botany Bay, in New South Wales.

Botany Bay — how the name rang in my ears! It became more and more familiar to all Newgate prisoners as the weeks and months passed. We heard it from the lips of officers of the Court, of keepers and turnkeys, of visitors from the outside who came to see friends and relatives in the gaol; for, at about the time we had been taken into custody, His Majesty's Government, after years of delay, had decided to establish a penal colony in New South Wales. Botany Bay was the place fixed upon. For more than a century and a half, England had emptied her gaols into the American Colonies, but the outbreak of the Revolution had put an end for all time to this practice: America wanted no more settlers of this kind. And so, for ten years, from the beginning of the war until 1786, England's convicted felons had been accumulating throughout the country. Conditions in the gaols and hulks had become so desperate, from overcrowding and disease, that the Government was at last forced to take action, and in the summer of '86, orders were given for the outfitting of a fleet of transports which were to carry to an unknown continent more than halfway around the world as many convicts as could be crowded aboard. I understood now why His Majesty's Home Office had ignored Mr. James Matra's petition for colonizing

American Loyalists at Botany Bay. They had New South Wales in mind as a penal settlement and, as the need to empty the gaols and hulks was greater than their sense of obligation to the Loyalists, the decision was made. It was, to me, a bitter reflection that, of all the American refugees in London who had dreamed of New South Wales as a future home, I alone was to have that dream fulfilled, and with a vengeance.

Thanks to Nick Sabb, Oakley and I had been spared the greater miseries of Newgate life, and he had opened his wallet as generously for Nellie Garth. In comparison with the friendless, penniless convicts, we lived like nabobs, and when our turn came, Sabb, Mortimer Thynne, Oakley, Ned Inching, and I, in a coach of Nick's hiring, made the journey to Portsmouth, where the transports lay, ready for their cargo. We had hoped that Garth and Mrs. Thynne could go with us, but women were kept separate from the men on these journeys, and all the influence of Messrs. Sabb and Thynne had not succeeded in gaining for these two the privacy of our coach. They were compelled to go in a great wagon drawn by four horses, and filled with Newgate's worst — shameless creatures who hooted and yelled as they set out for Portsmouth, whilst some of the more brazen lay in the straw and waved their shackled legs in the air. It was a wagonful of bawdiness and no mistake.

Our own party set out like so many respectable citizens off for a day of pleasure in the country. To be sure, we were in shackles and under guard, but folk in the streets could not see the irons. We left the women's wagon far behind before we had reached the open country. Every mile put between us and the miseries of Newgate was like a load lifted from the heart. It was glorious spring weather, with the birds singing, the trees in new leaf, and the meadows so fresh and green that I could have looked at them forever. Merely to draw in the clean rain-washed air was a joy past measuring; it was worth all we had suffered to have this heightened pleasure in the simple act of breathing. Tom was as lighthearted as myself; he sang, he whistled, and thrust his head out the window every other moment to call or wave to countryfolk in the lanes and fields. Ned Inching sat glum in his corner, and Sabb seemed in no better spirits.

"Aye, Tom," Nick remarked presently, "it's well enough for a pair of country louts like yourself and Tallant to take joy in the fields, but what about us?"

"Why, ye moon-faced gallows-load," said Tom, "d'ye mean to say ye're not glad to be quit of Newgate? God's truth! Here's the greatest rogue in London that's missed dangling in the sheriff's picture frame by the width of an eyebrow, and he finds nothing to be merry about!"

"Be damned to ye," said Sabb. "I was never in finger-post distance of the gallows, but I'd take the risk willing enough to bide in London." He shook his head with a heavy sigh. "When will I ever see it again?"

"When? Why, seven years from now, old guts-and-garbage! What's seven years to a man can live on his own fat the whole of the time if it comes to that? Shame to ye, Nick! Here's Hugh and me as lively as new fleas, and we've got life to serve. Cheer up, old cock! And ye too, Ned Inching, else I'll give ye a footing! Ye look as doleful as a pair of Scotch alley cats! . . . Look yonder," he added, as a handsome carriage drawn by four horses approached down the drive of a great park we were passing. "I'll take oath there's one of His Majesty's privy councillors inside that coach, and if he had his deserts he'd be riding with us.

"The little rogue the Law's last tribute pays,
    While crowns around the great one's chariot blaze . . .

Call me cut if that ain't sober truth, though who wrote the lines I couldn't say."

"Never call me a little rogue," said Sabb.

"Haven't I said ye was the greatest in London," said Tom with a grin, "save fellows like His Lordship yonder?"

"I can enlighten you as to the author of the quotation, Mr. Oakley," said Thynne. "It is no other than our distinguished poet laureate, Mr. Whitehead."

"Is it so, Mr. Thynne? Well, here's another to cap the first, and damme if I don't think it's the better of the two: —

> "The law doth punish man or woman
> That steals a goose from off the common,
> But lets the greater villain loose
> That steals the common from off the goose."

"Excellent, Tom, excellent!" said Thynne, with a chuckle. "More truth than poetry there."

"Aye, it holds a mort of truth," said Oakley. "The greatest villains in the Kingdom are the nabobs that go to His Majesty's levees. They've stole nine tenths of the country from the rest of us, and they covet the other tenth. It's them that take the people's commons and they do it by acts of Parliament. And if some poor lad poaches a rabbit in His Lordship's park, where does he land? . . . Hugh, d'ye mind the redhaired boy sent along to the transports last week? What was his name . . . Dugan, if I recollect."

"What of him?" asked Thynne.

"The lad might be fifteen, though he looked younger. *He* stole a goose, or was it a hen? What does he get? Seven years' transportation! There's the King's justice for ye! I mind another sample of it I saw when passing through Covent Garden Market, not a fortnight before Tallant and me was caught: there was two men being flogged through the streets, taking their air and exercise at the same cart's tail. For what, would ye say?"

"Misdemeanours, certainly, else we might have had the pleasure of their company to Botany Bay," said Thynne.

"So they call 'em, Thynne, and one was a small thing. The

man had stole a bunch of radishes, valued at sixpence. But the fellow beside him, taking the same punishment, had raped a girl of fifteen, his own niece. Is that justice?"

"I know a pair of brisk young highwaymen with no call to complain on the score of justice," said Sabb.

"Aye, we was lucky," said Oakley. "I'll warrant Tallant's neck is as sore as me own at thinking how close we was to wearing a hempen stock. . . . Ned Inching, brisk up, me lad! Look at him, Nick! He's got the pride of Satan and thought never to be nabbed."

This was, indeed, a sore point with Ned Inching, alias Tim Sidewise, and I don't know how many others, though Inching was the handle he went by in Newgate. He was as proud of his trade as though it had been the most honourable, as it was among the most ancient, in the land. According to Sabb, Inching had started picking pockets as soon as he was tall enough to reach them, and in forty years he had been caught but once before. Now he was for seven years' transportation.

He gave Oakley a sour look. "How far will it be, this Botany Bay?" he asked.

"Hugh, you're a scholar," said Oakley. "Where is the bloody place?"

"A matter of halfway around the world," I replied.

"Right, Mr. Tallant," said Thynne. "According to my computations, we will cover on the voyage a distance in the very near neighbourhood of fourteen thousand miles."

"Fourteen thousand miles!" Sabb exclaimed. Oakley laughed heartily at his doleful expression.

"So it is, Nick. Trust Mr. Thynne to know his geography, for he's been to Oxford, and Cambridge too, I shouldn't wonder. Now tell us, Thynne, what like of a land is it?"

"A very unpromising one, I fear, Tom."

"With naught but rocks and sand and the bush filled with wild beasts and naked savages?"

"Something of the kind, certainly."

"Good! Hugh and me will thrive there. But poor Nick! His guts will cry cupboard from morn till night; and what Ned will do is more than I can guess, for the wild men will have never a pocket amongst 'em. Never mind — hearts of oak, lads, hearts of oak!"

Little any of us knew about New South Wales, but Thynne had a copy of the *Morning Chronicle* of the day before, in which was a brief account of transports which were to take us there. He drew out the paper and read us the following: —

"It is now expected that the fleet for Botany Bay will sail within the week. The expedition is under the command of Captain Arthur Phillip, R. N., who will remain in New South Wales as first Governor of the colony. He will sail in H.M.S. *Sirius*, with H.M. armed tender *Supply* as an auxiliary vessel. The following transports will carry the felons:

1. *Alexander* — 213 male convicts
2. *Scarborough* — 208 male convicts
3. *Friendship* — 77 male and 20 female convicts
4. *Charlotte* — 88 male and 20 female convicts
5. *Prince of Wales* — 100 female convicts
6. *Lady Penrhyn* — 102 female convicts

Three store-ships, the *Golden Grove, Fishburn,* and *Borrowdale,* will carry most of the supplies for the colony. A company of marines, under command of Major Robert Ross, to form the military establishment, is already at Portsmouth, and it is expected that the last of the convicts will be embarked by Saturday next."

This notice, bald and dry as it was, gave us matter for discussion during the next hour; then we fell silent, and one by one my companions dropped off to sleep. As I looked from one to another of them, I thought of the strangeness of my fortunes in being of that company. Inching alone excepted, none of them bore the stamp of the underworld upon him. For all that he was a highwayman, Tom Oakley did not belong to that world, though he knew it well enough. Sabb knew no other, but he would have passed anywhere as a respectable merchant, rather too fond of good living. As for Mortimer Thynne, he might have been a schoolmaster, a parson, a barrister, a banker, for he could have fitted himself to any of these professions insofar as appearance went. Of all the convicts I had met in Newgate, Mr. and Mrs. Thynne had most interested and puzzled me. To see them in fetters was a shock to one's sense of probability; indeed, of possibility. Mrs. Thynne was a handsome woman of forty, half a head taller than her husband, with fine dark eyes and thick brown hair, and a complexion that needed no aid from art. Her manners were most correct, and her speech as genteel as though she had graced in her youth one of the most elegant of young ladies' finishing schools. She gave an appearance of delicacy in constitution, and yet she had borne the unspeakable conditions of Newgate with no appearance of sinking under them. To be sure, she had enjoyed there, with her husband, the best quarters and all the comforts that money could procure, for Mr. Thynne was as well provided with funds as Nick Sabb himself. Even so, it was a horrible place, and there was no paying for a single breath of pure air. I admired Mrs. Thynne's courage, and her gift for carrying her gentility with her. She was always handsomely dressed, and spent most of her time in Newgate in making her toilet for the appearance in the State Side court, late in the afternoon, and a veritable triumph she made of it. Thynne's own costume was always of the best materials, though more sober in taste, and I shouldn't wonder if it were not designed to set off to greater advantage the elegance of his wife. He looked like an Oxford don who had married a comfortable fortune, and for all I know that may have been the case. Husband and wife were, by profession, what is known as "gate-crashers." With spurious cards of admission to routs, balls, masquerades, and other assemblies of the fashionable world, they would lift jewelry, silverware, watches, diamond-studded snuffboxes, whatever of value came to hand. They were such accomplished thieves that they had practised their profession successfully for years, in both London and provincial towns. Aiming at ever higher game, they had finally been caught at one of the King's levees. Their case at the Old Bailey Sessions House caused a stir and there was a great deal about it in the newspapers. Upon conviction, both were sentenced to fourteen years' transportation. They were completely lacking in any appearance of hurt pride and accepted their changed condition with as much ease and self-possession as though they were going to New South Wales as free and prosperous settlers. As I looked at Mr. Thynne, opposite me in the coach, and sleeping like an honest gentleman bound to Portsmouth on business, it was hard to believe in our forlorn condition and the fate in store for the five of us.

To distract my thoughts I took up the newspaper and read again the item about Botany Bay. If the figures given were correct, 586 men were being sent out and but 242 women. Some Grub Street wag had noticed these figures, for there was a bit of verse below the news item, with one stanza reading: —

> Three husbands at once, Mr. Gaoler, you say,
> We females shall have when at Botany Bay?
> Punishment, this, to be sought after, courted?
> Before they transport us we're more than transported!

Oakley, who had been snoring loudly, awoke.

"What are ye about, Hugh?" he asked.

"There's eight hundred and twenty-eight of us for New South Wales if this tally is right," I said. "Have you thought of it? Except for a few stout fellows like ourselves, here's a cargo of misery that will be as helpless where we're going as babes in the wood."

"You're right; I was thinking the same thing myself. There never was such a crackbrained expedition as this sent out since England was a nation. But they get rid of us, and that's the main thing. I shouldn't wonder if the hope is they'll never see hide nor hair of us again. We're none so lucky, but I'd sooner be in my own shoes than in his that's to govern us. What's his name again?"

"Phillip."

Tom shook his head. "God help him! A merry time he'll have trying to make a settlement on the ends of the earth with eight hundred convicts! There'll not be above a score that knows any trade save that of knavery. But let him and them that's sent him worry about that." He glanced cautiously at the coachmen on the box and the guard beside him; then he added, in a low voice: "I'm thinking of ourselves. Transportation for life — it's just beginning to come in to me what that means. 'Tis a huge land, ain't it, this New South Wales?"

"No one knows the extent of it, but you could put a score of Englands in it, that's certain."

Tom stretched out his legs, regarding his shackles with a mingled air of disgust and contempt; then he gave me a hearty smack on the knee. "Man, it's good to be alive and fit for anything!"

I felt the same way about it, and as the coach rolled and jolted on its way to Portsmouth, we talked of the future as though we were free men and Botany Bay a promised bed of roses rather than a penal settlement.

We reached Portsmouth too late to be taken aboard one of the transports. Instead, we were carried to the town gaol for the night, and found it crowded to suffocation with others waiting to be embarked. It was an ancient three-story building of brick, more foul than Newgate itself. The keeper, a sergeant-at-mace, was one of those gaolers who serve without pay for the sake of the perquisites extorted from the inmates, but what he had provided in return for his fees I couldn't see, for the room into which he attempted to squeeze us had neither beds nor bedding; there was scarcely space to set foot between the men lying or sitting on the bare floor. The guards who had brought us from London were a pair of typical Newgate flunkeys, accustomed, for a suitable reward, to looking out for the welfare of their "gentlemen lodgers." Judging by their indignation as they peered into this crowded ward, you might have thought that they and not ourselves were to sleep there.

"Look ye, Master," said one, "this 'ere's a genteel party we've brought, and we'll not have 'em pigged in the like o' this. Have ye no better quarters?"

"I might have," said the warden.

"And what d'ye ask?" said Sabb.

"Ten shillings the night, gentlemen, with hot food at five shillings, and good ale at ninepence the quart."

"Then take us there," said Sabb.

"Ye must pay on the nail," said the warden. He led us to a dingy narrow room lighted by two small windows, and stood with his hands on his hips while Sabb drew out the great leather pouch I knew well by this time. I will not venture to say how many guineas, half crowns, and shilling pieces I had seen paid out of it, but there seemed to be no bottom to the pouch, the reason being that Sabb's nephew, in London, his right-hand man in business, kept him well supplied.

"Nick," said Oakley, when the money had been paid and the door locked behind the guards, "d'ye know how deep Tallant and me are in your debt?"

"Shut up or I'll wring your necks," said Sabb. "What's that to me?"

"Nothing, I know it well, but we're not the men to forget an obligation. Hugh, ye've kept tally. What's it come to?"

I consulted my pocketbook. "Not counting to-night, the total is forty-one pounds, seven and fourpence," I replied, "and how we're ever to get square with you, Nick, is more than I can see."

"Hush, now," said Sabb. "Who's said anything about payments? I've done naught ye wouldn't do for me in the same pinch, and where'll be the good of money in the place we're going?"

"Ha, ha, ha! Just so," laughed Thynne. "We shall be true children of nature in Botany Bay."

"It's good coin, Nick?" Tom asked, with a wink at me, as Sabb was about to return the pouch to his pocket.

"Good!" said Sabb, bristling up. He drew forth a half crown and dropped it to the stone floor. "Is that the ring of true sweet silver? Is it, Tom Oakley?"

"Aye, Nick — sweet as a bell's tone. I was wrong to question it."

Sabb's great belly shook with a silent chuckle.

"Lads, as ye know, I'm all but master of one of the King's mints, but since His Majesty don't know it, I take heed to carry with me none but coin that has his own approval."

"And a very sound practice that is," said Thynne.

Then, over a gallon of ale ordered up by our two bene-factors, we fell to discussing our immediate prospects, and our chances of being embarked together, on the same trans-port. Thynne surprised us all by saying that he had two daughters, one of whom was to accompany her parents to Botany Bay.

"Thynne, I've known ye, off and on, these five years," said Sabb, "but this is the first I've heard of the daughters."

"Mrs. Thynne and I make no parade of the domestic affec-tions, Mr. Sabb. They are charming girls, both, though I do say it. It is Phoebe, our baby, who is to go with us."

Barbarous as England's treatment was of her convicts, it was made somewhat less so by the provision that a father, or mother, or both, sentenced to transportation, could apply to have one or more of their free children sent with them. Per-mission was granted or not, according to circumstances, and whether or no room could be found in the transports. Thynne told us that permission for his daughter Phoebe had already been granted and that she and her elder sister, Doris, were to meet their parents in Portsmouth. Garth, as I knew, had applied for permission to take Nat and had been refused.

"And your eldest is not to go?" Sabb was saying.

"Doris? No, no," said Thynne. "She is adequately — I might say, splendidly provided for."

Sabb gave him a shrewd look. "There's a blessing," he said.

"Is it not? Dear Doris! She is Mrs. . . . ah . . . Mrs. Livingstone now. We had hoped to have our chick, our Phoebe, as well settled, and she might have been, there's no doubt of it. But . . . dear me, when it came to the thought of separation, it was not to be borne. Phoebe wished to come with us, and I can't say that we regret the decision. She'll be a great comfort to us. . . . My poor wife! What a day she will have had in the wagon, and Mrs. Garth as well!"

The women arrived at about eight in the evening. Somewhere on the way the more abandoned females had laid in a supply of gin, and the half of them were now howling drunk. Some stood in the wagon, clinging to one another for support while they yelled and jeered at the townsfolk and exchanged obscenities with bystanders no better than themselves. We first heard them from afar and stood at our upstairs windows overlooking the street to watch the arrival. The clear cold light of the May evening brought out every detail of the scene: the mean houses, for it was a wretched quarter of the town, crowded with drabs and slatterns; the shackled women, some with faces that seemed scarcely human, their hair hanging in tangled mops about their shoulders, posturing in lewd attitudes to the delight of the mob of hoodlums that followed them. It was a picture that Hogarth might have painted, and even he would not have dared to present it in its naked truth; only the well-fed, sweating horses could have been depicted as they were. We caught sight of Nellie Garth and Mrs. Thynne seated in one corner of the wagon, gazing straight before them, with stony faces.

"God help 'em!" Oakley exclaimed. "Sabb, we must get 'em out of that company if we have to wreck the gaol!"

A request was sent to the warden, and in return for a handsome fee he consented that Garth and Mrs. Thynne should come into our room. It was a long narrow chamber, and a piece of dirty sailcloth was stretched across one end to make an apartment for them. They were brought in a few moments later. Garth halted at the door and looked about her with a glint of humour in her eyes.

"What's this?" said she. "Mrs. Thynne, do they take us for a pair of trollops that they put us amongst the men?"

"God love ye, Nellie!" said Tom. "Ye look as happy as Hunt's dog! The beast of a time ye and Mrs. Thynne will have had since the morning!"

"Nothing of the sort, Mr. Oakley," said Mrs. Thynne. "Mrs. Garth and I did very well."

"My love," said her husband, "you're a woman of courage: I've always said it. But . . . dear me, this goes beyond my expectations. Mrs. Garth, my compliments and respects. You both look as cool and fresh as Roman matrons at the blush of a new day."

"And why not?" said Garth. " 'Twas a lovely day indeed as to weather, and we took the full good of it."

"But how could ye, with such shameless creatures for company?" asked Oakley.

Mrs. Thynne laughed. "They sang the most shocking songs!"

"There, my love, we'll speak of them no more. We'll hear songs and to spare, no doubt, before the night is done."

Mr. Thynne's prediction was more than fulfilled, for the women were lodged directly below us, and they made night hideous until the small hours. But Newgate experiences had inured us all to bedlam, and the Thynnes, with Sabb and Inching, played cribbage with as much pleasure and as strict attention to the game as though they were in some quiet country tavern. Nellie Garth sat apart, by the window, speaking to no one. She was thinking of Nat, of course. A bitter prospect it was to her, setting off without him. Oakley and I made no attempt to comfort her. We talked of the long voyage ahead, trying to form some picture of the land of our exile, and wondering where we would be that day ten years hence.

Some time after midnight Mrs. Thynne joined Nellie in their apartment behind the canvas curtain, and the rest of us prepared for bed by the simple act of taking off our shoes.

VI

PHOEBE AND DORIS

I HAD thought Newgate a foul place, but the conditions in the Portsmouth gaol were even worse. There was but one pump for the whole of the prison, in a brick-walled yard at the back. Oakley and I had tried to get a wash there when we first came in, but the crowd was so great we could not get near it. Early the next morning before the others were stirring we went down again and found the yard empty.

"The Lord be thanked!" Tom exclaimed. "Now, if only we could strip and have a proper scrub! The filthy beasts, to grudge us that small comfort!"

The irons we wore comprised a length of chain linked through collars about three inches wide which were fixed above the ankles with iron pins riveted in place, and they could be struck off only by a blacksmith. We had worn the cursed things since our arrival in Newgate, and only twice in all those many weeks had we been freed from them so that we could wash without being hampered by clothing. But we could have a bath of a kind by dropping our breeches whilst we soaped and scrubbed our bodies; then we would wash the breeches as well as we could, wring them out and let them dry on our bodies.

We were hard at this task when a strong-made fellow of about thirty crossed the yard leading a small boy by the hand. He stood looking on whilst we soaped and scrubbed our soiled shirts and put on fresh ones. Tom was humming to himself in the joy of being clean once more. The newcomer smiled.

"Aye, it's a rare treat, is water," he remarked.

"Ye wish to freshen the lad?" asked Oakley. "Come along; I'll pump."

The father removed the boy's clothes and stood him in the tub beneath the spout. Oakley pumped vigorously, and the lad jumped up and down for the pleasure he took, throwing back his head to catch the stream of water full in his face. He was about eight years old, a handsome little fellow, but with a delicate look about him.

"There, Tommy, ye shine like a new penny," his father said as he lifted him out and tossed him in the air at arm's length.

"Tommy, is it?" said Oakley. "Would ye believe it, now! There's two of us with that same uncommon handle!"

"I'm Tom Goodwin," said the boy.

"And a good name *that* is. Ye'll win through to anything, I'll be bound, when ye've growed a bit."

When his father had toweled and dressed him in fresh clothing, he said, "Run along now to yer ma whilst I have a scrub."

For the next five minutes the father thought of nothing but the treat of clean water. It was as good as having a wash all over again to see the delight he took in his own. He was powerfully built, his arms and shoulders knotted with muscle. His head, covered with short curly brown hair, was set on a short muscular neck.

"Dan Goodwin's my name," he said.

When we had given our own, Oakley said: "Ye don't look to have been in long."

"Long enough," said Goodwin. "Better than five years — in the hulks on the Thames. But I've kept my health, being abroad by day, working on the stone barges."

"And where away now? Botany Bay?"

"Aye." An expression of grimness passed over Goodwin's face. "And with scarce a year left to serve of the seven given. I'd hoped to finish it out here."

"Man, ye're lucky for all that, alongside of us. We're sent for life."

Goodwin made no comment for a moment; then he asked: "D'ye know the transport ye're booked for?" We shook our heads. "I'm for the *Charlotte*. We're to go aboard to-day."

"The lad goes with you?" I asked.

"Aye, and his mother, though she's a free woman. But she would come and bring the boy, for all I could say against it. She got the permit unbeknownst to me."

Goodwin put out his hand. "Well, lads, the best of luck! Mebbe we'll go in the same ship; but we'll meet down yonder, if not afore." Then, with a nod, he left us.

Oakley stood looking after him, thoughtfully.

"What d'ye think of him, Hugh?" he asked.

"The salt of the earth, if I'm a judge of men," I replied.

"Ye can lay to that," said Oakley. "No flaw in the metal there, whatever he's done. Let's hope we're sent in the *Charlotte*. We'll do well with a two-three like Goodwin for friends."

Upon returning to our quarters we found our companions gathered around Sabb, who was seated at the table, gazing dolefully at a sheet of paper he held in his hand.

"What's amiss, Nick?" said Tom. "Will there be nothing for breakfast?"

Sabb peered at us over the top of his spectacles, which he wore, I think, not so much for use as because they gave him so perfect an appearance of respectability. Seeing him now, you might have thought he was some honest merchant who had received news of a fall in stocks.

"The food's to come directly," he said, "but Tom, it looks to be the last meal you'll take with some of us for many a long day."

The warden had come in our absence, leaving the orders received for our going aboard the transports. The Thynnes, with Oakley, were down for the *Friendship;* the rest of us were to go in the *Charlotte*. This was sad news for all, for we had hoped to go in the same ship.

"Curse ye, Nick!" said Tom. "Didn't ye draw the pouch and jingle it about? 'Twould be worth a guinea or two, surely, to have us all together."

Sabb shook his head. "Money will mend nothing here. The orders came from above — the Home Office like as not. We must go as ordered."

"So be it," said Tom, cheerfully. "What can't be helped must be endured. Liven up, old pinch-guts! Mr. Thynne and I will have ye nightly in our prayers. Now then, where's breakfast?"

"Coming, Tom, coming," said Thynne, rubbing his hands in anticipation. "And *such* a breakfast!"

"As what?"

"Eggs, just minted, warm from the hens — let us hope. And rashers, and pig's liver, and grilled kidneys, and veal-and-ham pie. Is there something more you might fancy? There's still time to send out."

"Can we manage, Hugh, with what's ordered?" said Tom.

"We can try," I replied. "Mr. Sabb, Mr. Thynne, our hearty thanks. You've done more than well by us these many months. We'll do as well by you at Botany Bay, if there's fish and game to be caught."

"Just what Thynne and I was thinking," said Sabb, his eyes twinkling. "We're not so simple as we look, may be. Payment, with interest, at Botany Bay, eh, Thynne?"

"Precisely," said Thynne, with a laugh. "Fish and fowls and beasts of the forest, brought daily to our doorsteps, if doorsteps there will be. . . . What is it, my love?"

Mrs. Thynne, who was standing at the window, gave a little shriek of pleasure. "The girls, Mortimer! Here they are!"

Ever since Thynne had first spoken of them, I had been wondering what kind of daughters such a pair would have.

We hurried to the window to see an elegant coach, drawn by two horses in shining harness, pull up before the entrance to the prison. There were a coachman and a footman in tawny-coloured livery with gold braid to match the trimmings of the carriage.

Oakley, who was beside me, gave a gasp of astonishment as the girls got down; and well he might have, for they were lovely creatures as elegantly dressed as though on their way to take the air in St. James's Park. A striking contrast they and their equipage made in those wretched surroundings.

"Here we are, my loves!" Thynne called, thrusting a hand through the bars of the window and waving to them. "Tell the keeper to fetch you up directly."

In his excitement Oakley had pushed me to one side, so that I could not see them as they glanced up, but I heard one reply, with a merry laugh: "Gracious, Papa! Where's your wig? You haven't lost it?"

"No, no! Of course I've not lost it. Make haste! We're about to sit down to breakfast."

"Poor dears," said Mrs. Thynne. "I fancy they've only just come. They look dreadfully disheveled."

"Disheveled? Nonsense, Florentia! They're as fresh as rose-buds."

Sabb stood back, hands on his hips, gazing at Thynne with an air of wonderment and unbelief. "Thynne, they're your daughters?" he asked.

"Dear me! Whose else would they be? It's no great compliment you pay Mrs. Thynne, sir, to doubt it."

"I crave pardon, ma'am," said Sabb. "So handsome a mother would be bound to have daughters to match . . . but . . . well, I'm beat to think of their coming here."

"Where else would they go?" asked Thynne. "Phoebe is to share the exile of her unfortunate parents, and Doris wishes to bid us good-bye. You would not deprive us of a last re-union, Mr. Sabb?"

The Thynnes understood Sabb's bewilderment well enough, I think. At any rate, Mrs. Thynne smiled with a little air of triumph and flattered vanity. The lovely apparitions did not, certainly, fit the setting, yet neither of the parents appeared to think there was anything remarkable in their coming here. Oakley and I hastened to put on our neckcloths, waistcoats, and coats, and Tom stood waiting with an air of intense expectancy. I knew as well as though he had told me that he would have given the world and all to be dressed at the top of his bent at that moment.

A moment later the door was unlocked and the young ladies entered. Phoebe, the smaller of the two, was dressed in a little bonnet and a gown of pale blue silk that suited her to perfection. She had thick corn-coloured hair, meticulously dressed, and her eyes, of a deep blue, would have sent a flutter into the heart of any young man. She rushed to her mother's arms, and then kissed her father lightly on both cheeks. Doris had the brown hair and fine dark eyes of her mother and would have been about twenty-one or twenty-two at this time. Her mother held her at arm's length for a moment, regarding her critically; then she gave a little nod.

"You'll do quite well, my dear," she said; "quite well indeed."

"I'm so glad you think so, Mama. Heavens! What a place!"

"The 'Thynne's Arms,' my love," said her father with a gay laugh. "We've only just moved in, and the comforts are not yet all that could be wished."

"And Doris, love, I'd have you notice the Thynne's feet," said her mother. With a dainty movement she lifted her frock a little and thrust out her legs, stretching them apart to the length of the chain that shackled them, making the links rattle at a great rate. Doris's eyes widened, then she and Phoebe burst out laughing, their parents joining heartily, as though it were the greatest joke in the world.

"Now you must look at mine," said Thynne, and he did

a little caper that made them laugh even more. "I've a set of little bells ordered for your mama's, and I shall have mine handsomely gilded before we reach Botany Bay."

"What do you think of my bonnet, Papa?" Phoebe asked.

"Perfect, perfect. I could not have made a better choice for you myself."

"There, Doris!" said Phoebe, wrinkling her nose and thrusting her tongue out at her sister. "She called it hideous, Papa."

"It doesn't suit her at all," said Doris.

"Jealous thing!" said Phoebe. "She's eaten up with envy because she didn't see it first."

"There, my loves, no quarreling. You're both perfect. Now tell us: when did you come?"

The Thynnes, parents and daughters, seemed for the moment to have forgotten the presence of the rest of us. They had eyes only for one another, and seemed as carefree as though sitting cozily at home, the world shut out. Presently Phoebe raised her eyes for the most demure and winning glance at Tom and me. "Papa, aren't you forgetting yourself?" she asked. "You've not introduced your friends."

"Bless me, so I haven't!" Thynne exclaimed. "Mrs. Garth, ma'am — my daughters. Messrs. Sabb, Oakley, Tallant, and Inching — my daughters. The world at large — my daughters."

Nellie Garth was as taken by the strangeness of this domestic scene as ourselves. She greeted the girls very civilly, and the rest of us bowed with our best manners, Phoebe and Doris glancing from one to another of us with a slight inclination of their comely heads. Phoebe had the practice of looking at you, shyly and trustfully, then dropping her glance in a most demure and engaging way. Doris had the manners, at least, and the self-possession of a lady. Both daughters had their mother's fine complexion and teeth as white as milk. I was young and vain enough to feel a little stir of envy at the very particular, though discreet, regard Phoebe bestowed upon

Oakley. As for Tom, he had been hard hit from the moment of her coming and had eyes for no one else.

One of the turnkeys now appeared, followed by two female prisoners bringing our breakfast, in two large baskets. Places were made for the daughters, and Mr. Thynne, in honour of the occasion, took his seat at the head of the table, with his wife opposite. Phoebe sat across from Tom, and besieged him with such skill that the poor fellow scarcely noticed his food; but there was nothing forward or bold in Phoebe's glances. Instead, she gave the impression of a modest young girl whose heart had been caught for the first time, and who is all wonder and confusion at the strangeness of the experience. And for all I knew then, or know now, that may have been true.

Mr. and Mrs. Thynne were in their gayest mood. What always impressed me about them was their self-possession, their lack of any sense of strangeness or incongruity upon whatever occasion, in whatever company. Their daughters had it as well. On the present occasion they ignored the miserable room with its bare brick walls and iron-barred windows. They ignored the shouts and oaths and bawdy talk we could hear only too plainly, coming from the room below where the female felons were confined. Only once was notice taken of the latter. In a brief pause in our conversation, we heard one of the trollops, with a voice like a fishwife, yell to another: "Is it so, ye ha'penny upright! Ye've a Jack in the cellar at the very moment and well ye know it, but who was so daft as to board an old fire-ship like yerself is more than I could say!"

Mr. Thynne raised his eyebrows with an air of mild concern.

"Dear me!" he said. "The language is allusive, yet scarcely so veiled as might be wished."

"What creatures," Doris remarked, with a shrug of her pretty shoulders. "Mama, I hope you won't have to associate with them on the voyage."

Mrs. Thynne gave a little sigh. "I'm afraid I shall," she replied, "and Phoebe with me. Your father will be in the same ship with us, of course, but they tell us we shall be lodged in different parts. There's no avoiding it."

"Alas, no," said Mr. Thynne. "The orders are very strict, but I shall, of course, try what money can do, once we are embarked."

"How awful!" said Doris. "Papa, can't you *make* Phoebe stay behind? Her wanting to go is perfectly ridiculous!"

"It is, my love: your mama and I are of the same opinion."

"It really is absurd, Phoebe," said Mrs. Thynne. "You don't know how foolish you are. Why, there isn't even a town in Botany Bay. Nothing, I believe, but the empty land."

"I'm going," said Phoebe, quietly. "Doris may do as she pleases, but *I* love my parents, and I mean to share their hardships."

"You see?" said Doris. "Phoebe would have you think me a heartless, selfish creature, but I'm not, Papa, you know I'm not. I can do far more for you in London than ever I could in that wretched Botany Bay."

"You can, my dear child," said her father, patting her hand. "There, we'll call the matter settled and say no more about it. Doris shall be our urban goddess of plenty, mindful always of her dear parents in the wilderness, and sending us news from afar of the gayeties and splendours of London. Mind that you write whenever occasion offers!"

"Papa! To be sure I shall!"

"*If* ever occasion offers, which I doubt . . . And Phoebe shall be our nymph of the glades and forests. Even now, Phoebe my love, I see thee, the spirit of delight and youthful grace, in thy little kirtle of grasses . . ."

"That will do, you wretch!" said Mrs. Thynne, with a faint smile. "Would you trick us into thinking we are bound for a very Eden?"

"No, Florentia! But, Botany Bay . . . the mere name is a

promise. Doris, you have brought, I hope, your mother's things and mine, our poor trifles and oddments for the voyage?"

"Yes, Papa. Three huge boxes, with Mama's things in two of them and yours in one. Phoebe has her own in a fourth."

"Four boxes! My loves, I doubt if we shall be permitted to carry so many."

"Oh, but you will. They are already aboard the *Friendship*."

Her father gazed at her admiringly.

"Doris, I have always known your capabilities, but this surpasses expectation. How did you know that we are to embark in the *Friendship?*"

"I inquired, of course. Phoebe and I met a very agreeable young officer in the company of marines who are to guard you. He took us directly to a Major Ross, in charge of all the soldiers: such a nice man . . ."

"Oh, Doris!" Phoebe exclaimed, with a little laugh.

"But he is, Phoebe, you know he is." She smiled. "He was very obliging, at least. He gave orders for the boxes to be sent out immediately and we saw them go."

"You have done us a great service, my loves," said Thynne. "Now your mama and I can face the future in better heart. It is indeed gratifying to find benevolence amongst the military."

"She's to have supper with him to-night, Papa. At the Golden Cross. She promised," said Phoebe.

"Doris! Was it necessary?" her mother asked, reproachfully.

"Yes, Mama; but what does it matter? I know very well how to take care of myself."

Directly the meal was finished the girls hastened away to lay in an additional supply of comforts for their parents' and Phoebe's use during the voyage. No restrictions had been placed by Government upon what the convicts could carry with them in the way of extra food, clothing, and the like, and all but the friendless and penniless brought with them parcels, bundles, and boxes filled with articles to the limit of their means. The larger of these, too heavy to be carried by hand, were marked and taken in charge by the agent for the transports, to be delivered aboard ship. Sabb doubted whether their owners would ever see them again, but the chance of that had to be taken.

Mr. and Mrs. Thynne bustled about the room, busy with their own preparations. They must have felt as low-spirited as the rest of us but were resolved not to show it. Thynne was urging his wife to don her plainest, meanest gown, but she would not hear to the proposal.

"No, Mortimer. If the monsters have the inhumanity to lead a lady through the streets, the townspeople shall know, at least, that I *am* a lady. I will not shame my husband and my daughters on our last day in England."

"And quite right, ma'am," said Sabb, who failed to notice the odd nature of this display of pride. He stopped short to stare at Ned Inching, who was gathering his scanty belongings into a bundle. "Ned, what have ye there?" he exclaimed.

Inching glanced warily at the door, then turned his head toward Sabb.

"Bit o' luck on the way down from Lunnon," he said, and with that he displayed a fine gold watch and chain and an enameled snuffbox.

Sabb slapped his thigh and Mr. Thynne halted in the middle of the floor.

"Thynne, had I told ye he was clever?" Nick asked, proudly. "Let's have a look at 'em, Ned."

Inching laid the articles in his hand, standing by with a grin on his face while Sabb opened the case of the watch and examined the works with a practised eye.

"Wuth twenty guineas if it's wuth sixpence," he said. He

beamed at the pickpocket like a schoolmaster commending a promising scholar. "Ned, where and when could ye have nabbed 'em?"

"Four Crowns, in Petersfield, w'en we stopped to bait," said Inching. "Party in the blue velveteen coat, standin' by the pump."

Thynne paid his fellow artist the tribute of an admiring glance; then he turned to his wife, shaking his head wistfully. "Thynne, Inching, and Thynne — what a firm for business they would make, my love!"

"I fear it's a little late to suggest it," said Mrs. Thynne.

"Dear me, dear me!" her husband added, in the same wistful voice. "And with you, Nick, for the fence . . ." He became almost melancholy as he thought of this splendid combination of talent in the light of the present situation, but a moment later he was speaking eagerly and hopefully of the future, as though they were all at the close instead of at the threshold of their terms. Upon returning from transportation they would form such a combination, and draw in with them half a dozen more, the most gifted pickpockets in London. Sabb loved a discussion of this kind: he would forget time and place while laying plans for action against the movable property of London's more prosperous inhabitants. In the present case, he saw, in fancy, the firm of Thynne, Inching, and Thynne already at work, and a rich stream of watches, gold snuffboxes, jewelry, and such disposable treasure passing through his hands on the way to merchants in his own line of business in Amsterdam, Antwerp, and other Continental cities.

The dream was rudely broken in upon. The bolts of the door were shot back and the warden appeared with an officer of marines who held a sheaf of papers in his hand.

"All ready here?" said the warden. "Look alive then!"

We were taken down to the street where some fifty convicts were already lined up two and two, with a file of soldiers on either side of them. Directly in front of us were the females who had come with us from Newgate. They were of all ages, from women of seventy to girls in their teens, clad in the same filthy rags in which they had entered the prison months before. A few had shawls and bonnets that looked as though they had been salvaged from dustbins, but most of them were bareheaded and wearing for their one garment the quilted petticoat, of cotton or flannel, fastened high under their arms, the common article of dress for women of Wapping, St. Giles, and other miserable quarters of London. Several had infants in their arms and I noticed one big with child. These women had been culled out at Newgate as the lowest and vilest there and so to be gotten rid of first, and yet the sight of them would have stirred to pity the heart of any thoughtful observer. Their laughter, oaths, and shameless talk offered them the only means of defense they could find against a savage pitiless world that cared nothing whether they lived or died.

In our company behind were Mr. and Mrs. Thynne, Sabb, Oakley, Inching, and myself, with about a dozen other convicts, both men and women. Among the latter were Daniel Goodwin and his little boy, and a small, decently dressed woman with a sallow, sharp-featured face, whom I took to be Goodwin's wife. With this company he moved off toward Portsmouth Harbour. Although we proceeded slowly, the march was a torture to Nick Sabb, who weighed well over sixteen stone. Sweat streamed down his fat face, his lips were tightly set, and he stared glassily ahead. The rattle and chink of fetters made a dismal music for a fine May morning, but mingled with it, half drowning it came the yells and hoots of the women in front. I could see Moll Cudlip's shaven head well above those of her companions, and her screaming voice dominated all others as she shot taunting remarks right and left, giving back with interest what was sent by the crowds along the shop fronts, in entryways, or leaning on their elbows

from first-floor windows. For there are always people to make
sport of human misery, human degradation, and these Portsmouth crowds were no exception; but it would not be true
to say that such folk were in the majority. On the contrary,
most of the spectators stood in silence as we passed, and their
pitying glances and whispered comments were harder to bear
than taunts and abuse.

Nellie Garth was walking stolidly on, her gaze straight
ahead. Of a sudden I heard a cry of "Nellie! Nellie!" from the
crowd lining the footway. Garth stopped short, and turned
with an expression on her face that I can see to this day. The
voice was that of Mrs. Windle, her friend and neighbour at
Wood End, but before the little woman could push her way
through the crowd, Nat was in his mother's arms, clinging
to her without a word, his face pressed against her bosom.
Garth lifted the boy, holding him close, and walked on with
him held so.

"There, Nat," she said, in a trembling voice. "All's mended
now. You're here . . . God bless ye, Sarah Windle! I might
ha' knowed ye'd find me, soon or late."

Mrs. Windle was laughing and crying in the same breath.
"I was bound ye shouldn't miss him, but oh, Nellie, my
heart's sick to see chains to the feet of as honest and decent
a woman as ever drew breath! He's all right, is Nat, though
he's been to the point of death through grievin' for ye. Set
the lad down now and I'll tell ye the whole of it from the day
your letter came."

We moved on, Nat clinging to his mother's hand, and Mrs.
Windle talking as fast as her tongue could move. She began
with the day when we had left Garth's farm, but the sum of
the matter was that Nat had grieved his heart out during the
whole of the time he had been absent from Nellie. But I could
see that Mrs. Windle was holding back what she wished Garth
to understand but could not tell her in Nat's presence. She
tried to convey the information with nods and woebegone

shakes of the head and piteous glances at the boy, who seemed conscious only of the fact that he held his mother's hand once more. Then Garth understood, and a look of profound despair came into her eyes. Nat believed that he was going with his mother. Mrs. Windle had not had the courage to tell him the truth.

VII

THE FIRST FLEET

WE turned into a lane leading to Point Beach, the last bit of English ground our feet were to tread, and glad I was of that. Before us we could see the harbour sparkling in the morning sunlight, with pinnaces and barges plying back and forth, for many ships-of-war were lying there. Our transports were far out, on the Motherbank at Spithead. Some had already taken in convicts in the Thames and at Plymouth, and those of us now to be embarked were the last parties the ships would receive. We had walked better than a mile from Portsmouth gaol; Sabb was puffing and groaning, but bound he should make it to the beach without help. I doubt whether he had ever before traveled so far on his own feet. He had arranged in advance with his nephew, Timothy Sabb, and some of his old London cronies that they should come down by hired coach to see him off, and he kept looking from side to side, becoming more and more worried lest they should fail to appear.

A great crowd was gathered at the beach, surging against a double line of marines that had been thrown around the landing stairs. They were, mostly, friends and relatives of convicts already embarked, and many were half frantic with rage and grief because they had been given no opportunity to take leave of them. A marine officer was trying to pacify them, but his voice was lost in the uproar.

"Hush, good people," he shouted. "Let me speak . . ."

"Hush is it?" one woman screamed. "Ye've snatched my

man for the term of his life! I'll see him once more afore he goes!"

The clamour was renewed from all sides, and the officer stood with his arms folded, grimly waiting for silence. At last the crowd, seeing that nothing was to be gained by shouting, gave him leave to speak.

"You'll see your folk, I tell you," he said. "Boats will be here at midday to take you off to the transports."

"It's no lie, sir? Ye'll not deceive us?" someone asked.

"You can go at midday but not a moment before."

"But how can we know what ships our folk is on?" another woman asked.

"Officers will be here with the lists, to direct you. Now fall back and be quiet, else there'll none of you go."

The crowd had to be satisfied with this assurance, and the work of embarkation proceeded. While we awaited our turn, a dozen great wagons, filled with convicts collected from gaols all through the southern counties, arrived at the beach. The condition of these poor creatures was appalling. With few exceptions they were clad in rags that barely covered their nakedness. There were old men and women amongst them so wasted by disease and starvation that they could scarce stand, and girls and boys in their early teens. As I watched these miserable creatures being herded onto the barges, I wondered whether there was any other nation in the so-called Christian world so barbarous in their social relationships as the English. Ever since entering Newgate, being powerless to lighten such misery, I had tried to harden my heart and to close my eyes to the sight of it; but I was seized at times by such hatred toward those responsible that, even now, as an old man, my blood surges hot at the thought of it.

I had hoped until the last moment that Oakley and I would be in the same transport, but he and the Thynnes were called to the boat for the *Friendship*. We had time only for a hand-clasp and a hasty word of farewell.

" 'Tis cursed luck," said Tom, "but pills are to be swallowed, not chewed, and there's an end of it. We'll meet yonder, Hugh."

"To be sure we shall," said Thynne, gayly, "in the floral meadows of our wished-for haven, Botany Bay. Mr. Tallant, I am more and more firmly convinced that the name is one of good omen. I can scarce wait till we arrive there, to roam the dells and the lawny champaigns like children in the days of the world's innocence."

"Where's the daughters, Mr. Thynne?" Garth asked.

"They will come, ma'am. I have no uneasiness on their account."

"I would if they was my girls," said Garth.

"They will meet us on the ship, Mortimer," said Mrs. Thynne. "Doris told me as much."

"To be sure they will . . . Alas, my friends, we are called. Away, away, to Botany Bay; to the woods and fields away! Mr. Tallant, I'll thank you to have an eye on Nick Sabb during the voyage. See that he has his eggs and rashers every morning, else he'll fall away from a horse load to a cart load."

We watched them go with sad hearts. Thynne stood in the boat waving his handkerchief like some prosperous citizen off for a holiday in France. Sabb turned away with a sigh.

"There goes as honest a man as any in the cards when the four kings are out," he said, with a glum smile. "We'll miss him sore on the voyage."

The convicts for the *Charlotte* were embarked a few moments later, and a pitiful scene followed when Nat had to be told that he could not go with his mother. Not that he made an outcry; on the contrary, he merely looked at Nellie while she comforted him, explaining that he was to come to say good-bye with Mrs. Windle, later in the day. Of all the ordeals Garth had endured since leaving home, this was, certainly, the worst, but she kept herself well in hand and spoke quietly and cheerfully to the lad. He clung tightly to his

mother for a moment; then Mrs. Windle led him away while
we were marshaled down to the boats. Sabb, Goodwin, Inching, and I were the only men amongst twenty women, the
same lot that had come with us from Newgate. Moll Cudlip
was there, and while she was the unholy terror she had always
been, she had learned to beware of Garth. There was one, a
girl of sixteen, Mary Doyle by name, who belonged to that
company no more than did Garth herself. I remembered having seen her in Newgate when we first entered the place, but
she was now so wasted with grief and despair that I scarcely
recognized her. We four men sat on a thwart facing Garth,
Mary Doyle, and Mrs. Goodwin, who held their boy Tommy
asleep in her arms. Mary Doyle seemed far past the comfort
of tears, but Mrs. Goodwin was crying bitterly as she looked
back at the widening stretch of water between the boat and
the shore.

"Now, Bella, bear up," said Goodwin. "We'll be home
again afore ye know it, comin' ashore at this very place, like
as not. There's near six of my seven years gone afore we start:
think of that!"

"Home? We'll never see home or England again," she
sobbed. "God forgive ye, Dan Goodwin, for tearing me apart
from all I love and cherish!"

"Ye're a free woman, Bella. Ye needn't have come. 'Twas
not me that wished it."

"Free? With a convict for a husband? What can I do but
come?"

Mrs. Goodwin was to be excused, perhaps, under the circumstances, but she made a sorry spectacle of herself, heap-
ing reproaches upon her husband with such bitterness that
Garth was led to say: "Hush, ma'am! Have ye no pride, that
ye carry on so? Ye should be a help to your good man, not a
hindrance. . . . Ye're sent for smuggling?" she asked, turning to Goodwin.

He nodded.

"Then ye'd best honour and not abuse him, ma'am, for there's no shame in what he's done. Where would the poor be without the smugglers?"

Mrs. Goodwin raised her head to give her a resentful glance, but she was silent after that.

We were soon beyond the harbour and approaching Spithead, where we could see the transports, small ships of between three and four hundred tons burthen, anchored in a line, about a cable's length apart. Beyond them lay the three store ships, and this side the two ships-of-war, the *Sirius* and *Supply*. The *Sirius* was a vessel of 600 tons, painted a dull yellow, with a broad black band at the waterline. The *Supply*, which would serve as a tender to the *Sirius*, was an old naval transport, a brig of 170 tons: she looked small indeed for the voyage ahead. We passed near the *Sirius* and could see the people on her deck. One of the seamen said: "Yon's Captain Phillip on the quarter-deck," and all turned to stare, but we were too far off for a clear view. It was not until we were well on our way that I saw, close at hand, the man who was to be Governor over us, with the power of life and death in his hands.

There was no wind that morning, but the swell in the roadstead made it no easy matter for the women to manage the ladder up the *Charlotte's* side. For Sabb, the attempt was hopeless, and when the others had been gotten aboard, a boatswain's chair was let down and he was hoisted up and swung inboard amidst the cheers and laughter of the seamen.

The deck was all confusion and cluttered with last-minute stores brought off in lighters. No time was allowed us to enjoy the air and sunshine. The moment we had been checked off, the women were separated from the men and we were herded down to our quarters.

Before going further I had best describe, once and for all, how the transports were fitted out for convicts, for the manner of it in the *Charlotte* was the same as in all the others. On the upper deck, abaft the mainmast, and running from larboard to starboard bulwarks, was a barricade of thick oak plank, three feet high and topped with iron spikes. A second barricade crossed the deck abaft the foremast. The space between was for the use of the convicts in the hours they were permitted on deck, and gates, with a guard at each, led through them for the use of the seamen. All the hatches were strongly secured with crossbars, bolts, and locks, and railed round from deck to deck with oak stanchions. Sentinels stood at each of the hatchways, and a guard of marines overlooked us at all times from the quarter-deck.

We had no reason to hope that we were to make this voyage to New South Wales in any comfort, and I had prepared myself in advance for the trials to come; but as I halted at the foot of the ladder and peered into the semi-darkness of the 'tween-decks, my heart sank at thought of the weeks and months of confinement in store for us in that stifling hole. The men's quarters ran the width of the ship, with bulkheads fore and aft, separating us from the quarters of the women on one side and from the cabins of the marines on the other. It was like a narrow hall running athwartships, with double tiers of bunks divided by wooden partitions into sections seven feet six inches in width. These sections were to furnish sleeping accommodations for five men, giving each an eighteen-inch allowance of space. The bulkheads were provided with small ports through which the guards could overlook the place and fire amongst us in case of an attempt at mutiny or other trouble, but the openings were covered now with heavy lids and bolted shut. There were no outside ports to this dungeon; what light and air we received came through a single hatchway. Next to the hatchway was a cleared strip running the width of the vessel and eight feet wide, and this, with the narrow passages between the rows of bunks, was supposed to serve one hundred men with what room they needed for eating, recreation, and movement.

We were only a little more crowded, perhaps, than the guards themselves and the ship's company, for the *Charlotte,* a vessel of but 335 tons, had to provide room for 100 male and 24 female convicts, 40 marines and 31 seamen, counting their officers. In addition, three marines had their wives, with five children amongst them, so that 203 persons in all were crowded into a ship with room for scarcely half the number.

The light of a few candles in iron lanterns fixed to the beams seemed to make the gloom the deeper; it was reflected from the gleaming eyeballs of men lying half-naked in their bed places, gasping for air. The passageways were crowded as Sabb, Goodwin, Inching, and I pushed our way along to the single section of bunk space not yet occupied. This was at the end of a passage and against the bulkhead separating ours from the women's quarters. Glad we were that a fifth man was wanting for our section, for Sabb could never have fitted himself into eighteen inches of sleeping space, and had Ned Inching not been a mere sliver of a man, there would have been no squeezing even the four of us into so cramped a place.

Sabb stripped to the waist and slumped down on the bunk, puffing and panting, the sweat streaming down his huge legs and making little puddles on the floor.

"Ye mean to drown us, Nick?" said Inching. "I'd best fetch a slop tub for ye to run off in."

"Bear with me, lads," said Sabb. "At this rate I'll melt down to common size in a fortnight. Goodwin, how is this alongside the hulks — worse or better?"

"No worse," said Goodwin, "but in the hulks we was off to work the day long and had but the nights to suffer." He glanced at a cadaverous, hollow-eyed fellow lying head out in a bunk opposite.

"Ye've been long aboard?" he asked.

"Eight weeks," the man replied.

"Eight *weeks!*" Sabb exclaimed. "Ye tell us they've been filling the ship as long as that?"

The other nodded. "Longer. There's some here since February, and not an ounce of fresh food in the whole of the time."

"What hours do we have on deck?" Goodwin asked.

"There's been no order to it so far," the man replied, "but as a usual thing they give us an hour in the morning and again in the afternoon. They say we'll be better served once we get to sea."

Presently I walked through the passageways to get a view of the place and of the men we were to be cooped up with for the long voyage. The space between the lower and upper tiers of bunks was just enough to allow about six inches of headroom to those sitting in them. In some of the sections men were playing cards with candles stuck in bottlenecks for light, gambling for money if they had it, or for rations, articles of clothing, tobacco, or whatever had an exchange value. In others, men lay head out, their chins propped on their hands, in a kind of waking stupor. The place was so hot and the air so foul that I soon felt drugged and heavy-headed. I crawled into my bunk place and, despite the noise, fell asleep within five minutes.

I was awakened by someone shaking me by the shoulder, and found Goodwin standing in the passage.

"I'd not known ye was here," he said. "We've all been on deck this hour past. The friends and kinsfolk have come off to say good-bye. There's another half hour permitted if ye wish a breath of air."

I hastened after him up the ladder and was so blinded by the sunlight that I could scarcely see, at first. The deck was filled with people, wives and parents and friends who had come to make their farewells and to bring parting gifts to the convicts. The scene was one I shall never forget: pitiable, moving, sordid, comic, all at once. Gin, the one consolation of the poor and wretched of England, was flowing freely, and many of the people were now either maudlin or hilariously drunk. There was little to choose, in the state of the ship's company, between the convicts and their friends, and the marines and seamen with theirs, beyond the barriers. All discipline had been relaxed, according to the common practice in English ships ready for sea, whether navy or merchant vessel. Now and then, in moments of comparative lull in the uproar, I could hear faintly a band of music which was playing on the quarter-deck of the *Sirius,* but the only music in the *Charlotte* came in bursts of discordant song whose words left something to be wanted in point of elegance.

I found Sabb seated on a chest against the forward barricade. His friends from London had found him at last, Sabb's nephew among them. The nephew was as lean as the uncle was fat, dressed in a green coat with silver buttons. He had a sallow leathery face pitted by smallpox, and the only resemblance I could see in him to Nick was a pair of shrewd, intelligent grey eyes. Sabb had a bottle in one hand and a pork pie in the other and he was eating and drinking with a kind of fierce eagerness, as though convinced that he must store up provender inside him to last the whole of the voyage. Upon catching sight of me he rose unsteadily, waving his pie in a gesture of invitation.

"Come, Tallant," he called genially. "Fire a slug with us! Good cheer and good company! Strip-me-naked go down, and sorrow go drown, and be damned to Botany Bay!" His cronies, six of them, sat on the deck around him like the satellites of a bloated Bacchus, drinking slightly watered gin. I had no wish to disturb these old friends at such a moment, and so, after shaking hands all round, I moved on.

I spied Garth sitting on a coil of rope, with Nat in her lap and Mrs. Windle standing beside her. I knew from afar that Nat had been told that he was not to go. Mrs. Windle had come with one of the last boats from shore, and was still breathless with the excitement of getting aboard. She was showing Garth the contents of a large canvas bag she carried, filled with things she had bought for her in Portsmouth.

"And, Nellie, 'tis naught to all it was my heart's wish to bring; but there's tea here, and sugar, and two dozen of the best candles, and a dozen lemons and a smoked shoulder of mutton . . ."

"There, ye good soul," said Garth, close to the point of tears. "Ye should never have done it. Ye'll be going hungry the long road home, that's certain, without sixpence left in your pocket."

"The coach hire is paid, Nellie. God bless ye, never ye fret for me! How could I be hungry? I'm that heartsick I'll have no wish to eat for a fortnight. But I've some nice cold vittles for Nat, packed up for the journey home. Mr. Tallant, it's a comfort to know she'll not be friendless in a far land, with yourself and Mr. Oakley there, though a better-handed woman to do for herself I've never known."

"Never fear; we'll take care of her," I said.

"Will ye listen to the man!" said Garth. "Take my word for it, 'tis they will be coming to me when the pinch comes."

"They may so," said Mrs. Windle. "Ye'll be at no loss, that's sure, in a land where delving and planting and the like is wanted."

Nellie turned to her boy.

"Nat, look yonder at the great ships! Go stand by the rail for a bit where ye can see 'em better."

Without a word, Nat rose and obeyed.

"Now, Sarah, whilst there's time, I'd speak of my place," said Garth. "The rent is paid to next quarter day, and then it must go back to him that owns it. Will ye clear my house before then, and take my bits of things to your own?"

"That I will, and cherish 'em as you would, against the day ye come home."

"If ever we do come," said Garth.

Mrs. Windle laid a hand on her arm. "Never doubt it, Nellie," she said, earnestly. "Have patience equal to your pluck, and, God willing, we'll have ye back in His good time."

"Leave that," said Garth. "There's my horse and cow and the pigs. Has the sow farrowed?"

"She has, and oh, Nellie, two was et by the boar, but there's eight saved."

"They're yours, all," said Garth. "I wish ye to have 'em, Sarah, and small the payment is for the good friend and neighbour ye've been to me."

Mrs. Windle was so overwhelmed by the gift that she was speechless for a moment; then she protested against accepting it; but Garth was bound she should have the animals and so the matter was settled.

While we were standing there, a gaunt, sheep-nosed man dressed in threadbare black approached us, and, without waiting to be invited, raised a bony hand in a gesture of benediction.

"My poor brother, and sisters," he said, in a hollow voice, "are you able to read?"

Nellie gave him a cool glance.

"We can manage to spell out print of a large size," she said. "What d'ye wish?"

Garth and I, at least, guessed his errand in advance, having seen others like him at Newgate of a Sunday, laying up edification for themselves on Earth and treasures in Heaven by distributing tracts and pious exhortations to the inmates there. They were well-meaning people, no doubt, but their condescending manners and their assumption that all convicts were lost souls made them anything but welcome visitors. The fellow addressed himself first to me, saying how grateful I should be for the benevolence of a government that was sending me to a new land where I would be blessedly deprived of the temptations that had beset me in the old. He hoped that, by cheerful and humble submission to those set over me, who were earnestly solicitous for my correction and redemption, I would yet prove to be a useful

member of society. With that, he thrust a packet of tracts
into my hand and turned to Mrs. Windle, not having noticed that she had no irons to her feet. There was a glint of
mischief in Garth's eyes as she waited to see what her friend
would do. Mrs. Windle was torn between indignation at
being taken for a convict and the need to say nothing that
would hurt Garth's feelings, but she handled the matter very
well.

"I'll have ye know, sir, that I'm a free woman, and
whether bond or free there's none of us here in chapel to
sing psalms through our noses, so we'll thank ye to go where
your company is desired."

The man wished to say more, but both women turned their
backs upon him, and after a last glance, filled with sorrow-
ful unction, at myself, he was obliged to follow Mrs. Windle's
advice.

"What has he left with ye, Hugh?" Garth asked.

I passed her the bundle of tracts, and she glanced at the
titles, reading them aloud to us: —

"*Dissuasions from Stealing,* by Reverend Eben White.
Cautions to Swearers, by Mrs. Matilda Blodgett. . . . Hugh,
ye'd best carry these for reading amongst the men, though
I'll not say it's where they're most needed." Her eyes twinkled
as she glanced at the next. "*One Hundred Exhortations to
Chastity.* . . . Aye, this was meant for us ladies, past doubt,
but whether a hundred will be enough I'd not be able to
guess."

"Bless ye, Nellie," said Mrs. Windle, with a sudden gust
of feeling. "Ye've a brave heart and a merry one in your
quiet way, but can ye abide the company you're with?"

Garth glanced across the crowded deck and her eye fell
upon a group of half a dozen women, among the worst in
the ship, lying or squatting on the deck with an equal number of men who had come to see them off. One of them sat

with her legs stretched apart, her arms braced behind her
and her head thrown back whilst another held a bottle to
her lips as she drank.

"It looks as if I'm obliged to, Sarah. But never fret. There's
a few decent women amongst the rest as I've found already.
We'll manage."

A few moments later the sound of a bugle cut through the
air and the command: "Clear ship! All visitors ashore!" was
shouted from the quarter-deck. Immediately the tumult
rose to a higher pitch. A squad of marines, all of them far
gone in liquor, was sent amongst us. Wives clung desperately
to their husbands and had to be torn from their arms by
main force. Several women fainted and were handed down
insensible to the boats. Others, crazed by grief and gin together, fought like furies, scratching and tearing at the
soldiers who sought to drag them to the gangway. One woman
fell in a fit and lay writhing and twisting on the deck, her
teeth clenched and her eyes staring blindly while others stood
round her, looking on with blear-eyed interest, as though
this had been a spectacle arranged for their benefit.

Of a sudden a chorus of yells and shrieks was heard from
the far side of the deck, but in the confusion they were not
heard by many of the company. Garth, having caught the
name Mary Doyle, quickly pushed through the crowd to
the bulwark. She came back a moment later, her face grimly
set.

"There's one of us that won't see Botany Bay," she said.
"Poor Mary! Poor lass! She's thrown herself overboard."

A boat was immediately rowed round to that side of
the ship, but the girl's irons had helped to drag her down,
and the seamen, after rowing aimlessly here and there for
a quarter of an hour, abandoned the search.

Meanwhile, the convicts on the port side, ignorant of or
indifferent to what had just happened, lined the bulwark
as their friends and kinsfolk were herded down the side and

into the boats. The grief and despair of some was pitiable to see, making the greater contrast to others, too drunk or too callous to be affected by this final separation. These latter, and their friends in the boats, called back and forth to one another.

"Blubber away, Doll!" one voice shouted. "The more ye cry the less ye'll sweat!"

"Joe! Have ye a drop left in the bottle? Give 'er a kick in the guts! That's all the comfort she's wantin'!"

His friend, in one of the boats, waved a bottle in reply and held it to the lips of the weeping woman, who accepted it willingly, while those along the bulwark yelled with delight.

"Ain't it so?" laughed another. " 'Tis as great a pity to see a woman cry as to see a goose walk barefoot!"

"Good-bye, Mag!"

"Good-bye, Dickie! I'll meet ye at Peg Tantrum's!"

I stood by the bulwark amongst the most hardened and indifferent of the convicts during those last moments of contact between the ship and the shore. I had no wish to look on while Nellie was parting from her boy. When I saw her again she was standing alone, gazing stonily after the last boat to leave. A moment later all the convicts were herded down to their quarters.

VIII

ABOARD THE *CHARLOTTE*

On May 13, 1787, the eleven ships of the fleet for Botany Bay stood out through The Needles with the *Sirius* and *Supply* in the van. We were accompanied by yet another ship-of-war, H.M.S. *Hyena*, a 24-gun frigate which was to convoy us some two hundred miles on our way and return to Portsmouth with Governor Phillip's last despatches to the Admiralty and the Home Office. I doubt whether a greater load of human misery — or, as some would say, of human villainy — had ever before left the shores of England at one time. Thousands of convicts had, of course, been carried to the American Colonies in times past, but they had rarely gone in shiploads, and never, I believe, in fleets. In this first expedition for New South Wales, there were 756 convicts in all, and I have little doubt that His Majesty's Government wished that we might have been five times as many, for the gaols and hulks, filled with the accumulation of ten years, were far from having been emptied at our departure.

It had been Government's wish to send out in the First Fleet for Botany Bay strong young men and women fit for the hard labour of establishing a colony in a new land, but what happened was far otherwise. There were, to be sure, young people amongst us, but in many cases the wardens of the gaols and the superintendents of the hulks had selected for their quotas feeble old men and women, and with these, the greatest villains and trouble-makers whom they were only too glad to be rid of. In the *Charlotte's* company were

folk in their sixties and seventies, and boys and girls of fourteen, fifteen, and sixteen. Some might well have been called
human sacrifices to the savage penal laws of England, which
condemned them to seven years' transportation for such offenses as stealing a petticoat valued at four shillings, stealing
a teakettle, poaching a hare in a gentleman's park, cutting
down a tree for firewood, and the like. But it would not be
true to say that most of the convicts were exiled for offenses
of this nature. There were murderers amongst us, footpads,
housebreakers, coiners, and river thieves, many of whom
had missed hanging by a hair's breadth. During the long
voyage I came to know most of the *Charlotte's* company,
and I am obliged to say that a good half of them were as
complete villains as could have been found in the whole
of Europe.

We had no final glimpse of the shores of old England,
which mattered little in my own case, for I was glad to be
quit of a land which had given me few but sad or bitter
memories. The weather turned cold and stormy before we
left the Channel, and for a full week we were kept below.
The hatches were removed from time to time, else we should
have smothered there, but when the ship was rolling, in
heavy weather, the seamen were obliged to batten down,
and we had to breathe the same air over and over again.
Many of the convicts were seasick and the pleasures of their
near company in that confined place can well be imagined.
But it is surprising what miseries human beings can endure,
and how quickly they can harden themselves to the most
abominable conditions when circumstances force them to
do so. Once we knew what we were in for, we set ourselves
to meet it with as good heart as possible.

On a never-to-be-forgotten morning we were ordered on
deck, in batches of twenty, to have our irons struck off.
The sky was clear once more, and the wind fresh and abeam.
Goodwin and I were sent up in the same lot, and we filled

our lungs with the pure sweet air, too content to waste any of it in speech. The *Supply* and one other ship were far ahead, hull-down on the horizon, but the rest of the fleet were well within view, the *Sirius* not more than a mile astern of all, like an old hen worrying her brood on before her. The *Friendship* was just abeam, but too far off for us to see any of her people. I thought of Tom Oakley and the Thynnes, who might well have been thinking of us at the same moment, and wishing that we might close in to waving distance, at least.

The sharp clinking as our fetters were struck off was a sweet sound indeed to men so long burdened with the cursed things; and more went with the chains than their weight: something of the shame and ignominy they had fastened upon us was lifted from our hearts, and the good of that release was even greater than the other.

To be quit of them was blessing enough for one day, but Goodwin and I seemed to have been marked out for a second stroke of luck. When our fetters had been removed, we were lined up along the after barrier, and the *Charlotte's* boatswain and his mate went slowly along, scanning us critically. When they had passed down the line they returned to where Goodwin and I stood.

"Here's the liveliest pair," said the boatswain. He turned to Goodwin. "Been to sea afore this, ain't ye?"

"Times enough," said Goodwin. "It's my trade."

"Smuggling?"

"Aye."

"He'll do," said the boatswain. "And what of you?" he asked, turning to me. "Can ye reef and hand?"

"Yes," I replied promptly, for all my life, before leaving home, had been spent on or near salt water, and I had made a voyage or two to Boston.

The end of it was that Goodwin and I were chosen for duty with the *Charlotte's* company to replace two seamen missing when the ship sailed. We continued to mess with our fellow prisoners, and were locked in with them at night, but we had the great privilege of the upper deck through the daylight hours.

We began our duties on a day when there was little to do but stand by. The women convicts were brought up last to have their irons struck off and were permitted to remain on deck for two hours, after which the men came, fifty at a time, for the same period. I am obliged to say that the men were, generally, much better behaved than the women, for these latter took advantage of their sex — at least the younger ones did — and became increasingly bold and insolent. They taunted and tempted both seamen and marines, and, as some of them were far from ill-favoured, they played ducks and drakes with ship's discipline. At last their behaviour became so outrageous that Mr. Gilbert, captain of the *Charlotte*, was obliged to take notice of it. Captain Gilbert was an excellent seaman, quiet, even shy in manner, with a homely face and brick-red hair. Up to this time he had never appeared amongst the women, for the reason, doubtless, that he had never before carried such a cargo of depravity, and was at a loss how to act in the situation. But when, one morning, a good half of the women were found to be drunk upon being brought up for their two hours on deck, the captain came forward to inquire into the matter. No spirits of any kind were given the convicts, and the drunken women could only have gotten into that condition through the connivance of either the seamen or the marines.

They were separated from the sober ones, and these latter were first questioned, without result. Nellie Garth and Mrs. Goodwin, because of their respectable appearance and actions, were particularly questioned, but Nellie was no telltale, and Mrs. Goodwin, much as she despised the company she was in, had too much sense to draw upon herself the abuse and persecution that would have been her lot had she informed upon the others. Furthermore, she was so incensed that she, a free woman, had been forced to lodge with convicts that she was resolved to be of no service to those who had placed her in that situation.

The tipsy women were then questioned. They were scarce able to stand, but all stoutly denied that they had tasted so much as a drop of spirits, and were not in the least awed at being questioned by the captain himself. They sized him up at once as a man of mild disposition, shy of women, and made such sport of him that he became more and more confused and ill-at-ease.

One bold-looking wench had been fighting, for her face was scratched and bruised and one eye swelled shut.

"Now then," said Captain Gilbert, with an attempt at an authoritative manner, "what does this mean?"

"I ain't been fightin', Captain. Oh, no!" said the woman, with a leer at the others. "Ye see, I was standin' bitch to some of me lady companions in our handsome saloon, and just as I was dishin' out the tea, the bloody ship rolled, and I had the cursed luck to go arsy-varsy and tread upon me eye."

Yells of delight from the others greeted this bit of repartee.

" 'Tis the God's truth, Captain," one of them shouted.

"Never believe 'er, sir," yelled another. "She's a bawdy-house bottle got cracked for bein' empty!"

"Silence!" said Captain Gilbert, his face as red as his hair.

"Hip, Michael! Yer head's on fire!"

The captain again shouted for silence, but the women were all at him at once, now, seeing how vulnerable he was.

"Ye'd best come down and play rantum-scantum with us, old chicken-hams! There's many a good penny'orth amongst us."

"Ain't it so!"

"I'll have 'im first!"

"I'd fall on me back if he was to look at me!"

"Never heed that one, sir! She's a fire-ship!"

At this the woman so accused fired up in all truth, and before a hand could be lifted to prevent them, the two were at one another's throats, clawing and scratching as they rolled on the deck. The others joined in, and a squad of marines was needed to separate them. Six were again put in irons and sentenced to spend the next fortnight below.

One night shortly after this, a search was made of the women's quarters and four marine privates were discovered there, disguised in petticoats. They were kept in that garb until the following morning when they were ordered up for punishment — four dozen lashes each, laid on with such vigour by the boatswain's mates that the backs of all were flayed raw. Their companions amongst the women then received a dozen lashes each on the bare breech, in the presence of the whole ship's company, but they were such brazen hussies that so light a punishment served only to make them the more outrageous in their behaviour. Not a week passed before they were again caught, this time with some of the seamen who had bribed the men on guard. On this occasion the women, instead of being flogged, were made to "wear a keg," as it was called. Small casks with the heads knocked out were fitted over them with holes cut for their arms, and this contrivance was attached to them, with a harness of ropes; they could not sit down in it. The effectiveness of this punishment was slight, however. The women paraded the deck in so comic a way that the officers themselves could not keep from laughing, and presently all five, regardless of the risk to themselves, toppled over and rolled about the decks with the rolling of the ship, upsetting seamen and convicts alike, until the casks were staved in against the bulwarks. So rebellious were these women that, as a last resort, Captain Gilbert decided that all should have their heads shaved. This punishment was effective, and thereafter the ship was much quieter.

Day after day we proceeded southward, the fleet keeping well together, and on the third of June all came safely to an anchorage off Santa Cruz, the capital of Teneriffe. Here a week was spent while supplies were replenished, and during this time Captain Phillip refreshed the ships' companies, seamen, marines, and convicts alike, with liberal supplies of fruit, fresh meat, and vegetables. He inspected every ship of the fleet, and I well remember the occasion when I had my first near view of the man destined to lay the foundations of a new commonwealth. He was slight in stature, with dark eyes, a high-bridged nose, and a severe expression upon his lined, sallow face. He spent an hour aboard the *Charlotte*, and examined every quarter of the ship with a thoroughness that showed how much he had the well-being of the convicts as well as the freemen at heart. I have little doubt that, had Captain Phillip been given the charge of fitting the transports for the voyage, we would have been better accommodated. It was not his fault that we were so inhumanly crowded and starved for air below decks.

It was not until we were again at sea that I learned of two passengers transferred to the *Charlotte* at Teneriffe from the *Scarborough*. One was a convict, but in a different category from the rest of us. He was a political prisoner, David Munro, the only one carried out from England by the First Fleet. With him was his daughter, Sally, who had chosen to share her father's exile.

Mr. Munro received vastly better treatment than that accorded to the rest of the convicts. He shared a cabin with the master's mate of the *Charlotte*, and his daughter was berthed with the wife of one of the marine officers. Every day Mr. Munro and his daughter walked the quarter-deck, and I could see from afar how devoted they were to one another. The father was a frail man, in contrast to his daughter, who

was in the very flower of youth and health. She read to him for
hours at a time, but I had no close view of them until we were
well on our way toward Rio de Janeiro.

We were lying becalmed on a day so windless that the reflections of a few fleecy clouds lay on the sea as in a slightly
flawed mirror. Because of the stifling heat, the convicts were
all on deck, the men on one side, the women on the other. I
was standing alone by the bulwark, behind one of the boats,
when I felt a hand laid on my shoulder, and there was
Mr. Munro.

"Well, young man," he said with a smile, "you'll never get
us to Botany Bay at this rate. I thought you seamen were
skilled to whistle for a breeze?"

"They've tried it, sir," I replied, "but we seem to be holding to the slack, for all that."

I knew at once, by a kind of instinct, that here was a
thoroughly good man, one for whom the distinctions made
between different classes of society did not exist. I was pleased
and flattered to have been mistaken for one of the ship's company, but I could not leave him under this impression. I told
him that I was a convict, merely detailed for ship's duty
during the daytime.

"Well, and so am I," he replied. "Where is your home? In
England?"

When I explained that I was an American, his interest was
immediately aroused and he plied me with questions, in so
friendly a manner that I soon found myself opening my
heart to him as freely as though he had been an old friend.
I told him of my family's Loyalist sympathies, of my service
in the American War, and of my unhappy experiences in
England, which led to my being taken as a highwayman.
When I had finished, he said: "Young man, what a mistake
you made!"

"I realize that now, sir," I replied, "but I was desperately
anxious to leave England, and I had long tried without success

to earn the money for a passage home. I couldn't get a seaman's job; there were scores of men offering for every one
available."

"I'm not speaking of that," said Mr. Munro. "I mean, what
a mistake it was to side with the King against your own
countrymen. Would you make the same choice again?"

"No, sir," I replied, promptly. "England herself has
taught me better."

"Aye. The hope of the world, of all freedom-loving men,
is in America. . . . Was it known by the judges at your trial
that you are an American Loyalist?"

"No, sir. You will understand that I had no wish to bring
shame upon my family, or upon the other Loyalists in England."

"And none of them learned of your arrest?"

"I believe not. The only close friend I had in England returned to Canada before my trouble came. My mother is there,
but she will never know what happened to me. I wrote her
that I was about to sail for Bombay, for service with the
East India Company."

Mr. Munro then told me that he himself was an American.
He had left England, with his parents, when a small boy, and
most of his life since that time had been spent in Canada, in
or near Montreal. He was a fiery Republican, with deep sympathy for all underdogs, whether politically or socially op-
pressed. His enthusiasm for the revolutionaries of the American War had brought him many enemies amongst the official
classes in Canada, but he cared nothing for that. He organized
a Society for the Advancement of Political Liberty, whose
purpose was to work for the emancipation of Canada, with the
idea of forming a sister republic in the North. His labours
on behalf of this society had taken him to England, some time
after the close of the American War, where, at last, he was
arrested for seditious practices. It was a near thing that he

was not tried for high treason. The result of his trial was that he received a sentence to fourteen years' transportation.

This was the first of many talks with Mr. Munro as we proceeded toward Rio de Janeiro, and I believe he enjoyed our companionship almost as much as I did. We talked of America and made one another homesick by doing so. He hoped to return to Canada when his sentence had expired and was full of dreams and plans for that time, but I wondered, sadly enough, whether he would live to fulfill them. His body was not equal to the demands his eager, active spirit made upon it; the hardships of the voyage had told heavily upon him, but he seemed never to give a thought to his health. Munro was fifty years old at this time and looked forward confidently to his freedom and future work as though assured that he had another fifty years to come. I wondered what would happen to his daughter in case of his death in New South Wales. A strange and lonely situation it would be for her. I learned that her mother, who was of French Huguenot blood, had died when Sally was ten, and that her only living relative beside her father was an aunt on her mother's side, living in Quebec.

And then came my first meeting with her. It was another of those windless days when the *Charlotte* lay all but on the Equator. The sky was covered with a thin veil of cloud, tempering a little the heat of the tropical sun, and the deep silence of the sea lay over the ship as well. The convicts were sprawled about like dead men. Most of them were asleep; others lay with their heads pillowed on their arms, gazing at vacancy. Sabb and Inching had found a bit of shade beneath one of the boats and were playing cards with two cronies, without a word, as though the game were a part of some solemn religious rite.

Turning my head presently, I saw Mr. Munro and his daughter approaching the barrier that separated the convicts from the ship's company, aft. He spoke to the guard standing there, who let them pass.

So imbued was I, by this time, with the convict point of view that it had not occurred to me that I would ever meet and talk with Miss Munro. Though her father was himself a prisoner, he was set apart from us by the political nature of his offense, and I quite understood, without his speaking of the matter, that he would wish to keep his daughter free from any contact with the felons. I was so taken aback by his action in bringing her to our part of the ship that I stood like a lout as they approached.

"Tallant," said Mr. Munro, "my daughter has grown weary of being cooped up on the quarter-deck." Then, turning to her: "Sally, this is the young man I spoke of, an American like ourselves."

Miss Munro gave me her hand with a frank grave glance, but I thought I could detect a twinkle of mischief in her eyes, as though she were quite aware of my embarrassment and my awkward effort to appear at ease. And an effort it was, in all truth. Since leaving Canada and my own people there, with the exception of Mrs. Garth my companions had been exclusively male and I had all but forgotten how to behave in the presence of a well-bred young woman. I was so foolish and proud as to imagine that Sally was dissembling her feelings about me and my status in an effort to put me more at ease. Mr. Munro had given me Dr. Goldsmith's "Deserted Village" to read, and, seeing my embarrassment, he began to speak of it, but I was no better than a miserable combination of Silence and Justice Shallow. Never, surely, could a young man, eager to make a good impression, have made a more dismal failure, and when they left me I suffered one of the bitterest hours I had ever known. It was not so much because of hurt pride for the poor impression made. I was thinking, rather, of the gulf that lay between me and such a girl as Sally Munro. With the stigma of convict upon me forever, with a life sentence to serve in a penal colony, what did the future have in store? Some day, no doubt, impelled by need and loneliness, I would seek what Botany Bay could offer in the way of a wife.

I looked about me at the convict women sprawled on the decks, horrible creatures, most of them, learned in every kind of vice known to the underworld of London. And some woman of this kind I would have to choose as the mother of my children.

One brazen young trollop turned her head and caught my gaze. For all that it was forbidden, the women never lost an opportunity to speak with seamen, marines, or male convicts. This one, leaning back against the bulwark with her feet outspread, gave me a knowing leer.

"How d'ye do, Conkey Beau?" she said.

"Ain't he a proper Duke o' Limbs?" said another. "He'll make us some feet fer children's stockings at Botany Bay, eh, Cully?"

*   *   *   *   *

Once we were out of the doldrums and in the region of the southeast trades, we made excellent progress, and on August the sixth, a light breeze from the sea carried us within the islands that lie off Rio de Janeiro, where we anchored for the night, sailing into the harbour next day. A reshuffling of the convicts was ordered by Captain Phillip here; the rowdiest of our women were sent out of the *Charlotte* to the *Prince of Wales,* and six of our most villainous men were transferred to the *Alexander.* Among those sent to take their places were Mr. and Mrs. Thynne, Phoebe, and Tom Oakley. Not since leaving Portsmouth had we seen them or had news of them, and the pleasure of having our small Newgate company of friends together once more can well be imagined.

I noticed a change in Tom from the moment of his coming aboard the *Charlotte,* and the reason for it was clear almost at once: he had fallen head over heels in love with Phoebe

Thynne. He made no secret of the matter when, later in the afternoon, the two of us were talking apart from the others, with Garth. Nellie charged him with having lost his heart and something of his wits.

"D'ye blame me for that?" Oakley asked.

"There's no matter of blame," said Garth. "Ye mean to marry her?"

"Why not? Phoebe wishes it as much as myself. Nellie, she's a girl in ten thousand! Little I thought Tom Oakley would ever be touched here," and he struck his breast, "but . . . well, I'm fair daft about her, and that's putting it small."

"There's no need to tell us," said Garth, quietly. "Have ye thought of this, Tom? She's come with her parents on a mere girl's whim, ye might say. Will she be content to bide in Botany Bay her life long?"

"Aye, if it should come to that," said Tom. "She's told me as much; but look ye, Nellie! For all I'm sent for life, I've no mind to die in the cursed place. Soon or late we'll find a way to leave, eh, Hugh?"

"That's as may be," said Garth. "'Tis a long way from England. My belief is there's none of us will see home again."

"Come, come, Nellie," said Tom, clapping her on the shoulder. "Ye was never one to take the dismal side."

"Dismal or not, I'll look at facts broadside on," said Garth. "My belief — and I say this to the pair of ye though I'll not speak so to the others — is that there's no thought in England that any of us shall ever go home. Those sent for seven years are no better off than yourselves, with life to serve. We'll be free in the colony, it may be, when our time is done, but England? Never hope it."

"What d'ye think, Hugh?" Oakley asked.

"That Nellie may be right. But whether or no, we'll have something to say about settling for life in New South Wales."

"There, Nellie, hearten up," said Tom. "Ye'll not see the end of your own time if Hugh and me has our way. We'll pay our Botany Bay debts with a loose foretopsail. Will ye come along if the chance offers?"

"Would I not!" said Garth. "But I'll tell ye when that will be, Tom Oakley: to-morrow come never, when two Sundays come together."

We sailed from Rio on September the fourth, in a far healthier state than when we left England. For, at home, many of the convicts had been put aboard the transports weeks, even months, before they were ready to sail, and fed upon nothing but salt provisions. Scurvy had made its appearance even before we left Portsmouth, and had greatly increased on the voyage; but the abundance of fresh fruit and vegetables given us at Rio had restored all but a few of the worst cases. There had been sixteen deaths on the voyage thus far, which was considered a small number in so great a fleet of convict ships.

With westerly winds to speed us on our way, we sailed toward the Cape of Good Hope. This time was made memorable to me by the further talks I had with Mr. Munro. I was now on terms of real friendship with him, and, although I had come to think of his daughter as "Sally," I had the discretion never to address her in this familiar way on the occasions when he brought her to our part of the deck. Indeed, in my desire not to presume upon an acquaintance so generously permitted by her father, I went beyond reason in my attitude. When she was present I became so stiff and formal in manner that her father once remarked, after she had left us: "Mr. Tallant, you behave strangely for a young man. Does my daughter displease you?"

I was so taken aback by the question that I could only mumble, "No, sir," and fall silent again; but I thought — at least, I hoped — that he would understand how matters stood with me.

The days and the weeks passed, miserably enough for the most part, in a ship so desperately crowded, and the other transports were in even worse condition than ours in this respect. For all the favouring winds we made but slow progress, for none of the ships were good sailers, and it was necessary for the fleet to keep together, setting pace by the slowest amongst them, which was the *Charlotte* herself.

We reached Capetown on October 13, five months out from Portsmouth, and here a full month was spent in preparation for the last long leg of the voyage to Botany Bay. No doubt the time passed pleasantly enough for the officers of the fleet, lodged comfortably ashore, but for the convicts that month was weariness itself. The transports lay a mile and a half from the town, too far for us to see any of the life of the place, but we could, at least, watch the boats coming and going between the ships and the shore. The Cape being the last outpost of the civilized world, we took in, here, everything in the way of livestock and provisions that could be of use in establishing the new colony. In every ship the carpenters were making pens and stalls for cattle, goats, sheep, and swine, and crates for fowls. No inch of room that could be spared was wasted. Most of the animals had to be carried in the *Sirius,* the *Supply,* and the three store-ships, but the transports took the overplus, leaving only room on deck for working the vessels.

Nellie Garth was, I believe, the only convict in the entire fleet who either wished to, or did, buy an animal on her own account. She wanted a pig, and Captain Gilbert was so surprised and gratified to learn of a convict with such good sense that he informed Governor Phillip himself of the matter. Evidently Governor Phillip was no less pleased, for permission was readily granted. Nick Sabb furnished the money for the purchase, and Nellie insisted upon buying a sow big with young. A proud and happy woman she was on the day when her sow, in a strong crate, was hoisted aboard the *Charlotte.* "A body's the better for having a dumb beast to fend for," said she, "and there's none will be more useful where we're going than a pig."

"Nellie," said Oakley, "you're a forehanded, forethoughted woman, and I wish ye luck with the sow; but my belief is ye'll have your labour for your pains. She'll not survive the voyage."

"Won't she, now?" said Garth. "Tell me that at the end, Tom Oakley. I've a way with pigs. She'll have her feed, morning and night, if I must stint myself to give it."

A week later the *Charlotte* and her sister transports were crawling eastward, far beyond Capetown. There were days when men and animals alike suffered all the miseries which tempestuous weather can furnish. The ships, heavily laden, wallowed through the great seas, and many a time tons of water came pouring inboard, half drowning us. As I think of those wretched days and nights, I hear again the confused uproar of wind and sea, the bellowing of the cattle, and the faint plaintive cries of the terrified sheep and goats. And they were no more terrified than many of the ship's human freight, particularly those with no knowledge of ships or the sea, who believed, often enough, that their last hour had come. The pitiless majesty of the sea was brought home to them for the first time in their lives, and it appeared the more awful in that great waste of waters, so empty, and grey and lonely, that seemed to stretch on and on to infinity.

In view of the size of our convoy — eleven ships, all varying in seaworthiness and sailing qualities — our success in keeping together, in all kinds of weather, during so great a voyage, seemed no less than a miracle. Never since leaving England had any ship been separated from the others, but when we were six weeks out from Capetown, four of the ships parted company by design. Governor Phillip was anxious to arrive at Botany Bay in advance of the main body, that he might look out the best site for the future settlement and get the work of clearing and preparing the land under way, and he transferred from the *Sirius* to the *Supply,* which was considered the faster ship. Three of the better sailing transports, the *Friendship, Scarborough,* and *Alexander,* were ordered to accompany him, and on the twenty-fifth of November, 1787, the two sections of the fleet parted company. Many were the forebodings of those in the following ships as they watched the others drawing slowly away from us. We were far out on an ocean but little known at that time, with the hazards and dangers of six thousand watery miles still before us. Would we meet again? That thought was in everyone's mind as we watched the dwindling sails catching the gleams of sunshine far in the distance. By late afternoon all were hull-down on the horizon and at sunset they were lost to view.

Thereafter came the most miserable part of a voyage that seemed destined never to have an end. Conditions were bad enough for the people aft, but infinitely worse for the convicts. We had been seven months in the *Charlotte,* with never a chance to set foot on land, confined for the greater part of the time in a foul hole not fit for the habitation of pigs, to say nothing of human beings. In the storms met with as we crossed the vast southern expanse of the Indian Ocean, the seams of the upper deck opened up, and sea water trickled upon us night and day until there was not a dry spot in the place, nor a dry garment to wear. Scurvy made its appearance once more, followed by dysentery, until more than half our number were too weak and ill to stir from their bunks. Most of the convicts were far sunk in a kind of hopeless apathy, careless as to whether they lived or died. Goodwin and I were grateful indeed for the blessed boon of hard work — we had scarcely a moment of leisure the day long; the others, with few exceptions, had only their misery for company.

Many were the talks I heard at night, in our quarters, as we pushed farther and farther away from England. Even the most degraded of the convicts, whose life there had been wretched enough, looked back upon it with pleasure in the light of present circumstances. Some thought only of food, and they would speak of the fine feasts of tripe and pig's knuckles and cabbage they had enjoyed at the threepenny ordinaries. Others, who had had no taste of ale or spirits in all these months, were half-crazed for the want of it. They remembered the gin shops of St. Giles, Spitalfields, Clerkenwell, and Wapping, where a man could get blind drunk for twopence, sleep it off under shelter, start the round again the next day, and so live, stupefied for a week, on a capital of one shilling. They would talk of their Dolls, Mags, and Lizzies with details as to their qualities as doss house companions for cold winter nights. As I listened to the talk that went on interminably in our bunkhouse where the few candles would scarce burn in the foul air, I came to think of London as one vast warren of filthy courts and alleys, lined with gin shops, farthing fries, rag-and-bottle shops and penny lodginghouses, swarming with petty thieves, footpads, beggars, and prostitutes.

And I would think of the difficult, thankless, heartbreaking task that lay ahead of Governor Phillip. Could he ever succeed in founding a colony? Even though New South Wales should prove a very paradise, such a company as ours might well starve there. Many were scarcely above the brutes in intelligence. They had none of the qualities needed for colonists, and neither the will nor the capacity to acquire them.

And now I come to an event that stunned and saddened me for many a day to come. Mr. Munro, whose health was delicate at the best of times, was taken with a slow fever shortly after we left the Cape, and confined to his cabin. I little thought, at first, that the illness was grave, but as day followed day and he made no appearance on deck, my anxiety increased, and I made bold to ask Surgeon White for news of his condition. The surgeon told me he was sinking fast, and that he had little hope of his recovery. I was deeply anxious, then, and watched from afar, hoping to have word with Sally, but she rarely appeared on the quarter-deck, and then only for a moment. I could see — at least, I felt — that she had forgotten my existence, and a kind of bitterness filled my heart at the thought that she could consider me so indifferent to her father's welfare that it was not worth while to give me word of his condition. This was a most ungenerous thought, but in my sensitiveness it was, perhaps, a natural one to hold. But I quickly forgot my hurt pride in my pity and sympathy for herself, watching day and night in her father's cabin, with the shadow of death creeping ever closer.

I hoped against hope that her father would rally, but it was not to be. When the end came, Sally herself informed me of it. It was a still day, with the sky heavily overcast. We lay becalmed, fore and main courses clewed up, and all of our gear creaking faintly as we rode the long swell rolling eastward. A blood-red dawn had warned us that the swell was, probably, the forerunner of another gale. I had finished some small task when I looked up to find Sally standing beside me. Her face told me all I needed to know. As I think of that moment, I am again conscious of my feeling of despair, wanting to comfort her and finding nothing to say. I took her hand, then quickly released it, taken aback at my own presumption. She told me that her father had died in the night. It was the first time I had ever spoken with Sally alone. Not more than a dozen words were exchanged between us, but I have never forgotten that brief meeting, nor the desolate look she gave me as she turned and went back to her cabin.

Mr. Munro was buried the same afternoon. The wind had come up meanwhile and was gathering strength from moment to moment. Squalls of rain continually drenched the decks and the convicts were battened down below, but Goodwin and I were about our seamen's duties.

We watched the group of seamen and marines gathered at the gangway where Captain Gilbert, one of his officers shielding the book from the rain, read the burial service. A single albatross hovered over the ship on great motionless wings, gliding deeply down to pass astern, rising swiftly again as he turned to breast the wind. In all the world's oceans, there was no region more lonely, more remote from the world of men.

Sally stood by Captain Gilbert, heedless of the rain, not looking at the body of her father which lay at their feet, sewn up in a canvas shroud. I thought of her aloneness, her friendlessness, her only relative thousands of miles distant, on the other side of the world. What could she do now? What would she wish to do? Perhaps she would return to London, with one of the transports, and go from there to Canada — a formidable voyage for a young girl to make alone.

She turned quickly and gazed out to sea as the men stooped to lift her father's body to the plank. When she turned again it was gone.

IX

BOTANY BAY

ON the morning of the nineteenth of January, we sighted the coast of New South Wales, nearly twenty miles distant. We sailed northward throughout the day, with a fresh breeze at E.N.E., drawing in ever closer to the land. There was a stir in the ship, and all on board were heartened by the happiest anticipations. Even among the convicts, who could hope for nothing better than a life of forced labour under severe discipline, I was aware of a new spirit of content, at the conclusion of our long voyage, and the thought of setting foot on land once more.

Just before nightfall, when we were pretty close in, and could make out clearly the whitish cliffs to the south of Botany Bay, the *Sirius* made a signal for the convoy to pass one by one under her stern, and each ship was ordered to work offshore under easy sail until daybreak. The sea was calm and the summer night warm and cloudless; I would have given much to have been allowed to remain on deck. But all of the convicts were ordered below and the gratings made fast over our hatches.

I lay with my bundle for a pillow, with Tom Oakley stretched out beside me. Some of the men sat in groups in the passageway, speaking eagerly of New South Wales and the relief of going on shore. Others seemed indifferent to our glimpse of the new continent, or anticipations of the morrow, and fetched out their cards or dice to begin the evening's gaming. Many of the convicts, like owls or bats, seemed to come alive only at nightfall. The ship rolled with a light creaking of timbers, and the stench of her bilges, on this hot summer night, mingling with the odours of filthy clothing and unwashed human bodies, made Newgate a fragrant memory by comparison. Foul air, enfeebled health, and the desponding state of their minds made most of the convicts uneasy sleepers; they shifted this way and that on their hard planks, groaning, muttering, and scratching the whole night through. At last I fell asleep.

The sound of our grating being removed awakened me, and the voice of the marine on duty at the hatch, summoning me and Goodwin by name. "And up with a dozen more of ye," he added. "Look alive!"

There was no great scramble for the privilege, even on this final day of our voyage, for most of those below slept sounder at this hour than during the night. Goodwin, Oakley, and I were followed by the wanted number. The breeze still held, and the *Charlotte* was standing offshore on the starboard tack, under foresail and maintopsail. The stars, though fading, shone in a cloudless sky. It was dark to the west, where we had spied the land the night before, but there was an increasing brightness where dawn touched with faint rose-colour the tufts of fair-weather cloud along the horizon. As the light grew stronger, the *Sirius* tacked and stood in toward the land, making a signal for the ships of the convoy to follow.

Before an hour had passed the coast of New South Wales was visible from the deck, stretching away to the north and south as far as the eye could reach. It was a glorious morning. I felt my spirits rise at sight of the vast continent before us. Had I been a free man, engaged in an expedition to explore these unknown forests, plains, and mountains, my happiness would have been complete. Presently we opened the entrance to Botany Bay and followed the *Sirius* in between the heads. There, before us, to the relief and joy of all, we saw the brig

Supply at anchor, together with the *Alexander*, the *Friendship*, and the *Scarborough*.

All of the convicts were now permitted to come on deck, between the barricades, where they lined the bulwarks three and four deep, to stare at the land they had traveled so far to reach, and which was to be their home, in many cases for life. When the sails had been furled and all made snug, I stared as earnestly as the others. This was to be my home, too; for how long, I did not permit myself to speculate. Though Oakley and I often spoke of escape, we well knew how small our chances were. I am setting down these recollections in 1831, when ships from England are seen as commonly in Melbourne or Sydney as they were on the Potomac when I was a boy. All of the oceans have been explored and their islands and coastlines charted; a voyage to Australia to-day is little more of an adventure than a crossing of the Atlantic used to be. It is hard for young Australians to realize that at the time of which I write, New South Wales seemed little less remote than the moon. The nearest European settlement was in the Dutch East Indies, a thousand leagues distant, on a course beset with dangers which had nearly caused the loss of Captain Cook's ship. That we had reached Botany Bay safely was a tribute to the skilled seaman and nagivator in command of the convoy.

At first sight the shores of Botany Bay wore an aspect of beauty and fertility, but we soon learned that the green meadows were morasses, covered with coarse marsh grass, and that the rich vegetation of the wooded shores was rooted in mud. The bay itself afforded but indifferent anchorage, being exposed to the easterly winds which sent a great sea rolling in between the heads; it seemed to extend inland for several leagues, and to be four or five miles wide from north to south.

And then we had our first view of black men. There was a picture for an artist to have painted — the arrival in Botany

Bay of the first fleet of convict settlers, and, certainly, this scene will some day be commemorated and preserved for posterity. Even at the time I realized the strangeness of that first meeting between felons, outcasts, despised and rejected by society, and those members of one of the most primitive of all savage races, who would have rejected us in their turn, had they possessed the power. A dozen or more of the blacks emerged from the bush at the end of a low point. They were tall lean fellows, stark naked, who looked as black as coal in the bright sunlight. They carried shields and were armed with long slender spears which they shook defiantly, shouting "Warawara! Warawara!" in deep harsh voices. The convicts yelled and hooted at them, which only aroused them the more. We did not then know the meaning of this first word we had heard of the native speech, but we could easily guess it from the fierce warning gestures of the blacks.

"By God!" one of the convicts exclaimed. "We've been pitched out like dirt by them at home, and even the bloody savages won't have us!"

I have always remembered this incident. Like other old settlers, I feel a certain tenderness for the blackfellow, the original proprietor of the land. No man can say how long he has lived here, nor whence he came, but the continent was his by right of discovery, and he had peopled it as thickly, perhaps, as his mode of living permitted. If to-day he steals our sheep, or spears our cattle, it is because we have destroyed the game on which he once subsisted. The defects of the Sydney black were many, but he was a brave fellow, and often a merry one. The arrival of the transports in Botany Bay marked the beginning of a mighty change in the annals of the Australian Continent, and the blacks who shouted "Warawara!" (Go Away!) from the point may have had some prescience of the future.

Our interest in the blacks, and the near-by shores of Botany Bay, ended abruptly when we were told that we might make free with the water in the scuttle butts, and that more would be fetched on deck. It was a great luxury to have all we wanted of the element we had never had enough of, even to drink, during the course of the voyage. We drank deep, we bathed our filthy bodies as best we could, washed our clothing, stiff with dirt and crawling with vermin, and spread it in the morning sun to dry. I had scarcely finished when a dozen of us were ordered into one of the longboats.

"Off with ye, lads," said the bosun's mate; " 'tis a watering party — ye'll have a run ashore."

We sprang into the boat, delighted at our good fortune, and an officer and three marines took their places in the stern. Goodwin was beside me on the thwart, and I could see the pleasure it gave him to have an oar in his hands. We pulled along the northern shore of the bay, rounded a blunt point and entered a creek, bordered by marsh lands. At last the boat grounded and we rolled our casks for a considerable distance to a drain which carried a run of fresh water. Two convicts, Jurd and Mawson by name, were given cutlasses and ordered to fetch bundles of the best grass they could find, for what sheep and cattle we had left were at the last extremity.

Only a man who has been eight months at sea, without once setting foot on land, could understand our emotions as we felt the earth beneath our feet once more. I worked hard that morning and enjoyed my task; filling the casks with bucket and funnel, and helping trundle them down to the boat, as I had often seen our slaves do in Maryland, with the hogsheads of tobacco on our rolling road. Flights of wildfowl traded up and down the bay; immense flocks of white cockatoos passed overhead, screaming and chattering harshly. At midday we were ordered to knock off for a bite of food.

Jurd and Mawson had disappeared amongst the trees a quarter of a mile distant, after fetching in several loads of grass. Of a sudden, we heard an outcry and saw the two convicts running toward us pursued by three blacks, who halted and cast spears which flashed past the fugitives, missing them narrowly. A second party of blacks now burst from the woods, taking up the pursuit with angry shouts. Our marines were on their feet, muskets in hand.

"Quick, lads!" the lieutenant ordered. "Over their heads! Fire!"

The reports of the muskets were no doubt the first the blacks had ever heard. They halted in consternation, and as the marines reloaded and raised their pieces once more, they retreated to the cover of the bush. Glancing over his shoulder, Jurd slowed his pace to a walk, while Mawson sank down, unable to proceed further. I followed the marines at the double to where the wounded man lay. A spear had ripped its way through his left buttock, and the blood was flowing fast. Jurd stood in glowering silence by his companion, wiping his cutlass furtively on the leg of his pantaloons.

"What's this?" asked the lieutenant.

"Tried to spear us, the black bastards!" said Jurd.

"There's blood on your cutlass."

"Can't a man defend himself?"

"Disarm him, corporal!" ordered the officer, sternly.

Whether angered by his situation and the pain of his wound, or because of some long-standing grudge, Mawson now raised himself and pointed a shaking finger at Jurd.

"He's a bloody liar, sir! 'Twas all his fault!"

Jurd took a step forward, clenching his fists, but the marines seized him. "Speak out!" said the officer. "What have you done?"

"I'd naught to do with it," Mawson replied. "We came onto a black boy and a girl, cookin' some fish over the coals. Jurd grabbed the biggest fish and started to eat it, and the black boy snatched it from his hands. He had no weapon, and Jurd killed him where he stood, with the cutlass. The girl set up a squalling, and next thing I knew was this." He touched his backside gingerly.

"Take him in charge," ordered the lieutenant.

Jurd was a powerful fellow, and before his wrists were made fast behind his back, Goodwin and I were obliged to lend a hand. Leaving him with Mawson under guard, the officer ordered the rest of us to accompany him to the scene of the crime, half a mile distant, in the bush. We had no trouble in finding the glade. The blacks were about to carry away the boy's body when we emerged from the scrub, but they dropped their burden at sight of us and vanished among the trees. All was as Mawson had described it: the embers of the fire, the broken bits of fish, a pool of blood on the ground, and the dead boy, with a deep gash in his neck which had severed the jugular vein. He was a well-made little fellow not more than twelve or thirteen years of age. The officer turned to us with a stern face.

"You've heard Mawson's story. Observe and recollect what you see here. The Governor must be told of this at once!"

The sequel to the young black's murder was prompt and terrible. On the same afternoon, the Governor assembled his Criminal Court under a gum tree close to the beach, on the northeast extremity of Botany Bay. The Court consisted of Captain Collins — the Judge Advocate — and three naval and three marine officers. A boatload of the more hardened convicts from each of the transports was ordered ashore. Jurd stood sullenly by the tree, shackled, and guarded by two marines. The witnesses gave their testimony and when Jurd was required to speak in his own defense, he only growled out: "I've naught to say. What if I did kill the black bastard? There's one less to put out o' the way."

The scene in the lonely peaceful bay was one I have never been able to forget. The marines then on shore, about fifty in all, were drawn up on one side of the tree where the brief court-martial had been held. In front of them stood the officers of the Court with Governor Phillip at their head. The convicts summoned to witness the execution stood opposite.

The silence of the great empty land, intensified by the rustling of leaves and the faint hissing of the tall grasses as they bent and nodded to the fresh breeze, was like a visible presence, and, after the Judge Advocate had pronounced sentence, ". . . hanged by the neck until you are dead," the hush seemed to deepen as though we were all under a spell. Then Governor Phillip spoke, gazing sternly in our direction: —

"On this, the very day of your arrival in New South Wales, one of your number has committed an atrocious crime. It is a crime not only against the natives of this land who have harmed none of us: it is a crime against ourselves, and against the future welfare of the colony it is my duty to establish here. The news of this murder will travel far amongst the natives, who will fear and hate us from this day on, and seek to take a just revenge upon us. Let the fate of this wretched man be a lesson and a warning to every one of you."

Governor Phillip then glanced at the Chaplain, the Reverend Richard Johnston, who stepped to Jurd's side, but the murderer glared defiantly at him.

"To hell with ye!" he said. "I'll not die dunghill! Turn me off!"

He had his wish. Wanting the executioner's black bag to put over the man's head, a handkerchief was bound across his eyes, the noose quickly adjusted, and, a moment later, he was twitching and swaying high in air. The sun was low in the west, and the long shadow of the hanged man seemed to spread and deepen until it cast a gloom over all the shores of Botany Bay, an omen of dark days to come.

*   *   *   *   *

Botany Bay was soon found to be an unsuitable site for the foundation of the colony: the bay itself was shallow, for the most part, affording no anchorage where ships might ride un-exposed to easterly weather, and no deep coves where docks might be erected for loading and unloading cargo. The shores

were marshy, and what dry land was discovered nearby
seemed sandy and barren; worst of all, no sufficient supply
of fresh water had been found. Though he ordered his officers
to continue their explorations, and even selected a site for the
settlement, in case no more favourable place should be discovered elsewhere, Governor Phillip resolved to examine Port
Jackson and Broken Bay before disembarking the people
where we were. He set sail to the north on the following morning, with three rigged longboats, taking with him Captain
Hunter, Mr. Collins, the Judge Advocate, and the masters of
the *Sirius* and the *Supply*. Owing to an outbreak of scurvy
among the seamen, I was fortunate enough to be chosen to
pull an oar in the Governor's boat.

It was midmorning when we passed between the heads
against a fresh easterly breeze, getting a good offing before
Captain Hunter ordered the sails set to run northward with
the wind abeam. He held the tiller, while the Governor sat beside him, gazing at this coastline which no European, save
Captain Cook and his people, had examined before. A great
surf broke at the base of rocky cliffs, and level, barren heath
land lay above. At the end of two hours, we were pretty close
inshore and abreast of the south head of Port Jackson.

Nothing was known of the place, save that Captain Cook,
who had sailed past the entrance in 1770, at a considerable distance offshore, noted in his log that there appeared to be good
anchorage inside. We were to discover that the great navigator's instinct had not been at fault.

No man who sees Sydney for the first time to-day can form
the least conception of the harbour's unspoiled beauty at the
time of which I write, when all was as the hand of the Creator
had fashioned it, and the forests which clothed the whole
countryside to the water's edge had never felt the woodsman's
axe.

Sailing in past the southern head, with sheets slacked off,
we opened the vast, landlocked harbour which stretched

away for miles to the south and west. The wind was cut off
by the high land as we turned southward, and we furled our
sails. All gazed at the still waters opening before us in hushed
wonder and delight, scarcely venturing to speak in this enchanted place. The great harbour, sheltered from every storm
and ruffled only by light cat's-paws off the land, extended
before us, branching in coves and bays separated by wooded
points, as far as the eye could reach. As the boats glided westward in a silence broken only by hushed voices and the faint
dip and plash of oars, small islets came into view, their rocky
shores mirrored in the glassy waters of the harbour. Forests
of gum and cedar trees stood at the head of nearly every
cove. Clouds of snow-white cockatoos, their plumage gleaming
in the sunlight, passed from one wooded promontory to the
next; bright-coloured parrakeets rose in thousands from the
trees, with harsh chatterings, as if in protest at this violation
of their sanctuary. In one cove, a pair of black swans floated
majestically, and rose with heavy wing-beats as we passed.
We were the first white men to gaze on these scenes of un-
sullied primaeval loveliness, and I shall recollect them to my
last day.

Here and there in the coves we saw native fishermen, in
their canoes of bark, but they paddled away hastily at sight of
us. The Governor was eager to establish friendly relations with
them, but he had more pressing business to-day.

"Well, Hunter," said he, "we need search no further!"

"Aye, sir. There's no such harbour in the world! All the
fleets of Europe might ride safely here!"

The Governor hailed the other two boats, ordering them to
proceed westward, separating to explore the coves on the
north and south sides of the harbour.

"Captain Hunter and I will examine these coves near the
entrance," he said. "Look for a good run of fresh water,
tolerably flat, rich soil, and deep water close inshore, where
quays may be built. You may camp to-night and to-morrow

night wherever you see fit; let us meet here, by this point, on the following morning. I shall expect full reports, with charts, and as many soundings as time permits."

We now proceeded with our task of exploration. A party of blacks stood on a point as we passed, brandishing their spears and shouting their invariable greeting: "Go away!" Governor Phillip ordered a halt, and made it clear to the savages, by signs, that they should leave their weapons on shore and wade out to receive the gifts he displayed. They took his meaning at once, and, to our surprise, about a score of them made their way out to the boat, unarmed, and showing great courage and confidence in our good will. The Governor rewarded them with mirrors and beads; on account of their behaviour, I heard him say to Captain Hunter that he would give the adjacent bay the name of Manly Cove.

It was midafternoon when we entered the cove about which the town of Sydney now stands. We had six and seven fathoms down the middle of the bay, and four close to the beaches on either hand. In breadth and extent inland, the harbour was perfectly designed for an anchorage, and for working ships in and out. The forest, which at that time covered the slopes on both sides, grew to the water's edge, so that we stepped from our boat almost literally into the woods. Most of the trees were of the eucalyptus kind, some of them of enormous size in spite of the rocky nature of the ground, but at the head of the cove, bordering what was later called the Tank Stream, were clumps of magnificent cedars.

The Governor landed presently, and went in search of water, followed by a seaman who carried his musket, while Captain Hunter continued his task of surveying the cove. Governor Phillip returned in about an hour's time, saying that he had found a run of water sufficient for the settlement's needs.

"We'll encamp here for the night, Hunter," he announced. "I'll be surprised if we find a more promising spot."

"So I believe," replied Hunter. "We can moor the ships close inshore, with stern lines fast to the trees. I've found several places where quays could be built with no great trouble. . . . Shall we dine now, sir?"

"We've still a couple of hours of daylight; let us employ them in completing our survey. There's a pair of kangaroos yonder, one of them as great as a man. They seemed to have little fear, yet I could not come within musket shot. I'm no hunter, I fear!" He smiled. "What of yourself? Can you live up to your name?" The captain, eager to get back to his soundings, shook his head, and Governor Phillip glanced at the rest of us in the boat. "Who'll try for the kangaroo?"

I made bold to say, "May I, sir?"

"What's your name?"

"Tallant, sir."

He eyed me keenly for a moment, then turned to his servant. "Give him the musket and my pouch and powder-horn. . . . You'll find their tracks by the run of water yonder; when I last saw them, they were about a cable's length to the south. Do your best. There's a portion of grog for you if you bring one back."

I followed the shore of the cove to the stream at its head, a run of good water, shaded by fine old trees. The Governor's tracks were easy to follow in the damp ground, and I saw also, for the first time, the curious traces of the kangaroo, with the mark of the tail in one muddy place, where the animal had sat upright in alarm. Moving quietly and glancing steadily ahead, I reached higher ground, where the forest was more open; and there I had my first sight of an old man kangaroo, with his mate, feeding side by side, not a hundred paces distant. I crawled forward on my belly, as the Indians do in America, taking advantage of what cover there was. At last I looked to my priming and gave a low whistle. The kangaroos sat up abruptly and I shot the male through the heart, while his mate bounded away, going at a pace that astonished me. My quarry must have weighed eleven stone, or more, and when I got him on my back, with a hind leg over each shoulder, I had as much as I could do to carry him to the beach. For all that the others had heard the report of the musket, Governor Phillip, to forestall a disappointment, had ordered his men to lay out supper, the old wearisome fare of salt beef, rancid cheese, and wormy ship's biscuits. The cheer that went up when I hove in sight with the kangaroo warmed my heart.

Governor Phillip and Captain Hunter examined the animal with keen interest — as we all did, in fact; then, with the help of one of the soldiers, I skinned and cut him up into steaks and collops which the others broiled over the coals; and only those who have lived on ship's fare for months together will know how welcome the fresh meat was. Seasoned with salt and pepper, all pronounced the kangaroo as well-flavoured as good wether mutton. We ate like starved men and everyone had as much as he wanted. The rest of the meat was cooked to carry with us.

It was a warm, cloudless night, and when supper was over I made myself a bed of dry leaves and lay with my coat for a pillow watching the stars come out. Presently one of the seamen came to inform me that Governor Phillip wished to speak to me. He was sitting by the fire, chatting with Captain Hunter.

"Where did you learn to stalk game, young man?" he asked.

"In America, sir."

"You are an American by birth?"

"Yes, sir."

"And why are you here? What is your sentence?"

"Life, sir. For highway robbery."

"I see. . . . Well, good night to you. That's all I wished to know."

We spent the following day in exploring several near-by

coves, and when the three boats met on the twenty-third, I felt certain from the talk I overheard among the officers that Governor Phillip had decided to fix our settlement on the shores of the small bay he now named Sydney Cove, in honour of Lord Sydney, Home Secretary. Late on the same afternoon we returned to Botany Bay,

X

THE FELON PIONEERS

GOODWIN and I were on deck with the seamen before dawn the following morning. It was believed that the fleet would sail for Port Jackson in the course of the day, but at sunrise the wind made up, blowing hard off the land, so we were obliged to wait for more favourable weather. The time was employed in bringing back to the ships the supplies that had been carried ashore. In the *Charlotte*, we were washing down the decks as well as we could, in view of their cluttered condition, when there came a hail from a man working aloft: "A sail! Sail ho!"

Every man made a rush for the ratlines and we stared out to sea scarcely believing what our eyes beheld: the topgallants and royals of a large ship appearing on the eastern horizon. Captain Gilbert was summoned from his cabin and came on deck half-shaved, to examine the ship through his spyglass. Within half an hour a second vessel was spied, and by this time the rigging of every ship in the harbour was filled with men gazing toward the distant vessels which were standing in, close-hauled, for the entrance to Botany Bay. Everyone was overcome with astonishment at this unexpected sight. We had been at anchor less than a week, in a harbour only once before visited by white men, on the coast of an unexplored continent thousands of leagues from the nearest European port, and here were ships making in for the land when we had supposed there were none save ours closer than China or the Cape of Good Hope.

Despite the heavy weather, the *Supply* weighed anchor

and sped out under foresail and maintopsail to reconnoitre. Meanwhile, the strange vessels, finding it difficult to close with the land because of the offshore wind, tacked and bore off and were soon lost to view; but the *Supply* contrived to work her way back some hours later, bringing word that the strange ships were either French, Spanish, or Portuguese. We saw no sign of them the next day, but Governor Phillip, fearing that they might discover and lay claim to the beautiful harbour he had just visited, set sail in the *Supply* as soon as the tide served, and anchored in Sydney Cove, leaving word with Captain Hunter that he was to follow in the *Sirius,* with the rest of the fleet, at the earliest possible moment.

At eight o'clock on the morning of January 26, the strange ships came in sight once more round Cape Solander. They entered the bay and dropped anchor not far from where we lay, displaying the royal ensign of France. They proved to be the *Boussole* and the *Astrolabe,* commanded by the Count de la Pérouse, sent out on a scientific and exploring expedition. After paying a visit of courtesy to the French Commander, Captain Hunter lost no time in following Governor Phillip to Port Jackson. Our six transports and the three store-ships made a brave show as they stood out to sea in the wake of the *Sirius.* Between six and seven o'clock on the same evening, January 26, — the date is now celebrated as Anniversary Day, — the entire fleet lay moored in Sydney Cove. Convicts and freemen alike lined the bulwarks of the various ships, gazing stolidly, or glumly, or with awe and wonder and delight, according to their natures, at the densely wooded shores, the islets and rocky promontories, the mirrorlike bays and inlets of this harbour. Our small vessels were dwarfed to insignificance within it, but the cove where we lay was snug enough, about a quarter of a mile wide at the entrance and half a mile in depth.

The marines and some of the seamen from the *Supply* were already ashore, and a flagstaff had been erected on the east side of the cove, near the spot where we had roasted the kangaroo. At about seven in the evening we saw Governor Phillip and his officers gathering by it. Presently the Union Jack was run up. A volley was fired by the marines, whereupon those on shore gave three cheers, answered by cheers from the ships. Another outpost of Empire had been claimed for England. The sound of the volley echoed away and away along the rocky shores; then, as the sun set and the last light faded from the sky, the silence of the land seemed to be flowing in again like a measureless tide from the vast unknown interior, to meet and mingle with the silence of the sea.

Although the next day was Sunday, the healthier of the male convicts were ordered ashore, under guard, to begin the task of clearing the land along the borders of the cove. Oakley, Goodwin, and I were among those chosen, and I shall never forget our satisfaction as we made bundles of our meagre belongings and quitted the crowded, evil-smelling *Charlotte*, never to return on board. The confusion that prevailed during the first weeks of the settlement was indescribable. The supplies had been carried in various ships, and many of those needed first were not to be got at until others had been removed. Orders and counter orders were given and men were sent here and there on useless errands.

More than half of the convicts had become so enfeebled as a result of the long voyage as to be useless for labour, and many of the marines were in the same condition. Before us lay a hundred tasks requiring the skill, energy, patience, and endurance of hardy woodsmen and pioneers, and where were the men for them? Governor Phillip's heart must have quailed as he looked about him on the shores of Sydney Cove, thinking of the wretched human material he had to work with. Had the King's ministers in London resolved, with malice aforethought, to put every stumbling block possible in his way, they could scarcely have done more than they did to hamper and impede him from the outset. No experienced farmer had

been sent with the expedition to supervise the work of preparing the land for gardens. Scores of carpenters were needed,
and amongst the convicts only twelve could be found with
some small knowledge of the trade, and the half of this
number were too sick to be of use. Masons, sawyers, brick-
makers — artisans of every kind were wanted, and wanted
in vain. Governor Phillip had to make shift with men who
had never held a tool in their hands, save those used by housebreakers to pick a lock or jimmy open a window. As for tools
— the saws, axes, hammers, picks, shovels, crowbars, and
the like, furnished by the contractors, were all of the poorest
quality, and even so there were not enough for the work in
hand. Our axes would not hold an edge for ten minutes, and
the hafts were of miserable cross-grained wood which often
broke after half a dozen strokes. In the confusion of that time
the men would deliberately throw away their tools, or lose
them by design, and everything was in such a state of chaos
the wonder is that anything got done. I can truthfully say that
the amount of work gotten through with in the first three
months of the New South Wales settlement could have been
accomplished in as many weeks by one fourth the number of
free men.

And yet, little by little, but at a rate painfully slow, some
progress was made. Saw pits were dug, trees felled, tents
erected, and a few plots of land cleared for gardens. In my
own case, had I not been a convict, I might well have called
myself happy. The great empty land with its golden sunshine
and its winelike air was all and more than I had hoped it would
be. It was a harsh land and a barren land, compared with the
American wilderness, with far less game than is to be found
in America; for all that, it had a beauty and a character of
its own that appealed to every drop of my blood.

Tom and Goodwin knew nothing of the woodsman's craft,
but they wielded their axes heartily, and with as good effect
as such poor tools permitted. In those first confused days after

the landing there was no orderly supervision of the convicts. Groups of men were assigned to particular tracts of forest and ordered to set about clearing them; the amount of work done depended upon the strength and good will of those engaged upon it. Goodwin, Oakley, Sabb, Inching, and I had managed to get ourselves assigned to the same job, the clearing of a tract at the head of Farm Cove. Governor Phillip ordered several such tracts cleared at some distance from the settlement that he might discover where the soil was best suited for gardens. We considered ourselves lucky to be working together, at a good distance from the main body of convicts. We built a shelter of boughs, thatched with reeds, and it served our purpose very well.

In view of my knowledge of such work, I was chosen overseer for the five of us, and I favoured Sabb and Inching in a manner that might have lost me the job had it been known to the authorities. But there was good reason for this: two men with less knowledge of manual labour, or more averse to acquiring it, could not have been found. It was truly comical to see this pair with axes in their hands. They were never at a loss in the thickets and forests of human society, such as London, but Nature's forests were another matter; so Oakley, Goodwin, and I let them loaf to their hearts' content; we were well repaid by their company. The only work they did was to walk to the settlement to draw our rations. Nick had his well-thumbed cards and his cribbage board and the two of them played in deep content, keeping a wary eye out, however, for possible inspection visits. I see them at this moment as clearly as I did on an afternoon when, having prepared for themselves a snug nest of grass and fern, at the foot of a huge tree, they settled themselves into it with sighs and grunts of content. They reminded me of Sir John Falstaff and Slender taking their ease, and not in the least ashamed of their idleness.

"Hugh, by God, it's all come out as promised," said Nick.

"D'ye mind how yourself and Tom said ye'd work out the footin' I staked ye to in Newgate?"

"That I do," I replied.

"Wouldn't ye know he'd hold us to that?" said Oakley with a grin. "But mind this, ye four hundredweight o' guts! We said naught of working out Ned Inching's! Call that debt canceled, else we'll report the pair of ye and a good hiding ye'll get."

"Canceled? Never in the world!" said Nick. "I pay ye at the rate of convict wages, which is three farthings a day. Ye can keep the score and tell me when ye've worked it off. By then Ned and me will be through our time and for London again."

Inching was about to speak in his turn when we heard voices in the distance. We had laid plans in advance for such emergencies. Sabb and Inching immediately seized their axes and took places at a tree the rest of us had nearly cut through while we attacked another. And none too soon; a moment later Governor Phillip himself appeared, accompanied by Mr. Collins, the Judge Advocate, and two marine officers. Sabb and Inching rested from their labours, puffing and blowing, as though they had been hewing steadily since daylight.

The Governor halted and looked about him, surprised and gratified at the extent of our labours.

"How many of you are at work here?" he asked.

"Five, sir," I replied.

Again he looked about him with more than evident satisfaction.

"You five have felled all these trees alone, without other help?"

Sabb and Inching stood with downcast glances, patterns of modest worth.

"Yes, sir," I replied.

The Governor remembered Goodwin and me, and he asked all of our names, making note of them in his pocketbook.

After a few additional questions he turned to the Judge Advocate, then acting as his adjutant.

"Mr. Collins," he said, "these men are to carry on here without supervision." He again turned to us. "You have done very well. As long as you merit the trust I am placing in you, you shall have it," and with that he walked on.

This was a fortunate meeting for us. We were left at full liberty during those first days on shore, and the time was to come when Governor Phillip would remember us to our great advantage.

*   *   *   *   *

On February 3, 1788, the second Sunday after the arrival of the fleet at Fort Jackson, divine service was held by the Reverend Richard Johnston. The meeting place was under a great tree near the shore of the cove, and all the people, officers, marines, and convicts were gathered for the occasion. Only the male convicts were ashore at this time, the females having been kept on board until arrangements for their shelter could be completed. I well remember the hot and muggy morning and the strange assortment of human beings gathered to hear the first divine service ever held on the Australian Continent. The convicts resembled an assemblage of beggars from a London workhouse, for the shoddy clothing supposed to last them for a year was already in rags, and some of the men were barefoot. The Chaplain's text was taken from the 116th Psalm, the twelfth verse: "What shall I render unto the Lord for all his benefits toward me?" I will do the convicts the credit to say that, on this occasion at least, they were quiet and orderly, the reason being, perhaps, that all were trying to recall what benefits they enjoyed to be grateful for. At the end of the service the Chaplain informed us that, by the Governor's orders, those convicts whose conduct merited approval and who found mates amongst the women would be permitted to marry, and he exhorted them to show, by sober, industrious behaviour, that they were deserving of this indulgence.

That same afternoon, Goodwin, Oakley, and I, having worked like draught horses for more than a week, felt justified in taking French leave from the settlement, so we set off together, carrying our supper rations with us. Having gone inland for a couple of miles, we came out on the shore of another cove, later called Blackwattle Bay. This place, although close to that chosen for the settlement, was a complete solitude, its stillness broken only by the calls of gayly coloured birds and the whir of their wings as they passed close overhead. The forest was not so dense here as at Sydney Cove; clumps of gum and cedar trees were scattered over the ground rising in a gentle slope from the water's edge. At the head of the inlet was a beach of smooth yellow sand checkered with the shadows of overhanging trees, and a little stream trickling down its rocky bed made the silence seem the deeper at that spot. We seated ourselves, enjoying to the full the peace and beauty of the afternoon, and the pleasure of being free, for a few hours at least, in the great lonely land. Oakley lay on his back, his hands beneath his head, gazing into the pools of blue sky between the piled-up masses of cloud that seemed to hang motionless there.

"This is something like," he said, presently. " 'Twill be none so bad, this New South Wales, if we can steal away now and again to be with ourselves."

"It's easy done," said Goodwin.

"Aye, for the present," said Oakley, "with everything upside down, but once they get some order into the place, I doubt if we'll go and come as we please."

"If they'll set me to the work I can do best," said Goodwin, "I'll not be bad off for liberty. Fishing was my trade at home when it wasn't smuggling. I'm thinking there'll be few here knows that business as well as myself."

"There'll be none," said Oakley. "Ye can lay to that."

We were silent for a time, then Goodwin said: "Lads, here's a plan that's popped into my head. My belief is that them who show a willing hand will have more liberty than Tom thinks. In the miserable good-for-nothing lot we've been sent out with, a man with any skill at a trade will be wanted bad, and he'll be put at the work he knows best."

"Aye," said Oakley. "That'll be fishing for you, and hunting for Tallant, since he's already bagged a kangaroo for the Governor himself. But where's the work for me? I'll be kept hacking down the bloody gum trees."

"No," said Dan, "not if ye work it right. What'll be wanted here most is food, and fresh meat even above fish. We've already been told they're to choose hunters for the settlement. What's to prevent Hugh from asking to be made one, and you with him?"

"By the Lord, we'll do it!" said Tom, eagerly. "Ask for the chance, Hugh! I warrant we'll get it. I'm a good hand with a fowling piece, if I do say it."

I had a plan of my own in mind at this time, but said nothing about it. Instead, I agreed heartily.

"We'll not miss the chance for the want of asking," I said, "and the sooner the better. What more, Dan?"

"This," said Goodwin. "Governor Phillip is a man of his word. He'll favour them that work for the good of the place. If we're given jobs to hunt and fish, we'll bide our time and ask to be sent down here to live by ourselves. What d'ye say?"

Oakley and I were heartily in favour of this. The cove offered a perfect anchorage for a boat, and the trickle of water that came in at the head would furnish a dozen families. The soil was a sandy loam and there was good pasturage for live-stock at hand. We explored the land all round and selected sites for dwellings as hopefully as though permission to settle here had already been granted. We would build a house for Oakley and Phoebe and another for the Goodwins, and I was to decide whether I would live with one household or the other, or have a hut to myself.

It was at this time that Oakley confessed to Goodwin and me what, of course, we already knew, though we had waited for him to speak of the matter. During that part of the voyage when he was in the *Friendship* with the Thynnes, he had gotten Phoebe with child.

"But mind ye, lads," he said, " 'twas no trifling matter on either side. And I'll make her a husband as true and steady as though we'd been married aforehand, with bell and book."

"Ye will and all, that's certain," said Goodwin. "Well, Tom, ye'd have had to go far to find a prettier lass. I shouldn't wonder but she'd make the best of wives and mothers. When does she expect? I'd guess ye'd not long to wait."

"I was well beforehand with my courting," Oakley said, mantling a little. "It's a matter of another three months. Hugh, if it's a boy, I'd wish him to have your name. Would ye object?"

"Object? Never in the world!" I replied heartily.

"Then it's done in advance, for I've made Phoebe promise a boy. . . . There's one more I'd wish to see for our little town here, if we're allowed to build it . . . Nellie Garth."

"Aye," said Goodwin; "she's a thriving woman, is Mrs. Garth. She'd make a champion manager for a little farm."

"Champion?" said Tom. "She's beyond that, even. There never was such a hand to make things grow. No better turnips, pumpkins, cabbages, and the like came into Covent Garden Market than Nellie Garth's. We must have her amongst us if the thing is possible."

The sun was setting by the time we finished our rounds of the cove. We halted again by the little stream to eat our salt pork and wormy biscuit, talking of the good meals we would have here in future if our plan carried through. Then, in the golden light of early evening, we started back to Sydney Cove.

When halfway back we halted to wait for nightfall, for we wished to return unseen to our quarters on Farm Cove. As we were sitting there, we caught sight of a man walking in the direction from which we had come.

"Damn my eyes! It's Mortimer Thynne!" Oakley exclaimed.

Thynne turned quickly at our hail, and, with wave of the hand, strolled toward us. He smiled as he came to a halt.

> "Can'st tell me, gentle foresters,
>   If shepherd's cot, or some rude shelter, else,
>   Lies hidden in the depth of this drear wood?"

Thynne could be counted upon to have some quotation from the poets pat to whatever occasion. He admitted that he was lost and had supposed himself walking toward Sydney Cove instead of away from it. We had seen nothing of him for more than a week, for he had been kept aboard the *Charlotte* to help one of the assistant commissaries in making out lists of supplies to be sent ashore. He told us that he had come on land only that morning.

"And all the ladies as well," he added. "The last of them were set ashore at midday."

"What!" said Tom, getting hastily to his feet. "Then we must make haste to see that our own are safe. I'm astonished, Thynne, that ye could leave your wife and Phoebe at such a time as this."

"Set your mind at rest, Tom," said Thynne. "Mrs. Thynne and my daughter are under the protection of Captain and Mrs. O'Day, in their tent. Miss Munro, I am happy to say, arranged for this. Your wife and the lad with them as well, Goodwin, and Mrs. Garth. There is quite a tentful, in fact, for the O'Days have taken in others amongst the younger women who desired to come. As for the rest . . . dear me! It seems that protection is the last of their wishes."

"Thynne, there'll be the devil an' all afoot now," said Tom, soberly. "The men will be wild to get at 'em. Are they to have leave?"

"It seems so; at any rate, they've taken it," said Thynne.

Let me speak of this night — it was the sixth of February — in the light of my later knowledge of what had been decided upon by Governor Phillip and his staff. It must be remembered that most of the convicts, men and women, were the scum of England's worst. It must also be remembered that, during a voyage of more than eight months' duration, the men and women had been kept rigorously apart except for a few occasions when they were permitted to be on deck at the same time. There was no intention, of course, to keep them forever separate, and the Governor let it be known that some liberty of intercourse was now to be granted; in the chaotic situation that prevailed during the early weeks of the landing, no other course was possible. His hope was that, under Government encouragement, the steadier convicts would marry. The others would be no more of a problem here than elsewhere in the world. As for the first meeting, ashore, orders had been given the marines to stand aside and let convict nature and human nature have its way; but those women who desired protection were to have it.

As the four of us walked on toward the settlement, Thynne told us of this, for he had heard the news current aboard the transports. He also told us that the women had been able to smuggle ashore a large quantity of gin and rum given them by the seamen.

I'd best draw the veil as quickly as possible over the scenes that met our eyes as we came through the forests to the shores of Sydney Cove. The light of many fires cast wavering reflections across the still waters of the bay and outlined in clear silhouette the trunks of the tall forest trees. Two hundred women and three times as many men were rushing here and there with howls and yells that sounded like nothing human. In the scarcity of women, men battled for them, the women, some stark naked, egging them on with taunts and promises for the victors. They were worse, even, than the men; they resembled furies escaped from some lowest circle of Dante's hell.

I have no wish to dwell upon this scene which exceeded in bestiality anything I could have conceived of as possible. It would have continued the night long, no doubt, had not Nature herself taken a hand to bring it to an end. Some time after midnight there came on a violent storm of wind and rain accompanied by vivid flashes of lightning that seemed like the thunderbolts of the wrathful God of Israel, directed at these degraded beings who had come to establish a new Sodom in the wilderness. The condition of the settlement, with more than a thousand people on shore, can well be imagined. The rain fell in solid sheets, and those under canvas were but little better off than those for whom no shelter had yet been provided, for most of the tents were laid flat before the storm came to an end. The revelers, their fury well dampened if not extinguished, huddled in sodden misery beneath the trees. Oakley, Goodwin, and I were set at work helping to raise the fallen tents, and many of them were blown down a second time before the fury of the wind was spent. The peals of thunder seemed to split the very heavens. I remember seeing, in one particularly blinding flash of lightning, an old woman leaning on a stick, her scraggly hair streaming with rain and her dress plastered against her skinny body. She might have flown to Sydney Cove in the wink of an eye, from some blasted heath in England, for if ever I have seen a veritable witch, it was she. She raised one bony claw in malediction, shaking it at a group of half-drowned women huddled in the open, at her very feet, and too frightened to move.

"Ye sluts!" she screamed. "Burn, would ye? Ye'll burn in hell afore the night's done!"

XI

SENTENCED TO PINCHGUT

THE following morning there was not a cloud in the sky; the drenched earth steamed in the sun, and a fresh breeze quickly dried the ground. There was no more liberty now, to say nothing of license — every convict save those too sick to stir was set at work in the attempt to bring some order into the settlement in preparation for the events of the afternoon when Governor Phillip's commission was to be read. At midday we were ordered to make ourselves as decent as possible, and an hour later we were assembled in two companies, the men in one, the women in the other, whereupon we were marched to the cleared land later to serve as a parade ground for the soldiery. By the Governor's orders, the events of this Proclamation Day, when Government and Law were to be formally established in the colony, were conducted with impressive solemnity. All officers and seamen of the eleven ships in the harbour who could be relieved from duty were ordered on shore, and stood in a company at one side of the parade. The marines, under arms, in their dress uniforms, were drawn up on the opposite side, and the company waited in deep silence for the Governor to appear. He came, presently, accompanied by the Lieutenant Governor, the Judge Advocate, the Chaplain, and other officers of the Civil Establishment. They walked slowly down the parade to the spot where a camp table had been placed, with the commissions, in two morocco cases, resting upon it. Here Governor Phillip exchanged formal courtesies with the marine officers, and, this ceremony con-

cluded, the soldiers, with fifes and drums playing, fell into
columns, marched around the parade, and were formed in a
circle around the body of convicts. We were then ordered to
sit down, and, as the commissions were drawn forth and
opened, the soldiers discharged their muskets three times over
our heads. This was to signify our position, as felons, in the
colony. Captain Collins then opened and read His Majesty's
Commission appointing "our trusty and well beloved Arthur
Phillip, Esquire" to be Captain-General and Governor-in-
Chief in and over the territory of New South Wales and its
dependencies. It was a lengthy document, defining the Governor's powers and duties, and while it was being read, the
Governor stood with his hat beneath his arm, listening with
as keen attention as though he had not already known its
contents. He then made a short address to the military, thank-
ing them for their good conduct, reminding them of the great
trust imposed in them, and of the sacred duties and responsi-
bilities which this honour entailed. He next turned in our
direction, gazing in stern silence over the assemblage of convicts whilst three more volleys were fired over our heads.
After another interval of silence, prolonged to make the
solemnity of the occasion the more impressive, he addressed
us, and for all the years that have passed, I believe that I can
quote his remarks very nearly in the words in which they
were given.

"There are, in this place," he began, "more than seven hundred of you, men and women, convicted of crimes against
society and condemned to exile by the just laws of our country. Throughout our voyage from England, and during the
past twenty days since our arrival in New South Wales, I
have watched you, and tried you, that I might know what
manner of folk you are. I had hoped that you might have a
desire, at least, for improvement; that you might wish to
mend your evil ways and habits and be ready to accept the
opportunity I would be only too willing to grant, to become

decent and useful members of the community to be established here.

"A few — a very few — have justified that hope. By far the greater number have shown me, only too clearly, how mistaken it was. You have taken advantage of every indulgence granted you. You have believed that the kindness shown you by my officers, upon my authority, might be abused with impunity. You have fought like the brute beasts amongst yourselves. You have robbed one another and stolen from the Government stores. You have hidden or destroyed the tools given you to work with at a time when all our hope of some rude comfort and security from the elements depends upon those tools. When, yesterday, I permitted the women to come on shore to take their part in the life and work of this colony, giving you all freedom to rest and refresh yourselves after so long a voyage, how have you employed this freedom? By a night of riot and debauchery that would make the black savages of this land hang their heads in shame at thought of being compared with you."

Governor Phillip paused to let his glance travel slowly over the assemblage of convicts listening to him dully, impudently, sullenly, or with some degree of concern, according to their natures. Then he continued: —

"Be assured, I know you now. Be assured, also, that I shall know how to deal with such depraved, licentious, vicious animals as you have proven yourselves to be. Since you will not be ruled by kind and generous treatment, you *shall* be ruled by grim justice, and I warn you that it will be grim indeed toward those whose conduct warrants such treatment.

"We have come to a new land which offers us little or nothing in the way of food until such time as we can produce it for ourselves. We are dependent for our very lives upon the supplies we have brought here with us. Yesterday, several of our fowls were stolen. In England, such an offense, serious though it is, would not be punished with death, for fowls are plentiful there and easily supplied. Here, I warn you, the theft of a fowl, or a pound of rice or flour, is a matter of the gravest consequence. The person found guilty of robbing our stores shall be hung.

"We have a great labour before us in making this wilderness habitable. You shall not be worked beyond your capacities, but I insist, I demand, that each of you contribute his full share to the welfare of this colony. Those who do shall receive just and liberal treatment. Those who do not, shall not eat."

At the conclusion of these remarks Governor Phillip reviewed the companies of marines, while the band played different airs, concluding with "God Save the King." The convicts were then dismissed to their quarters.

*   *   *   *   *

Ever since the morning when the French ships had dropped anchor in Botany Bay, one thought had dominated every other in my mind — escape. The French had built a small temporary fort on shore, armed with a couple of light cannon, to protect their carpenters, who were at work on a pair of longboats fetched out in frame. It was known that the *Boussole* and *Astrolabe* would sail as soon as the boatbuilding was done. This task occupied the whole month of February, and early in March I learned that Count de la Pérouse planned to sail within a week. My time, eagerly waited during many an anxious hour of thought, had come at last.

Until now, I had taken no one into my confidence. Much as I liked and trusted the Goodwins and Nellie Garth, it seemed best that they should know nothing of my plans, but Tom Oakley was different. I could not go without taking leave of him and suggesting that he accompany me. It had been agreed between us that we would seize the earliest opportunity to escape, but now that he was planning to marry Phoebe and awaiting with such happy anticipations the birth of their first child, I doubted that Tom would want to join me. I had decided to make my escape on a Sunday, when I would not be missed until evening roll call, and on the afternoon before, when work was over for the day, I broached the subject to Oakley. We were alone in the lean-to shelter we had erected on the edge of the clearing where we had worked ever since coming ashore. Our week's rations had been drawn, and Tom was baking a hard flat cake of something resembling bread, on the blade of a shovel which also served as a frying pan. He was silent for some time after I had told him of my plan.

"D'ye think the Froggies'll have ye?" he asked.

"They might. I heard Captain Hunter say that the *Astrolabe* had lost ten killed and twenty wounded in the Navigator's Isles."

"Aye — they'll be shorthanded. Ye're hopin' to make friends with some of the seamen and talk 'em into stowin' ye away on board?"

"Yes. And to keep out of sight of the officers until we're at sea."

"Can ye talk the lingo?"

"Not a word."

"No matter, ye'll make 'em understand." Tom paused. "In my belief, ye've a good fightin' chance. Damn my eyes! If it wasn't for Phoebe . . . but no, I'm stoppin' here. Ye've no idea how I love the lass; I'm daft about her, and that's the plain truth."

"I understand."

He tossed his cake into the air, allowing it to fall back on the unbaked side, and smiled awry at me. "I'll miss ye sore, Hugh! . . . Look! Here's Mortimer."

Thynne was coming along the path from the far side of the cove. He was our chief source of news concerning what went on in official quarters. Governor Phillip was so poorly supplied with clerks that he had been obliged to seek among the felons for men capable of preparing records and reports. Thynne's intelligence, his pleasing presence and more than respectable attainments, had all worked to his advantage. Having been brought to the Governor's attention on the voyage out, he was appointed to the clerical staff shortly after our landing in Port Jackson, and now had a desk in Phillip's portable canvas dwelling, already known as Government House. Thynne strolled up to us, swinging his rough cedar staff as jauntily as if it had been a gold-headed walking stick.

"I've good news for you, lads," he announced. "Your petition's to be granted."

Tom sprang to his feet. "Ye mean it? Ye're sure?"

Thynne nodded. "I heard His Excellency talking with Surgeon White. There's desperate need of fresh food, with all this scurvy. You two are to be appointed hunters, and Dan will have a boat for fishing as soon as one can be spared."

"God bless ye, Thynne!" exclaimed Tom, heartily. "Will we have leave to stop in the other cove, like ye wrote down?"

"That you will. And Nellie Garth, too. Nothing's too small for the Governor to recollect. 'Twas the sow she bought in Capetown got her in his good books. She's to try her hand at a little farm of her own."

"Ye've done Nellie a kindness she'll never forget," said Oakley. "She'll call it heaven to be quit of the sluts she's had to make shift with!"

Thynne smiled and dismissed the subject with a wave of his hand. He turned to me. "I'm forgetting the principal part of my errand here. Tallant, Miss Munro would be pleased if you would step around to see her for a moment at Mrs. O'Day's tent."

When I had made myself as tidy as conditions permitted, I set out with Thynne for the marine camp. The sun was near to setting, the golden light revealing the havoc wrought by men's hands in this once beautiful and lonely place. Trees hacked down in any fashion by unskilled axemen lay in every

direction, and groups of tents were crowded together at
haphazard in the clearings. The soft earth at the mouth of the
Tank Stream had been churned into quagmire by the passing
of many feet. Along the shore of the cove were great piles of
stores, covered with old sailcloth, and the acrid smoke of
brushwood fires filled the air. We crossed the stream higher
up, where the huge old gum and cedar trees had been left
undisturbed. I halted and turned to Thynne.

"Is Miss Munro alone at the O'Days' tent?" I asked.

"No. Mrs. O'Day is there, and the Captain himself, unless
he has gone since I came away."

"Thynne, I'm not going on. Make some excuse for me, will
you?"

"Nonsense, my dear fellow. It was Captain O'Day himself
who sent for you, at Miss Munro's request. You're no more
free than I to disobey an order."

I did so, nevertheless, persuading Thynne to ask Sally if
she would be good enough to come to the spot where I waited.
A convict's natural embarrassment would, I thought, be considered a reasonable excuse.

During Thynne's absence, I composed myself as well as I
might. Little as I had seen of Sally Munro since our coming
to Sydney Cove, I had thought of her with a tenderness that
I knew must be conquered. I had no slightest reason for supposing that she took more than a friendly, half-pitying interest in me. What pain and humiliation she would feel if I
should betray my feeling toward her! My heart was bitter
at the thought that, had I met her in America, or in England
before my arrest, I would have had every right to speak. But
now . . . I imagined myself saying: "Miss Munro, you have
lost your father; you are far from home and friends. But
here is Hugh Tallant, who offers you his steadfast heart, and
the inestimable privilege of sharing the cabbage-palm hut of
a convict for life."

I acted as my own physician, and felt well out of danger by

the time I spied Sally coming along the path, escorted by Thynne. I was more than glad of his presence; in his easy, offhand manner he broke the ice, for me at least, for Sally appeared to need no such service. She greeted me in the friendly manner of our first meeting on board the *Charlotte,* yet I could see that she was moved at the thought of her father, the only bond between us.

"You needn't wait, Mr. Thynne," she said; "I'll ask Mr. Tallant to walk back with me, part way, at least."

Once we were alone, my embarrassment melted away. It was Sally's doing. Her simple, friendly manner, and forgetting or wishing away the barriers I had been so conscious of, made me forget them as well. She told me why she wished to see me. Shortly before her father died he had asked that I be given some of his books, among them a little volume containing Dr. Goldsmith's "Traveller" and "The Deserted Village," which he knew I loved. She had made for them a little canvas case so that I might keep them safe.

Little by little all sense of constraint vanished and we stood talking as naturally as though we had been friends for years. Sally spoke of the O'Days, of the warmth of their Irish hearts and of what their protection and friendship had meant to her since her father's death.

"You showed great courage," I remarked, "in coming out here to the ends of the earth."

"Courage? Not at all." She smiled faintly. "It was ignorance of what lay ahead. But I would have come in any case. My father was my comrade from babyhood."

"You've an aunt in Canada?" I said.

"Yes, my mother was French. My aunt in Quebec is her sister."

"You must be eager to get back to her. . . . Do you find this a dreadful place?"

She shook her head. "The country's lovely — I long to see more of it. But it is dreadful that . . ."

"It had to be a convict settlement?"

"Yes, you understand?"

"Of course. I feel as you do. I could love the land, too, as a free man."

"How long . . . must you stop a long time?"

"Only as long as I live."

She laid a hand on my arm. "Forgive me. I didn't know. Well, I'm as much of a . . . of a prisoner as yourself. I'm not permitted to go anywhere alone."

"I'm surprised that you were allowed to come here."

"Why not? Captain O'Day knows you."

"May I ask what your plans are, Miss Munro?"

"I'll go back to Canada, as my father wished. But I don't want to make such a long voyage alone. The O'Days are ordered to Norfolk Island, when the *Supply* returns. They want me to go there and stop with them until their return to England."

I was deeply moved at the thought that this was to be my last meeting with Sally. On the morrow, I would make my attempt at escape; I could not bear to part from her without something more than a casual leave-taking. I glanced up and down the path, to make sure that we were unobserved.

"Miss Munro," said I.

"Yes."

"I'm afraid we shan't meet again. I can't leave you without saying how much it has meant to me to know your father and yourself. And I want you to know something else — to-morrow I shall try to escape."

"Gracious heaven! How? In one of the French ships?"

She listened with keen interest as I explained my plan to her, and exclaimed: "They might take you! Can you speak French?"

"No."

She paused to reflect for a moment. "Come with me. I'm going to write a letter you can present to one of the seamen when the time comes. Oh, I hope you'll succeed!"

We walked back along the path and Sally asked me to wait

for her not far from O'Day's marquee. Presently she returned
and handed me a folded paper.

"That's to give the French," she explained. "It says that
you are an American, unjustly imprisoned and eager to get
home. They don't like the English, and may help you only
for that. And here is my aunt's address in Quebec. Who knows
but we might meet there someday? Now I must hasten back
before the Captain returns." She took both of my hands in
hers and pressed them. "God bless you, and take you safe to
America."

*   *   *   *   *

Next morning, when the drums beat for the roll call, I
was present to answer to my name, and knew that the whole
day would pass before I would be missed. Tom and I strolled
back to our hut, saying nothing until we were out of earshot
of the bands of convicts on the path. Then Oakley pressed
into my hand a pair of silver shoe buckles, and a heavy gold
ring.

"What's this, Tom?" I asked.

"Ye'll need 'em, lad. They'll grease the way when ye talk
to the Frogs." He grinned. "They was honest come by, too."

He forced me to accept the gift, and presently when I had
made a bundle of clothing and food and taken up a heavy
cudgel which would be my only weapon in case of attack by
the blackfellows, I clasped Tom's hand.

"Time I was off."

"I'm fair sick to go! But I can't do it, lad. Ye'll write if ye
get off safe?"

"That's looking a long way ahead."

"So it is. Ye're takin' on a chancey job, but never say die!
Off with ye, Hugh, afore Nick gets back. Good luck! I've no
mind to stop here for life. Mebbe we'll meet up one day."

He squeezed my hand hard and I turned away southward,
into the bush. Once across the clearing, I was safe from

observation, and found my way to a native path I knew, which led through the woods, avoiding the open heath land along the coast. I walked warily, stopping to listen from time to time, for I had no wish to fall in with a party of blackfellows. Grieved as I was to part with Sally and my small group of friends, my heart lightened as the day advanced. I was free, for the time being, perhaps for good, and had everything to gain and little to lose, I thought, in attempting to board one of the French ships. If the seamen would have none of me, and I found escape impossible, I would make my way back to Sydney with some story which would explain my absence from roll call. But I put this thought out of mind.

It was midmorning when I reached a tongue of woods jutting out toward the marshes near the creek where we had filled the *Charlotte's* water barrels. It seemed likely that the French might be watering for their departure, and the woods gave me a vantage ground from which I could reconnoitre the bay without being seen. Though the season was early autumn, the sun was bright and the northerly breeze agreeably warm. I stole through the woods without a sound, passing the glade where Jurd had killed the black boy, and coming to a halt in the fringe of underbrush close to the run of fresh water. I parted the rank growth and peered out.

There were two boats in the creek about half a mile distant — one returning to the ships, and the other approaching, laden with empty casks. The *Boussole* and *Astrolabe* lay at anchor inside the northern head, looking enormous to eyes accustomed to our smaller ships; I could see the breastworks where the guns were mounted, and the large canvas fly beneath which the longboats had been put together. The watering party drew near with much good-natured shouting; I was convinced that there was no officer in the boat, and that the men, in charge of a bosun's mate or quartermaster, were in the best of humours at the prospect of a run on shore. The boat grounded at the head of the creek.

The men seemed to know the place well, and were in no hurry to set about their work. Two, whom I took for marines, put down their muskets and filled their pipes; the others, numbering half a dozen, rolled the barrels to the watering place and sat down on the bank to drink wine, with which they seemed well supplied. One short, strong-made fellow, with a cutlass at his side, wandered off in my direction, examining the plants growing on the edge of the marsh. He came ever closer, and when I was sure that he was within earshot, I called in a low voice, as Sally had instructed me: —

"*Ami!*"

He gave a start and laid his hand on his weapon, but I rose to my feet, parted the bushes, and smiled as ingratiatingly as I knew how. "*Ami!*" I repeated, holding out the letter Sally had written. The French seaman asked me some unintelligible question; I shrugged and shook my head.

"*Tu ne parles pas français?*"

I made it clear that I could not, and when a quick glance had assured him that I was alone and unarmed, he took the paper from my hand. I do not know all that Sally had set down, but as he read the note the fellow's manner changed.

"*Toi américain, hein? Anglais pas bon!*" He paused to reflect for a moment, and pointed to the ground at my feet. "*Attends ici.*"

I offered him the little gift I had prepared: the things Tom had given me and one of my own pair of razors, but he shook his head, smiling in a friendly manner. "*Attends!*" he repeated. With that, he left me to stroll back to his mates.

I watched them while my paper passed from hand to hand and they seemed to consult among themselves, with many gestures, as to what should be done. Four began to fill the barrels at last, while my new friend, accompanied by an elderly fellow with a grey moustache, wandered casually toward my hiding place.

The newcomer spoke enough broken English to make himself understood and questioned me at some length, making sure that I was an American and that I had been to sea. The two then spoke together rapidly before the elder man turned to me once more. He said that they would risk hiding me on board the *Astrolabe*, and that as soon as night fell, I was to make my way along the shore to a sandy point near the anchorage, there to await a boat. They took leave of me with smiles and friendly claps on the shoulder.

I was overjoyed at this good fortune. No one resents a shorthanded ship more than the seamen themselves, a fact which accounted for their willingness to stow me away; but they were good-natured fellows for all that, and my heart warmed to them. I opened my bundle and ate with good appetite the salt beef and Tom's unleavened bread; then I settled myself to wait through the long hours until nightfall.

The Frenchmen were as good as their word. It was past midnight when a small boat stole in to the beach and ferried me out to the bows of the *Astrolabe*, where I climbed a rope to the rail. I was then led down a ladderway, past gun deck and orlop and into the hold. We groped our way in the darkness amongst bales and casks. The old English-speaking seaman showed me an empty puncheon in which I might hide when any of the ship's people entered the hold, and informed me that he would find means to fetch me food and water when only the anchor watch would be on deck. If discovered, I was to say that I had stolen on board unknown to anyone, in a bark canoe. Once at sea, I might rest assured, he said, that Captain Clonard and his officers would be glad of an extra hand.

I spent four days in the hold of the French ship, in company with innumerable rats. They squeaked and scurried about by day, and made sleep almost impossible at night. The hold was pitch-dark, save when parties of seamen came down with lanterns to hoist out casks of provisions. At such times I crawled into my puncheon hastily and remained there until the workers were gone. On the last day, when the faint glimmer of light coming down the hatchway told me that the sun was up, there was a great stir and bustle in the ship, a blowing of bugles and the tramp of many feet on the decks above. I flattered myself that we were about to sail, and was stretching my cramped limbs when the sound of voices warned me that some of the people were coming down the ladderway. There was nothing for it but to crawl into my puncheon, like a rat into its hole.

The voices drew nearer; presently I heard footsteps in the hold and saw a yellow gleam of light on the carlings. Several Frenchmen were speaking, as if in protestation. Then a voice close at hand — as English as roast beef and Yorkshire pudding — stiffened me with alarm.

"He *must* be on board. We caught the other fellow in the *Boussole*."

"We 'ave question' all ze seamen; zey know nozzing."

"I'll have a dekko, in any case."

"As you wish, Lieutenant."

For a long time I heard them moving empty casks and prying about among the stacks of firewood. The Frenchmen were weary of what they considered a useless search, but the English officer was indefatigable, and I cursed him heartily under my breath. At last he seemed satisfied.

"It's plain the fellow's not here," he remarked; "the blacks may have knocked him on the head before he could get to Botany Bay. . . . Hello, what's this?"

The devil himself must have directed the officer's eye to my puncheon, half concealed in the shadows behind a pile of wood.

"Empty, you say? Fetch a light."

I was caught. Next moment strong hands dragged me out, none too gently.

"*Sapristi!*" exclaimed the astonished French officer. "How you come here?"

I told the story agreed upon, which seemed to satisfy him, and was prodded up the ladderway to the upper deck. A curious crowd gathered about us; Captain Clonard himself ordered me questioned further, thinking that some of his people might have helped me to stow away. But I stuck to my story, heartened by the looks of sympathy many of the seamen bestowed upon me. Presently I was ordered into a boat and taken ashore.

A corporal's guard of Sydney marines stood on the beach, with fixed bayonets, about a burly young convict, a former seaman, whose tattooed arms were manacled behind his back. He was a fearless fellow who boasted openly of his thefts from the men and exploits among the women.

"So they catched ye too?" he remarked, with a leer. "It's a red-checked shirt at the gangway, for the pair of us. . . ."

While they pulled my arms behind my back, and snapped handcuffs on my wrists, the lieutenant asked curtly: "You're Tallant, eh?"

"Yes, sir."

Several French officers stood near by, and the Englishman now turned to his corporal. "March them back to Sydney. Tell the captain I'm stopping to dine with these gentlemen."

I had risked all and lost all. Escape had been just within my grasp, only to be snatched away by the very worst of ill-fortune. That I would be severely punished, I had little doubt. As my fellow prisoner had predicted, we would almost certainly be flogged. Heretofore, I had been a model convict, noticed and praised by the Governor; from now on, my status would be very different.

We arrived at the settlement during the noon hour of rest, and a little crowd of friends and acquaintances followed us to the tent where we were placed under guard. The sergeant dispersed these people, once we were inside. We were given bread and water, and strictly guarded throughout the long, dismal afternoon. At nightfall the sergeant notified us, with a kind of cruel relish, that the Governor had ordered us to be flogged, three hundred lashes each.

Flogging has always seemed to me the most inhuman of all punishments. I had been an unwilling spectator at such scenes on more than one occasion in the past, and felt a sense of fierce, dark humiliation at seeing the manhood scourged out of a fellow creature. The physical pain of a flogging often extends beyond human endurance, but the pain of the soul is worse. It was agony to think that Tom, Goodwin, and Nellie Garth would know that I was being flogged; worse than agony to think of Sally Munro. Had it been possible I think that I might have taken my own life.

The fellow in the tent with me snored on, wasting no time on useless forebodings. I was still wide-eyed when the sun came up, and the drums beat for morning roll call. Even my callous companion was silent and thoughtful during the morning hours. The corporal came to fetch us at noon.

The flogging pillory stood near the barracks of the marines. None of my friends was present, of course, but a crowd of convicts and marines had assembled about Surgeon White, a burly corporal and the sergeant I had seen the night before. The convict women enjoyed these spectacles even more than the men, and there was no lack of them among the audience. There was a hush as we were ordered to halt, and the sergeant glanced down at a paper in his hand.

"James Saxton," he commanded, "step forward!"

My fellow prisoner did as he was told, and the sergeant went on: "By order of His Excellency, Governor Phillip, three hundred lashes, for attempting to escape. Corporal, do your duty!"

The handcuffs were removed from Saxton's wrists, and he was ordered to step into the tall narrow box at the foot of the pillory, which would prevent him from moving his feet. He was helped to take off his shirt, and his hands were confined in the two holes provided for that purpose, at the level of his shoulders. The burly corporal rolled up his sleeve and drew the tails of the cat through his left hand.

"Proceed!" ordered the sergeant.

The corporal drew back his cat and brought it down with all the strength of a brawny arm, to strike Saxton's back with a thudding sound. The breath flew out of the man's lungs with a loud "Ugh!" and a great red stripe appeared on the bare flesh.

"One!" announced the sergeant.

The corporal struck again. "Two!" The flesh quivered as the injured muscles contracted, and the red stripes turned purple. "Three!" . . . "Four!" . . . "Five!" Now the bright blood came welling out and began to trickle down the man's back. I turned my head. An hour seemed to pass, and still the flogged man, whose one virtue was courage, had made no sound but an occasional low moan. The convict spectators watched in silence.

"Hold!" interrupted Surgeon White. "That's all the man can bear for to-day. Carry him back to the tent."

I glanced at the poor fellow as they removed him from the pillory. He had lost consciousness and his back was a red slough from waist to shoulders.

The sergeant glanced at his paper once more. "Hugh Tallant, step forward!"

There was black despair in my heart as I stood with my arms outstretched while the guards removed my handcuffs. At that moment a marine orderly came running across the parade at top speed.

"Sergeant!" he called. "Orders from Major Ross!"

The sergeant glowered at the man, but took the folded paper, spelling out the words silently with his lips, like a schoolboy. He gave me a sour glance as he looked up.

"Call yourself lucky," he said, grudgingly; then, to the corporal: "Take him off to Pinchgut. He's to have three months."

XII

GOODWIN'S HOMECOMING

PINCHGUT is a rocky islet in the harbour, between Kirribilli Point and Garden Island. In those early days it was a penal colony within a penal colony: it was often remarked that the three quarters of a mile of calm water separating Pinchgut from Sydney had a more wholesome effect upon convict character than the four thousand leagues of stormy ocean between Port Jackson and England.

There was no water there, no shelter of any kind, nor shade against midday sun save for a few bushes and stunted trees. Garden Island is only four hundred yards away, and from there to the land the distance is even shorter. The most indifferent of swimmers could have made his escape had there been no sharks. These fish, of great size and ferocity, inhabited the harbour in scores. Several convicts, driven to desperation by existence on Pinchgut, had attempted the short swim to land. But not one had reached it.

Bread and water was the diet on Pinchgut. The place was visited once a week by a corporal's guard, who filled the keg and left seven days' supply of wretched bread, barely enough to sustain life. To a man of active mind and habits, the life there was more terrible than I can make clear in words. In those days there was seldom more than one convict at a time on the islet, and the solitude was a torture in itself; there was nothing to do but indulge in one's own sad or bitter thoughts. When it rained, the hermit shivered all night long, exposed like an animal to the weather. When the summer sun beat down, making a veritable furnace of the rocks, his only refuge from the heat was in the scant shade of one of the stunted trees, or in some tidal pool. After a month on the islet I looked back upon the life in Sydney as our first ancestors, after their expulsion, must have reflected upon the delights of the Garden of Eden.

The usual sentence to Pinchgut did not exceed a fortnight, and during that time, as I said, the diet was bread and water. At the end of the second week, however, I was given a little salt meat and pease, as well as a piece of old sailcloth for a shelter. Without these small indulgences my lot would have been a hard one indeed.

My sentence on the island would expire on the eighth of June, and I kept count of the days by means of scratches on a rock. Long after dark, on the last night of May, I was over-joyed to have my first visit from a friend. Winter was coming on and the night was too cold for sleep. Huddled in my blanket where there was a little shelter from the breeze, I heard a cautious voice hailing me: —

"Hugh! Hugh! Where are ye?"

It was Goodwin, paddling a native bark canoe close in-shore. I guided him to the north end of the islet, where we made ourselves as comfortable as we could among the rocks.

"How be ye, lad?" he asked.

"Still alive, as you see."

"Did ye think we'd forgot ye?"

"Of course not."

"I'm to have a boat next week. It's the devil and all to get hold of a canoe. I've tried a score of times afore now."

He handed me a bundle, containing the first decent food I had tasted for three months, and I fell to ravenously.

"Eat hearty," said Dan. "Nellie and my good wife fixed it for ye."

Presently I leaned back against the rock with a feeling of

pure animal content. For the first time in three months my belly was full.

"God bless you, Dan," I said. "Now give me your news."

"There ain't so much to tell. Tom's a father now."

"He is! A boy?"

"Aye. Born on Saint Patrick's day. Mrs. Thynne was for callin' him Paddy, but he's to be christened Hugh Thynne Oakley."

"Tom and Phoebe are married?"

"Long since. All shipshape and Bristol fashion."

"Do you see Miss Munro sometimes?" I asked, casually. "How is she?"

"Well enough. She's leavin' to-morrow."

"Leaving!"

"Aye, for Norfolk with Captain O'Day and his lady. The *Supply* sails around midday."

I had hoped to have at least a word with Sally before her departure, and Dan's information disappointed me cruelly. "You're sure it's to-morrow?" I asked.

"Certain. I had it from Thynne. Ye should see him, Hugh — he's that proud to be a granddad!"

"You got leave to move to the other cove?"

He glanced at me in the darkness, seeming to hesitate before he spoke. "I hate to speak of us, lad, while ye're in a fix the like o' this . . . yes, the Governor gave us leave. We've been a buildin' our cottages. Tom's a hunter now, and I'm to have a boat, and nets. Hugh, ye must ask leave to live with us."

"I'm not likely to get it with a black mark against my name."

"Who knows? There's worse crimes than tryin' to run away."

We talked on in the dark while the small waves slapped against the rocks below, and we shivered in the chill breeze. At last Goodwin rose.

"I must be off, lad. The moon'll be up in half an hour. Ye'll be ashore in another week. There's a black family helping us these days. If they don't make off with their canoe, I'll slip up to see ye first chance."

*   *   *   *   *

The breeze was at northwest next morning, and I knew that the *Supply* would pass between Pinchgut and Garden Island, on her way out to the Heads. Sally must never see me, yet I wanted a last glimpse of her. I chose a spot where I could lie at full length among the rocks, unseen by those in the ship, and peep out through a clump of bushes.

It was midmorning when the brig came around Bennelong Point, half a mile distant. Her jibs and topsails were set, as well as the forecourse and driver; once clear of the point, she bore off, slacking away her braces to run almost free for Bradley's Head. She came on fast, and I flattened myself against the rock, never taking my eyes from the group standing on her quarter-deck. Now I could make out Sally, and Mrs. O'Day's short, stout figure at her side. The *Supply* increased her speed as topgallants and royals were loosed and sheeted home.

Now she was abreast of Pinchgut and less than a hundred yards distant. Sally gazed fixedly at the barren islet, turning to stare back after the brig had passed. I did not move until the vessel bore up and disappeared beyond the high land more than a mile away. How many months or years would pass before I might hope to see Miss Munro again, I made no effort to compute.

Dan came twice during the nights that followed, bringing gifts of food, and the news that Garth was making progress with her little farm. The family of blacks seemed to have settled in the cove. The woman was a help to Nellie, Dan said, and her man was useful at hauling the nets. On the last day of my exile, Goodwin passed close to Pinchgut in the launch Governor Phillip had allotted him for his fishing, and grinned as he pointed to the black man with him, who was learning to pull an oar. Next morning, promptly on the day set for my release, the marines came to carry me to Sydney.

As we pulled into the cove I could see that some progress had been made, though the improvement was pitifully small, considering the number of men at work. A few acres had been cleared, particularly about the head of Farm Cove; the observatory on the point was finished; wattle-and-daub huts had replaced many of the convicts' tents; barracks of a sort had been erected for the marines; the hospital had been enlarged and I saw the beginnings of a permanent residence for the Governor. The shores of Sydney Cove were commencing to assume the aspect of a permanent settlement.

Thynne was waiting for me on the wharf by the flagstaff; he nodded to the corporal and clasped my hand.

"Come, Tallant," he said, "His Excellency told me to fetch you. Prepare yourself for good news."

The Governor's house was close by, surrounded by cultivated land fenced with stakes. He looked up from his writing as Thynne ushered me in, past the sentinel, and informed me briefly that while my attempt to escape had not been forgotten, I was to have one more chance. My petition to be a game killer would be granted, and I could live with my friends in Blackwattle Bay. My future would depend upon my conduct and success at hunting.

I was so overjoyed at this good fortune that I could only stammer out a few words of thanks. Thynne was ordered to see that I got a week's rations and a musket and fowling piece.

"You're in luck, eh, Tallant?" said Thynne. "You know whom you owe it to?"

"No."

"To Miss Sally Munro. And 'twas she who saved you from the flogging as well."

Thynne glanced at me quizzically, relishing my astonishment. "Quite so," he went on. "She'd been off on a three-day trip, with some of the officers and their wives, to the head of the harbour. They returned on the very morning when you were to have been flogged. Miss Munro had heard nothing of your attempt to escape. The moment she learned of it, she came to Government House to ask for an audience with His Excellency. I heard every word that passed between them."

"What did she say?"

"A good deal that I hadn't known before. That your father and brother gave their lives for the King in the American War. That you were wounded in one of the last battles. That your loyalty cost you the family estate. You couldn't have had a more eloquent defender or a prettier one. She told how your compensation had never come through; how you were driven to commit a crime in order to get to Canada. The end of it was that His Excellency sent an urgent message to Major Ross. You know the rest."

I glanced at Thynne's lean, intelligent face. "See here, Thynne, I suspect that you had a hand in this, too."

He smiled. "Why not? I had no wish to see you flayed alive. And I couldn't think of a better advocate for you than Miss Munro. . . . Now, Tallant, I must hasten back to my inkpots. There'll be a warm welcome for you at Blackwattle Bay."

Thynne proved the best of prophets. I reached the small, new settlement an hour later, and the pleasure with which Nellie and the others greeted me warmed my heart. They had accomplished wonders at the head of the beautiful and lonely cove I had not seen for so long.

The cottages stood close to the beach. The walls were of cabbage palm, plastered with clay; the roofs were neatly thatched with reeds of the gum rush, and the floors were of clean, hard-packed sand. A path led from the landing where Goodwin's boat was moored and his nets hung to dry. They had cut down the brush roundabout, leaving only a few fine old trees to shade the dooryards in summertime. Behind the houses was the fenced enclosure where Nellie kept her pigs, and next it a paddock for two cows and a young bull entrusted to her care by one of the marine officers. Some progress had been made on a clearing where Nellie hoped to plant maize and vegetables as soon as the proper season should arrive. The family of blacks of whom Dan had spoken lived in a bark hut near by: a man, his wife, and a boy of fourteen. The fellow's name, Pattagorang, signified "kangaroo" in the local dialect, but Goodwin called him Pat.

I was taken into the Goodwin household; Tom and Phoebe, and their child, lived with Nellie Garth. It was plain from the first that Phoebe was never designed to be a mother. There was no doubt, I think, that she loved her little son. She would be seized by moods of the deepest tenderness and affection for him, and I have never seen a young mother who had more engaging, more touching ways with her first-born. Then, of a sudden, she would tire of the child, turn him over to Garth or Mrs. Goodwin and go off to see her mother at Sydney Cove; often she would be away for a day or two at a time. Tom was shocked at this indifference, and more than one stormy scene took place when Phoebe would return; but it would all pass quickly, for Tom could never be angry with her for longer than five minutes. What hurt him most was that Phoebe refused to suckle her child. She proposed turning him over to one of the convict women to rear, but both Tom and Nellie Garth said no to that. The event was that Garth reared the baby herself, feeding him on cow's milk with a little sugar added.

Nellie knew by instinct what others were forced to learn by experience. The Government's wheat and Indian corn had been planted too early in the year; the young shoots withered for lack of rain and were killed by the hot sun. Garth waited until late in July before planting the seed given her, and the result showed how wise she had been. By mid-October the corn was tall and green in her little field.

Oakley and I were up every morning before daylight to set out with musket or fowling piece in search of game. We became skilled in the habits of emu and kangaroo, learned what lagoons were visited by black swan, duck, and other wildfowl, building hides in the marshes where we could lie in wait. Sometimes, but not often, we would come back empty-handed; at others we would bring down a dozen or more duck at a single discharge of our guns. Our chief duty was to hunt for the sick at the hospital, but we would have been more than human if we had not reserved a small share of game for ourselves. The fresh meat, with the weekly rations we drew from the Sydney stores and the fish Goodwin fetched home, kept us in the best of health. When fish were plentiful, Goodwin often pulled round to Sydney with the boat laden to the gunwales. His work took him to many a remote reach and cove seldom visited by any but himself, and he came to know the ramifications of the vast harbour better than any man of his time.

*   *   *   *   *

Though he liked the country and was content with the work assigned him, Goodwin lived with but one thought in mind — a return home. When we sailed from Portsmouth, only a year and a half of his sentence remained to be served. This was, I think, the chief reason why Mrs. Goodwin had insisted upon coming with him to New South Wales. She was devoted to Dan, despite her somewhat peevish, complaining ways, and she made him a good and loyal wife. Bella was a splendid cook and housewife and kept their cottage as neat as a Dutch kitchen. But there is no doubt that she enjoyed her sense of martyrdom, endured for his sake. I had great respect for Mrs. Goodwin, but I must admit that she lost much of the virtue of self-sacrifice through speaking of it so often. But that was her nature; we all have our faults, and I have no wish to dwell upon the flaws in the character of an excellent woman.

Goodwin's time would be up in November, and both he and his wife were in a state of almost painful anxiety and impatience for the day to come. For, during these months, the transports and store-ships that had brought us out had sailed, one by one. Some had gone by way of China for cargoes of tea for the East India Company, others had sailed direct for the Cape and home. Only one, the *Fishburn*, remained in Sydney Cove; she was now upon the eve of sailing, and the Goodwins hoped to return in her. The question was, would his time be up before the *Fishburn* left?

The rest of us were almost as concerned about the matter as the Goodwins themselves, for if they missed going by the store-ship they would have a year at least, perhaps two years, to wait, as no other ships were expected within that time. The thought of separation was painful to all, and Dan said little of it. He had the most thoughtful consideration for others, and leaned over backward, as the saying goes, in his efforts to conceal his own happiness at thought of freedom, knowing that we must be left behind.

And then came the long-wished-for day when, according to Goodwin's own careful reckoning, his seven-year sentence expired. I remember well: it was the twenty-seventh of November, and I must have been awakened by Goodwin shortly after midnight on the morning of that day. I opened my eyes to find him standing beside my bed with a candle in his hand, and I could feel the joy in his heart before a word was said.

"Hugh, I'm off to fish now, and Oakley's coming with me. If we've luck we'll carry the catch direct to Sydney afore comin' home."

"Is it morning?" I asked.

"Aye," said Dan, his face beaming; "though a mite early,

I wished to have the full good o' this day from the start."

I sprang out of my bunk and clasped his hand, as happy for him, I verily believe, as I could have been for myself, in his place.

"God bless you, old lad!" I said. "And you're a free man! How does it feel?"

"I couldn't rightly say, but I feel it, here," and he struck his chest.

The whole of our little settlement was stirring within the half hour. We felt justified in proclaiming a holiday for ourselves, but Goodwin was so mindful of his duties that he was bound to go fishing. He and his son and Tom set off in the boat a little before sunup, and I went inland, afoot, with my fowling piece, to hunt for ourselves and no one else, on this occasion. I returned at midday with four leash of wild duck that Mrs. Goodwin roasted to perfection in our clay-covered oven. We had our rations as well, and Nellie and Mrs. Goodwin were busy throughout the afternoon preparing the feast we were to have, keeping a sharp lookout the while for the return of the others. It was not until toward evening that we spied the boat coming round the point from the direction of Sydney.

"There's Phoebe with 'em," said Garth, in a relieved voice.

"And high time, too," said Mrs. Goodwin, disapprovingly.

Phoebe had been absent three days on one of her periodical visits to her mother's house. She was subdued and quiet upon first arriving, but that passed off. She took her son from his crib, fondled and played with him and tossed him in the air till the little fellow crowed with delight.

A happy occasion that was, for Dan had learned, at the settlement, that the *Fishburn* would sail for England on the Friday. Before ever leaving England, Goodwin had put away the money for their passage home. He had it safely hidden in his cottage.

Our meal was now ready, and Governor Phillip himself

would have been pleased to sit at such a feast. The ducks came on, basted with their own rich gravy, with roast turnips, and carrots to go with them. There was grilled mullet for another dish, and boiled salt beef and cabbage for a third, enough and to spare for all. Even tea was not wanting, brewed from the leaves of a shrub that grew wild in the forests, and called, for want of its true name, the sweet-tea plant.

Mrs. Goodwin was all but out of her senses with joy and excitement over the news of the *Fishburn's* early departure. She hurried back and forth between the house and the cook shack at the back, talking a steady stream.

"Nellie, I can't hardly believe it! Wouldn't ye say it's all been ordered by the will of God? Here's Dan's time out the very day, for I mind well he was judged and sentenced the twenty-sixth of November, seven years gone, and I never thought to see the end of 'em; I never did. And now they're past and done with! And there ain't but a week to wait! . . . Dan, are ye certain about the *Fishburn?*"

"Aye, she'll sail Friday, certain sure, for the word is posted at Government House."

"And the captain'll take us? There ain' no doubt about it?"

"If all's shipshape with my papers, and it will be, for I've made no mistake in my reckoning. I asked to see Governor Phillip this morning, but he's that busy I must go again to-morrow."

"Goodness me! I don't rightly know *where* I be, I'm that stirred up," said Mrs. Goodwin, her eyes shining. "I can't relish my vittles the way I'd wish."

"Just ye calm down now, Bella," said Tom, "and enjoy 'em hearty, for ye'll taste no roast duck on the voyage home."

"That ye won't," said Garth, "nor none of yer good soft bread. If 'twas not for the mouldy flour, and that's no fault of yours, I'd say I'd never et better. . . . Phoebe, what's amiss with ye? Ye're scarce eatin' a bite. . . . Bless me, if the lass ain't as glum as a mute at a funeral!"

Garth laid a hand on the girl's shoulder, and of a sudden Phoebe burst into tears. She buried her head in her arms, her whole body shaking; then, rising from the table, her face still hidden in her hands, she went quickly out the door.

Tom gazed blankly after her. He put down his fork, and with a quiet nod to the rest of us followed her.

"God forgive me!" said Mrs. Goodwin. "God forgive me for the selfish creature I be! Takin' joy in my good fortun' with never a thought for the rest of ye!"

Her eyes filled with tears, and a moment later she herself was crying.

"There, ye good soul," said Garth; "we'll not have ye blamin' yerself. It's not in reason to hide the joy ye feel. We'd be the same in your place."

"I should ha' tried, Nellie," sobbed Mrs. Goodwin. "But I was thinkin' only o' Dan and me and little Tom. I should ha' tried, for your sakes as well as Phoebe's. I'm selfish and unmindful, for you're to bide here and we're to go."

"We'll do well enough," said Garth, "and it ain't as if we was yonder in the settlement. Take comfort, now, Phoebe'll have her cry out and be all right, after. She's had 'em before, in her homesick times."

Mrs. Goodwin raised her homely, tear-stained face, wiping her eyes on her sleeve.

"I know, but she's such a young thing, Nellie, and it's a rough hard life for a girl."

"She'll settle down to it, in time, I shouldn't wonder," said Garth.

Mrs. Goodwin shook her head. "No, never — not Phoebe. I'll say this, amongst ourselves: she shouldn't ha' married Tom Oakley, for she'll never be happy here."

"Hush, now!" said Goodwin, sternly. "It's not for us to

say what Phoebe should ha' done. And don't ye put the notion in her head she can't be happy!"

"I've no thought of it, Dan! I wouldn't for the world! But a body that ain't blind can see it, clear as daylight. And she with as handsome a little son as ever was born! Even that ain't made her content."

Goodwin and I carried benches outside, and seated ourselves by a great cedar tree that stood in the dooryard. It was a glorious night, with the moon an hour up, and not the wisp of a cloud to pass across it. The shadows beneath the trees were pools of blackness, and before us lay the peaceful cove, like a silver mirror, with Goodwin's boat at anchor there to give the bay a homely touch, and seeming to keep the great silence and loneliness of the land at a little distance.

"Hugh," said Goodwin, presently, "I'll miss ye sore, ye and Tom. I will, so."

"Away with that," I said, with an attempt at lightness, though my heart was heavy indeed. "Tom and I have no mind to give you two thoughts, Dan, once you've gone. We're resolved to forget you, straight off."

"Aye, that'll be best, if so be we can manage it," said Goodwin. "I take small comfort in going, for the thought of ye two, and Garth."

Tom returned and took a seat beside us.

"She's all right now, and will be along directly," he said. "Phoebe's a soft heart, Dan. She was upset to think we're to lose Bella and yerself so soon."

"What'll you do, Dan, once you're home?" I asked.

"We'll not speak of that," Goodwin replied. "Bella's said enough to spare of home."

"Ye fear to sadden us?" Tom asked. "*We're* not softhearted! As far as that goes, Hugh and me's getting to love this land. We'd think twice about leaving, even if the chance was to come."

"It's not a bad life here, the way we're fixed now," I said. "Come, Dan! Tell us what you'll do, at home. You won't go back to smuggling?"

"I will and all," said Goodwin, quietly.

"Then we won't say good-bye if ye're set for that work again," said Tom. "Mind ye, Dan! It'll be twice seven years, and mebbe life, the next time ye're caught."

"No fear! . . . Lads, smugglin's my trade; 'twas my dad's and my granddad's afore me. There'll be Goodwins at it in the generations to come."

Their work finished and the kitchen made tidy, Garth and Mrs. Goodwin joined us presently; then Phoebe came, quiet now, and well over the fit of homesickness. Bella took care to say nothing that might touch her there again. We talked of the bad times and good times we'd had together, and of Nick Sabb and Ned Inching, who had settled into the life at Sydney Cove with better heart than ever we thought they would. Sabb had been made sergeant in charge of the convict patrols that policed the place at night, and had made a snug little home for himself at the guardhouse, with old Maggie Shinn to wash and mend and cook for him. Inching, through Sabb's influence, had been given a post that suited him well — that of sexton for the settlement: he had charge of the burying ground. This churchyard, without the church, lay back from Sydney Cove in open sandy ground covered with scrub. It was a forlorn spot, with its own native air of desolation, but Inching seemed to take a kind of sour pleasure in being miserable there, and in seeing the lodgings in this part of the settlement increase. He had a helper for grave-digging, and they had made final homes for twenty men and eight women since the month of January.

Presently Goodwin asked Phoebe to sing, and we all seconded that proposal. She had a lovely voice, sweet and clear, and she knew scores of songs, both grave and gay: she never came to the end of them. Phoebe was in a sad mood that night and she sang one song I have never forgotten and never will: —

> "Shall I go walk the woods so wild,
>   Wand'ring, wand'ring here and there?
> As I was once full sore beguiled . . .
> Alas for love! I die with woe.
>
> "Wearily blows the winter wind,
>   Wand'ring, wand'ring here and there
> My heart is like a stricken hind;
> Alas for love! I die with woe."

None of Phoebe's songs touched Tom Oakley to the quick as this one did. She had only to sing it, on a night of full moon, or one with the sky a glory for stars, and his eyes would fill with tears and a flood of tenderness well up in his heart. And well Phoebe knew it!

The next day was Sunday, and both households were astir early. The Goodwins were up before the rest of us, Dan making himself tidy, with his wife's help, for his walk to Sydney, where he was to see Governor Phillip. He was dressed in his best blue coat and trousers, and shoes with silver buckles, which he had never before worn in New South Wales.

"A fine upstanding fellow ye look, Dan," said Oakley, admiringly. "I'm proud to know ye."

"I mind well when I first saw him in the coat," said Mrs. Goodwin, with a happy smile. "Ye recollect, Dan? 'Twas the day we was married. The cloth is as good as it was then, thanks to me, for I've took the best of care of it."

"So ye have," said Goodwin. "It gives me a queer feelin' to be wearin' it again, like as if all the grief that's come since had never been. . . . Lads, what'll I do at the settlement, yonder?"

"Do?" said Oakley. "Walk straight along to the Governor's house like the free man ye are, and tell him ye've come for the release paper."

"No," said Mrs. Goodwin; "I know how it'll be with Dan.

He's like to be that tongue-tied not a word will come out as it should. Ye'd best see Mr. Thynne, first, and ask him to come along to explain all in proper fashion."

"So I will, Bella; 'tis good advice. I shouldn't wonder if I'd be gone till evenin', for I wish to see the captain of the *Fishburn* when I'm through at the Governor's, and lay down the passage money. I'll feel better when it's safe in his hands and all's settled for us but the going aboard."

"Oh, Dan, a happy day this is!" said Mrs. Goodwin, giving him a last brush with her hand. "Go along, now, and come home the minute ye can. I'll have supper waiting and ready."

"Leave that," said Goodwin, "for there's no saying how long the business will take. I might have to spend the night, and if I do, I'll bunk in at Nick Sabb's. So don't wait up for me."

A long day it was for Mrs. Goodwin, but she got through the better part of it in making preparations for departure. In the afternoon I found her, with Garth, sitting on the floor beside the sea chest which Mrs. Goodwin had brought, packed with clothing and other necessities, from England. She glanced up quickly when I appeared in the doorway.

"Dan's not coming yet?" she asked.

"Now, Bella, how could he come as soon as this?" said Garth. "The time will go soonest if ye forget Dan till we see him. I shouldn't wonder if he'll be obliged to stay the night, like he said."

"I know; like enough he will, but gracious me! It *is* hard, the waitin'. There couldn't be no hitch, think ye, to our being allowed to go?"

"Hitch? Never in the world. Didn't Dan himself say he'd seen the captain?"

"There, I'll think no more about it," said Mrs. Goodwin, with a happy sigh. "Now, Nellie, here's a box not even touched yet, of the best black and white thread; there's four dozen spools of each, with papers of needles, both the large and small. And this cloth bag has twenty pounds of the best wool yarn. This ye shall have, for the patching and mending of Hugh's things, and Tom's, to say naught of yer own."

" 'Tis more than kind," said Garth, "and I'll not say no, if they can be well spared."

"They can, and I'd wish ye to have them, whether or no, for a starved place this will be, soon, for cloth and thread. I was told by Mr. Palmer, the commissary, there's not enough in the stores to last another three months, not to speak of the lack of needles. This petticoat I wish to lay out for Phoebe. There's good wear in it still, and 'twill serve in the end for cutting into little suits for the baby."

"Poor thing," said Garth; "she's still that low-spirited. I could wish she'd stayed at her mother's till the ship's gone. A lonesome time we'll have here till we can settle down to it."

I left them for an hour's stroll in the moonlight, and when I returned to the house I found Nellie Garth seated at one side of the table and Tom at the other, with Goodwin's home-made lamp, filled with shark-liver oil, burning between them. They were writing letters home for the Goodwins to take with them for posting in England. Mrs. Goodwin was more than commonly excited and "stirred up" to watch them at work on the very letters she was to carry. Phoebe was sitting near Tom, holding the baby, asleep in her arms.

Nellie gave me a quick friendly glance as I came in.

"Come, Hugh," she said. "Be a good lad and write for me. I'm no hand at letters, and do naught but spoil good paper. Will ye help me?"

Tom had prepared a little heap of quills, from the flight feathers of the black swan. I selected one and took Garth's place at the table.

"It's to my old neighbour at home," she said. "I'll speak and ye can set it down: 'Mistress Sarah Windle, Wood End, Middlesex, England. Dear Friend Sarah . . .' Have ye got that down?"

Nellie went on till my hand was weary, telling of New

South Wales, of our little settlement apart from the others, in Blackwattle Bay, of the wonderful climate of the country, of her pigs and fowls, and the bull and the two cows entrusted to her care — all the homely things in which she took so deep an interest; and her concern about Nat showed in every other line. At last she was done, and took the pen to write in her own sprawling hand: "From your old neighbour and gossip, Ellen Garth."

"I'd wish to be set this moment where my letter's bound," said Tom, looking up from his writing. "Ye mind Dick Waller, Nellie, landlord of the Bell in Hand, at Northolt? It's to him I'm writin'. Many's the pot of ale I've had in Dick's company. . . . Hugh, have ye none of yer own to write? The *Fishburn's* our last chance for letters. God knows when there'll be another!"

"No," I said, "I'll wait for the next one, whenever it comes."

I had more than once been tempted to write, in confidence, to Mr. Fleming, making a clean breast of my present situation. I longed for news of my mother; my anxiety about her, the uncertainty as to whether she was living or dead, was indeed hard to bear. But when it came to the point of writing, I could not bring myself to do it. I knew that I could depend upon Mr. Fleming to guard my secret; but there was no knowing what had happened to him. He might be still in Canada; he might have returned to England. The possibility I most dreaded, when I was tempted to write, was that my letter would fall into the hands of someone else, and be opened in his absence. The news of my fate would then become known to my mother, if she still lived, and to our friends in Canada. It seemed best to keep silence; to let my friends and relatives believe that I must have died in India, the grave of so many hopeful young men who had gone out to make their fortunes.

The hour grew late and Goodwin had not come, but we all waited up for him until at last we were sure that he could not be expected until morning.

"That'll be it, depend upon it," said Tom. "Dan's not been able to finish the business to-day, else he'd ha' come well afore this. Bella, ye'd best go to bed and take your rest."

Phoebe and Garth had already gone, and Tom soon followed; but Mrs. Goodwin and I sat by the table, talking and waiting until well past midnight. At last, overcome with drowsiness, she laid her head on her arms and fell asleep.

I was more than sleepy myself by that time, and took a turn outside before going to bed. I walked down the path toward the bay and stopped short, for there was Goodwin, sitting on the little pier we had built over the shoal water. He didn't see or hear me until I stood beside him.

"What is it, Dan? How long have you been here?" I asked.

He got heavily to his feet, and walked slowly along the beach, I following. When we were out of earshot of the house, he stopped. My heart smote me as he turned his face toward me in the moonlight.

"We're not to go," he said.

"Not to go? You mean the captain of the *Fishburn* won't take you?"

He stood staring dully at the sandy shore, as though he had not heard me. Then he shook his head, slowly.

"It's not that . . . I'll not be allowed to go, the Governor says." Of a sudden he roused himself, and his voice was cold and hard as he spoke again.

"Will ye believe this? The convicts' papers was not sent out with us from England! That's what the Governor says. It's a lie! It must be a lie!"

"Wait, Dan," I said. "The Governor himself told you that?"

"The Governor himself told me that. The fault's none of his, he says. The papers wasn't sent. He's wrote for 'em, to England. Till they come, he can take no man's word for the time he's served."

I could think of nothing to say. What comfort could have been offered in the face of so bitter a disappointment? A moment later Goodwin added, in a heartsick voice: "And it's no lie, what he said. I could ha' told, if it had been. No . . . Governor Phillip's an honest man. He spoke fair and looked me straight in the eye. . . . But how am I to tell Bella? How? It'll break her heart."

XIII

THE UPPER HAWKESBURY

"WE'RE not to go." . . . Goodwin's words, and the dull, embittered, hopeless voice in which he had spoken, sounded in my ears as I walked away northward along the beach of Blackwattle Cove. I could see that he wanted to be alone, and I had no wish to be present when he should rouse his wife and break the news to her. I glanced back as I turned from sight, around a wooded point. Dan was standing where I had left him, as though powerless to move from the spot.

I walked slowly along in the bright moonlight, following the windings of the beach; then struck across the land till I came into the path leading from our place to Sydney Cove. Convicts were not supposed to be abroad at such an hour, but with Nick Sabb in charge of the patrol that policed the settlement at night, I knew that I ran little risk. The marines policed only their own barracks and the storehouse, so I gave these places a wide berth and made my way to the cabbage-palm hut that served both as a guardhouse and as a lodging for Sabb. This stood back from the cove on the west side of the Tank Stream. A light was burning there; the door was open, and looking in I saw Sabb, Mortimer Thynne, and Ned Inching seated at a table lighted by a single candle, their shadows huge on the walls of either side. Sabb and Inching were at their old diversion, cribbage, and Thynne was looking on. Sabb glanced round quickly at the sound of my step.

"What's this?" he exclaimed. "Thynne, didn't I say 'twas

an uncommon quiet night, with not a man fetched in to the guardhouse? Here's one that walks in without waiting to be fetched!"

"Am I under arrest, Nick?" I asked.

"So ye are," said Sabb, with a grin, "and I'll just shut and lock the door so's ye won't run out on us. . . . Sit ye down, Hugh! Now then, what are ye up to, prowlin' round the settlement at this hour?"

"Ask Thynne," I replied.

"Ye speak of Dan Goodwin?" said Sabb.

I nodded.

Thynne gave me a sober glance.

"Tallant, if ever I've felt sorry for a man, it's Goodwin," he said. "I might have told him, in advance, but I hadn't the heart to do it."

"What do you mean by that?" I asked.

"Did he say nothing of what he was told by the Governor?"

"Yes; that, by some mistake, the Home Office had failed to send out the records of our terms, and the Governor could take no man's word that his time was out until the records came."

"That is true; that is absolutely true," said Thynne.

"How can you be so sure?" I asked.

"Because, Tallant, I made the fair copies of the very despatches Governor Phillip sent to Lord Sydney by the first transport that sailed for home. You will understand the impression made upon me by the paragraph which mentioned the missing records. I can quote the Governor's very words: 'I urgently request the necessary information respecting the time for which the convicts were sentenced, and the intentions of Government respecting those convicts who, when their time shall expire, may refuse to become settlers and demand liberty to return to England!' . . . It is hard to believe in such gross neglect on the part of the Home Office. The fact remains that none of our papers were sent out."

"Neglect, d'ye call it?" said Sabb, grimly. "I've my own belief about that."

"Aye," said Inching; "the papers wasn't meant to come. We're sent for life, the lot of us, them with seven years as well as the rest. None of us will see England again. They've made sure o' that."

Thynne shook his head.

"See here, Thynne," said Sabb. "Is it likely they'd forget to send so important a thing as our papers? No, by God! We're naught but rogues, the main part of us here; but there's rogues with human feelings, like ourselves, and there's rogues in high places with stones for hearts. What do they care about justice? They've got rid of us, and they mean to stay rid of us, be our terms what they may."

"No," said Thynne. "Our papers will come, but God knows when!"

"Meanwhile, here's Goodwin, as free a man this minute as Governor Phillip, or Lord Sydney himself. A heap o' comfort he'll take in thinking his papers may come, someday!"

"There's nothing we can do about it," said Thynne. "Tallant, it's fortunate, your coming round to the settlement. I was to send for you the first thing in the morning. I've news for you and Oakley."

"Good news?"

"*I* would not call it so, but you and Tom will. You recollect the fellows who took to the woods a fortnight back?"

"Yes. Haven't they been found?"

"Only fancy! They thought China lies just beyond the mountains and hoped to reach it on foot!"

"Mebbe it does," said Inching. "Mebbe they're safe there by now."

"God save us, Ned Inching!" said Thynne, giving him a wondering look. "You tell me you really think the Celestial Empire is a part of New South Wales?"

"I know naught of the Celestial Empire, but I shouldn't

wonder if China was not far off yonder. They'd never tell us, for fear we'd *all* hop it."

Thynne shook his head with a give-it-up expression. "By the Lord! Here's a geographer!" he said; and turned to me. "A detachment of marines was sent in search of the missing men," he went on. "They got lost, and a second detachment of six went in search of the first. They would all have died of starvation if they had not fallen in with some friendly blacks who guided them home. Both parties came in yesterday, half-dead. As for the convicts, heaven knows what has happened to them. I suspect it's no case of half-dead, there."

"What has this to do with Oakley and me?" I asked.

"*You're* to go in search now. Governor Phillip's orders. He does you the honour of thinking you will be able to learn what has happened to the poor devils, and to find your way back with the news. You are to take the tame black, Pattagorang, with you."

Ten minutes later I was away on the road for home. Tom and I had long wished for an opportunity to explore the country inland from Port Jackson, and had been tempted, more than once, to take French leave for the purpose. But, as we had to report at Sydney twice weekly for roll call, we had decided that the risk was not worth the chances of losing favour with the Governor, and our jobs as hunters with it. I half dreaded reaching Goodwin's house, thinking of the state Bella would be in, after the news Dan had surely broken to her by this time. Day was at hand as I came within view of the cove, and saw that the boat was gone. Mrs. Goodwin spied me from the door and came to meet me.

"Dan's gone off to fish," she said, quietly. "He wished for the day alone. I fixed him a bite o' food to take with him. We wondered where ye'd got to."

For a moment I thought that Goodwin had not told her, but Mrs. Goodwin put that fear out of my mind at once.

" 'Tis a cruel blow to him, Hugh — a hard, bitter blow,"

she said. "My heart's that sore for him . . ." Her eyes filled with tears. "Come along, now, and I'll get yer breakfast."

I was so astonished at Mrs. Goodwin's fortitude that, of a sudden, I took her by the shoulders and gave her a hearty kiss on her sallow cheek.

She broke down at this and cried a little, but soon recovered herself.

"Hugh, I've been a peevish, naggin', worryin' wife to him, but God help me, I'll be so no more! When I think of the sharp-tongued, hateful creature I've been, blaming him for bringin' me here . . . A poor helpmeet he's had in me for anything but the housework. But I'll comfort him now, if so be as I can, and make the waitin' easy instead of a torment. . . . But his papers will come someday, won't they, soon or late?"

I never thought to see such a change as that in Bella Goodwin. She had spoken nothing but truth in calling herself a peevish worrying wife, for that she'd been from the day I'd first seen her at Portsmouth gaol, blaming Goodwin endlessly for dragging her off from home and friends to be the wife of a convict. But from this day on she forgot herself in thinking of her husband.

I found Tom having his breakfast, with Phoebe and Garth. Phoebe listened to my account of what we were to do with an air of almost painful interest, puzzling to me then, though I understood the reason for it later.

"And you'll be gone a full week?" she asked.

"Longer, perhaps," I said. "We're ordered to continue the search until we can come back with definite news of what's happened to them. We're to carry rations for ten days."

"Oh, Tom! You'll not be here to see the *Fishburn* sail!"

"What of that?" said Tom. "I've no wish to see her go, but we can think of that with better heart since Dan and Bella won't be aboard. Their hard luck is our good."

"So it is," said Garth. "Bella's bearin' it in a way I never thought to see."

A strange happy light came into Phoebe's eyes.

"I'm so sorry for them," she said, quickly, "but it would have been terribly lonesome here without them."

"Phoebe, you little vixen," said Garth, giving her a sharp look. "You're not sorry at all."

"Oh, but I am, Nellie! I am indeed!"

"We're all that selfish and may as well admit it," said Garth. "As Tom says, we think of our own good above theirs."

Tom and I lost no time in making our preparations, and within the half hour we were ready to go. Pattagorang was awaiting us in his canoe, by the pier. Phoebe came with us down the path, and as I stepped into the canoe, she threw her arms around Tom and clung to him, her face hidden against his breast.

"What's this, Phoebe?" he said, patting her shoulder. "D'ye think I'm off for good? . . . There now, lass! Bear up! We'll be back afore ye know it."

She glanced up briefly, her eyes streaming with tears.

"Tom, be very careful, won't you? I'm so afraid that . . . that something may happen."

Drawing down his head, she kissed him, then turned quickly and ran back to the house. Tom stood gazing after her for a moment, and as he took his place in the canoe he said: "Hugh, lad, I've got a wife in a thousand — aye, in ten thousand!" He grinned. "But like enough ye've heard me say that afore now."

We paddled round to the settlement in the cool of the morning, both of us deeply content with the prospect before us, of a full week, perhaps a fortnight, of complete freedom. In that mood, even the rough little settlement at Sydney took on a new aspect. It seemed more cheerful and promising, and I realized, for the first time, I think, that the colony Governor Phillip had founded under such discouraging conditions might yet prosper. The slopes on either side of the cove had been pretty well cleared by this time, leaving only a few scattered trees. The rows of huts for male and female convicts, the hospital, the storehouses with their thatched roofs, the Governor's cottage, the marquees and the newly built cottages of the officers, the barracks of the marines clustered around the parade ground, made a far from mean impression of man's handiwork under the rough hard conditions of pioneer life.

Leaving Pattagorang with the canoe, we walked up the beach to Thynne's hut. For all the fact that Thynne had sat up till the small hours yarning with Nick Sabb, he appeared as lively as though refreshed with a full night's rest. Half a dozen convicts, both men and women, were waiting in his dooryard, for Thynne combined with his official duties that of letter writer to the felon population. Most of them could neither read nor write and all those who wished to send letters home by the returning transports came to him for help. At this time, with the *Fishburn* soon to leave, he was doing a thriving business. We found him at a table in his small office.

"Come in, Tallant, come in," he called, cheerily. "Tom, the top of the morning to you! One moment and I am at your service."

He was just finishing a letter for a thick-set, low-browed fellow, all rags and tatters, who stood, barefoot, in the middle of the room turning his cap round and round with great horny hands.

"There," said Thynne, with a final flourish of the pen; "is that all you wished to say, my good man?"

"Did ye tell the old devil, me fayther, I ain't sick, but workin' like a bloody slave in the brick kiln?"

"I did."

"And ye wrote about the sarpents and the murtherin'

blacks? And I'd call the worst bog in auld Ireland Hiven itself alongside o' this New South Wales?"

"It's all in," said Thynne.

"Then I'd thank ye to read it over to me," said the man.

Thynne cleared his throat, and with a glance, half triumphant, half apologetic, for ourselves, began: —

Honoured and Well-beloved Parent: We are informed that the store-ship, *Fishburn*, is to sail for England within the week, and I hasten to take my pen in hand, to inquire after your welfare, and to assure you of my own. May this message of filial solicitude find you as well as it leaves your devoted son. Although separated from you by half the circumference of our Planet, and set down in what is, after all, a wilderness, be it never so blooming and romantic, my health leaves nothing to be desired. Our simple repasts, partaken of in quantities a more prosperous society might consider inadequate, together with an abundance of wholesome out-of-doors employment, make for a sound mind in a healthy body. I am at present engaged in the honourable and useful task of brick-making. One day, soon or late, these same bricks will rise in noble edifices, monuments to the foresight and architectural genius of our Governor.

What manner of land is New South Wales? — you may ask. A veritable land of promise, I reply, though in some respects, perhaps, it suffers by comparison with our own dear Emerald Isle. The aborigines, I must admit, are not unjustly incensed at the white strangers who have usurped their hunting grounds; and serpents, both large and numerous, await the day of their banishment by some Patron Saint who has yet to make his presence known amongst us. But time flies on winged feet, and I am now called to my not unpleasant labours at the brick kiln. Not a day passes, my honoured parent, when your name is omitted from the thoughts and prayers of

Your dutiful, obedient, and affectionate Son

The man listened with an air of bewildered admiration as Thynne read this flowery epistle. The latter then put the quill in his hand and guided his fingers while he signed his name.

The fee was one shilling, and the convict seemed well pleased with the bargain.

"Thynne, that was worth a good half crown of any man's money," said Oakley, when the convict had gone out.

"Was it not?" said Thynne, with a bright smile. "But we must temper the wind to the shorn lamb. I sometimes write them for sixpence."

He rose, put on his hat, and, informing the convicts waiting in the dooryard that he would be back directly, he led us to the Governor's house. It was little better than a cotter's dwelling at home, but it seemed almost luxurious beside the wattle-and-daub huts of the convicts. The Governor was writing at a large table covered with neat stacks of documents and papers. Around the walls were shelves for books and records. An open door gave a glimpse of another room that was, apparently, the Governor's combined drawing-room and study.

He glanced up, gravely.

"You have explained, Thynne, the purpose of this mission?" he asked.

"Yes, Your Excellency."

"What I wish you to do," said the Governor, "is to find these men. The chances are that you will discover only their bodies, for they left the settlement with little food, and they have now been missing for a fortnight. How far west has your hunting taken you?"

"Not far, sir," I replied. "Three or four leagues out from the Crescent."

"You'll have the black with you?"

"Yes, sir."

"I understand that you have never been molested by the natives in your hunting?"

"No, sir."

"Good. What trouble we have had with them has been of our own making. We can scarcely complain if they attack men who steal their gear and break up their canoes. Thynne!"

"Sir?"

"Write an order on the commissary for a fortnight's rations for three men. And they'll want a supply of powder and ball."

It is about five leagues by water from Sydney to Rose Hill. Governor Phillip had long since realized that there were no tracts of land near the coast suitable for growing the crops needed so urgently. Having explored the country round about, he fixed upon a region then known as the Crescent as offering the most likely land for farming, and already there was a little settlement in the making here, at the place called Rose Hill. It was from this place that we were to start on our search. We concealed our canoe where we had often hidden it before, on the shore of what is now called Homebush Bay, near the eastern end of Elizabeth Farm. At the new settlement, Captain Campbell, in charge of the marines, informed us that the tracks of the fugitives had been followed as far as Bellevue, or Prospect Hill, which was a considerable distance farther inland. Campbell was surly and short with us; far from pleased that two convicts were now set to a task in which his own men had failed. He predicted that we would have our labour for our pains. We had our own ideas about that, and might have made some more than pertinent remarks on the worthlessness of marines for anything but garrison duty; however, being convicts, we held our peace.

During the following week we proceeded farther and farther into a wild, rocky, wooded country that we first viewed from Prospect Hill. Not a black man did we see save Pattagorang himself, and he went forward at such a pace that it was as much as we could do to keep him within view. How he followed the trail of the missing convicts after so long a time is still a mystery to me, but he went forward with an assurance that convinced us he knew what he was about. On the second day out, we came upon the remains of two convicts, their bodies half eaten by dingoes and so badly mutilated that we could not know whether they had been killed by natives or had died of starvation.

No white men, save the missing convicts we followed, had ever set foot in the country we now traversed. Our general course was south-southwest, and before noon of the next day we had found three more bodies lying as they had fallen. This left but one unaccounted for. The trail, if trail there was, for we saw no signs of one, now became more difficult for Pattagorang to follow. We turned this way and that but proceeded in the same general direction, and late in the afternoon emerged from the forest country into the bottom lands of a broad unknown river, the Upper Hawkesbury, or Nepean, flowing north, which watered a region far more fertile and beautiful than any we had yet seen in New South Wales. The land here was open, bordered with low hills, and carpeted with rich grass. Scattered groves of stately trees, free from undergrowth, gave the landscape the appearance of some nobleman's park. Kangaroos bounded away at our approach, and we saw emus far in the distance, grazing on the rich grass of the meadows that bordered both sides of the river. Away from the stream, and at a higher level, were other far-reaching flats, with small lakes among them fringed with reeds and green bush and reflecting the glories of the evening sky. Pat, wholly unmindful of all this lonely beauty, led us on a long circuit, through the open grass land and back toward the river once more, and then, by some instinct possessed only by his countrymen, brought us to the remains of the last of the missing men, lying beneath a tree. It was no pleasant task to bury the man, and we wasted neither time nor sentiment upon the poor wretch who lay there. Tom remembered him, for he had come out in the *Friendship*, but he remembered no good about him, and no prayers were muttered over his grave.

Pattagorang built a fire, and when it had died away to a

fine bed of coals we roasted a couple of swan to a golden brown, and a better meal I've never enjoyed. When we had finished, the black made him a nest in the grass and Tom and I stretched out in our blankets near by. The night was cool and starlit; we could hear the quacking and chattering of the waterfowl and the music of their wings as innumerable flocks passed overhead.

"Hugh," said Oakley, presently, "we'll say naught of this place, eh?"

"Not a word," said I.

"We've small hope of clearing out from New South Wales," he added, after a silence.

"I catch your drift, maybe," I replied. "You're thinking we might get lost, ourselves, and settle here."

"Man, if it wasn't for Phoebe and the lad, ye'd not have to speak twice of such a plan!"

"What's to prevent our fetching 'em, and Garth and the Goodwins with 'em? We could shift our gear up here on the quiet. A month would do it."

Tom sat up, his hands clasped around his knees. "It might be done," he said. "It might well be done! But we'd be found, soon or late."

"What of this, Tom! We might do it all open and above-board. Suppose we went to the Governor himself, told him of the place, and asked leave to come here. We're in his good books now. If he said yes, we could come with tools, and seed from the Government stores, and livestock that we'd never be able to fetch, otherwise. What a place for sheep, or cattle!"

"And horses — don't forget the nags! I'd a picture in my mind's eye just now — a cottage by the clump of trees yonder, with smoke risin' from the chimney and Phoebe on the door-step, and me and young Hugh walkin' out after supper for a look at the colts and fillies. Lad, ye're right! It must be done with the Governor's help. If he's the man I think he is, we'll have it. . . . But would Phoebe be content in such a lonesome place?"

"You should know that better than I."

"She's London born and bred, but ye've seen her change. . . . I can't say she's much of a mother; mayhap that'll come. Phoebe's young."

We talked on half the night, and the more we discussed this bright prospect, the more convinced we were that it might become reality. We spent the following day in making a thorough exploration of this delightful region, and were four days on the homeward journey as far as Rose Hill. As it was no business of ours to make a report there, we went on to the place where we had hidden our canoe. We came down on the ebb tide, and Tom's vigour in wielding a paddle showed his eagerness to reach Phoebe and home. I rallied him about this as we were rounding Long Nose Point, with Goat Island less than a mile ahead.

"Take it easy, Tom. You'll be in a sweat, and that's no state for appearing before the Governor."

"What!" said he. "Must we report to the Governor tonight, think ye? He'll not expect us, that's sure, at this hour."

I agreed with that, and he glanced back with a grin.

"Ye rogue!" he said. "Wait till ye've a wife of yer own. Ye'll know how to haste, then, on yer homecomings."

Night was falling as we passed between Goat Island and the mainland and turned south. Goodwin's boat was tied up at the pier, and lights were shining in both houses.

"They've not seen us," said Tom, happily. "By the Lord! I *am* in a lather. Go along, Hugh. I'll have a dip, first. But don't go to our place. I wish to surprise her."

As I opened the Goodwins' door, I found Bella and Garth sewing by the table, with the lamp between them.

"Hugh! Where's Tom?" asked Garth.

"Coming . . ." I stopped short. "What is it, Nellie?"

Mrs. Goodwin put her head in her arms and burst out

crying. Nellie got to her feet and, going to a little cupboard, returned with a bit of folded paper which she handed to me in silence. I opened and read it.

NELLIE: —

I am leaving for England by the *Fishburn*. I can't bear it here any longer. No one knows I am going, not even my father and mother. Ask Tom to forgive me if he can, and please help him to take care of little Hugh.

Your sorrowful
PHOEBE

Garth seated herself again at the table. A moment later we heard Tom's quick step on the graveled path, outside.

XIV

SALLY

EVERY man, as he looks back over the road he has traveled from youth to the threshold of old age, will recall a stretch of the road that lies deep in shadow; when the misery of the journey was relieved by scarcely a gleam of light ahead. There was such a period in my own life, shared indeed by all the inhabitants of the Port Jackson settlement; from the dreary summer of 1789 — winter in the Northern latitudes — until well into our winter of the following year.

More than two years had passed since our arrival in New South Wales and no ship had come out from England to relieve our distress. The people of Sydney Cove, convicts and freemen alike, sank more and more deeply into a kind of hopeless apathy and despair. It is hard for the best of men to live and work without some pleasant prospect to cheer them; how much harder is it for felons, with scant resources of courage and energy, weakened by half-starvation, living in wattle-and-daub huts that scarcely offer a shelter from the elements, to face a future which promises nothing but the continuation and deepening of their misery.

In the month of November, the ration of the entire settlement had been reduced to two-thirds allowance, and five months later it was again reduced, to less than one-half. Each male convict now received, as provision for seven days, two and one-half pounds of flour, two pounds of salt pork, and two pounds of rice, or pease. The rations of women and children were even less. This food had been loaded into transports or store-ships more than three years earlier. Of poor quality at best, its condition after so long a period can well be imagined. It had lain in the steaming holds of leaky vessels during the eight months' voyage. It had been handled and rehandled, and had suffered all the damage that time and exposure could work upon it. The flour was mouldy and alive with weevils; the pork was no more than pieces of rancid fat, so nauseating that only starving men could have swallowed and kept it down — the few lean bits boiled away to nothing; the rice was a grey powder, filled with worms. Governor Phillip was compelled to order that rations should be issued daily, instead of weekly, for many of the convicts could not command themselves, and would devour their week's provisions at one meal. Then, in defiance of the most severe penalties, they would steal the food of their mates, or plunder the poor gardens of the settlement. The country about Sydney Cove was so barren that the Governor was forced to order the greater part of the swine to be slaughtered, because of lack of food and herbage to keep them alive. In March 1790, it was known through the settlement that the food remaining in the public stores would be exhausted in three months' time. Failing the arrival of ships from England, our colony of near one thousand inhabitants would face starvation.

We would have been more than human, at Blackwattle Bay, had we not fared a little better than the inhabitants of Sydney. Nellie's vegetables, and our game and fish, went to the hospital or into the public supplies, but when I shot a wild dog or Dan captured a shark, we felt justified in saving the almost inedible flesh for ourselves. As many as a score of men were hunting for the settlement in those days, and game became more and more scarce in the region of Port Jackson. On many a day Tom and I came home empty-handed. All of Goodwin's fish was now needed for the inmates of the hospital, fifty or sixty poor creatures who were more the victims of starvation than of disease.

A change had come over Dan; he went about his duties in the same quiet way, but the light of hope had gone out of him. There were several others whose terms had expired; all shared Dan's belief that Government had no intention of permitting any of them to see England again. Like Goodwin, Tom Oakley had become embittered and taciturn. He believed, at first, that Phoebe had left him with her parents' connivance, and refused to see or speak with them from the day when we had returned home to find Phoebe gone. I was thoroughly convinced, on the other hand, that the Thynnes had known no more of their daughter's plans than Tom himself. Feeling certain of the injustice Tom did Mortimer and his wife, I played my part in bringing them together, and in the end the old friendly relationship was resumed.

During the months of February and March, our relations with the blacks became seriously strained. Gangs of the rougher sort of convicts were in the habit of wandering about the country on Sundays or holidays, ostensibly searching for the herb they called "sweet tea." In spite of the Governor's warning and the severe punishments inflicted on men known to have plundered the aborigines, the hungry convicts never missed an occasion to steal fish or game from them, carrying home their weapons and implements, and oftentimes breaking up their bark canoes. More than one of the felons was murdered by the incensed blacks; the convicts retaliated in kind, and it became dangerous for an unarmed person to go into the bush alone. The natives had great fear of a musket, though they knew that firearms were harmless, once discharged. Pattagorang grew more and more uneasy; he warned us to be on our guard and contrived to make us understand that it was dangerous to separate when visiting distant hunting grounds. The most hostile of all the tribes was that known as "Bideegal," who inhabited the northern shores of Botany Bay.

Game had become so scarce and wary in the vicinity of the

settlement that we were obliged to go far afield. One day, late in March, after a week of unsuccessful hunting, I set out at dawn to the southward, resolved to spend a night in the bush rather than come home empty-handed. When I ate my wretched midday meal I had seen no more than a single small kangaroo, far out of range, and going at a great pace, but toward evening, as I was circling to the west, I came on a pair of emus, picking at the grass in a little glade. They had not seen me; I began to stalk them, taking advantage of what cover there was, and without the least suspicion that I was being stalked in my turn, by men far more deeply versed in woodcraft than myself.

At length I crept within range. The male bird raised his head suddenly, as if alarmed. I fired; he fell kicking in the grass while his mate went off like the wind. My ramrod was in my hand when I heard some small sound behind me and turned about. At that moment a spear struck me, entering the right shoulder with such force that the barbed head was driven clean through behind the shoulderblade, close to the backbone. There was a wild yelling as half a dozen blacks came bounding toward me. The blow of the spear had nearly knocked me down, and the weapon's twelve-foot haft, dragging from my shoulder, caused great pain, but I seized my musket by the barrel, preparing to defend myself as best I could. Then I felt a crashing blow on the head, and knew no more.

*　　*　　*　　*　　*

When I regained my senses, my right arm and shoulder were afire with pain, and I was so pitiably weak I could not stir. At first I could not even guess where I lay. A man's voice asked: —

"How does he do?"

A small, cool hand was laid on my forehead and a woman's voice replied: "No worse."

"The lad's as tough as oak. Such a crack on the head might have killed an ox! I've no fear of the shoulder; the inflammation's going down. But he may never recover from the concussion."

"You say he's a chance, though?"

"Aye. His skull's an inch thick. . . . I've a power of work to-day; will you change the bandages, Miss Sally?"

Even then my numbed brain told me nothing. The patched, mouldy canvas of a tent was overhead, with the afternoon sunlight streaming in through a dozen small rents; I lay on a cot, with blankets pulled up to my chin. Sally Munro was standing with her back to me, leaning over a basin in which she was washing some cloths.

Presently she turned, and, seeing me conscious, gave a little cry and came running to the bedside, to take my uninjured hand in hers.

"Don't try to speak, Hugh," she said. "It's all right."

I could do no more than give her a puzzled stare as she dipped a cloth in cool water, wrung it out, and placed it on my forehead. Then she began to feed me water with a spoon. My throat was parched with thirst and my body seemed to absorb the water faster than Sally could raise the spoon to my lips. She smiled.

"Drink," she said. "Surgeon White says you may have all you want."

I wanted to speak but Sally put her fingers over my lips. "You mustn't talk. You're going to get well, Hugh. I'll tell you all in good time."

My eyes closed once more, and that is all I recollect until the morning of the next day. The water Sally had given me worked some sort of miracle, for when I awoke the fever was down, the inflammation of my wound reduced, and the pain much less than on the preceding day. And I was hungry, which I took for a good sign.

The sun was casting level beams of light through the holes

in the wall of my tent. There were the faint hum and bustle of the awakening settlement, distant shouts, the barking of dogs on the other side of the cove. I heard the drums beat and the voices of the convict overseers, far and near, calling the rolls of the men about to start their work. I wondered whether Sally were up and about, and listened eagerly for her footstep outside the tent. I knew now that I was in Sydney, in one of the old tents pitched when the hospital became overcrowded. I raised my hand and fingered the great bruise on the back of my head.

Memory returned by slow degrees. I recollected shooting the emu, miles distant from Sydney, on the northern shores of Botany Bay, and the attack of the aborigines, but I could recall nothing that had happened since. I wondered dully how much time had elapsed, and how Sally came to be here, instead of on Norfolk Island with Captain O'Day and his wife. Then I saw her slender figure in the doorway. She came straight to me, leaning over to touch my forehead with her lips.

"You're better, sir. The fever's down, by half."

She gave me water, all I wished to drink, removed the bandages from my shoulder, spread fresh ointment on the wounds, and bound them with the clean cloths she had washed the day before. Gentle as her touch was, the slight movements I was forced to make hurt abominably.

"There, that's finished," she remarked. "I know how it must hurt. Your shoulder's not nearly as red as it was."

"I'm hungry," I whispered.

"Splendid! Surgeon White says you may have some broth whenever you want it. Tom Oakley fetched in a fine kangaroo last night. Did you see him this morning?"

I shook my head, and she went on: "He's slept beside you every night. And Nellie Garth and the Goodwins have come often. You've staunch friends, that's certain."

"When did you come, Miss Sally?"

"Only a day or two after you were hurt. The *Supply* came to Norfolk to bring back the officers and seamen marooned there when the *Sirius* was wrecked."

"Wrecked! The *Sirius?*"

"Yes; on the reef at Norfolk, but no lives were lost. . . . I must go, now; the hospital is filled with sick. I'll fetch your broth when it's ready."

The morning hours wore on, while I stared at the canvas overhead or at the glimpse of the cove through the tent's open fly, dozing off from time to time, and grateful merely to be alive. Surgeon White looked in for a moment when Sally brought the broth.

"Well, young man," he said as he took my pulse, "you can thank God for a thick skull. I wish all my sick had your constitution."

When he had gone Sally fed me the broth. Never have I enjoyed a meal as I did that one, though my enjoyment owed more, perhaps, to the pretty hands that fed me than to the excellence of the food itself. Each spoonful seemed to give me fresh strength.

Sally was in and out of my tent throughout the day, but with the hospital so crowded she had little time to herself. I slept the afternoon long, and when I woke I found Oakley sitting beside me.

"So ye're out of the woods, lad?" he said.

"That I am — better every hour."

"Damme if I'd have believed, ten days back, that I'd ever see ye on the mend, like this. I thought ye was a job for Ned Inching."

"Not this time. Ten days — have I been here as long as that?"

"Miss Sally didn't tell ye?"

"She hasn't allowed me to talk more than a minute or two at a time."

Tom nodded. "She's promised me a half hour, granted ye

let me do the talking. Aye, it's been nip-and-tuck with ye, lad."

He went on to tell me how I'd been found in the bush.

"And ye can thank old black Pat for that. Without him to track ye down, ye'd ha' been dead long since and yer carcase et by the dingoes. Ye must ha' broke the spear when ye fell; I found the after end of it. The blacks wanted to keep the barbs, I reckon, and pulled six feet of it through yer shoulder, point first. Then they stripped ye naked and made off with the musket and the emu ye'd killed. . . . Has Miss Sally told about the *Sirius?*"

"Only that she was wrecked on Norfolk Island, and no lives lost."

Tom nodded, soberly.

"There *was* a loss, for the lot of us. God knows what'll come of it! She was to go on to the Cape of Good Hope for flour and pork. Now there's naught but the *Supply* between us and starvation. It's believed whatever supply ships has been sent from England must ha' been lost as well. . . . But away with that. We'll manage somehow, like as not." He gave me a keen glance. "Ye're pleased with yer nurse, I take it?"

"That I am!"

"Ye owe life to her, lad — no question there. I hope ye know what use to make of it, now ye have it again?"

"What do you mean by that?" I asked.

"Answer that for yerself, if ye're not stone blind and have a tongue to speak with," said Tom.

Those long weeks in the hospital proved that I had friends beyond any man's deserts. Garth and Bella Goodwin prepared little dishes for me out of their own scanty store of food. Goodwin and Oakley rarely missed a day in coming to see me; Sabb and Ned Inching would drop in of an evening, and the Thynnes as well. Sally's duties in the hospital were far from light, yet she found time to spend many a half hour with me. Sometimes she read to me; at others we spoke of the

past, particularly of our childhood days, hers on the fringes
of the Canadian wilderness, mine in the Maryland colony. I
opened my heart to her as I had done to no other, and acquainted her with every circumstance that had led to my
imprisonment and transportation. I knew, long before this,
that I loved Sally, and often, as I lay awake at night, my heart
would be filled with despair and bitterness at thought of my
situation. It was unthinkable that a felon, a transportee for
life, could aspire to the hand of such a girl, but I resolved that,
as long as I lay ill, I would try to forget all but the joy of her
daily company.

I grew stronger rapidly, until I was at last permitted to
walk out for a little and bask in the afternoon sunshine. I had
the feeling of rebirth common to every man who has been at
the brink of death. The world took on a new beauty; the
most commonplace objects appeared in a new light, as though
I had been gifted with new vision to behold them with.

One Sunday morning I had walked as far as Dawes Point,
where I found Inching and Nick Sabb stretched out at ease,
enjoying their day of complete idleness with a gusto which
always seemed greater, in the case of this pair, than with
commonplace folk. "Sit ye down, Tallant, sit ye down," said
Nick, heartily. "Damme, if ye don't look as good as new
again!"

"So I am," I replied. "Surgeon White says I can return to
Blackwattle Cove, to-morrow."

"And Ned, here, had a place all marked out for ye at the
buryin' ground!"

"Aye," said Inching, with a grin; "as pretty a place, Tallant, as ye'd wish to see, right alongside of old Mag Pallcat."

"What! Is she dead?" I asked.

Inching nodded, with an air of satisfaction.

"Them bones shall rise no more. And bones was all I had
to bury. Ye mind what a mountain of sin she was in Newgate? She would ha' weighed all of fifteen stone. Aye, New

South Wales is the place for alley cats and Pallcats: makes angels of 'em in no time."

"How is it, Ned, that you don't mark the graves?" I asked. "You must have forty or more in the burying ground by this time."

Inching nodded. "My town's growin' fast. Where's the need o' markers? I ain't seen any weepin' kinfolk there of a Sunday. Far as that goes, I know where every one of 'em's planted. I can call 'em by name, and give ye a full catalogue of their good deeds. Do it before ye can spit."

"*I'll* have a marker, mind that!" said Sabb.

Inching's face brightened.

"What, Nick! Ye mean to give me the joy of planting ye?"

"No, by God! Ye've done me dirt enough already, trap-sticks! Ye'll not have the pleasure of shovelin' six feet more on my carcase. I'll outlast ye, no question o' that, but not for long mebbe, if the ships don't come from England. I've clean forgot the taste o' food."

"What will ye have for the marker?" asked Inching.

"Somethin' neat, with a proper verse on it."

"No fear — I'll furnish it," said Inching.

"Here lies Nick Sabb, taking his rest,
Of many a cully he got the best."

"Aye, that wouldn't be far off it," said Sabb. "Ned, tell Tallant about Pallcat. Ye mind the man she was livin' with, Hugh?"

"Tooley, the lumper, wasn't it?"

"That's the one. Tell him about Tooley's mournin', Ned."

"He'd thieved a full quart o' gin off the marines," said Inching, "and damn my eyes if he didn't come to the buryin' ground to share some of it with Pallcat! He'd half finished the bottle afore he come, else he'd never been feelin' so gen-erous-like. Down he squats on Pallcat's grave and begins to talk to her like she was still alive. 'Mag,' says he, 'how is it wi' ye where ye are? Thirsty, ain't it? Ye'd relish a dollop, I shouldn't wonder? How's that? . . . Ye old bawdy-house bottle! Don't I know it as well as yerself? Ain't I seen ye drink two quarts o' gin in less'n two minutes? But Mag, mind where I be. 'Tain't much better than where ye are. But I don't forget ye, lass.' With that he pulls the cork and pours mebbe three drops on Pallcat's grave. 'Twouldn't have wetted a gnat's hair. 'There's a handsome kick in the guts for ye, Mag,' says he; then he up-ended the rest of the bottle down his gullet in one swig!"

*　　*　　*　　*　　*

I returned to Blackwattle Cove the following day, and now I come to an event of such sacred memory, a time of such deep happiness, that I shall pass it over with the briefest possible mention. It is not to be shared with strangers, at any great length.

Since her return from Norfolk Island, Sally had become Surgeon White's greatly valued assistant at the hospital. She had worked so hard, under the primitive conditions of that place, that, at the end of a month, she was herself in a condition to be a patient there, rather than a nurse. At last Surgeon White had ordered her to rest, and she came to Blackwattle Cove for the good of the air, and to be away from the wretched, depressing life of the settlement. She stopped with the Goodwins, and many a day did I pass in her company. In Pattagorang's canoe, with himself for a paddler, we made excursions along the lonely winding shores of the innumerable bays and coves of the great harbour, and it was then that I learned what I had never dared to hope for — that my deep love for Sally was as deeply returned. I have called this a time of great happiness, but this is not wholly true, and the fault was mine. Foolish man that I was, I could not forget that I had no right to the happiness Sally offered me from the depths of her loving, generous heart; and I went beyond all reason in pleading against myself, in reminding her, over and over, of the future in store for the wife of a transportee for life. My intentions were of the best, of course, but I did my dear girl scant justice in supposing that she had not considered this matter for herself, long before I brought it forward with such wearisome repetition.

And so it was not until she was about to return to Sydney, to resume her work in the hospital, when I had spoiled what might have been the pure joy of our companionship by my anxiety lest she should discover, later, that she had made a mistake in loving me, that we had the matter out for the last time. I could go to the very spot, on Blackwattle Cove, where Sally, having once more listened to my heart-burnings and heart-searchings on her account, halted and faced me, her eyes filled with tears.

"Hugh, I am not a child. I know my own mind and heart better than you can know them. But if you won't have me, speak out and be done with it. I can say no more, for very shame."

And there and then I put an end forever to my doubts and fears. That day was the tenth of June, 1790, and I have celebrated it with thankfulness for more than forty years.

XV

THE SECOND FLEET

ONE day, shortly after Sally's return to Sydney, I had been out with my fowling piece on a fruitless search for game. Returning home, I found the Thynnes at Goodwin's house. They doted on their grandson, now more than two years old, and were miserable indeed if a week passed without their seeing him. They had brought their own poor rations to be contributed to our midday dinner, and Bella Goodwin was in tears as she regarded the miserable portion of flour and so-called pork to serve as a meal for eight people.

"Hush, now, Bella," Goodwin was saying. "There's no good cryin' over the vittles. We'll just have to make out the best we can with what we've got."

"It's slow starvation!" said Bella, miserably. "We'll die in this poor mean land! That's what the Governor wishes, I'll warrant, so there'll be more for his officers and the soldiers."

"Mrs. Goodwin, no," said Thynne, shaking his head soberly. "Governor Phillip fares like ourselves. I've seen the food prepared for his own kitchen, and it's no worse and no better than every convict has. And I'll add this: he brought out from England three hundredweight of flour, at his own expense, for his own use. He has given the whole of it to the public stores, to be served out to all."

"Ye know that, Thynne?" asked Oakley.

"I do, for I heard it from the Commissary."

"He's an honest man, that may be said for him," Mrs. Thynne remarked. "He's doing what he can to make the food last till the ships come from England."

"Ships, ships, ships!" Mrs. Goodwin exclaimed, bitterly. "They lie when they tell us of ships to come! There's none been sent, to my thinking. If they have, they've been lost at sea."

"No luck, Hugh?" Goodwin asked.

I took my game bag by the bottom end and shook out one small cockatoo; it wouldn't have weighed a pound, bones and all.

"What do you think?" I asked. "Must I carry it all the way to the hospital? It wouldn't go far, amongst sixty."

It was agreed that we might add this poor bird to our unnamable stew, and Bella accepted it with as much enthusiasm as the gift deserved.

Whilst the meal was being prepared the rest of us took seats outside to enjoy the warmth of the midday sun. Thynne sat with Tom's boy on his knee. A fine sturdy lad he would have been, with decent food to grow on. As the matter stood, he had not done badly, for Garth gave him a gill of milk morning and night, the rest of our scant supply going to the hospital.

"He's not a Thynne, my love," said Mortimer, holding the boy at arm's length, and regarding him fondly. "At least, he's not a perfect Thynne."

"I should think not, indeed," said Mrs. Thynne, with a tight smile. "Neither is his grandfather."

Tom laughed heartily.

"I'd never have believed it, ma'am, without your word for it. Like enough, that's just as it should be."

"So it is, so it is," said Thynne; "but Tom, the boy is your very image. I see it more and more. . . . Hugh Thynne Oakley — there's a happy combination of names! Hugh for true, Thynne for win, and Oakley . . . bless me! What does Oakley rhyme with? No matter; I'm convinced that little Hugh will combine in his character all the virtues and none of the faults, small as these are, of his namesakes."

Bella had gotten over her fit of despondency by the time the meal was ready. We didn't linger over it — each one downed the nauseating mess as quickly as possible; then Goodwin and I set out in the boat for the signal station on the South Head, calling at Sydney Cove on the way. It was one of Goodwin's tasks to carry the weekly relief to the lookout station on South Head, where a constant watch was kept for the ships that never came. On this occasion we carried down a midshipman from the *Sirius,* Southwell by name, and four marines that made up his detail. Southwell was an intelligent young fellow, but so desperately homesick that he had sunk into a state of chronic melancholy. His four companions were as dejected-looking as himself, and climbed down the ladder at the pierhead in glum silence. Duty at the signal station had once been welcomed, but the monotony of keeping watch over that empty sea had long since ceased to make it so. We rounded Bennelong Point and headed east for the four-mile run to South Head. Goodwin held the tiller. Southwell and his men sat facing aft, as though to avoid until the last moment the sight of the lookout where they were doomed to spend another week of useless vigil.

Presently Goodwin said: "Look yonder, Mr. Southwell. Will they be having a game with us at the station?"

I was staring ahead at the same moment, so taken aback I could not believe in what I saw — the ensign run up the halyards of the tall pole on the Head, and now fluttering out in the breeze.

Southwell turned in his seat, then rose to his feet, steadying himself by the mast. The flag was undeniably there. Southwell turned to us again, an expression of incredulity, of blank astonishment, upon his face.

"The ships," he said, in a trembling voice. "It can mean nothing but that! The ships from home!"

"I'd not be too sure, sir," one of his men replied. "It might be the *Supply* comin' in again."

Governor Phillip, despairing of the arrival of the long-awaited store-ships from England, had been obliged to send the *Supply* to Batavia, in the Dutch East Indies, for a cargo of rice, salt beef, and whatever other provision might be had there, for the food in the public stores was so nearly exhausted he dared wait no longer. The *Supply* had been in constant service, without overhaul, for more than three years and was in no fit condition for so long a voyage. We now feared to learn that it was, indeed, the *Supply* returning; that she had met bad weather and been compelled to put back for repairs.

But as we neared the station, our doubts vanished. We saw one of the men from the station hastening down the path to the cove on the west side of the Head, and we could guess, from his behaviour, that it was not the *Supply* that had been sighted. He ran back and forth along the shore waving his arms like a madman and shouting with joy as we came to a landing.

"What do you see, Thompson?" Southwell called.

"They're in view from the Head, sir," the man shouted. "It's the fleet from England, certain!"

"How many?"

"Two so far. They're hull-down, but comin' up fast!"

We made the boat secure and hastened up the rocky path to the station. The officer Southwell was to relieve had the spyglass trained on the distant vessels, and we all examined them in turn. Small they looked against the measureless floor of sea, but as they neared we agreed that they were of greater tonnage than any of the ships, save the *Sirius*, that had come out in the First Fleet, and there was no doubt that they were English. The breeze was fresh and from the north, and they came steadily on, the sunlight of late afternoon gleaming on the sails from time to time. A blessed sight it was to the eyes of men in our condition, who had all but lost belief in the existence of an outside world.

Southwell and his men took over at the signal station, and

the relieved detail, having waited until the ships were no more than three leagues off the entrance to the harbour, hastened down to the boat to carry the news to Sydney. The flag had been seen from Bennelong Point, and we met Governor Phillip's boat with himself and the Judge Advocate on board, coming out of Sydney Cove as we entered it. They passed close alongside, and we gave them what news we had.

Every man, woman, and child in the settlement able to stir abroad was at the waterfront as we tied up at the pier. As we made our way through that throng of half-starved scarecrows who all but mobbed us in their pathetic eagerness for news, I wished that His Majesty's ministers, in England, might have looked upon the scene. It was one to have touched even their hearts; to have made them more mindful of their duty toward the wretched folk they had exiled and forgotten, at the far ends of the earth. Famine was written plain in every face — in the hollow eyes, the sunken cheeks, the blotched and sallow skin stretched tightly over the bones. Their bodies were mere skeletons, having scarcely any protection against the cold of this winter season. Not one in a score had even the remains of shoes to his feet. Shoulders, elbows, knees, hip-bones, showed through shreds and rags of clothing that would have been scorned as garments by the poorest beggars of London.

"Aye, they're coming — 'tis the ships from England, certain — they're not five miles off by now," we repeated over and over again to the forlorn beings who plied us with questions from all sides. The day being Sunday, all the people were at liberty, and marines and convicts alike milled along the inner shore of the cove or hastened out to Bennelong Point in the hope of catching sight of the ships as they came down the harbour; but no ships appeared, and late in the afternoon the Governor's boat returned with word that, owing to the failing of the breeze, the ships were standing off till morning, outside the Heads. At sunset the convicts were ordered back to their quarters and Goodwin and I were about to set off for home when we received word, from Mr. Palmer, the Commissary, to leave our boat at Sydney and return, with Oakley, at dawn the next morning ready to help in the work of unloading stores.

It was a night of nights at Blackwattle Cove. Nellie Garth — stolid, patient, long-suffering Nellie — let the tears flow unchecked at thought of the letters she would receive from her old neighbour, Mrs. Windle, with news of her dear Nat.

"There'll be a dozen, that's certain," she said. "Sarah Windle's not one to forget any small thing I'd wish to hear about the lad and the place and all."

"A dozen?" said Tom. "God bless ye, Nellie, there'll be twice the number and more, I shouldn't wonder."

"I never thought to see the day; I never did," said Mrs. Goodwin, walking the floor of the small bare room. "Dan's papers will come, and we'll be free to go home by one of the ships that's fetchin' 'em! Glory be, there's many a poor creature here will be made happy the morn, one way or another!"

I will now tell, as briefly as I can, what happened on the following day. I have no wish to dwell upon the events of it, for the memory of that day, and those immediately following, is a horror that has remained with me these forty years. I thought I had seen, in Newgate prison, as black an example of man's inhumanity to man as England could furnish; but it was not until the arrival at Port Jackson of the Second Fleet of convict transports that I realized to what depths of ferocious cruelty one species of the human animal can sink. Three transports, the *Neptune*, *Scarborough*, and *Surprise*, with the store-ship *Justinian*, anchored in Sydney Cove after a five months' voyage from Spithead. They had left England with 1017 convicts on board. Of that number, 281, above one in four, died on the passage, by far the greater number victims of the cruelty of the masters, or, better, monsters, of the transports, and their underlings.

Before proceeding, I had best explain the iniquitous system for the transportation of convicts prevailing at this date. Some months before the time set for an emptying of gaols and prisons throughout the Kingdom, His Majesty's Government would advertise for bids from firms of merchants and shipowners for the carrying of the convicts to New South Wales. The firm making the lowest bid would, commonly, be given the contract and would engage, upon the payment of a fixed sum per convict, to provide transportation and food for the human cargo. Nothing was stipulated as to the kind of provisions to be furnished — this was left to the tender mercies of the contractors themselves; but the worst feature of the bargain struck was that the merchant contractors received payment from Government for the convicts embarked: no clause in the agreement required that they be delivered, alive, at the end of the voyage. Therefore, no interest for the preservation of life was created in the owners or charterers of the transports, and the dead were more profitable (if profit alone was consulted and the good name of their house was no consideration) than the living.

The convicts in the First Fleet did not suffer by this vicious system, for Governor Phillip, a humane and honourable man, was present to see that they were not starved and misused. The case in the Second Fleet, of which I am now to speak, was far otherwise. The Government contract had been awarded to a London firm, Messrs. Calvert, Camden and King, and every convict who survived the voyage in their ships, or who witnessed the arrival of the fleet at Sydney Cove, will wish that their names, and those of their ships' captains, may be infamous forever.

Goodwin, Oakley, and I, walking fast along our well-beaten path from Blackwattle to Sydney Cove, knew nothing of all this at the moment. It was a clear winter morning, almost cold enough for frost, and the land lay shadowy and still in the first faint light of approaching day. Although we had decent clothing of our own brought out from England, we were sparing of its use, and wore, commonly, the garments of the Government issue, coarse Osnaburg shirts and trousers, so patched and mended by Garth and Mrs. Goodwin as to be past even their skill for further repair. They offered little protection from the biting air of early morning, but we took no thought of cold as we hastened toward Sydney. We believed, as did everyone else, that the coming ships were not transports but store-ships bringing us the long-awaited supplies: food, clothing, stout shoes, tools, medicines for the sick, soap, blankets — all the innumerable things which most folk take for granted in life but which had been lacking with us for many weary months.

"Lads, think of it!" said Tom. "Full bellies again for all! Clothing for all! By God! The Governor should make this a holiday. If I was master here, I'd give the starved frozen people a day to remember for once in their lives!"

"Like enough he will," Goodwin replied.

"I'd think first of the empty bellies," I put in. "Double rations all round for the start."

"Aye," said Tom, "with the fresh clothing to come directly after. And then I'd say: 'Good people, ye've done well enough in these cruel and bitter times; better than I expected. Ye've been half-starved and half-frozen in the midst of winter, through no lack in my power to remedy. I promised ye relief when the ships came, and that ye shall now have. Here's shoes for yer naked feet, stockings for yer naked legs; shirts and trousers for the men and blouses and warm flannel petticoats for the women. Bring the filthy rags ye may now put off to the parade, and we'll burn 'em in a common fire.' "

"There'd be little enough to burn," said Goodwin.

"Hugh, will ye look at him," said Oakley, giving Goodwin a clap on the shoulder. "He's near to bursting with the joy he feels at thought of home. Speak up, Dan! Take the full good of it. There's no call to be so delicate for our sakes."

"Ye think it likely the papers will come?" Goodwin asked.

"No doubt of it," said Tom, with such conviction that Goodwin's face lighted up. "It's not a thing would be twice neglected. Ye mind what Thynne told us of the Governor's despatches sent home by the transports we came out in? Thynne copied 'em himself, and there was full mention of our missing records. The letters from the Governor would have reached London well before these supply ships sailed. Aye, the papers have come. Take that as certain."

"I'll wait and see," Goodwin replied; "and say naught to Bella till I'm sure. I doubt she could bear a second disappointment."

We hurried on, impatient to reach the rise of ground where we could overlook the settlement, and there we halted to take in the welcome sight below. We were puzzled by the appearance of the crowd that thronged the shoreline on both sides of the pier.

"Aye, the Governor's given 'em liberty for the day," said Tom, "else there'd be no such swarm as that."

"Quiet, ain't they?" said Goodwin. "Like as if they can't believe the ships has come."

There was no stir and movement in the crowd as there had been the previous afternoon; no running here and there for a better view, and not a shout or a hail, from ship or shore, broke the morning stillness. We looked at one another, not knowing what to make of the strange frozen silence, then pushed on at a faster pace.

We were skirting the burying ground, with its forlorn hillocks of unmarked graves, when we saw Ned Inching coming up the path from the settlement. He spied us at the same moment and halted.

"What news, Ned?" Tom called. "There's naught amiss, yonder at the beach?"

Inching had a gnarled and calloused heart, well able to withstand the heaviest shocks of time and circumstance, but we always knew when he was moved by the sour smile that wrinkled his leathery face.

"They ain't store-ships," he said.

"What!" Oakley exclaimed.

Inching shook his head.

"Wait. Ye'll see summat, directly. No, they ain't store-ships. They're transports. They been chuckin' the dead into the cove. They's six bodies washed in, up to now. We'll have work aplenty today, me and my men."

We were about to hasten on, when a procession of a dozen men, bearing canvas-covered litters fetched from the hospital, appeared around a turn in the path. Each litter was carried by two men, and upon them lay the pitiful remains of a woman, a boy of fifteen or sixteen, and four men. Three were stark naked; the others had some remnants of filthy rags, dripping with sea water, clinging to the huddled forms.

The men put down the litters, and we stood staring at them in silence.

"God in heaven!" Oakley exclaimed, in a low voice. "Who could ha' done this!"

"Who?" said one of the bearers. "Who but the bloody masters of the ships? The poor bastards has been starved to death."

"Food, lads!" another put in, with a harsh laugh. "By Christ, here it is! Forehanded, ain't they, in sendin' it ashore?"

Goodwin, Oakley, and I waited to hear no more. At the waterfront, convicts and marines together were staring like folk possessed at three more bodies just then being dragged in from the shallows to the beach. Mutterings now began to be heard, and shrill cries of grief and rage and horror from some of the women. Offshore, we saw the Governor's boat lying alongside one of the transports. A moment later he appeared at the gangway with Colonel Johnson of the marines, and came down the ladder to embark for shore. Two six-oared boats lay by our pier, their men standing by for orders. Goodwin, Oakley, and I, with a fourth man detailed to go with us, waited with the rest.

Several officers of the Civil Establishment were on the wharf when the Governor returned. They conversed apart there, for a moment, and then came toward us, the crowd falling back on either side as they approached. The Governor's face was pale and hard-set and he looked straight before him as he passed through. We learned that the transports had brought, not only convicts, but the first contingent of soldiers of the New South Wales Corps, sent out to replace the marines of the First Fleet whose period of service would soon expire. Presently our soldiers marched down from their barracks to the music of fifes and drums. They had prepared to meet the newly arrived Corps as best they could, but they were a sorry-looking company in their ragged faded uniforms. Their last-issue shoes, like those of the convicts, had long since been worn past further mending, and nine in ten of them were barefoot. The convicts were herded back from the beach and the marines drew up in platoons to one side of the wharf. The boats from the transports were now coming ashore with the members of the new Corps, and through the next hour the work of disembarking them, with their wives, children, and baggage, continued.

An effort was made to mark this memorable occasion with a show, at least, of pomp and circumstance, but the attempt was a dismal failure. Officers and soldiers alike, of the New Corps, looked about them with expressions on their faces that revealed only too plainly their astonishment and disappointment. Scattered along the shores on both sides of the cove they saw lines of wretched mud-plastered hovels, and around them was a crowd of ragged, emaciated beings, the very children of famine, giving them a foretaste of what their own life was to be in this outpost of Empire.

Long before the last of them were ashore, rumours were spreading swiftly, from mouth to mouth, through the crowd: all of the ships were floating hells, filled with dead and dying; of more than one thousand convicts embarked, half the number had died on the voyage; the bodies we had already seen were of convicts who had died during the night and had been thrown overboard by the captain of the *Neptune*, who expected the ebb tide to carry them seaward before they could be washed ashore.

It was not until nearly midday that our shore boats were ordered out to the transports to help in the work of disembarking the convicts. Goodwin's boat was sent to the *Neptune*, where, we were told, Surgeon White would give us our directions. We found him awaiting us at the gangway. As a usual thing, he had an excellent command over his feelings, but on this occasion I could see that he was holding them in check only with the greatest difficulty.

"This way," he barked. "Come along, now! Make haste!"

He led the way to the forehatch, and there we were halted by the appalling stench that poured up from below. I had believed that five months in Newgate and eight months aboard the *Charlotte* had hardened me for all time to horror of that smell, but I quailed before it once more, as did the others. The surgeon gave us a grim look.

"It's got you, has it?" he said. "You'll heave your insides out before this day's work is done. Men, I'm warning you: the 'tween-decks of the *Charlotte* was heaven itself compared with what you're about to see here. Work as fast as you can. When you can stand it no longer, come up for air. Now follow me."

Down we went to the orlop deck, and it was like a descent into hell. There had been packed into this horrible place 530 men and women. Death had mercifully taken nearly one third of the number before the vessel reached Port Jackson, and those who remained were so frightfully reduced by dis-

ease and starvation as to have neither the will nor the power
to help themselves. By the dim light of three or four lanterns
swung from the beams we saw forms that looked scarcely
human, some half, others quite naked, lying in bunks without beds or bedding. I do not believe that the worst slave
ship that ever sailed from Africa could have shown so terrible
a scene of human misery. Men whose bodies were mere skeletons lay in their own filth, their rags of clothing alive with
vermin. Many had no longer the strength to cry out; others,
who wished only to die where they lay, begged us not to
touch them, and groaned pitifully, cursing us in feeble voices
as we took them from their bunks. Not one in a dozen had
the strength to climb the ladder to the upper deck. Most of
them were dragged or pushed up from hand to hand, and
swung over the ship's side in slings to the waiting boats. Some
fainted when brought to the open air, some died upon deck,
and others in the boats before they could be carried to the
beach. Upon reaching the shore many were not able to walk,
stand, or stir themselves in the least. Some crept up the beach
on their hands and knees; some were carried upon the backs
of men waiting to receive them.

All through the afternoon the work of unloading these
miserable beings continued, and night had fallen before the
last of them had left the transports.

From what I have already written of the starved condition
of the settlement before the coming of this Second Fleet of
transports, my readers will be able to picture for themselves the
desperate situation on this night of June 20. The small rude
shelter that served as a hospital had accommodation for no
more than sixty inmates, and at this time it was filled with the
sick from the settlement itself. Between three and four hundred of the convicts just landed needed immediate medical care
and there was not even shelter for them unless the old half-
rotten tents in which we had lived at first could be called
shelter. One hundred of these tents were brought out from the

storehouse and quickly erected in lines along the beach. Each had accommodation for four people, and in these the sick were compelled to lie on the bare ground, through a bitterly cold night, with one blanket among four for covering. The Sydney convicts forgot their own misery in the presence of these others whose sufferings were so much worse than their own. They showed a humanity, a generosity, in sharing their poor rags of clothing with the naked frozen people in the tents that did them honour. Themselves enfeebled by hardship and long privation of the most elementary necessities, they laboured the night long, fetching grass for the sick to lie on and wood for the fires that were lighted along the rows of tents.

During the early part of the night, Goodwin, Oakley, and I were employed in carrying some of the weakest of the convict women to huts in the settlement where room was made for them to lie out of the bitter cold. We were returning from one of these journeys when we heard a forlorn cry, "Dan! Dan!" and saw Bella Goodwin running toward us. She and Nellie Garth had come over from Blackwattle Cove early in the afternoon to see the ships, and none had worked harder than themselves, or to better purpose, in caring for the sufferers.

Bella clutched her husband's arm, unable to speak for a moment. She hid her face against his breast while Dan patted her shoulder, gently. We thought she had been overcome, for the moment, by the pitiful sights on every hand, and there were enough, certainly, to challenge the stoutest heart.

"There, Bella," said Dan. "Ye'd best take some rest now. Ye and Nellie have done yer share and more for the poor creatures."

"Dan, it's Nellie Garth's boy! The lad she's told us about time and again! He's here!"

"What are ye saying, Bella?" Oakley broke in. "Ye tell us . . ."

"It's him . . . her lad, Nat! Nellie's just found him, yon-der in one of the tents!"

She buried her face in her hands. "Oh, the poor little fellow! I doubt if he lives till day!"

*   *   *   *   *

It was about three in the morning when we set out for Blackwattle Cove. There were the Goodwins, Oakley, Nellie Garth, and myself. Dan and Tom carried Nat Garth on a litter, Nellie walking beside him, with Bella Goodwin and I following. The waning moon was shining in a clear sky, and our breath came out in clouds of frosty vapour. I don't recol-lect that a word was spoken save by Goodwin, who held the front handles of the litter. "Mind the stone," or "Mind the log," he would say over his shoulder to Oakley as we wound this way and that over the uneven ground.

Bella halted and took me by the sleeve; the others moved on, not heeding us. "Wait," she said, in a low voice. "Let them get ahead. . . . They'll find him dead when they reach the house. I'd not see Nellie at the moment."

She seated herself on a stone by the side of the path and covered her face with her hands. When she had recovered a little, we went on.

"Hugh, if ye'd seen her when she first knew the lad!" she added in a heartsick voice. "Miss Sally was with us, and we was givin' what help we could, like the others, amongst the tents. We come to one where five was laid, with but a bit of old canvas to cover them, and the one who was strongest amongst 'em had hogged it all for himself. The tent was old and rotten, all holes and patches, and the light come through from one of the fires beyond, but naught of the warmth. The four others lay on the bare ground, perished with cold, and one poor skeleton — that was Nat, but she didn't know it then — had not a rag to his body. We thought he was dead till he moved a little. Miss Sally had gone to the hospital then.

Nellie slipped off her under petticoat to cover the poor naked body. 'We'll carry him out to the fire, Bella,' said she, but first we took the rag of canvas from him that had it all and covered the others again. Then, with her petticoat round him, Nellie lifted the boy, and 'twas not till she'd brought him to the fire that she saw 'twas her own lad. And he knew her, and put his poor sticks of arms around her neck. I came to seek Dan directly I knew the truth, though I can scarce believe it yet. The poor lad! The poor abused little creature! How can it be he's here? Would he have leave to come, to seek his mother? Oh, the pitiful sight of him! He'll not live, that's certain!"

The others had a fire going when we arrived and a kettle of water heating over it. Nat was in Nellie's bed in the next room. She came out, presently, to fetch the water, but she wanted no help. There was no door between the two rooms, only a canvas curtain, and we heard the splashing of the water as she washed him. Then Nat spoke, only a word or two, and we heard Nellie say: "There, Nat. Rest, lad. It's all right now. It's all right," and there was silence after that. Half an hour later she came to say that he was sleeping. Goodwin, Oakley, and I went to the other house, leaving the two women to keep watch.

XVI

GARTH'S VENGEANCE

It was on a Monday night that we brought Nat to our place. All the rest of the week Nellie nursed him, never leaving the room for more than a moment or two. She knew from the first, I think, that there was little hope, but she clung to his life for him, heartening and encouraging him in every way she could. Nat was conscious all the while, but so weak that he scarce had the strength to speak above a whisper. He died on the Saturday morning, with Nellie sitting by him, holding his hand, and we buried him the same day, on a green rise shaded by one tall gum tree, overlooking the cove. Garth shed no tears in our presence, then or later. She walked away while Goodwin and I were filling the grave, and was gone till nightfall. Mrs. Goodwin was the heartbroken one, if tears are ever an indication of true misery, but she understood that no comfort we might offer could be of service to Nellie.

On the next day, Sunday, Garth had gone to the grave to plant a border of shrubs around it. She wanted no help in this task, and Tom and I were sitting in the dooryard, watching the distant lonely figure. Presently we saw Nick Sabb coming along the path from Sydney, accompanied by a man and a woman, whom we guessed were convicts arrived in one of the transports. The man was a big-framed fellow, pale and hollow-eyed, who looked as though the walk from the settlement had all but exhausted him. The woman wore a patched and faded shawl over her shoulders and an old quilted petticoat hung at an angle from her bony hips. Her scant grey hair was twisted in a tight knot at the back of her head, and her quick squirrel-like movements and small harsh voice revealed a tough spirit in the shriveled little body. Their name was Peters, and they had come out in the *Neptune*. Mrs Peters made it known at once that she was not a felon, but a free woman who had accompanied her husband, condemned to seven years' transportation for stealing a fishnet. Before the transport had left Portsmouth she had been entrusted with a letter for Mistress Nellie Garth, and she was bound to deliver it into the hands of no one else. Mrs. Goodwin and Dan, seeing the visitors, came over from their house, and Tommy Goodwin was sent for Garth. Sabb explained that Mrs. Peters had been given the letter by a woman who came to see Nat the day before sailing. "But ye say ye can't call her name?" he asked, turning to Mrs. Peters.

"It'll come in a minute," said Mrs. Peters. "She was that grieved, cryin' over the lad and wringin' her hands, I thought 'twas hers till she told me the mother was here."

"That would be no one but Mrs. Windle," said Oakley.

"So it was, sir, and she give me five shillin' to see the letter was give to the mother's own hands, and that I'll do. The young 'un's here with her?"

"He's dead," said Mrs. Goodwin, her lips trembling. "We buried him yesterday."

"I looked to hear it," said Mrs. Peters. There was no emotion, in voice or manner, as she spoke. "The wonder is we ain't all dead with him. Look at my man! Fourteen stone he weighed when he was catched. Who'd ever think it! . . . Be ye all convicts here? Ye've a sight better lodgin's than them in the town yonder."

"I'd say naught about the voyage to the boy's mother when she comes," said Goodwin.

The little woman sat forward with a jerk, and her black eyes snapped.

"No more we won't, if she don't prick us to it; but if she's bound to know we'll not scant the truth. 'Twas murder, murder, murder, from first to last! And so I'd tell the Governor of this place if the chance was given."

"That we can believe, ma'am, from them we've seen brought ashore," said Goodwin, "but 'twill serve no turn, now, to tell Mrs. Garth."

"What is it ye say, Dan?" And we turned to find Nellie standing in the doorway. She nodded to Sabb as she entered the room and stood looking at the strangers.

"Be ye Mrs. Garth?" asked the woman.

Nellie nodded, without speaking.

"Then this letter's yourn, ma'am, and its none so clean, as ye see, for I had no means to keep it so."

Garth took the letter, turning it over slowly in her hands; then she put it in her petticoat pocket, and took a seat facing the bearer of it.

"Ye came in the *Neptune?*" she asked.

"So we did, ma'am."

"And ye saw my boy, times, on the voyage?"

"Not me, for I was amongst the women, but my man was chained next to the lad the five months long."

"Chained?" asked Nellie, in a cold hard voice.

"Nellie, there's naught to be gained in speaking of the voyage," said Tom, "for it's done with and past mending. Will ye tell us, Mrs. Peters, or yer husband, if ye know, what the lad was sent for?"

"Wait," said Garth, in the same cold even voice. "This is my affair, and I'll know what happened to my boy. . . . Chained?" she repeated, turning to Peters.

The man now spoke for the first time, in a dead voice, contrasting strangely with that of his wife.

"We was all in chains, ma'am, from the time we left England till the day afore we fetched the land here."

"Homeless dogs was never so starved and misused!" Mrs. Peters broke in, clenching her small bony fists. "Hearken to this: there was above five hundred of us in the *Neptune*, in the dark stinking hole deep in the ship, with but two hours in the twenty-four to be on deck. It was horrible for us women, but a hundred times worse for the men. They was chained from first to last and lay body against body, with no room even to turn on the boards."

"What is he called, the captain of the ship?"

"Called? I'd call him beast, devil, murderer, and his officers with him. They never came near us to see if we lived or died."

"Ye lay next my boy?" Garth asked, turning to the man.

"Nellie, there's no need to go into it now," Tom began, but Garth cut him short.

"Hush! I'll have the truth."

"Then ye shall have it, Mrs. Garth," said the woman, "for if ever a lad was murdered, 'twas yer own son, and scores with him. I can't give ye the true numbers, but I'll say one in three died on the voyage and their bodies were cast into the sea like filth. Dick, speak up now and tell her the whole of it."

Then, in a dull voice, with the air of one so beaten down by hardship and privation that he no longer had the strength to feel grief or anger or horror, — only a kind of helpless melancholy, in the relation of past events, — the husband told us the story of the voyage. I shall not repeat it here. It was a tale of cruelty, greed, and indifference on the part of Captain Narker and his underlings in the *Neptune* the truth of which has long since been made public. Human history has few darker pages to show than that which concerns the treatment of the convicts who came out to New South Wales in the Second Fleet.

Garth heard him through, asking a question now and then as the story touched upon Nat, and Mrs. Peters prompted her husband lest any detail of the horrors should be forgotten or passed over. At the end of it Nellie thanked Mrs. Peters for her kindness in bringing the letter; then she went off alone to read it.

That same evening, after Sabb had returned with the visitors to Sydney, the Goodwins, Oakley, and I, having finished our supper, were waiting for Nellie, who was alone in her room at the other house. She came in presently, for a moment only.

"Ye'll wish to see Mrs. Windle's letter," she said. With that, she laid it on the table and went out again.

"Read it aloud, Hugh," said Oakley.

This was the first letter received by any of us since we had left England. Mrs. Goodwin lighted our homemade lamp and set it at my elbow. The letter was dated from Portsmouth, January 16, 1790, the day before the *Neptune* sailed.

Dear Nellie: —

When this letter comes to your hand, I hope and pray ye'll not think hard of your old friend and neighbour for what's come to poor Nat. I did the best I could to comfort him and do for him like as if he was one of my own. But oh, Nellie, I could see how it was with him from the day ye was parted, though he said not a word of it. He grieved his heart out day and night, and he come to the point where he couldn't abide the waiting. That's all there is to say of it. He was bound to come out to ye, somehow, and took the only way there was.

Last July he went off without a word to any of us here. I was at my wit's end with worry and hunting high and low. Then we found he'd gone to London and was took up by the constables for stealing three silk handkerchiefs hung to dry in an areaway. He was held for the Quarter-Sessions at the Guildhall, and being such a lad and his first offense, he was sent to the Fleet for three months. And not a Sabbath, Nellie, one of us didn't go to visit him and take him what little comforts we could.

I knew why he'd done it. A better, honester lad never lived, and he'd no more steal than you or me or one of my own lads, save he saw no way but that to be sent to ye. When I had him home again I talked and talked with him and begged him to wait, but there was no way I could get him to promise he would. And it wasn't a fort-night till he was away again. This time he was took up for stealing draper's goods to the value of thirty shillings from a shop in Great Hart Street. For that he's sent for seven years.

Oh, Nellie, like enough it's my fault, but still I don't see how I could have stopped him. He had but the one thought, to see his mother, and seven years is forever for a boy to wait.

I write this from Portsmouth and the transports will sail to-morrow if wind and weather permits. I've brought Nat comforts and clothes and all needful for the voyage, and if he wins through to ye, safe and sound, I'll say it was God's will and all for the best he should go. Nat can give ye the news of all here. I'm that heart-sick I can say no more.

Your Friend,
SARAH WINDLE

Feeling ran high in the settlement toward the masters and officers of the transports, but none was so deeply hated as the captain of the *Neptune*. What the officials of the colony were thinking we did not know, having little connection with them, but it was believed by the convicts that Governor Phillip would, surely, set an inquiry afoot to fix the guilt for the ill-treatment of convicts which had resulted in 281 deaths in a total of 1017 embarked. And this was not the full num-ber, for many, as in Nat Garth's case, survived the voyage only to die on shore. And five hundred more were so wasted by disease that the poor resources of the settlement were taxed to the uttermost to take care of them. But no inquiry was made, and it soon became clear that none was intended. We did not know, then, that Governor Phillip was to make a full report to the Home Office of the horrible conditions in the Second Fleet, and that his indignation equaled our own. The convicts, with the fatalism of their kind, accepted a situa-tion they were powerless to remedy.

All but one, and that was Nellie Garth; but before I speak of that I will tell, briefly, of the events following the arrival of the ships.

Goodwin, Oakley, and I were busy the whole of this time, helping to carry ashore the supplies brought by the *Justinian*. All the people were put upon full rations once more, and every convict, male and female, received a new blanket, a pair of shoes, and an outfit of clothing. A portable hospital, in frame, came by the *Justinian*. This was speedily set up, and as many of the sick as could be accommodated were transferred to it from the tents where they had lain from the day when they were brought ashore.

Somehow, the word got about that the missing papers with the dates of conviction and the terms of service of the First Fleet convicts had arrived with the despatches from the Home Office, but no word of the matter was given out from Government House. Goodwin waited with what patience he could muster, but as day followed day, and none of the orders or proclamations mentioned the freed men, Goodwin gathered half a dozen of those whose time, like his own, was out, and a petition was prepared and signed by them humbly begging an audience with Governor Phillip. This was granted, and once more Dan, with Bella's help, dressed himself in his old wedding suit and set out for Sydney.

He returned late in the evening; it was like the other time when he had gone so hopefully to see the Governor, thinking that he would be free to return home by the *Fishburn*; but on this second occasion there were none of us asleep when he came home. Bella ran to the door when we heard his step, and the moment we saw his face we knew what he had to tell.

"Dan . . . they . . . they didn't give ye the paper?" Bella asked.

Goodwin fumbled in his coat pocket and drew out a document which he handed to her in silence. She quickly opened and read it, her face lighting up as her eyes ran over the lines.

"But . . . ye're free! Here it is, writ out, with the Governor's name, and the stamp and all!"

"Aye, so it is . . . but we're not to go. We're not ever to

go, if so be they can hold us here." He seated himself by the table, gazing dully before him for a moment; then he struck the board a mighty blow with his fist, and his eyes blazed with anger.

"The villains! The dirty rogues! I'm free; there's the paper to say it. I've paid seven years of life for what I've done, and my time's out. But home's thousands of leagues off, and how are we to get there?"

"But ye've money for the passage, Dan," said Oakley. "And here's the ships . . ."

"Aye, but they won't take us. I been to every one. They say it's not allowed, in the charter, to carry any freed men home. It's all clear now! I see why we've been sent to the world's end. It's not meant that any of us shall see England again. Seven years, fourteen years, life — it's all one. We're here till we die."

Garth sat with her elbows propped on the table, gazing at him stony-eyed.

"I could ha' warned ye what to expect," said she, "for I feared it from the first."

"Hold hard," said Oakley. "I'll get this straight. Tell us what was said by the Governor."

"He had the records brought of the five of us there present," said Goodwin, "and he looked 'em over and over, like as if he wished to find we'd mistaken in thinkin' our time was out. In the end he acknowledged 'twas as we said."

"And then, what?"

"He spoke to me first. 'Goodwin,' said he, 'ye'll wish to stay on here as a free man, no doubt?' "

" 'No, sir,' said I. 'I speak for all of us here. We wish to have the discharge papers and go home by one of the transports returning.' 'And what would ye do at home?' says he. 'There's tens of thousands idle and their wives and children in the workhouses. Here, in this great empty land, ye can make new lives for yerselves. Ye shall be given plots of land and tools to work them, and seed for the plantin'. And ye may draw rations from the public stores till such time as ye can support yerselves.'

" 'I've my wife and three bairns in Yorkshire, sir,' said one. 'I've no wish to settle here and see 'em no more.'

" 'It might be they could come out to ye at a later time,' said the Governor, and he went on to tell how it would be, mebbe, some day, with freed men on their own land. We caught the drift of it soon enough. Government had no wish that any of the convicts should return to England. We was to stay, willin' or not."

"Did ye task him with that?" asked Garth.

"I did, for my blood was hot, but I spoke slow and respectful. 'Sir,' said I, 'ye don't tell us we're obliged to stay here against our wish?'

"He didn't answer, straight off, and he didn't look at us as he thought what to say to that.

" 'You're not obliged,' said he, 'but I urge it for your own good. Ye'll fare far better here, in the long run, than in England.'

" 'We wish to go, sir, for all that,' said I, and the others spoke to the same end. I'll not say 'tis the Governor's doing, for I doubt it is. He's had his orders from home, and as sure as I speak, the orders is to keep us here, justice or no justice, if the thing can be done."

"He forbade ye to go by the ships?" asked Tom.

"He said he had naught to do with the ships, once they was discharged of the troops and convicts and cargo. For the voyage home they're under charter to the East India Company. When we'd left the Governor's, we spent the day going from one ship to the other. We showed our discharge papers, signed by the Governor and stamped with the Great Seal. None but me had money, but the others hoped to work out the passage home. We was told they had no need of men, and for all I offered to lay down the money in advance for Bella and

Tommy and me, they'd have none of it. 'Twas against the terms of the charter, they said, to take any passengers.

"I went last to the captain of the *Neptune,* and hard I found it to ask a favour of the black-hearted rogue. I put it off and put it off till late afternoon. At last I was about to go out to the ship when I spied him comin' ashore, with his purser. As ye know, they've set up a shop in a marquee on the west side of the cove, to sell ventures they brought out on their own, and the food they stole on the voyage from the convicts. I followed 'em there, and waited outside, biding a chance to see the captain, for there was many there, marine officers with their wives and all, to buy; and they paid through the nose, for the price of everything was four or five times what they'd be in London.

"At last I saw my chance and spoke to this Captain Narker, and cursed myself, after, for doing it, for what he said was as bad as spit in the face. He said we could rot here, and be damned to us. None should go home in his ship."

"He was at the marquee when ye left?" Garth asked.

"He sleeps there," said Goodwin. "He'll not trust his own men to guard the place at night, for they're as great villains as himself."

Tom, Garth, and I walked over to our own house, with no word spoken amongst us save Nellie's "Good night to ye" as she went into her own room. It was about nine o'clock and the air biting cold; I was grateful for the new blanket to add to the old one on my bunk. I lay awake for half an hour, perhaps, thinking of Dan, and Bella, whom we'd left seated by the table, her head in her arms, crying her eyes out; and the next thing I knew it was morning.

Nellie was nowhere about. We called at her door, but there was no answer. Her bed was made up, but she always did that the first thing in the morning. The Goodwins had not seen her, and we thought, at first, that the young bull or one of the cows might have broken from the pasture and strayed

off, but we found the animals safe and no sign of Garth. We'd
no thought that anything was amiss. Since Nat's death,
Nellie had kept to herself when she could. She would go off
and be gone for hours to fetch firewood, to give a reason for
avoiding company. We had breakfast without her, none of
us inclined to talk for thinking of the events of the day before. Bella was hard put to keep from breaking down every
time she looked at young Tom. They'd not told him yet, but
the lad took it as settled they would go home now that the
new ships had come. He begged his father to take him to
Sydney to see them. Goodwin promised he should go the next
day, and as soon as he had finished his breakfast, Tommy went
off to look at some snares he'd set for birds.

Goodwin went to the door, following the lad with a mournful glance. He was about to return to the table when he
stopped short, looking to the eastward where the path came
down the slope from the direction of the settlement. "What's
this?" he said. "Here's Mortimer Thynne comin'! There's
summat in the wind, by the look of him."

Thynne was a frequent Sunday visitor with us, but never
on a weekday, and least of all at so early an hour of the morning. He was coming down the path with an air of desperate
haste. Tom hailed him from afar but he made no reply.
Upon reaching us he was so winded he couldn't speak for
a moment, but stood puffing and blowing, with his hands
pressed against his chest. At last he managed to gasp out.
"You've not heard?"

"Heard what?" asked Tom. "Catch yer wind, man. Come
in and set ye down."

"Garth," said Thynne. "Nellie Garth. . . . She's killed
the captain of the *Neptune!*"

XVII

THE RIOT AT THE GUARDHOUSE

ONE week later, at eleven o'clock in the morning, Nellie Garth was brought from the guardroom at the marine barracks to the building near Government House where the Criminal Court was held. There had not been so great a crowd gathered at a trial in Sydney since the settlement was made. Many of the officers and seamen from the four ships in harbour were present, together with the people of the Civil Establishment and the soldiers off duty. And on the outskirts of the throng were the convicts, some hundreds of them — the old and infirm, and those still too weak, through disease and semi-starvation, to be set at labour. These forlorn members of the community were under little supervision in the daytime and they wandered about the settlement like homeless dogs, with nothing to look forward to from day to day but the hour for drawing rations.

The Court was held in a large bare room with whitewashed walls, furnished with benches for the spectators, and in the rear of the room was a place where convicts might stand, for it was considered advisable that some should witness the trials of their fellows, to carry the news to the others of the moving wheels of Justice. Directly the doors were open there was a rush for places and the room was packed in an instant. Goodwin, Oakley, and I managed to enter. Those unable to come inside crowded about the open doors and windows. The judges sat on a platform at one end of the room beneath a portrait of His Majesty George the Third, and the clerk sat at a table below them. To one side was a small railed box for the prisoner and near it a bench for the witnesses.

In those early days of the colony, the Criminal Court was composed of seven members. Captain Collins, the Judge Advocate, presided, and six officers of the military establishment served with him. Although His Majesty's Government had made provision for both civil and military courts for the colony, it had failed to send out with Governor Phillip any officers familiar with the Law. Captain Collins was merely a marine officer selected for the office of Judge Advocate for want of anyone better qualified, and the officers who served with him were even more ignorant than himself of methods of procedure in criminal trials. Therefore, in the absence of anyone able to instruct them, the Court conducted its proceedings by its own improvised methods. Justice was served, but an English magistrate would, I suppose, have found much to criticize.

I have spoken of the high feeling prevailing in the settlement at this time against the masters and officers of the Second Fleet who had so cruelly abused the convicts under their charge. This was true not only of the convicts: I believe that every decent freeman from the Governor down felt the same indignation, but their sentiments were kept under cover, of course; whatever the provocation, they would never make common cause in any matter with felons. The latter, seeing that the guilty officers were received at Government House and entertained by other members of the Civil and Military Establishments, felt themselves betrayed and abandoned, but in their helpless situation they could do no more than brood over their wrongs and mutter amongst themselves. To them, Garth had become a champion, the one convict with the courage to act in their behalf, and they awaited the outcome of her trial with intense interest and anxiety. Mortimer Thynne had asked for and been granted permission to appear as Garth's attorney. This was the first time that a convict had been represented by counsel.

Deep silence spread through the densely packed room as the clerk rapped for order.

"Ellen Garth, stand forth!" said the Judge Advocate.

Nellie stood with her hands resting on the rail in front of her as the charge was read. There was a great black bruise over one cheekbone, and a ragged cut, partly concealed by her hair, extended down the forehead over her left eye. A loud murmur of sympathy was heard from the crowd at the windows, but this was silenced by a sharp reproof from the Judge Advocate.

"Ellen Garth, you have heard the charge against you. Are you guilty or not guilty?"

"Guilty, Your Honour."

"Call the first witness," said the Judge Advocate.

This was the purser of the *Neptune*, a low-browed, heavy-jowled man of forty or thereabout, with small, cruel, crafty-looking eyes.

"You are Martin Dowd, purser of the transport *Neptune?*" asked the Court.

"I am, Your Honour."

"Relate the circumstances, on the evening of June thirtieth, when you last saw the captain of your vessel."

"On the afternoon of that day, sir, I come ashore to the marquee we set up to sell the bit of trade we brought out from England, at great trouble and expense to ourselves, for the good of the colony here. Captain Narker was about his business in the town. He went off to the ship for his supper and came back about eight o'clock. We took turns sleepin' in the marquee to see all was safe with our goods, and that was his night to stay. He said to me: 'Purser, I'll take over now, and ye needn't come back till noon to-morrow.' Them was the last words I ever heard him speak, Your Honour. I went off to the ship, et my supper, and turned into my hammock directly after. I was roused by the second mate at four in the morning. He told me the captain had been murdered in the tent by one of the convicts. That's as much as I know of it, sir, save what's known in a general way to all."

"Was Captain Narker alone in the marquee when you last saw him?" the Court asked.

"Yes, Your Honour."

"Mr. Thynne, does the prisoner wish to question the witness?"

"No, Your Honour."

"You may step down," said the Judge Advocate.

The next witness was a young convict woman who had come out in the *Neptune,* and was known to have been the captain's mistress during the voyage. She was a well-dressed, bold-faced wench, and it was plain, from her buxom appearance, that she had shared none of the hardships of the other women on the voyage from England.

"What is your name?" asked the Court.

"Flo Billings, please Your Honour."

"You were acquainted with Captain Narker, of the transport *Neptune?*"

"I was, Your Honour, in a manner of speakin'."

"You were with him on June the thirtieth, the night of his death?"

"Yes, Your Honour."

"Relate to the Court what happened on that night."

"Well, sir, it's known what a young woman has to put up with wherever she goes, on land or sea, and I won't say I was against doin' as well as I could for myself for the voyage, seein' as I knew I had a better chance than most, and I'd heered the officers wanted to draw lots for me."

"Leave that aside," the Court interrupted. "Tell what you did and what you saw on the night of Captain Narker's murder."

"If I'm to come to that, sir, I was in the tent I was told

off to live in with five more, and Captain Narker sent word I was to slip out, come dark, and go to the *Neptune's* marquee. So I picked up when the others was sleepin' and done as I was told. The captain was settin' by a box of his goods used for a table. He had a bottle of spirits on it. 'It's a cold night, Flo,' said he, and I said, 'So it is, sir.' 'Would ye relish a good stiff tot of rum to warm ye up inside?' said he, and I told him I'd not say no to that. We drank the bottle betwixt us and . . . well, sir, if ye'll excuse me, he blowed out the light and took me off behind the bales and boxes was piled up in the tent. His bed was there and that's where we went.

"It might ha' been an hour after, he wanted another drink. He said, 'Stay where ye are, Flo, and I'll bring ye a dollop directly.' He got up and lit the candle, and he must ha' sat by the box again, for I heered him pourin' out the spirits, but he didn't come back where I was.

"I was that sleepy I dozed off, and then I was roused by some queer noises I couldn't make out, but I heered him groanin' and it was like a chokin' and stranglin' for air. The light was still burnin' where the captain had set the candlestick, on the row of boxes betwixt where I was and the other part of the tent. It was two o'clock, for I heered four bells strikin' from the ships in the cove. I was scared, though I didn't know what was amiss, and shakin' all over. I was afeared to move for a bit, but I got to my hands and knees and looked past the boxes to the other part of the tent. I seen the captain down on his back, and the woman in the box yonder settin' astride of him with her hands around his neck. Blood was streamin' down the side of her face and she was breathin' hard. Her back was to me at first, but she got up directly she knowed he was dead and I saw her plain, though she didn't see me. She looked at the body for a minute; then she was gone. I was that scared I couldn't speak, and I couldn't ha' moved from the tent if it was to save my life. But when I'd got my wits together, I began to yell 'Murder! Murder!' and I kept screamin' till the soldiers come."

"You recognize the prisoner as the woman who was in the tent?" asked the Court.

"Yes, Your Honour. I saw her as plain as I see her now."

"You say that blood was streaming down her face. Do you think she was struck by Captain Narker?"

"It stands to reason he'd fight for his life. He had the barrel of his pistol closed tight in his fist. He must ha' bashed her with the butt end."

"Questions?" asked the Judge Advocate.

Thynne turned to Garth, who shook her head.

"No questions, Your Honour."

The third witness was a lieutenant of the Marine Corps. When he had been sworn, the Court said: "Tell the Court what you saw of the prisoner on the night of Captain Narker's murder."

"I was officer of the guard on that night, sir. A sentinel was on duty in front of the guardhouse. I was in the officers' room, reading the newspapers brought from England by the transports, when the man on duty outside appeared with the prisoner. She was bleeding badly, as the last witness has testified. I asked the guard what had happened. He said that the prisoner had come up to him out of the darkness, and that she wished to give herself up. I questioned the prisoner. She told me that she had killed Captain Narker, of the transport *Neptune*, and that we would find his body lying on the floor of the *Neptune's* marquee. When the prisoner had been locked in the cells, I went at once to the marquee where I found the woman, Billings, screaming 'Murder!' and half out of her senses with fright. Captain Narker's body was lying on the floor of the tent. He had a pistol clutched by the barrel, in his right hand, as the witness has said. Captain Narker's throat was black and bruised, and the fingermarks on it showed plainly that he had been strangled. The convict,

Billings, was then brought to the guardroom for questioning. She told the story already related to the Court."

The Court asked: "You examined Captain Narker's pistol?"

"Yes, sir."

"Had it been discharged?"

"No, sir."

"Do you think he had attempted to discharge it?"

"I could not be certain as to that, sir. I tried to discharge the pistol, outside the guardhouse, but it would not fire. I found the priming damp."

"When you questioned the prisoner, did she give any motive for killing Captain Narker?"

"Yes, sir. I remember her words. She said: 'I have killed the villain who murdered my boy by his cruelty, and scores of poor creatures with him.'"

"She said nothing more?"

"No, Your Honour."

Again no questions were asked, and this brought the testimony to a close. The Court was cleared of the spectators and Garth was taken back to the guardroom. It was a day of bright sunshine, with a fresh northerly breeze ruffling the waters of the cove. Flocks of cockatoos, and small parrots with their brightly coloured plumage, passed overhead, screaming and chattering, and, in the bay, the boats from the transports plied back and forth between the shore and the ships, unloading the last of the supplies brought from England. The crowd outside the courtroom gathered in groups, talking in low voices as they awaited the verdict. Goodwin, Oakley, Nick Sabb, and I stood together, too sore at heart for speech. Thynne, who had walked with Nellie as far as the guardroom, returned and joined us.

"Will there be any hope, Thynne?" Oakley asked.

"Very little," Thynne replied. "One chance in a hundred, perhaps."

"Thynne, be honest," said Sabb. "There's not one in a thousand. They'll hang her, certain."

"Poor Nellie! Poor woman!" said Tom. "Aye, she's done for. 'Tis foolish even to hope."

"Had it been a common seaman, there would be an excellent chance of an appeal for mercy being granted," said Thynne. "But the captain of a vessel in His Majesty's service . . . all the provocation in the world will not weigh against the man's rank. Nevertheless, I shall do what I can."

"God grant ye the gift of tongues!" said Goodwin, fervently.

Scarcely a quarter of an hour passed between the clearing of the courtroom and the reopening of the doors for the announcement of the verdict. This time, as she passed with her guards, Nellie saw us and gave us a grim smile. "God bless her!" said Oakley in a low voice. "She's lookin' death in the face, and knows it!" It was now midday, and the crowd outside was greatly increased in numbers by the convicts coming in for their noonday rest. Garth stood quietly facing the Judge Advocate as he rose to announce the Court's decision.

"Ellen Garth, this Court finds you guilty of willful murder. Have you anything to say before sentence is pronounced upon you?"

Garth shook her head.

"You have leave to speak. I ask you once more: have you anything to say in your own behalf before the sentence of the Court is pronounced?"

"I killed him, sir," Garth replied, in a clear steady voice, "and I'll abide the punishment. As for why it was done, ask my dead boy and the many murdered with him by the captain of the *Neptune*. I'll add this, Your Honour. If it was to do over again, I'd not stay my hand. I have no more to say."

As Garth finished speaking, a woman convict in the crowd by the open door shouted: "Free her! Let her go!" and immediately a babble of voices rose in a tumult of shouting: "Free her! Free her!" "Hang the bloody captains!" "Hang the villains!" "They're the murderers!" "Free her! Free Garth!" "Hang the purser of the *Neptune!*"

The clerk pounded with his gavel, and the Judge Advocate shouted, "Silence! Silence! Order! Do you hear?" but his voice was all but lost in the clamour that came from the convicts crowded at the doors and windows. This was the first time in the history of the colony that they dared to assert themselves as a body. The soldiers stationed outside the courtroom rushed amongst them but were overwhelmed by the angry shouting mob. At last quiet was restored, but the convicts, who had been driven back from the doors and windows, pressed forward again, despite the efforts to hold them back, to hear sentence pronounced. The Judge Advocate was both shocked and frightened by the boldness and determination of the half-starved felons. He stood, grimly waiting for quiet to be restored; then he said: "If there is any further disturbance here, every one of you shall suffer for it! Bear that in mind, for I mean what I say!" His voice was shaking as he turned to Garth to pronounce sentence.

"Ellen Garth, this Court, having found you guilty of the crime charged against you, doth order that, on July fifth, next, at ten o'clock of the morning, you shall be hanged by the neck until you are dead, and may God have mercy upon your soul!"

I thought there would be another outburst at this moment, but not a voice was raised. Thynne, who was standing beside the prisoners' box, stepped forward, and the convicts waited, in painful silence, to hear him.

"Your Honour, have I leave to speak?"

The Judge Advocate nodded, and Thynne made his plea for clemency. This was another man from the one I knew, or thought I knew: he showed a side of his character that had remained hidden beneath the light, bantering manner that was his daily wear. He was deeply moved, and spoke with a quiet eloquence the more impressive because of the sincerity that lay behind his words. He was one convict pleading for the life of another.

"Your Honour," he concluded, "I well know that, by the just laws of our land, the honourable members of this Court, having found the prisoner guilty of the crime charged against her, have no choice in the matter of sentence. They are compelled to condemn her to death. But it is within their power to make a recommendation of clemency, of mercy; and surely, sir, if ever a prisoner, standing before the dread bar of the Law, has deserved mercy, it is the unhappy and truly good woman for whose life I plead."

Three days passed with no news as to Garth's fate, but on July 4 we learned that no plea for clemency had been made by the Court, and that sentence would be carried out on the following morning. Since the night when she had given herself up, Nellie had been kept in solitary confinement and our requests to see her had been refused; but on the morning of the fourth, a boy came from the settlement with a note from the chaplain informing us that we would be permitted to see the prisoner at three o'clock on the same afternoon.

Bella Goodwin, overcome by anxiety and grief at Garth's fate, was in no condition to go, but Dan, Oakley, and I were at the gaol at the appointed hour. The Reverend Mr. Johnston was then with Garth, but he retired, that we might be alone with her for the time of our visit.

"Nellie, we've tried hard to get here afore this," said Oakley. He broke off, abruptly, not trusting himself to say more.

"Ye needn't tell me," said Garth, laying her hand upon his. "I knew ye would come, if ye could."

Goodwin sat with his elbows on his knees, gazing at the floor. Garth alone had herself well in hand.

"I wish ye all to set yer minds at rest," she said. "It had to be as it is, and I'm not afeared of what's to come. But I've one thing to ask, and then we'll say no more of it."

"What is it, Nellie?"

"I've a dread of lying in the burying ground, here in the settlement. I wish to rest yonder, beside Nat, if they'll grant it."

"That ye shall, Nellie. We promise," said Goodwin.

"There — I'm content, for I know ye'll manage it," said Garth. She then spoke calmly and quietly of other things, as though we had been sitting on the bench in the dooryard of Goodwin's house, and when we left her she had managed to convey to us something of her own courage so that the bitterness of the parting was spared us until the moment had passed.

Goodwin and I returned to Blackwattle Bay, leaving Tom at the settlement to arrange for bringing home Garth's body. The Reverend Mr. Johnston had offered his help in this, though he could not promise that permission would be granted. I remember my feeling of despair and unbelief as Goodwin and I took the path for home. With Nellie's quiet words of farewell sounding in my ears, it was impossible to bring home to the mind the fact that less than a day of life remained to her.

When we had finished the evening chores, we sat in the Goodwins' small living room, talking little, in low voices, as though we had been in the presence of Garth's dead body. I went back in thought to the winter afternoon when I had first met her, accusing myself, in anguish of mind, as being the cause of all the grief and misery that had come to her since that day. Consider the matter as I would, I could not but see how heavy was the burden of responsibility I must bear for the chain of events leading to the bitter present moment.

Bella Goodwin sat, chin in hands, gazing stony-eyed at the flame of the lamp.

"Is the Reverend Johnston with her?" she asked.

"Aye," said Goodwin.

"They'll not refuse her last wish, surely," said Bella.

"Who knows what they'll do? We must wait for Tom."

"There's hope . . . there is, there is!" said Bella fiercely. "I'll not give her up; not till the last minute!"

"Ye've no great time to wait, then."

"But there is, Dan! D'ye mind the two men was to be hanged for stealin' from the stores a twelvemonth back? They was led to the foot of the gallows and had the ropes around their necks; then word was brought their lives was to be spared."

"I mind well, and a cruel way it was to show mercy, if mercy was to be shown. One's been no better than an idiot, since."

"But they was spared, Dan, on the very edge of death. And so may Nellie be."

"There's no chance, I say! None. A blacker-hearted villain never lived than this Narker. The worst convict in the colony is a saint beside him. That's known, it must be, to the Governor himself. But he was master of a ship in the King's service. There's naught to weigh against that."

The time dragged on toward midnight. Bella, worn-out by grief and anxiety, went to her bed. Dan and I were dozing in our chairs when Oakley burst into the room.

"Wait," he said, breathing hard. "I've run all the way home . . . Lads . . . she's out! Free! . . . No, not pardoned. . . . There's been a riot . . . gaol delivery. They broke in the door and set her loose. . . ."

"Take it slow, Tom," said Goodwin, pushing him into a seat. "How's this, now? Ye tell us they broke into the gaol?"

Tom nodded. "By God, ye never saw such a mob! The soldiers was too late. . . . Wait; I'll tell ye how it was from the start. I went with the Reverend Johnston to arrange for the body. The Governor was off to dinner with the captain of the *Justinian*, store-ship, and there was none to give permission for the burial without his say. The chaplain told me to stop at Thynne's place. He was to see the Governor and send me word. Like enough he missed him, for I waited till close to ten o'clock and no word came.

"The town was quiet as the grave by then; ye'd never have guessed there was trouble afoot. I had young Hughie in my lap and presently I carried him off to his cot. Thynne and I waited another half hour, thinking the chaplain might come, late as it was. Then all hell broke loose amongst the huts across the end of the cove. 'Twas like that — one minute so still ye could hear a dog barkin' from Bennelong Point, and the next a yelling and shouting to stir the dead. Will ye believe it? We never guessed what was up, at first. I thought it was a free-for-all amongst the huts like the time they all but murdered the marines for trying to steal some of the women. But it wasn't two ticks till we knew this was something beyond a fight. We heard a crashing and banging from the direction of the gaol, and the drums began to beat the alarm from the barracks. Then it clicked with me. 'Thynne, it's Nellie,' I said. 'It's a gaol delivery!' 'It may be,' said he. 'Tom, for God's sake stay where ye are! There's naught they can do. Keep clear of it!' Mrs. Thynne came running out in her nightdress. She grabbed my other arm, but I shook them off and away I went, cursing myself for knowing naught of such a plan before, and them that had it in hand for saying naught of it to me, the oldest friend Nellie's got."

"Likely there was no plan made," said Goodwin. "But who could have egged them on to it?"

"I'm coming to that. Black as the night is ye couldn't see a yard ahead and I bashed into a tree and all but knocked myself silly. As ye know, 'tis a good half mile from Thynne's place to the gaol. Every convict able to stir was packed around the place, and they paid no heed to the drums beatin' the muster at barracks. Those next the gaol was bashin' at the door with the trunk of a tree, and before I could get near, down it went. A rush was made then. There was no getting near the door for the mob, but I knew by the cheers and yells that Nellie was out and away into the bush. And Moll Cudlip as well."

"Moll Cudlip?"

"Aye, for 'twas Moll that led the crowd that broke in the door. Hugh, d'ye mind the thrashing Nellie gave the woman in Newgate? Who'd ha' thought Cudlip would pay anyone back with good? But she was one of the leaders, certain."

"Where was the soldiers?" Goodwin asked.

"Dan, 'twas the neatest trick was ever turned! Over and done with afore ye could say 'damn my eyes!' The guards at the gaol put up no fight. They was loosed when two squads from the barracks came at the double, with bayonets fixed and torches to light the way. The crowd melted into the dark on both sides, back to the huts, and no one the wiser as to who was who."

"But some must ha' been seen," said Goodwin.

"There'll be no floggings for this; that's my guess," said Tom. "Cut rations, mebbe, but no more, for the whole place was in it, women and men. Cudlip was seen and close to being took, for she was swaggerin' and yelling by the gaol when the marines came. She broke loose, though, and has gone bush herself, like as not. I didn't wait to hear what happened after. Good luck to her! She's Satan's own, but we've her to thank that Nellie's free, if what they say is true."

Goodwin shook his head, glumly.

"Free . . . aye, for to-night, to-morrow, but where can she go? To starve in the bush? They'll take her."

"Never, Dan. The getting loose was none of Nellie's work, but now that she's clear, she'll not be took again. She'll die first. . . . God bless her! If only there was some way to get track of her!"

"No hope of that," said Goodwin. "She'll never give us the chance."

"No . . . she wouldn't."

"I'd give my life to save her," said Goodwin, quietly. "Hearty and willing. Lads, we'd best turn in. Mark my words — they'll be here searchin' for her, come day."

Goodwin was right about that, except in the matter of the hour. We were no more than in our beds when a party of eight marines in charge of a lieutenant came to search the place. The men lay concealed for the rest of the night and the following day, lest Garth should steal back for food or help. Blackwattle Bay was kept under close watch for a week thereafter, and parties of marines searched all the bays and coves on both sides of Sydney; but no trace was found of either Garth or Moll Cudlip.

XVIII

THE AMERICAN BRIG

ONE Sunday, a fortnight after Nellie Garth's escape, Sally had come to spend the day at Blackwattle Bay. Whether the others knew how matters stood between us, we didn't know. Likely they did, though we had said nothing about the matter. Bella Goodwin seemed ready to burst with curiosity but managed to keep from putting the direct question. I could see Goodwin's hand there: he was never a man to pry into another's affairs, least of all those of a friend. Sally and I had decided to keep our understanding a secret for the present. There were rumours abroad that the Governor was planning to put some of the steadier convicts on farms of their own, and my hope was that all of us at Blackwattle Bay might be permitted to settle on the fine land Oakley and I had discovered on the upper Hawkesbury. If that should happen, Sally and I planned to marry without further delay.

The Thynnes were so attached to their small grandson that they had persuaded Tom to allow them to take the boy to live with them. This seemed the best arrangement that could be made, now that Garth was gone and Bella left alone to carry on the work of the two households, though she had been the one to protest against the plan. She seemed as fond of Tom's son as she was of her own.

Goodwin had had good luck with the fishing that morning. He returned at midday with the boat half filled, and directly dinner was over he and Tom had gone with the fish to the settlement. Sally and I spent the afternoon together, and when we returned at dusk we found Bella sitting on the bench by the doorway. She was feeling low-spirited, and Sally and I tried to cheer her, with no great success.

"Come, Bella," I said; "it isn't as though we'd lost the lad for good. The Thynnes will bring him down often."

"I know, but it ain't like it was afore. I don't rightly know how I'll manage here without little Hugh. What with Nellie gone and Tommy off with his father all the while, there ain't a body for me to talk with. I don't see what keeps Dan at the settlement. I'll warrant him and Tom has gone to gam with them good-for-nothings, Sabb and Inching."

We waited another hour, and as they had not returned we had supper without them. It was not until late in the evening that we made out the boat, shadowy in the starlight, coming round the point at the head of the cove. We went to meet them on the beach, and Tom called out: "Hugh, are ye there? We've news and to spare, lad! There's a ship from America lying in Sydney Cove."

"Make haste, now, the pair of ye," said Bella. "Your supper's been waitin' these two hours."

"Did I tell ye, Dan?" said Oakley. "They'll not believe us. Damme if I believe it myself, for all I've seen her with my own eyes."

"What's the man saying?" Bella asked. "There's no ship, surely?"

"Aye, but there is," said Goodwin, "else I'd have been home long since."

"He clean forgot ye, Bella," said Tom; "and small wonder with an American ship in the cove."

"She was signaled early this morning and sailed into the cove whilst we was giving in the fish at the stores," said Goodwin. "Ye'll know the stir that was made when we spied her coming round Bennelong Point. A bitter disappointment it was to all when we found she was not from old England."

His wife gazed blankly at him, and Sally and I were

scarcely more ready to believe. The sense of our remoteness, of the thousands of leagues of empty sea lying between us and the outside world, had grown upon us as the months passed, and America seemed as remote as the moon.

" 'Tis no game ye're having with us?" Mrs. Goodwin asked, once more. "There is a ship, as ye say?" But little by little even Bella was convinced. Speaking in turn, Dan and Tom gave us the news. The ship was the brig *Harriet* from Boston, homeward-bound now from China. The captain had learned, before leaving America, of the new settlement then being made at Botany Bay and had brought with him three hundred tons of cargo, both salt beef and spirits, on the chance of selling it there. He knew nothing of Port Jackson, and having called at Botany Bay he came north along the coast, and was about to square away for Cape Horn when he saw the flag at the signal station. The report was that Governor Phillip was more than willing to buy the stores offered, and the ship was to leave as soon as they could be taken ashore.

We talked until past midnight, then went to our beds, but I had no wink of sleep and needed none. Escape, escape, escape — the word kept repeating itself in my mind. Here, if ever, was the chance for Sally and me. I did not, then, think of Oakley or the Goodwins; my stirred and heated mind seemed, at first, to have room for only one image: Sally standing at the rail of the American ship and I beside her, our hearts too full for speech, as we watched the rocky headlands of Port Jackson receding in the distance.

And why not? For Sally the opportunity seemed as good as certain. She was free to leave the colony whenever an occasion presented itself. She had money and to spare for a passage, for her father had been no impoverished prisoner. He had left her, as I knew, about three hundred pounds which Captain O'Day had placed, for safekeeping, in the strong-box at Marine headquarters. Much as the O'Days would regret her going, they would be far from trying to dissuade her against such an opportunity as this, for it might never come again. From Boston she could take ship direct to Quebec, to her father's sister. As for me . . .

It was impossible to lie quietly in bed under the impulse to action of these reflections. I rose, dressed hastily, and was going toward the beach when I saw Sally coming toward me from the pier. She put her hands on my shoulders and her voice trembled a little as she spoke.

"I knew you would come, but I couldn't have waited longer. Hugh, we're going. You've come to tell me that, haven't you?"

Before I could speak she put her fingers over my lips.

"I know what you would say: I am to go in any case. Never! Not without you. Is that understood?"

"Sally, it may well be a chance for you, but . . ."

"No, no, no! We go together or not at all! We must and we can! Believe that, as I do."

"Have you forgotten the French ships that came to Botany Bay?" I said. "There may be a slightly better chance for me in an American ship, but I doubt it. We don't dare allow ourselves to hope too much. The ship will be searched from stem to stern as the Frenchmen were."

"I know it."

"Well, then?"

"Can you think of no other way?"

"How could there be another? My chance will be one in a hundred, perhaps."

"Hush! It is far better than that. To-morrow I will return to the settlement. I will tell the O'Days that I wish to take this chance to return home. They will understand that and help me in it. As soon as it can be arranged I will see this American captain. Open and aboveboard, with Captain O'Day himself to ask for a passage to America."

"And then, what?"

"Later, I shall make an occasion to see him alone. That will be easy. And I will tell him about you . . . about us."

"It won't do, Sally. Governor Phillip is sure to warn him against hiding or harbouring convicts. The ship will be so thoroughly searched before she sails, not even a rat could escape being found."

"I said nothing of hiding in the ship."

"Then I am to walk boldly aboard, with you, and wave my hand to the soldiers as we leave the cove?"

"Hugh, how slow-witted you are! You are a tolerable walker, I know. You could, perhaps, walk as far as Botany Bay?"

I stared at her.

"By the Lord! It might be done! It might well be done!"

"It will be done," she replied, quietly. "I will be in no haste in speaking to this captain. I must see him first, make friends with him. He will be a hard man indeed if I cannot persuade or bribe him to send a boat ashore for you at Botany Bay."

"There is a chance that Governor Phillip, or Major Ross, will think of such a plan to escape and forestall it."

"I don't think so. The convicts in the settlement will be carefully guarded on the day the brig sails. In any case, the chance must be taken. We're going, I know it," she added, with such confidence that I could almost believe, myself. "There is a Providence watching over us, Hugh. Think of this: I would have told the O'Days about us, if this ship had not come. Sooner or later I would have been forced to tell them. And now . . . you see?"

"Yes. You could not have gone without arousing their suspicion that I would try to go as well. As it is, you are sure they suspect nothing?"

"How could they? I have not worn my heart upon my sleeve. They know my father liked you, that I have been kind to you for his sake — nothing more."

"Sally . . ."

"Yes?"

"Supposing it succeeds, as we plan . . ."

"It will! It must!"

"Think of the Goodwins, of Tom Oakley. If the captain will consent to take me . . ."

"Why not the others? I was thinking of that as you spoke. I could ask, perhaps . . ." She broke off, and then added: "Hugh, we must not. The risk would be too great. Call me selfish, if you like, but I think of you first. Supposing a party of marines should go to Botany Bay, and Major Ross might send them, as a precaution. We must prepare for that possibility. We can, I am sure, if you come alone. With more, the chance of failure would be far greater."

"There will be no need to go to Botany Bay, if the others come. We can avoid that danger altogether."

"Avoid it? How? . . . Oh . . . I see it! You would come in the boat!"

The moment I spoke of the plan, Sally was as strongly in favour of it as myself. We could steal out at night, the Goodwins, with young Tommy, Oakley and I, and meet the brig well off the coast. Late as the hour was, we were too impatient to wait for day to discuss this matter with the others. Sally went to wake the Goodwins whilst I routed Tom out, and a few moments later we were gathered in the small bare living room at the Goodwins' house. It was a frosty night, and the air was nipping cold. Dan made up the fire on our dry-stone hearth and we drew our benches around it.

"Now, Hugh, what's this?" he asked. "What have ye to say that wouldn't keep till morn?"

Together, interrupting one another as we spoke, Sally and I outlined our plan, the others treasuring our words as though their lives depended upon not missing a syllable. Tom edged his stool closer and closer as he listened. Goodwin nodded his shaggy head from time to time, and there was a light of joy in his eyes I can see to this day. Bella turned from one to another of us, with timid wondering glances. When we had finished, I turned to Goodwin.

"Well, Dan?"

"It's champion, champion," he said, quietly.

"Do you see any flaws in the plan?"

"There's naught amiss with it from our end. It's as good as done, the slipping out at night. But I fear to take hope. If the captain says nay . . ."

"But he won't! He can't!" Sally broke in. "Here you must depend upon me."

"And glad we'll be to do it, Miss Sally," said Tom. "We would ask no better than yourself to speak for us. And with Hugh an American like himself, there's a point to make. Lad, ye must lie like a good one about your part in the American War. A Yankee from Boston would have fought against the King, not for him as ye did. If he learned the truth he'd say, 'Let him rot here, and be damned to him!' "

"Never fear for that," I said. "I'll know how to play my part."

"Ye know the Yankees. It's all a matter of rhino with them, ain't it? He'll not take us for nothing, we can be sure of that."

"If money can win him, I have three hundred pounds, and he shall have it all," Sally said.

Tom's eyes widened. "Three hundred pounds! God bless ye, Miss Sally! It's done, then. We're gone, as certain as sunrise!"

"We know naught of the man," said Goodwin, "but it does look fair promisin' with hard money to offer. I've better than sixty pounds brought out for our passage home when my time was out. . . . Bella, ye'll wish to go if the thing's possible?"

"I don't know what to say," Mrs. Goodwin replied, in an

anxious voice. "But I don't fancy it, stealin' away like a thief, and you as free as the Governor himself."

"And whose fault is it I'm obliged to?" said Goodwin grimly. "Not mine."

"Aye, but if we was to be catched trying to leave unbe-knownst . . . they might hold ye for another seven years."

"We'll not be catched if the man will take us," said Goodwin.

"Dan's right, Bella," said Oakley. "There's no risk to scare a rabbit."

Mrs. Goodwin rocked to and fro on the bench, clasping her thin shoulders.

"Oh, Dan! It ain't what I'd wished! I thought to see ye walkin' aboard a ship with yer head up and none to gainsay the right. But if ye say go . . ."

"I do say it," Goodwin replied. "I'll have the freedom I've earned, and I'll have it now."

"And how will we manage yonder, in a strange land? With another great ocean betwixt us and home?"

"We'll think o' that when we get there," said Goodwin. "Miss Sally, ye plan for to go to Sydney, come day?"

"Yes, and I'd best see little of you after that. I'll find means of getting word to you, in good time."

"There'll be little time needed on our side," said Goodwin. "We'll be waiting and ready well aforehand."

We then discussed how best to avoid the need of any communications on Sally's part, and it was agreed that Goodwin should go to Sydney with Bella, on the day the brig sailed. If we had no further word from Sally, we would understand that the captain had agreed to take us. In that case we would steal out in the boat the night following the sailing of the brig and meet her off the white cliffs to the south of Botany Bay. With a light easterly breeze, we could reach that place in four hours. If there should be no wind, we could still manage the distance, rowing, in from six to eight hours. Sally was to beg the captain to wait twenty-four hours, in case of need, and if he consented to that, she was to whisper the word to Bella when she said good-bye to her before going off to the ship.

Hope and love of life revived in all of us during the days that followed; had not the thought of Nellie cast a shadow over our hearts, we would have been almost gay. When we received word from Sally that all was arranged with the captain of the brig, none gave the possibility of failure a thought.

It was agreed that young Tommy must know nothing of what was in the air, lest he inadvertently let drop some hint of our plans, and his father was so insistent on caution that Bella led the boy away whenever our preparations might have aroused his curiosity. As a gift for the brig's captain, who had been unable to purchase a shilling's worth of fresh provisions in Sydney, we decided to take one of Garth's pigs, a crate of fowls, and as many vegetables as we could collect from our garden. Tom and I resolved to take our muskets and all the powder and ball we had.

On the Monday we went out with our nets as usual, returning in the afternoon with more fish than we had caught for some time. Dan remained in Sydney, to learn the time set for the brig's departure, not yet announced, while Tom and I sailed the boat home.

"I shouldn't wonder it'll be to-morrow, or the day after," Tom remarked. He was silent for a moment. "Hugh, I'll be obliged to speak to Thynne. I can't go like as if I was desertin' my boy. What d'ye think?"

"He can be trusted, that's certain," I replied. "But who knows? He might want to sail with us."

"Thynne? Not him! He's digged in here like a badger. He's told me he'll never return to England. Mortimer's no man's fool; he'll own Sydney when he's done his bit."

"Tell him, then, by all means. Dan will say the same."

"I'm glad ye feel so. I've a cousin he could write to in England, to tell me all's well. If we come safe through, soon or late I'll find a way to send for the lad."

Presently Goodwin arrived. "It's to-morrow, lads!" he said.

Tom's eye brightened. "Certain?"

"I saw Miss Sally at the hospital. She was lookin' at our fish, and found the minute to tell me."

Tom glanced keenly at him. "Then what d'ye look so glum about?"

"I'm worried aplenty, though it may be naught. Captain Campbell's sent word we're not to fish to-morrow. He wants the boat, an hour afore noon."

"What for?" I asked.

"He didn't say."

Tom laughed. "Be easy, Dan. It's naught. Like as not he's begged the boat from the Governor, for a picnic with some of the officers and their ladies."

Our boat had been used for such excursions several times in the past, and I said: "Tom's right. Ten to one they're going to Cockatoo Island to come home in the evening. We can leave well before midnight."

"No doubt ye're right, lads," said Goodwin. "I'd a kind o' forebodin' . . . I'm that set on getting away!"

We talked late, that night, after Tommy was in bed, making our final plans and attempting to provide against every emergency. We refused to be worried over the order for the boat, believing that it meant no more than a picnic, or an afternoon's shooting party. Even if the officers kept us until long after dark, we could set out as late as three or four in the morning with reasonable hope of passing the signal station unobserved. Should they sight us at sea, hours would pass before a messenger could reach Sydney to send a boat in pursuit, and meanwhile we would be safe in the brig and headed for Cape Horn. I fell asleep that night feeling as certain of escape as if New South Wales were already a hundred leagues astern.

The sun was an hour up when we reached Sydney. A light southwesterly breeze carried us as far as Dawes Point; we then furled our sails and pulled into the cove, passing close to the *Harriet's* side. The Governor was on board and the quarter-deck thronged with Sydney's notables. In spite of myself, my eyes were fixed on Sally, standing in talk with Mrs. O'Day and the Reverend Mr. Johnston's young wife. She gazed at me without a sign of recognition, and turned away once more.

As we tied up at the pier the visitors were coming ashore. Everyone in the settlement not at work stood on the beaches to watch the brig sail. An hour had passed when I heard the chant of the men at the windlass. She was well-manned; sail after sail was set with a smartness which would have done credit to an English man-of-war. The *Harriet* gathered way, parting the calm water with scarcely a ripple. The foretopsail halliards were let go in salute as she passed the *Scarborough* and a few moments later she was lost to view around Bennelong Point. Oakley went off to see Thynne. He was then to return home and have all in readiness when we came with the boat.

A corporal of the New South Wales Corps was approaching us. His boots were neatly blacked, his belts pipe-clayed, and he had the ruddy, well-fed look of a man newly out from England.

"Is Goodwin here?" he asked.

"That's me."

"Ye're to wait for Lieutenant MacArthur. Captain Campbell's orders."

"Where are we bound, Corporal?" I asked.

"Rose Hill. They're sendin' some hard cases from the *Scarborough* to work there. Stop here till ye're wanted."

He shouldered his musket and marched off, leaving us to

exchange glances that were more than glum. Rose Hill was many miles distant.

The sun crawled toward the zenith while we waited in our boat, fretting anxiously at the delay. The convicts trooped in for the noon hour, from the fields, the quarry, and the brick kiln, and at one o'clock the drums beat the signal to resume work. Dan and I munched our bread and salt beef without relish. It was midafternoon when a file of convicts was marched down to the pier, led by an officer and guarded by a corporal and six men. Each of the prisoners carried a blanket and a small canvas bag with his belongings. Their evil, pasty faces and cruel mouths branded them as a hard lot. The officer sprang into the stern when we had loosed the sails.

Lieutenant MacArthur, destined in later years to play so great a part in the history of New South Wales, was at the time a young man, in poor health, with a hot, irascible eye, a pugnacious nose, and an air of brooding over some grievance.

"Get them on board," he ordered the corporal, harshly. "Four to a thwart. There's plenty of room! Now come aft here, with your men."

The soldiers squeezed into the stern sheets. Dan held the tiller, while I found a place where I could manage the foresheet. There was scarcely enough breeze to fill the sails.

Once out in the harbour, the tide carried us slowly westward, each mile and each hour that passed adding to my uneasiness. We took to the oars, but the boat was too crowded and heavy-laden for rowing. The sun set, and it was night when we reached the Parramatta landing place. MacArthur had been staring ahead, hoping to see a light. It was his first trip inland.

"Now damn them all!" he exclaimed. "They were to have met me here. We'll have to camp for the night."

"If ye'll follow me, sir," Dan put in, "I'll guide ye to Rose Hill. I can find the path in the dark."

"It's a long way through the woods, I'm told."

"Aye, sir," Dan admitted, "a fair bit, but I'll have ye there in no time."

MacArthur thought for a moment and then said: "No — we'll camp here."

I spoke up from the bows. "I'm a hunter, sir. There's not an inch of these parts I don't know. Let me guide you to Rose Hill."

"That'll do, whoever you are! When I want your help, I'll ask for it!"

We were told to build a large fire, and fetch enough wood to keep it burning through the night.

"You'll stop here with the boat," the officer informed Dan, "and take the guard down to fetch another load of these rascals to-morrow."

I overheard this stunning announcement as I tossed a log on the fire, and my heart sank. Dan and I made a pretense of going to sleep in the boat, though we did not close our eyes for a moment. The convicts groaned and muttered where they lay, complaining of the cold, while four marines, with bayonets fixed, stood guard within a few feet of us. Mac-Arthur was as sleepless and vigilant as his men, rising to inspect the guard at intervals. The whole scene was illuminated by the bright flames of the campfire. The night was the longest, and the most anxious, of my life.

A detachment of marines from Rose Hill came down to the landing place just after daybreak, and the corporal and his men were ordered to return to Sydney with us, to fetch the second load of convicts. Every hour of that seemingly endless day was a torment.

We returned to Sydney, reaching Parramatta with the second lot of convicts before dark, and were ordered to wait until morning, when Lieutenant MacArthur would return. But this time the boat was left unguarded. The corporal went off at the head of his men. We waited, while the sun set and the new moon followed the same westering path. The short winter evening gave place to night.

No time was wasted. We pushed off silently, floating down-river with the ebb while we set our sails. A light northerly breeze was making up, and the warm air from far-off tropical regions was grateful to our chilled bodies. Three hours later we sailed into Blackwattle Bay. As we approached the jetty, Tom appeared from the shadows.

"By God, I'd all but given ye up!" he said.

"Now lads, work fast!" said Dan.

We stowed his chest with the provisions amidships, and fetched the muskets and our own canvas bags. The pig and the four fowls were stowed in the bow. I made a bed of blankets for young Tommy, forward, and lifted the boat's water keg to make sure that it was full. Dan came down from the cottage, carrying the boy and followed by Bella. We pushed off with scarcely a glance behind.

Bella took the tiller while Goodwin, Oakley, and I pulled mightily. From Blackwattle Bay to Dawes Point, we followed the windings of the harbour in a two-mile pull, all to wind-ward. Directed by her husband, Bella now steered for the northern shore, to skirt the land as far as Kirribilli Point, op-posite Sydney Cove, and only a few hundred yards distant. We had the wind abeam by this time, but dared not hoist sail lest we be sighted in the starlight. Sydney was asleep at this hour. Only a few lights showed. Of a sudden the dogs of the settle-ment began to bark, far and near, as if the breeze, coming in puffs off the land, had borne our scent to them. A cock crowed, clear in the distance, followed by others of his kind, and our bird in the crate answered with a cry, muffled in thick folds of sailcloth. The *Scarborough's* bell rang clearly, and the voice of a sentinel reached us from far across the still water — "Midnight! And all's well!"

Pinchgut Island lay directly in our path. A few of the more desperate convicts were marooned there and we gave it a wide berth. At last we got up sail and laid a course to pass just south of Bradley's Head. An hour later, we were breasting the long Pacific swell at the harbour mouth, and soon bore off for the run south to Botany Bay. The breeze held fair and steady from the north.

We breathed easy now. Dan settled himself comfortably at the tiller. "We'll fetch Cape Solander by eight bells. Lay ye down with Tommy, Bella."

"Ye think I could sleep?" she replied, going forward, nevertheless. "Ye'd ha' done well to listen to me, Dan. We're too late."

The same fear must have been in all of our hearts, though no one had spoken out until now. A hundred times I had imagined the brig hove-to at dawn on the day before. Sally would have been on deck straining her eyes westward as the light grew in the east; staring at the barren coastline while the sun rose behind her, and bright hope gave place to doubt, and doubt, after many long hours, to despair. The Yankee captain would have been at her side on the quarter-deck, his spyglass aimed at the Port Jackson heads, sweeping the coast, scanning the entrance of Botany Bay. I could imagine how the hours had dragged, and Sally's feelings when night fell. She would have urged the captain, implored him, to wait longer. Yet as they considered every aspect of the situation, what could they suppose had happened? I could almost hear the Yankee's nasal voice, saying with respectful firmness: "Wall, Miss, I've done my best for 'em. They've been caught, you can lay to that! I can't hang on here forever!"

"What d'ye think, Hugh?" asked Tom Oakley, in a voice too low for Bella to hear. "Would he wait?"

"God knows!"

"We can hope, can't we?" put in Goodwin, impatiently. "Stow yer doubts, lads! We'll sight the brig, come daylight!"

Dan steered close to shore until we made out the capes, toward four o'clock, then ordered the sheets trimmed as he bore up to head southeast. We had sailed little more than an hour, on this offshore course, when the breeze began to slacken, dying away at last to a flat calm. We were then four or five miles south of Botany Bay, and as many from the land. The sails were lowered and we sat staring to the eastward in silence, as if the intensity of our gaze might hasten the coming of the new day. At last the stars paled and the horizon grew luminous with dawn. Goodwin rose stiffly to his feet.

Slowly, the black sea turned misty blue, while the faint grey light in the east was touched with rose, and brightened to dazzling gold as the sun came up. Stare as I would, I could see nothing that broke the horizon from south to east.

"There she is!" Dan exclaimed. "Look! Just right o' the sun!"

Gazing in the direction indicated, I made out a pair of tiny projections above the horizon line, which disappeared as we sank into the trough between two swells. The light was so dazzling that I put the palms of my hands to my eyes.

"Her fore and main royals," said Dan. "Bella, take the tiller. To the oars, lads!"

No watermen on the Thames, rowing in a regatta for a great prize, ever pulled as we did or had a tenth as much at stake. The heavy boat leaped forward to breast the seas while we set our teeth and made the stout ash bend at every stroke.

"Hearty does it!" Dan panted. "With a will now! Break yer backs! They're on their way. We must get in sight afore the wind makes up!"

Young Tommy stood in the bow, staring ahead as intently as his mother. A long time had passed when he turned, excitedly.

"Look, Father!" he cried. "We're bringing her up!"

Dan glanced over his shoulder. "So we are, her t'gallants is showin'. Pass yer shawl forrad, Bella. Now son, can 'ee climb the mast and make this fast to the truck?"

Sweat streamed down our faces and plastered our shirts to our backs, but the brig, on which we had gained for a time, seemed further away than before. Now and again, when boat and vessel rose simultaneously on the swell, many miles apart, we had a glimpse of her royals, ever smaller and more indistinct. I knew only too well what had occurred: The north wind had made up offshore, and had reached the brig well before we could hope to have it; but we pulled on, never slackening our stroke. Bella stared ahead, closing her eyes at intervals to rest them from the glare, speaking to Dan in a low voice each time she sighted the *Harriet*. Presently she bowed her head in her arms.

"It's no use, Dan! She's gone," she sobbed.

"Hold that tiller!" he commanded, harshly.

We rowed grimly on for another half hour, but at last Dan rested on his oar. "Avast pullin', lads," he said in a dull voice. "We've lost her."

XIX

ESCAPE

WE sat slumped down on the thwarts, weary and heartsick. The boat slid gently over the long smooth swells. Bella still held the tiller, moving it back and forth unconsciously, as if to scull on in pursuit of the brig. Oakley was the first to speak.

"What's to do? Is it back to Master with our tails between our legs?"

In her despair, Bella forgot Tommy, who was standing in the bow still staring seaward.

"Now we'll never see home — never, never, never!" she cried, in an anguished voice.

"Hush!" said Goodwin sternly, with a warning glance. "Take the oars, lads." He spit on his hands and gripped his own.

"Where to, Dan?" Mrs. Goodwin asked, apprehensively.

Before he could reply, our rooster, despite his cramped quarters in the crate, managed to clap his wings and crow.

"Yon's a brave little fellow," said Dan, quietly. "I've a real likin' for a cock. 'Never say die' is the word with them. . . . Steer for Botany Bay," he added, to Bella.

We hoped that the northerly breeze which darkened the sea to the east would work in toward shore, but it came no nearer.

As the sun rose the heat became intense, but we pulled on, turning our heads now and again to estimate our slow progress toward the land. Weary, weary work it was, dragging the heavy boat toward Botany Bay, and we had little heart for it now. Only the unspoken thought of pursuit, in all of our minds, kept us doggedly at it. Midafternoon found us within the bay. With anxious hearts, we searched every part of it within our view. It lay before us, as solitary as though, before ourselves, sea birds alone had visited the place.

Dan had a smuggler's eye and a smuggler's memory. We headed into a narrow winding drain he had spied when we had gone with the watering party on the day the convict, Jurd, was hung. It was a mile or more from the fresh-water creek where we had filled the casks, and screened by tall sedge grass. With our oars, we poled the boat well into it, then, wading in knee-deep mud and water, hauled it yet farther, around a bend where we could lie completely hidden.

"Tide's at the ebb," said Goodwin. "There'll be water aplenty by nightfall."

There was firm ground a short distance inland. Dan took Tommy on his shoulder and carried him there, returning to fetch Bella. Tom and I brought the crate of fowls, the pig, and the sack of vegetables we had thought to give the captain of the brig. We found a snug dry place to make camp, well concealed by thick clumps of bush.

"Rest here, Bella, with Tommy," said Goodwin. "Hugh and Tom and me will have a look inland. We'll be back directly."

He led us on till we were well out of earshot. There we halted.

"Well, Dan?" said Tom, presently.

"Speak first," said Goodwin.

Tom shook his head, with a rueful smile.

"If ye ask me, we're beat. No more roamin' the country, huntin', fishin', and the like. We can hide out for a month, mebbe, but they'll nab us, soon or late. And then . . . aye, we'll be for it, proper!"

"Hugh?" said Goodwin.

"I'll not go back," I said, "never! But Tom's right — we're done for. When our powder and ball are gone there'll be no supporting life in the bush."

"I say, starve it out to the end!" said Oakley. "But there's Bella and Tommy. . . ." He got to his feet and strode back and forth for a moment; then he halted to face Goodwin.

"Hark ye, Dan! There's only one thing to do. Ye must go back to Sydney with Bella and the lad."

"Me? Go back?" said Goodwin, with a grim laugh.

"Wait, now! Let me finish. . . . Ye're a free man: that's known to all. Ye have the paper to show it, stamped with the Great Seal and signed by the Governor himself. It's my belief he's a real sympathy in his heart for them, like yerself, that's served their time and forbid to go home. I'll warrant it's not his fault ye've been kept. It's the black-hearted devils in the Home Office that won't allow ye to go. Well, then . . . if ye go back to the settlement with Bella and Tommy — ye see how it'll be? It's certain ye'll get off light."

"And what of yerselves?" asked Goodwin.

"Never fret for us," I put in. "Dan, it would be three hundred lashes each for Tom and me, even if we came in of our own will. And after that, hard labour for years to come. I'll not suffer it! I'll die first!"

"Ye won't suffer it," said Goodwin quietly. "No more will I go back with Bella and little Tom."

Tom glanced up.

"What d'ye mean by that?"

"We're not beat! No, by God! . . . Lads, we'll clear out of here this same night, but not for Sydney. We're going to make for the Dutch East Indies."

"What!" I exclaimed.

"In the boat?" said Tom.

"Aye, in the boat. Now let me tell ye summat I'd ha' spoke of afore save for what's come between. . . . When I knowed there was to be no goin' home for me, for all I'd served my time out fair and square, I done some hard thinkin'. I was bound I'd have the freedom I'd earned, and I could see no way but to take what was held from me. The boat was that way, and the only way. I knowed the Dutch East Indies was the nearest place I could fetch up. 'Twould be a hard cruel voyage in a little boat, and there was Bella and Tommy to think of. For all that, I was set to go and layin' my plans. Then the American brig come, and . . . there's no need to say more."

We stared at Goodwin as though he had been speaking in a foreign tongue.

"Well, is it go?" he said.

I could find no words, for the moment. Tom spoke for both.

"Hugh," he said, "d'ye mind the night in Newgate, after we'd been sentenced to swing, when the Recorder came with the word we was to have life? God bless ye, Dan! No need to ask!"

"Then it's settled," said Goodwin. "I knew well enough where I'd find the pair of ye."

We settled down to a discussion of the prospects. Goodwin had both a compass and a quadrant in his sea chest; and beyond this he had a little rough knowledge of the northern part of the New Holland coast, gained from an old seaman from his own village in England who had sailed with Captain Cook on the voyage when he discovered Botany Bay.

"Many a tale I heard from him," he said, "and I treasured every word as a young man will. The most of what I recollect was about the voyage when they'd got inside the Great Reef, and the wonder of the lagoons all along the coast till they fetched the Cape York Peninsula at the northern tip of New Holland."

"If only we had a chart!" I said.

" 'Tis no matter for that," said Oakley. "We've naught to do but follow the land till we come to the end of it and then head west."

"Hugh, will ye listen to him!" said Goodwin, shaking his head wonderingly. "Tom knows horses from stem to stern, but I've never seen his beat for lack o' knowledge of the sea . . . but there's a chart, only I ain't got it here. I laid my plans careful for this same voyage afore the brig come. I knowed that Captain Cook's own chart would be in Governor Phillip's office, but how to get a copy? There was but one man could help me there — Mortimer Thynne. I made a clean breast to him of what I hoped to do, and Thynne, God bless him, for all the risk to himself, copied the chart and no one the wiser. But devil of it's this — the copy's still at Thynne's house. The comin' of the brig and all put the thought of it clean out o' mind. We're obliged to go fetch it; there's no two ways about that."

We decided that we must run in to Port Jackson, under cover of darkness, and land in Rushcutter's Bay or Wooloo-mooloo; then one of us would make his way to Thynne's house. We had yet another reason for taking such a risk. We had in the boat but one small five-gallon cask for water. We would need another twice the size, and we hoped that, with Thynne's help, we might add something to our scant stock of provisions.

"How far will it be, Dan, the whole of the voyage from here to the Dutch Indies?" Tom asked.

"I can make only a guess at that, but Thynne's figured it out as well as he can by the charts. He says it's around seven hundred mile to the tropic where we'll strike the Great Reef. If we can manage to get inside, we'll have another thousand to the Cape York Peninsula, but that should be tolerable smooth sailin'. Once we're clear o' New Holland, we'll have another thousand to Timor, first Dutch settlement we'll fetch, if we do fetch it. Call it a thousand leagues all told. That'll be near it."

Oakley whistled under his breath.

"Once I boated down the Thames to Margate, and damme

if it didn't seem like the ends o' the Earth," he said. "A thousand *leagues!*"

"Or six hundred lashes for the pair of us," I added.

"And it's not certain I wouldn't get three hundred to add to yours," said Goodwin, "for it's me would be charged with stealin' the boat. What d'ye say, is it leagues or lashes?"

"Be damned to ye for askin'," said Oakley, dryly. "Does Bella know of the plan ye made for the boat?"

"No, I was leavin' that to the end when all was ready . . ."

Dan broke off, glanced quickly over his shoulder, and sprang to his feet. There was a rustling in the bushes behind us. Before we could speak or act, the undergrowth parted and there stood Nellie Garth.

With a whoop of joy, Tom sprang forward and threw his arms around her. "Nellie, Nellie, Nellie!" he cried, brokenly. "Is it yerself and all?"

" 'Tis not," said Garth, with a grim smile. "I'm a good four stone light, but I can eat the weight of it back, if ye've vittles at hand?"

She was gaunt and sunburned, her clothing in rags, and her eyes bright and hollow, but with the same old dauntless twinkle in them. Five minutes later we had her at the camp, and Bella was clinging to her so overcome that not a word could she say. Tommy, who had been awake all through the previous night, was now sleeping soundly with his father's watch coat for a pillow. Nellie's eyes were bright with tears as she knelt beside him, took his hands and pressed them to her cheeks. The lad scarcely stirred. As she rose, she caught sight of the pig, tethered to a tree near by and trying hard to reach her.

"God bless me, 'tis me own little blackie!" she said, and a moment later she was nursing it in her arms. Meanwhile, Bella had set out the food. We had half-a-dozen roast fowls, and two of them she placed before Garth and started feeding her as though she had been a child.

"Now, Nellie," Tom was saying, a quarter of an hour later, "tell us the whole of it, from the day we last set eyes on ye."

"I've as little to tell as there's been to eat," said Garth. "Bella, I couldn't well say how I relish the cold fowl, but take it away now, else I'll be hoggin' the whole of it.".

"Ye poor starved creature," said Bella, "ain't that why it's set afore ye? Oh, Nellie darlin'!" And she hugged her again.

Then, briefly, Garth told us her story. She had lived on raw crabs, oysters, and other shellfish, and had slept in the bush wherever night had overtaken her. "And the nights was the worst," she said. "I'll never again take the blessing of a fire as a common thing. There's been times I all but perished with the chill."

"But why didn't ye steal in to us?" asked Goodwin. "There's not been a night, Nellie, we ain't slept with one eye and one ear open for ye."

"Did ye think so mean o' me, Dan Goodwin? As if I'd not caused grief enough without gettin' the rest of ye in a peck o' trouble for my sake."

"What's become of Moll Cudlip?" I asked.

"Did ye battle with her, Nellie, like the time in Newgate?" Tom asked, with a grin.

"I did not. I'll say this for the woman. Though she's not one I'd choose for company, I'd go far to do her a good turn if the chance was offered."

"But where is she?" Mrs. Goodwin asked.

"I should think ye might guess," said Garth, dryly. " 'Tis not a thing to speak of, but . . . ye must ha' known, Bella, she had a fancy-man amongst the blacks?"

Mrs. Goodwin gave a gasp of horror.

"Nellie! I never did! Ye tell me . . ."

"I do," said Garth. "She's with him now, or was, when I saw her last. I had a kind invitation to go along with 'em to the black's tribe." Her eyes twinkled as she added, "I wasn't so tempted as ye might think."

It was scarcely necessary to explain to Garth the reason for our presence here. She had seen the brig coming out from Port Jackson and knew it was none of the English transports. When she spied Dan's boat coming in from sea, she had guessed the reason.

"And now — what? Dan, ye're sure to be took, soon or late. There's no livin' in the bush for long. I've tried it."

With a glance at his wife, Dan now spoke of the boat voyage. It was curious to watch the two women. Garth leaned forward, her eyes shining, watching Dan's lips as if for double confirmation of what the voice was saying. Bella sat with her hands tightly clasped against her breast. Her thin body trembled convulsively. She might have been listening to one condemning her to death. Dan was still speaking when Tom, who stood guard at the border of the firm land, came back at a run. "Lie low!" he said. "The Governor's longboat's just coming through the heads!"

Our camp, as I have said, was well hidden. Goodwin, Oakley, and I stole down to where we could lie, screened by a thick fringe of bush, and overlook the bay. The longboat was still far distant, a light breeze from the south filling her sails. Half an hour passed before we could make out the marines on board. An officer stood in the stern, spyglass up, as he scanned the shore slowly and carefully. Presently they slacked away for the creek at the head of which we had filled the *Charlotte's* water casks so long ago. There was a tense moment as she passed the outlet of our drain, but she held on, sailing in with the tide until she grounded in the shallows, a mile distant. Twilight faded to full night, and we saw the gleam of a fire where her people were encamped. "Now, lads," said Goodwin, "we've not a moment to waste!"

We hastened back to the others. Goodwin took Tommy in his arms, and Bella held his hand. Nellie carried her pig with her hand over his snout. Tom and I followed with the other provisions. We waded slowly across the marsh to the boat, and poled down, stern first, till the salt drain widened. In the open bay we stepped our masts, and headed for the entrance.

The night was so dark that I could see nothing but the black water rippling under the chill breeze, but Dan steered confidently. At last we heard the roar of breakers and made out the dim bulk of Cape Solander. The wind freshened outside. In two hours we were abreast of the signal station where a light showed in the hut by the flagpole. We bore up to enter Port Jackson, ghosting in with the cat's-paws that came down off the land. It was not far from midnight when we eased our grapnel into shallow water at the head of Wooloomooloo Bay.

"Tom, stop here with the womenfolk," said Goodwin. "Hugh and me will go to the settlement."

"Oh, Dan! I'm so afeered for ye!" said Mrs. Goodwin, in an anguished voice. "If ye're catched . . ."

"Hush, now! We'll be safe back in two hours, mebbe less." We waded ashore and there halted for a moment.

"Hugh," said Goodwin, "Ned Inching's our man. We'll go by the buryin' ground and send him to Thynne."

The distance from Wooloomooloo to Sydney was less than a mile. Inching's hut was dark, but we stole in, felt for his bed, and wakened him.

"Shhh, Ned! It's me — Tallant."

A more ready, nimble-witted man than Ned Inching could not have been found. He fumbled for me, then put his lips to my ear. "What's to do?" he whispered.

In two minutes I had explained the situation. He slipped into his clothes. "Wait here," he said. "I'll be back in a tick."

Dan and I sat on the bed. The silence was as deep as the grave — as the graves of all Ned's convict family sleeping six feet underground. The first we knew of his return, he was there before us, unseen in the darkness.

"Thynne's wi' me, and Nick Sabb," he whispered. "I'll fetch 'em in."

"Damn my eyes!" said Nick, in a hoarse whisper, and puffing hard. "Ye've got the courage of lions, and me sergeant of patrol that ought to hook ye and be made High Constable for life! Dan, it's true, what Ned says?"

"Aye, we're off, and no time to lose. Thynne, are ye there? Ye've brought the chart?"

"I have," said Thynne, "and a bit of beef and flour that may, perhaps, be acceptable. Four days' rations."

What this gift meant, only a Sydney convict of those days could understand.

"Thank ye, and hearty," said Goodwin. "There's another thing we're obliged to have: a ten-gallon cag, for water."

"Take mine," said Inching. "Ye can fill it from the little run at Wooloomooloo."

"There's need for haste," said Nick, "but let me speak for ten seconds, Dan, and all ye need to say is Yes or No. Would ye take Ned and me?"

"Ye wish to go? D'ye know where we're bound to, man?"

"Aye, the Dutch Indies, wherever they be, but speak quick, Dan! If I think twice I'll make lard o' my vitals."

"Done," said Goodwin. "Thynne, would ye wish to join us?"

"Good heavens, *no!*" said Thynne. "Nick, think what you do! Stay here, and I promise we'll be the most prosperous and respected citizens in the colony ten years hence."

"God's name, don't ask me to think!" said Sabb, desperately. "Haste ye, Dan, and Ned and me will whisper 'London! London! London!' till we're well out to sea."

Inching had scurried like a terrier under his bed.

"Reach me the sack," he whispered. "I've eight bottles o' rum here."

"Ready?" said Goodwin.

I have never forgotten that hurried, whispered leave-taking. Thynne was not even a shadow in the blackness as he gripped my hand.

"Hugh, if you reach the Indies, would you send us a parcel of spices? We'll know by that you've won through, and Mrs. Thynne is partial to a bit of seasoning in her food."

That commonplace remark brought a gust of deep warm feeling into my heart so that I choked up and could scarce speak, but I managed to say: "God bless you, Mortimer! That I will!"

"And tell Tom he's to have no fears for little Hugh."

Half an hour later we were gliding down the bay with no sound but the faint plash of the oars, and dawn found us ten miles to the north of Port Jackson, our hearts lightening with every mile we put behind us.

XX

A THOUSAND LEAGUES

Our boat was of the kind furnished to many of His Majesty's ships, and known as a launch; her length was twenty-two feet, and her beam six; she was remarkably dry in ordinary weather. We had reason to be grateful to the men who designed and constructed her. She was rigged with two masts and lugsails. We were eight on board, but she would easily have carried twelve and sailed the better for it.

We had a little beef and pork, a bag of flour, and a small one of corn fetched for the fowls. As I have said, we had a pig, the rooster, and four hens. The vegetables, carrots, turnips, onions, and cabbages amounted to about fifty pounds' weight. Tom and I had our muskets, a fowling piece, and a good supply of powder and ball, while Goodwin had fetched a fishing net, as well as hooks and lines, saw, axe, hammer, and nails, in the sea chest where his chart, compass, and quadrant were stowed. For water, we had one five- and one ten-gallon keg; and — a most important item — Ned Inching's eight quarts of rum. Last of all, and most useless so long as we should be at sea, Nick and Dan had their bags of sovereigns stowed away in the chest.

At dawn the wind made up stronger. We lowered the mainsail, unstepped the mast, rigged a pair of stays to brace the foremast, and set to work to make all snug. With the folded mainsail, we made a bed for Bella and her son in the bows, where they lay, wrapped in Dan's watch coat. An icy spray was beginning to blow over the quarters each time a wave overtook us; Goodwin sat at the tiller while the rest of us disposed our chilled bodies as best we could on the bottom boards, sheltered in some degree from the wind.

And so it went, throughout that day, and the night, and the day that followed. On the evening of the second day, Dan estimated that we had run two hundred miles or more. We had been edging in toward the land all afternoon, while he studied the coast attentively. Just before sunset, he pointed to the surf-battered shore.

"Get forra'd, Hugh," he ordered. "There's an inlet yonder. Trim the sheet while I bear up a bit."

A headland lay close to larboard, with what appeared to be an inlet beyond, guarded by a bar on which the sea ran very high.

"It looks ugly, but we'll chance it," said Dan. "It's not breakin' so heavy at the far end."

The change in course made the boat roll violently, while spray and solid water sluiced over the rail. The boat flew on, as if eager to reach a sheltered anchorage.

Presently we rose on a great sea and shot forward into the turmoil of waters on the bar. For a long minute it was nip and tuck, despite Dan's quick eye and steady hand on the tiller; then, with water ankle-deep in the bilges, we sped forward on even keel into a landlocked bay, or river mouth, bordered by low hills clothed in bush. We rounded-to in the lee of a long, wooded point and paddled till the keel grounded on sand.

We soon had a fire going at the foot of a low cliff. When we had cared for the livestock, we gathered by the hearty blaze, turning this way and that to let the heat soak into stiffened joints. We were weary and chilled to the bone and gave little thought to food. As soon as we had dried our blankets, we stretched out on the sand and fell asleep.

I have never revisited that northern coast and do not know to this day whether our refuge was Harrington Inlet or the great bay behind Smoky Cape. During the week we spent there I saw no sign that the country was inhabited, and the birds and beasts were so tame they seemed unacquainted with their enemy, man.

There were no kangaroos about, but the smaller animals of the same kind, called wallabies, were plentiful among the rocks. One of us hunted every day, while the others plied the fishing net and scraped up a supply of dirty reddish salt from the rock pools above the reach of all but the highest tides. Garth was forced to go off out of earshot while we slaughtered her pig; his flesh was cut in thin strips, well-rubbed with salt, and hung in the sun, with wallaby meat and what fish we were able to secure. When we set sail on a fine morning with the breeze at southeast, we carried full water kegs and a fortnight's supply of food.

Four hundreds of miles of open sea still lay between us and the Great Barrier Reef, and the distance was increased because of our need to hug the coast. We met with no great storms and were deeply thankful that wind and sea refrained from showing the full majesty of their might. Only at intervals, when we discovered a bay or inlet which enabled us to land, were we able to refresh ourselves on shore. We saw the sun but rarely, throughout this part of our voyage; the sky was as grey and cold as the sea. Sometimes, for forty-eight hours together, we sat huddled on the thwarts, drenched with rain and spray, the strong southerly wind seeming to freeze the blood. And we bailed until our weary hands could scarcely hold the scoops. There were days when we had little to eat, and others when we had nothing at all, but Nellie was bound our cock should not lack. She fed him a few grains of corn at a time, and stowed his crate forward, in the driest part of the boat. The spirit in his little bedraggled body was never daunted; on rare mornings when the sun came out and he was placed on a thwart to warm himself, he would flap his wings and crow with a right good will, as if to encourage the rest of us. His small heart seemed a reservoir of courage as boundless as the sea itself.

Throughout this time, we had the prospect of the Great Barrier Reef to cheer us. Its southern extremity, we knew, lay somewhere about the twenty-fifth parallel; once we were within its shelter, we could promise ourselves a voyage of comparative ease, for more than a thousand miles, until the time came to leave the continent of New Holland behind, and push out across the open sea once more, toward the Dutch East Indies.

We fell in with the Great Reef which shelters the coast from Moreton Bay to Cape York, and passed three days and nights of misery while searching for an entrance. The wind held strong at S.S.E., so that we were able to skirt the formidable Barrier closely enough to gaze beyond it at the calm waters within, the wooded islets, with their promise of rest and refreshment, and the faint, blue outlines of the distant main. Safety was there, but between us and the longed-for haven stretched the reef, where the great westward-rolling combers piled up in awe-inspiring fashion, crashing upon the Barrier in geysers of foam and broken water. Twice we thought we had found an entrance, and came so near to disaster upon discovering our mistake that we needed all of our resolution to approach so closely again, especially since the wind now shifted to full east, blowing directly onshore.

But Providence was with us. Late in the afternoon of a cloudless day, we found an entrance, all of a quarter of a mile wide, and sailed in without mishap. There before us, only a few miles distant across the lagoon, lay an islet that seemed heaven itself to our weary hearts. It was scarcely a mile in extent, rocky and barren, covered with clumps of harsh scrub, but at one end a sandy spit sheltered a little bay as smooth and clear as the waters of a mountain lake. More than a week had passed since we had last set foot on shore. Of water we had plenty, thanks to the rains that had so drenched and chilled us, but not a morsel of food remained in the boat save Nellie's bag of corn. Weak and stiffened as we were, we made shift to gather oysters and other shellfish before night set in, finding them so abundant in the rocky shallows that half an hour sufficed to obtain more than we could eat. We rested and refreshed ourselves at this place for two days, and set sail with life and hope renewed.

We sailed on to the north, day after day, in the midst of a silence that seemed never to have been broken since the beginning of time. I was conscious of a feeling of mingled awe and exhilaration in traversing these unknown regions. So far as we knew, no white man had ever passed this way before. Captain Cook, after his discovery of Botany Bay, had sailed north well offshore, not entering the Barrier until he had reached latitude thirteen or thereabouts, near the Endeavour River, where he hove down his ship for repairs.

Good fortune now followed us as if in recompense for the miseries we had endured. We were within the tropics, and cold weather a thing of the past; the trade wind held warm and steady between S.E. and E., speeding us on our passages between the islets where we camped almost every night. Water was to be found on many of the larger islands; only on rare occasions were we obliged to risk a brush with the blacks by filling our kegs on the main. It was now spring in these latitudes and the sea birds were beginning to lay; their flesh and eggs, boiled or roasted, provided us with many a meal. Great flocks of bronze-wing pigeons flew out each evening to roost on the islands, and a single discharge of my fowling piece often brought down half a dozen fine birds. We ate shellfish until we wearied of them, and when we drew our net we often liberated the half of the catch. Fish of a hundred wholesome kinds were here, in numbers that made us think with regret of the poor folk in Sydney. Twice we captured huge turtles, come on shore to deposit their eggs, and feasted like aldermen on the rich greenish fat and flesh.

In memory I can see our boat at anchor in any one of a dozen snug island harbours, our camp pitched, our beds of dry grasses ready prepared under the stars, and all hands gathered about the fire to roast our birds or fish. The rich juices dripped upon the coals with sharp hissing noises, sending up spurts of vapour that made our bellies quiver with anticipation. And the best sauce to whet our appetites, if whetting were needed, was the recollection of Port Jackson fare. Our brave little cock throve with us. Once within the Barrier, his grain was saved for the lean times ahead, but he grew sleek on fish and flesh and oysters, and the tidbits he discovered for himself as he roamed at will on shore. There was no fear of his straying. A call from Nellie would bring him back as fast as legs and wings could carry him.

One circumstance of our voyage within the reefs both surprised and reassured us: the small numbers of aborigines to be met within these regions. Sometimes, after dark, we could make out the faint points of light that marked their fires on the mainland; now and again, when the breeze was light, we saw smoke rising from some promontory. We had learned enough in Port Jackson to know that white men have no reason to fear these people in small numbers, provided that nothing is done to arouse their anger or suspicion. Though we had firearms in case of need, we were well content to avoid meeting parties of the natives, and only met them close at hand on two occasions.

Once, in a bay on the main, we surprised a small party whom we took for three generations of a single family. Their astonishment at seeing us was increased when we shouted greetings in their own speech or something akin to it. They lost their timidity by degrees, and before nightfall we were able to place ourselves on friendly terms with them. We camped on the shores of the bay for two successive nights, and while we kept watch, I think that we might have slept in perfect confidence, for they were as quiet and peaceable as country folk in England. On the last day, we drew our net and shared the catch with them, much to their delight, and when we set sail they accompanied us in their canoes, shouting and laughing in their efforts to keep pace with us, till the wind freshened and we left them far astern.

On another occasion we were camped on an island well off the coast, and three or four miles from a second larger island to the east. Shortly after daybreak, when we were making ready to sail, Tommy Goodwin came running to say that he had spied five canoes, approaching from the direction of the main. As always, we had taken care to screen our fire from view the night before, but we now believed that it must have been seen, and that the savages were bound for our island. For all our muskets, the prospect of facing so large a party was disquieting. Our boat was hidden in a cove below the camp, but we could not reach her without exposing ourselves to the view of the blacks. Carrying our weapons, Goodwin and I crept to a rocky promontory whence we could look down upon the approaching flotilla. To our great relief, it was soon clear that they were bound not for our island, but for the larger one beyond it, though they passed directly beneath our hiding place and not thirty yards offshore. We were well screened by bushes, and I have never forgotten that strange and intimate view of a savage tribe going about its affairs in complete ignorance of any observers. The canoes were made of bark, and larger than any we had seen; each carried fire, built on sand contained in the shell of a giant clam. The folk of all ages were naked and several of the women had infants at their breasts. One ancient crone was broiling fish over the coals in her clam shell and tossing them aft to her companions, who doused them in salt water and gobbled them up, bones, entrails, and all. A tall, skinny fellow stood in another canoe, polishing the haft of a spear, talking with great animation as he worked and making strange comic gestures which set the others to laughing heartily. A small boy sat behind him, with his head resting against an old woman's knees. He had a white sea bird, tethered by a long string of bark, and watched it intently as it fluttered back and forth high overhead. There was much talk and laughter and shouting as the flotilla glided swiftly by. Presently the canoes vanished to the eastward, in the dazzling track of the sun.

That was our last sight of the aborigines. A sense of our loneliness drew us more and more closely together as we moved slowly northward between the twin immensities of land and sea. For all save Bella Goodwin this was a time of increasing hope and confidence. She seemed to have lost all interest in living, to be fading gradually under the influence of an illness which was more of the mind than of the body.

Many an evening on shore, when Tommy was asleep at his mother's side, the rest of us would gather for talk of plans for the future, taking it for granted that we should succeed in reaching England. I recollect one night in particular, our twentieth inside the reefs, when these matters were discussed until the small hours. We sat by our dying fire on the shores of the bay, whose still waters were like a nether sky, bright with the reflections of the stars. According to Goodwin's calculations we were no more than two hundred miles from Cape York, the northern tip of the continent.

"Are ye certain of the reckoning?" Garth asked.

"I'm not far off," said Goodwin. "If the breeze holds, we'll be clear of New Holland in four-five days."

"Damn my eyes!" exclaimed Tom Oakley. "As close as that? Can't ye smell home in the air, lads?"

"That's the smell I'll live on, the rest o' my days," remarked Sabb.

"What d'ye mean by that?"

"Grant we win through, and with Dan to lead us, I'll warrant we will. What then? Ye know what happens to convicts escaped from transportation."

"Aye, if they're catched," said Inching. "But they'll never nab *me* again!"

"Ye'll go back to London, and picking pockets?" Sabb asked.

"What else? It's my trade, ain't it?"

Nick shrugged. "Suit yerself, Ned, suit yerself. I've nothing but good words for the trade; but if ye're set on climbin' a ladder to bed, go back to London. Ye'll not have the pleasure of my company. I'm for Holland."

"What'll ye do there?" asked Oakley.

"My nephew's carried on in London, if he ain't been hooked. I'll set up a branch in Rotterdam. Holland's a brisk market for jewels, and trinkets too pretty to melt down. There'll be a rosy future for the pair of us. . . . Where are ye for, Tom? Ye mean to run straight?"

"Ye can lay to that!" said Oakley, with a grim laugh. "I'm for Wiltshire, once we reach home; ye'll see no more of me in London! I'll work hard and save every sixpence, and soon or late, Tom Oakley, under another name, mind ye, will have his own string of horses, and money put by. . . . What of yerself, Dan? Will ye be safe in Suffolk?"

"That's to be seen," replied Goodwin. "I'd the luck not to be took at home, but on the Norfolk coast." He turned to me. "Would there be work and a decent living yonder in America?"

"Work?" said I. "You'd find it the day you landed. New England's the place for you, Dan: Boston, or Salem. They can't build and man ships fast enough to keep up with their trade!"

"Say ye so? We might do worse," said Goodwin, thoughtfully.

Presently the others stretched out on their beds of grass, under the stars. I walked down to the beach, where our boat lay in the shallows. Here, in the coolness and vast hush of the night, I found myself truly believing, for the first time, that we might yet reach England. Heretofore I had not permitted my thoughts to stray beyond the boat itself, the camps we made, the events of our daily progress. Now I found pleasure in letting them fly on before us, traversing in a flash of time the thousands of leagues of sea that stretched away ahead, to England, to America, to Canada; and so real were the scenes conjured up by imagination that I seemed to breathe the fragrance of Sally's very presence, to feel her nearness in an all but physical sense. Quebec . . . it was there I would go from England, as fast as ships could take me. In my longing for the day to come I dreamed myself already there, stepping along some narrow street of the ancient town, on the last five minutes of my quest for Sally. I fancied myself standing on the doorstep before her aunt's house, raising the brass knocker to announce my presence, seeing the doorknob turn . . . but even in fancy I could go no further. Time and space widened again on the instant, and I felt a pang that was close to despair as I returned to an awareness of the present moment. In the mind's eye I saw the American brig far out on the Pacific, with Sally standing at the bulwark, thinking of me, perhaps, as I was thinking of her. And the huge round bulk of the planet must yet be placed between us before ever our paths could begin to converge.

*   *   *   *   *

For eight days we had camped in a cove sheltered from easterly winds, where a run of sweet water found its way down to the beach. To the north the sea, as far as the eye could reach, was strewn with reefs and bars innumerable. To the west was a great opening set with mountainous islands, which Goodwin declared must be the passage through which Captain Cook had worked his ship twenty years before. If he had not mistaken his reckoning, this would be our last camp before pushing out to open sea and the Dutch East Indies. Both fish and game were plentiful here, and we soon laid in and salted provisions sufficient to carry us through the last leg of the voyage to Timor. Of bread or breadstuff we had none, save for two or three pounds of corn, and we had no intention of depriving our cock of this scanty ration. Our fish and wallaby meat was well salted and dried and ready to stow in the boat. Water was our chief concern, but we estimated that, by allowing a pint a day to each person, our fifteen gallons should last us as many days. If the trade wind held, Timor should be no more than ten or twelve days distant. Had it not been for Mrs. Goodwin, our prospects would have seemed brighter than at any time in the past.

Although we avoided speaking of her condition, we realized that Bella had come to the end of her tether; she would die here, or on the passage to Timor. She had sunk rapidly during the previous fortnight. Each time we went ashore, Dan had carried her, for she was too weak to stand, and now she lay in a kind of stupor, scarcely conscious of what was taking place around her. Whatever his feelings, Dan had kept his own counsel until the evening when all was in readiness for proceeding.

Tommy was already asleep at his mother's side. Garth sat on watch by the sick woman, who had taken no food the day long. Dan rose, with a nod to Oakley and me, and we followed him to the beach.

"Lads," he said, "this is our last camp. It's open sea, now, to Timor, with never a dot of land between, laid down on the chart. I wish your advice. Can Bella support the voyage?"

"No," said I.

"We must wait, Dan, till she picks up a bit," said Tom.

"That would be my wish," said Dan, "but I've the rest of ye to think of. The season's far advanced, and the monsoon due to shift. With luck we've a fortnight to fetch Timor before the westerlies set in. If we don't clear out quick, we're stuck here till May or June."

"Dan," said I, "this is a thing for you to decide."

" 'Tis bitter hard . . . but Bella's done for: that's plain truth. God help her, I doubt she lives through another night." He walked up and down before us for some little time; then he said: "We're obliged to go on, but for Bella's sake I'll ask ye all to stop here two days more."

That length of time was not required. Bella died the following morning, with Goodwin and Nellie Garth sitting by her. The rest of us had gone with Tommy to a sandy islet half a mile beyond the entrance to the cove. Garth met us at the beach, upon our return, and we knew at once what had happened. She went off with Tommy to a rocky headland at the far end of the beach, and her warm motherly heart found the way to break the news to the boy, and comfort him.

We buried the lad's mother in the night, when he was sleeping, and marked the lonely grave with a border of sun-bleached coral fragments. North, south, east, or west, there were no other white folk within a thousand miles. The sun had just risen when we rowed out of the cove. The breeze was blowing fresh and fair. We hoisted sail and bore off to the westward.

*   *   *   *   *

The memory of the sixteen days' voyage to the Dutch Indies is still such a horror to me, for all the intervening years, that I shall pass over the events of them with the briefest possible mention. The horror was concentrated in the last three days of the passage, although the anxiety, the weariness, the hard struggle to fetch land, then within view, began on the tenth day. Nothing went amiss during the first week, once we had groped our way through Endeavour Straits to the open sea. The breeze was light but fair, and so it held until, by Goodwin's reckoning, we were within two hundred miles of our destination. It then became lighter, but at the end of seventy-two hours we had on our starboard beam a glorious sight: the shadowy outlines of a mountainous land, so far distant that the bulk of it was below the horizon. At first we doubted the land was there. The sky was clear, but the moisture-laden air, shot through with dazzling sunlight, played tricks with vision. The faint bluish outlines would vanish, and we would again see, or think we saw, the empty horizon line before us. So it went all that day, but a little before sunset we doubted no longer. Away to the north we saw what appeared to be a group of small islands, but we had good reason to believe that they comprised the highest peaks of a single body of land. It was thanks to Tommy Goodwin's sharp eyes that we had not missed it altogether, for it lay abeam and far to the north. We did not then know that it was not Timor, but the neighbouring island of Roti that we saw.

No sooner had we hauled our wind to fetch it than the breeze failed us. We must have been a good twenty leagues off at the time. We took to the oars and toiled under a sun that seemed to suck all the juices from our bodies. The breeze made up at nightfall but came right in our teeth, and we made boards all that night and the following day, but I doubt if we gained three leagues in the direction we would go. We were just at the change of the monsoon and what little wind there was came from north to northwest. Then it fell dead calm and remained so.

For three days we had not been able to touch the remains of our fish and wallaby meat. Of necessity, they had been so imperfectly dried and salted that they had gone rotten in the heat; the mere sight and the smell of them set us to retching. But thirst, not hunger, was the torment. We had so little water left that we were obliged to cut down the ration to a quarter of a pint, issued at noon. Our brave little cock that had gone through so much with us had his just share; indeed, he had more than the share needed to keep life in his small body. We were bound that he should survive with Tommy and favoured them both in issuing the ration. With one of the blankets we made a shelter for them in the bow where they could lie protected from the pitiless sun. Of the six adults, Ned Inching best supported the horrors of thirst. Sabb's was the most alarming condition. The thick bitter mucus on his lips and tongue made it all but impossible for him to speak.

I have only a nightmarish recollection of the last thirty-six hours of a voyage of a full thousand leagues. I recall, vaguely, Nellie Garth kneeling beside me as she poured a few drops of water between my swollen lips, and my feeling of shame that she, a woman, should have outlasted myself. But, God bless her faithful, generous heart, knowing the woman she was I might well have been ashamed of being ashamed.

The last thing I remembered was Nellie lifting me to a sitting position on the floorboards.

"Hugh, look yonder!" she said, thickly.

A large ship lay becalmed about two miles distant, her dingy brown sails hanging limp from the yards. And between her and ourselves, a boat, rowing four oars or six, I couldn't be sure which, appeared and disappeared as she approached us over the glassy sea.

XXI

THE PARTING AT SNAPENESS

THE ship was the Dutch barque *Amstel*, homeward-bound from Timor, via Batavia and the Cape of Good Hope. Her captain was named Dykstra, a broad-beamed, broad-faced man of fifty, with the heart of a saint hidden in his squat body. Castaways in our desperate condition might well have aroused the pity of any ship's company, but Captain Dykstra and his men showed us a humanity that, by reason of our long experience as convicts and outcasts, gave us a renewed faith in the innate goodness of the generality of mankind. At the end of a week we were all fully recovered.

We were letter-perfect in the story we had planned to tell in the event we reached one of the Dutch settlements. We were castaways from the American brig *Rappahannock*, from Baltimore, in Maryland, with a cargo of rum, tobacco, and tierces of beef which we had expected to exchange in Peru for silver and hides. But the Spaniards would not permit us to trade there, and James, our mythical captain, had laid a course across the Pacific to India via the island of Otaheite, in the South Sea. We had found our way through Endeavour Straits, and just beyond, on a dark stormy night, a strong current had set us on a reef where the ship was lost. Captain James had been killed by the falling of the mainmast. At daybreak, the rest of us had managed to launch our three boats, but we had become separated from the others within the week and had never seen them again. Nellie was supposed to be the captain's wife.

Captain Dykstra, who spoke a little broken English, accepted this story without question, and when we reached Batavia, where we lay for the better part of a month, he was good enough to offer us a passage to Europe. We had informed him of the extent of our resources. Nick Sabb's leather guinea bag was far from its old weight, but he had remaining one hundred and eighteen pounds. Goodwin had the sixty pounds brought out from England — not a penny of it had he spent. Captain Dykstra agreed to take us for the sum of one hundred pounds down, the rest to be paid when we reached England. This left us with a sum sufficient to buy what clothing we needed and to pay for food and lodging during our stay in Capetown. At Batavia, owing to the pestilential climate of the place, Captain Dykstra permitted us to lodge on shipboard.

We had a good passage to Capetown, and on an evening early in December came safely to anchor within half a cable's length of the place where the *Charlotte* had lain, on the passage to Botany Bay. British, Dutch, and French Indiamen were at anchor in the bay; great numbers of scoots plied between them and the quay at the east end of the town, loading and unloading cargo, or fetching water and provisions from shore. Dykstra informed us that he was obliged to stop here for the better part of a month whilst the *Amstel* underwent repairs. Both Goodwin and I had made ourselves useful as seamen during the passage to the Cape, and now Dan, who was a first-class shipwright, offered his services to the captain, who gladly accepted them. Tommy remained aboard with his father. As soon as permission was received from the authorities, the rest of us went on shore to one of the humbler lodginghouses on the outskirts of the town.

Capetown, in those days before the English occupation, was a bit of Holland, set down in Africa, and inhabited by a greater variety of races than could be found in any European city. The wide streets were laid out at right angles with the greatest order, and the houses, of whitewashed masonry, in their well-tended gardens, looked as if they were scrubbed every day, from ground floor to attic. The burghers strolled along the waterfront in the cool of the evening, or sat in their gardens, drawing in stolid content at their great porcelain pipes. Seamen of many nationalities wandered in bands and crowded the public houses to drink the fiery Cape wine. Heavy wagons drawn by several span of oxen, and laden high with casks and bales, rumbled through the streets, managed with great skill by their Kaffir drivers, who cracked long whips of rhinoceros hide. The Dutch had brought numbers of Malays from the East Indies, and they gave a touch of gay colour to the scene, in their embroidered jackets and bright-coloured kilts.

We were more than wary when we first came ashore, fearing that other transports for Botany Bay might be lying in harbour, or, worse still, that some of those of the Second Fleet, homeward-bound, might appear in the offing. But our luck held. The only English ships in harbour were four outbound Indiamen, and three of them sailed within the week.

Captain Dykstra had made his report of our rescue to the Dutch authorities. Goodwin and I were called in to give further details, which were all written down with Dutch thoroughness. Our chief concern thereafter was to make no slips in conversation, for the names we gave the Dutch authorities were, of course, fictitious. But as we knew no one in the town save our landlady, who spoke no more than a dozen words of English, we managed very well.

Nellie, Oakley, and I passed many a pleasant afternoon walking out to the open country where we were free to talk over old times and make plans for the future. It was at this time that I pleaded hard with them to go on with me to America. Garth considered the proposal with deep seriousness. She knew that she could never again feel safe in England, but I could not draw a definite promise from her. Oakley would play with the notion of joining me; sometimes he would say: "By the Lord, Hugh, I'll come, and I'll fetch Nellie if I have to drag her along by main force!" Then he would think of England, and if ever there was a man who loved his country, it was Tom. His enthusiasm for America would fade, and he would outline plans for his future as a breeder of fine horses, once he had gotten on his feet again.

Sabb and Ned Inching passed their time soaking in sunshine in the garden at the back, and playing cribbage for hours together. With the excellent and more than abundant Dutch food provided by our landlady, Nick's belly began to resume its old proportions. He wore the same wide cowhide belt I remembered so well when I first saw it enclosing his huge paunch in Newgate. His "belly-gauge," he called it, and he had a name for every hole the full length of it. Three holes from the outer end was his Cloak Lane hole which marked his girth at the time he was nabbed and sent to Newgate. Two holes farther in was the Newgate State Side girth. Then, in succession, toward the buckle end, came the *Charlotte* hole, the Botany Bay hole, and last, a truly astonishing distance toward complete deflation, was the Famine hole, where he had fastened the belt when we were living on one-quarter rations of powdery, worm-eaten rice and rancid pork.

One afternoon, Sabb and Inching went into the town for the first time since we had come ashore. We were all in a happy frame of mind, for Goodwin had come to tell us that the *Amstel* was again ready for sea, and that Captain Dykstra planned to sail in two days' time, weather permitting. Dan had left Tommy on board; the lad loved nothing so much as a ship, and was the pet of all the *Amstel's* company. Dan stayed for supper and spent the evening with us. Nellie had gone to bed, and Goodwin was about to return to the *Amstel* when Sabb and Inching arrived. Nick's round face was flushed and beaming, and he had one arm around Inching's neck, the latter striving hard to hold him on even keel.

Nick Sabb "shaking a cloth" was as merry a sight as a man could wish to see; there was nothing mean or savage in his character. I had seen him in a doleful humour more than once, but never in an ugly one. His usual mood was one of bland, imperturbable good spirits, and when he was in his cups this heightened to a quiet, belly-shaking gayety: every man was his friend, and every passing moment a joy to live through. Inching liked his glass as well as another, but I never saw him drunk. He could pour an astonishing amount of liquor down his skinny throat and still be as sober as Sunday.

Sabb halted just inside the door, and in leaning back to get us into better focus he would have lost his balance had not Inching, who was behind, braced himself to receive Sabb's weight.

"Steady on! Ned, are ye there?

> "Oh-h-h, 'tis for our good, me hearty lads,
> We pass the hours away.
> We'll have a frisk without the risk
> Of a squabble or a fray,"

sang Nick, in a voice as melodious as that of a costermonger's donkey.

Ned peered round from behind.

"Fetch 'im a chair, Tallant," said he.

"Aye, Hugh, ye cloud-pushin' giant, fetch me a chair! Call me cut if I walk another step!

> "Oh-h-h, 'tis for our good, me hearty lads,
> We sing the hours away . . ."

Nick sank into the chair with a thump that only the stoutest piece of furniture could have withstood.

"What's this, Pinch-Guts?" said Tom. "Where've ye been?"

Sabb sat with his hands clasping his broad knees, mellowing us like a harvest moon.

"Well may ye ask, Tom! Well may ye ask!

> "Oh-h-h, we'll have a frisk without the risk
> Of a squabble or a fray."

He peered cautiously around the room where the candle-light cast wavering shadows upon the walls. "Are we all friends here? Who's the broad-as-long yonder?"

"It's Dan," said Tom. "There's none here but ourselves."

"Good! More than good! . . . Ned, ye weasel!" Sabb broke off and his belly shook with a hearty chuckle. "Lads, it's been a night of nights! I ain't enjoyed myself so much since the time, years gone, when I buried the old woman."

Inching, who had been standing by this while with a proud grin on his leathery face, now took a chair. His skinny form, or, better, the coat with the roomy pockets which hung upon it, seemed to be all lumps and corners.

"Now sit ye quiet, Ned," said Sabb, "whilst I praise ye to the heights of heaven. . . . It was like this, Tom. As ye know, Ned and me has sat in this house as demure as a pair of mutes at a funeral, and ye've me to thank for it. All the yearnin' for a pocket that wasn't his came back to the shrimp yonder the minute he first set eyes on the fat Dutchmen strolling along the quays, flashin' their silver snuffboxes, with the gold fobs to their han'some gold watches hanging from their waistcoat pockets, and the watches tickin' 'Take me! take me! take me!' so loud ye could hear 'em a good half-mile away; leastwise, Ned could. None of ye marked him, mebbe, as we was comin' through the streets the day we landed, but I did. I feared I'd never get him safe indoors, and when 'twas done I kep' him here. 'Ned,' says I, 'we've been saved by the Dutch, fetched here by the Dutch, fed by the Dutch, and we'll be carried home by the Dutch. If ever I see that quick little hand weaselin' toward a Dutch pocket, I'll shout "Thieves!" as sure's me name's Nick Sabb!' I made him see the light o' reason, but he'd ha' gone blind again, to all but the pockets, if I'd not kep' him alongside o' me day and night.

"Then comes this Hugh Tallant, three days back, to tell us the last of the India ships was to sail for Calcutta this very night. Says Ned, 'Nick, there ain't no harm thievin' from them that's been robbin' the poor folk of India these fifty years past and cartin' the loot home by the shipload.' Says I, 'Never in the world! They're our own kinfolk ye might say, and if they had their deserts they'd be carted by the fleet o' shiploads to Botany Bay.'. . . And that's why I've give the lad a run out for a breath of air."

"And air is what he's fetched home?" asked Tom.

Sabb peered around the room once more. "Ye're certain all's safe here? Landlady abed?"

"Hours since," said Tom.

"Then, ye blessed little Satan's apprentice, show 'em what we took," said Sabb. "Quiet, now!"

Ned began to disgorge. First came three handsome snuff-boxes, two of silver and one of blue enamel, with a picture on the lid of a sea fight between two first-rates. Three gold watches followed, and a dainty little round-bellied scent bottle of crystal glass, such as a lady would carry in her reticule, overlaid with gold filigree work of the most exquisite design. A superb brooch came next, a miniature of His Majesty, George Third, set round with sapphires mounted in a narrow gold band. All of these articles were wrapped in handkerchiefs, and the last item of the loot was a dozen solid-silver apostle spoons. The latter were fine examples of the silversmith's art, the handles being the figures of the apostles. These were wrapped in a large linen napkin splotched with fresh wine stains.

Oakley stared, first at the loot, then at Sabb, then at Inching.

"Have I said he was the neatest-handed rogue in the trade?" asked Sabb. "Away with 'em, Ned! Here's the key to my chest. Hide 'em well toward the bottom. Was it a good night's work, Tom?" he added, as Ned climbed the staircase to their room.

"I'll warrant that," said Oakley, gravely. "There'll be a hue and cry raised the morn that'll land the lot of us in quod. Aye, a fine night's work! And us all but safe home!"

"Never ye fret," said Nick. "We saw the last boat, with all the nabobs and their servants aboard, pull off to the ship. She'll be gone, come daylight."

"That's to be seen," said Goodwin, grimly. "If we're caught and sent back to Botany Bay, I'll save the hangman a job for the pair of ye."

Sabb sobered at once.

"Dan," said he, "the fault is mine; I know it well. I shouldn't ha' let him out o' my sight. But, damn my eyes, he worked on me sympathies, so I said he could have a buzz through the streets if he'd be back in an hour's time and promise he'd lift no more than a handkerchief or two, just to be certain his hand was in as good as ever."

Oakley laughed in spite of himself.

"And he comes home with a load to break a horse's back! Where the devil could he ha' took the apostle spoons?"

"I'm comin' to that," said Nick. "This being the last night afore the Indiaman was to sail, the officers, with the nabobs and their ladies goin' out as passengers, hired the han'some supper room at the tavern up against the public gardens. Ned ran into the crowd lookin' on from outside. All the light there was in the street came through the windies where the nabobs was dancin', with the cold collation to come. There could ha' been no holdin' Ned then save I'd been by to put him down and sit on his head."

"And why wasn't ye?" Tom asked.

Sabb had his excuses ready, but they boiled down to one: he was still too weak in the legs to walk far. He admitted, however, that he had had a hand in the taking of the apostle spoons. Ned had rejoined him at the public house, and they were just on the point of coming away when two of the stewards from the Indiaman, who had waited on the guests at supper, came into the public house with the hampers containing the linen and silverware brought ashore from the ship.

"They was sloppin' over with the wine they'd drunk arter the nabobs left," said Nick, "but they came in for a nightcap on the way to the boat landin'. And w'ile I talked with 'em, Ned was improvin' his mind with the twelve apostles."

There was no sleeping for Oakley, Goodwin, or myself that night. Tom and I were at the waterfront at the crack of dawn, where we found Goodwin staring out to sea. A fresh breeze was blowing, and far down the bay we saw the Indiaman outward-bound, with all sail set.

"God be thanked!" said Tom.

*   *   *   *   *

Our passage north from the Cape was a tedious one. The broad-beamed old *Amstel* was almost as slow as the *Charlotte,* but we were homeward-bound at last.

The incident I best remember on the voyage occurred on the day we left Capetown, when the lot of us were standing at the bulwark with full hearts, watching the coast vanishing in the haze. The day before, when Tom was laying in a few comforts for the voyage, he had discovered an old copy of the *London Chronicle,* evidently left at the Cape by some English vessel. It contained a long item about the sailing of the Second Fleet from Portsmouth, and beneath it was a treasure of poetry and unconscious humour — to us, at least — under the title: —

BOTANY BAY

or

The Felons' Farewell to England

May we, sad exiles to a barb'rous shore,
Removed from all that lured to guilt before,

With cheerful hearts the horrid journey speed
And learn to make a virtue of our need.
Atone our crimes to Britain and our God
By useful labour in that drear abode;
With patient toil the dismal desert grace,
Improve its wild, uncultivated face;
Mark the rude site of our Colonial town
And earn the willing settlers' modest crown.
Th' untutored Blacks shall faith and friendship find
And own we left our vices all behind.
England, farewell! Thy stern though generous hand,
Granting us mercy in a distant land,
We kneel to bless, while fresh and favouring gales
Convey us to our haven, New South Wales.

There was delightful reading indeed for us. As Nick said, he could all but weep at the thought that we were bound in the opposite direction.

I think that Captain Dykstra had a pretty shrewd notion before the voyage was over as to how matters stood with us, but he never so much as hinted at this. He had taken a great liking to Goodwin, and the two often sat in the great cabin till past midnight, smoking their pipes. They may have opened their minds to one another concerning the smuggling transactions in which Dutch and English seamen so often joined forces. It was late in March when the *Amstel* wallowed through the Strait of Dover, edging in toward the Suffolk coast when we had passed the Thames Estuary.

The sky was overcast that afternoon; the North Sea was grey and calm, and the light westerly breeze barely enough to fill our sails. Harwich and Felixstowe were off in the haze on the larboard beam. Goodwin stared at the flat Suffolk coast without a word. It was his own land where he was born and bred; he knew every hidden path, the windings of every salt creek in the marshes. The sun set and the grey light faded. The *Amstel* lost steerageway, turning slowly eastward as if she longed to be off for Holland and the end of her voyage.

At the time we were rescued, Captain Dykstra had taken our boat on board, and now, in exchange for it, he gave us a little boat of his own to go ashore in. Our leave-takings were of the briefest. It was pitch-dark, but I can well believe that the eyes of the others were as moist as my own as we shook Sabb's hand.

"Good-bye, ye rogue," said Tom. "Where do we meet again?"

"Not in England, Tom. No, no! But ye can get word o' me from my nevvy. Ned'll be able to find him."

"And now ye'll rob the Dutch in Rotterdam, the folk that's been so kind to us?"

"Never in the world," said Sabb. "What I do is this: my nevvy'll send me the lurries took from them that can well spare 'em, and I sell 'em to the Dutch for half their worth." He chuckled as he added: "Damn my eyes if I ain't got a pretty little stock to start with, thanks to Ned."

"See to it, Nick, that you send your address to your nephew," I said. "Tom and I won't be easy till we've paid you what we owe."

"Will ye hush about that?" said Nick. "I got the worth of it ten times over when ye was hackin' down the gum trees yonder in a place I'll spare to mention."

The boat was lowered and the ladder put over the side. Nellie climbed down with our little cock under her arm. Thanks to her excellent care, he was as full of life as ever he'd been. Nellie said she meant to breed a new race of fowls with him as sire. We made our hearty, grateful farewells to Captain Dykstra and his men, and followed into the boat. Dykstra leaned over the bulwark.

"Gootvin," said he, "if efer you vant a jop, come to me."

"Aye, aye," said Dan, and we pushed off.

Lights were few on this lonely stretch of coast, but Dan

steered confidently. Nearly two hours had passed when we entered a wide shoal inlet where packs of widgeon whistled on the tidal flats, and plover wailed in the darkness overhead. The tide was beginning to flow once more. The channel wound inland through a desolate region, half sea, half land. We turned into a creek that led off the main channel, and presently, glancing over my shoulder, I felt rather than saw dim trees on a slope of rising ground, the masts of a lugger stranded on the tidal shore, and the lights of a few distant scattered cottages. Steering with uncanny skill, Goodwin turned the boat into a narrow drain through which the tide was flowing soundlessly, and brought up alongside a jetty of piles driven into the mud. A slimy ladder led up to a plank walk.

"We're home, lads," he said, quietly.

He led the way along a well-footed path, through a copse and across a field. We passed a cottage where dogs barked and a door was flung open, but Dan gave a peculiar whistle, and the door closed once more.

"That's old Jasper's cottage," he said. "I can't get it through my head I ever been away."

We halted before a cottage at the far end of this tiny village. Dan pounded on the door and entered without waiting for a response.

Sitting in a low chair with a candle on the table beside her was a little old woman with snow-white hair showing from beneath her cap. She wore a pair of steel-rimmed spectacles and was bent over a worn, silver-clasped Bible which she held on her knee, her finger moving slowly along the lines as she read. She glanced up vaguely, peering over her spectacles, but finished the verse she was reading before she laid the book aside. Goodwin strode across the room and lifted her in his arms, as though she had been a child.

"Well, Granny," he roared, putting his lips close to her ear, "here I be again!"

He set her down, and the old woman stood with her hands on his shoulders, looking up at him.

"I ain't surprised, Dan'l. I ain't a mite surprised. I knowed ye'd come, soon or late. Where's Bella and Tommy?"

She was very nearsighted and had not observed the rest of us standing by the door. Even as she spoke, Tommy had his arms around her neck, hugging her close. The scene was the more affecting because of the restraint shown. You might have thought that Dan had come home after an absence of seven days, instead of more than eight years. She greeted us with just the little touch of homely formality which the occasion demanded, and listened in silence while Dan told her of Bella's death. But there was no display of emotion over the news. Suddenly she got briskly to her feet.

"Bless me, ye pore starved creatures! Here I be a gossipin' and ye'll be wantin' yer tea!" And away she bustled to the kitchen.

We were soon seated around a spotless deal table with two huge platters of smoked herrings before us, with plenty of bread cut in thick slices, and sweet country butter. There was tea for Nellie and Tommy, and a pitcher of home-brewed ale, refilled three times, for the rest of us. Oakley's eyes glistened as Dan poured out a foaming pot for him. He took a long pull and set down the pot with a sigh, wiping his lips with the back of his hand.

"Now I *know* we're home," he said.

Old Mrs. Goodwin was so deaf that it was all but impossible to converse with her, but she chattered on to Dan, trying to give him the gist of eight years' news in as many minutes. She would skip round to press her cheek against Tommy's and urge more food upon him.

"Bless my soul, ain't the boy growed! And he ain't forgot his granny, have ye, Tommy? Dan, he pledges to be a bigger man than yer father. He does, so!"

"Where's Howard?" Goodwin roared, when we had finished supper.

"Up yonder with the horses. They ain't gone yet. They'll be comin' by directly."

"Now ain't that just the way it ought to be!" said Goodwin. "Granny, there's naught amiss with my lugger?"

"She's just as good as when ye left. Trust Howard for that."

Howard was Goodwin's younger brother. We had a brief glimpse of him a few moments later when a pack train of a dozen horses, each of them well loaded, passed the cottage in single file, with as many men walking with them. Goodwin went out to meet them and was gone the better part of an hour. When he returned, he closed the door after him and stood by it with a well of content, all of eight years deep, in his heart.

He shook his head wonderingly. "There ain't no use," he said. "I just can't bring it home I ever been away."

We stopped for two days at Snapeness. The village was like a score of others on that east coast. The life of its people, ostensibly farmers and fishermen, had been based on smuggling for generations past. There was a little public house, and a dozen or more cottages. Two fine luggers belonging to the Goodwins lay in the creek, and nets hung on frames to dry. The arm of the Law, long as it is, did not appear to reach into these hidden tidal creeks and estuaries.

Nellie Garth, at the warm insistence of Dan and his grandmother, decided to stay on at Snapeness until she could lay plans for the future. Oakley was for Warwick and Inching and I for London. Dan ferried us across the broad tidal river to set us on our way.

"Yon's the path through the ma'sh," he said. "It'll fetch ye to the lane where ye turn left to come out on the Ipswich Road. The best o' luck to ye, lads. I needn't say there's a hearty welcome here whenever ye choose to come."

We gripped his hand and hastened on, not wishing to linger over the parting.

Tom was for the village of Weston, between Leamington

and Coventry, by way of Stowmarket and Cambridge. We had a hurried meal together at Ipswich, and had no more than finished when Oakley's coach arrived.

"Well, lads?" said Tom. "Hugh, look to yerself in London! I could wish ye was able to make yerself invisible, like Ned here. Above all, mind this: there's knaves and to spare like that police sergeant, Kneller, would give their eyeteeth to nab any one of us. It's forty quid they get as blood money for any man caught who's returned from transportation. No need to say what *we'll* get if we're took."

"Never fear," I said. "I'll not be long in London. Where will I get news of you, Tom?"

"I'm blessed if I know, yet. . . . See here — how'll this be? I've heard ye speak often of the New England Coffee House, on Threadneedle Street. It'll be a good safe place to send ye a line. How'll I direct for the name?"

"Write Hugh Bagehot. That was my mother's name."

Tom climbed to an outside seat, the guard played a strain of "All Ye Bright Faces" on his horn, and away they went. Oakley stood waving until the coach vanished at the bend of the road.

Ned and I reached London late that same night. As we drove along Cheapside we were held up by a crowd gathered around another coach, outward-bound, that had collided with a market gardener's wagon. There must have been a hundred people looking on as the guard and the driver of the wagon stood cursing each other with something past eloquence. The fronts of houses on either side stood out clearly in the light of a pair of torches, and I could see heads in the upstairs windows regarding the spectacle as though seated in boxes at the play.

"Tallant, I'm off," said Inching, with a grin, and before I could say a word in reply, he slid down from the coach and vanished in the crowd.

XXII

AT TOWER HILL GARDENS

I REACHED London with four pounds, eight shillings and sixpence, and a decent outfit of clothing, bought in Capetown with Nick Sabb's money. To make my small capital last as long as possible, I took cheap but respectable lodgings at four shillings a week, over a saddler's shop in Parker's Lane, not far off High Holborn. Knowing from past experience that I might again be reduced to a state close to beggary, I resolved to perform my one important errand whilst I could present a respectable appearance. This was to call at the New England Coffee House in hope of getting some word of Mr. Fleming. I knew that he had planned to return to London and felt certain that he would have come long before this. But when I called at the Coffee House I found everything changed. Of the servants, there was not one I remembered, and Mr. Fleming's name was unknown to the new management. My conclusion was that either Fleming had come and gone long since, or had not come at all. I felt more than ever forlorn and lonely. Although I had never admitted it, even to myself, I had cherished the belief that I would surely find him.

I had not needed Tom Oakley's word of caution to realize my danger in London. The eyes of the city's constables and their recollection of a face or figure were sharpened by greed, for there was at this time an iniquitous system of rewards known as "blood money" by means of which police constables were spurred on to add to their meagre wages. A partial

list of these rewards is as follows: For taking a housebreaker
— fifty pounds. A murderer — fifty pounds. A counterfeiter of gold or silver coin — forty pounds. A counterfeiter
of copper coin — ten pounds. A robber of the King's stores
— twenty pounds. Apprehending a felon illegally returned
from transportation — forty pounds. And so down to a five-
shilling reward for taking into custody any idle or disorderly
person.

It was not, of course, iniquitous for a constable to be mindful of his duty. The evil of this blood-money system lay in
the fact that the police would leave petty criminals at large
until their arrest became profitable. They would keep a pro-
prietary eye upon them in the early stages of their criminal
careers; even encourage and "build them up" in crime. "He
doesn't weigh forty pounds yet" was the common saying
amongst them; and so they would wait, encouraging the
wretches they meant to seize later, giving them a false sense
of immunity until they "weighed their weight." Then they
would pounce upon them and suck in the blood money with
the ferocious delight of the spiders they were.

There was one such spider whom I particularly loathed and
feared. His name was Kneller; I had often seen him at the
Old Bailey Sessions House during our trial there, and also in
Newgate. He haunted the prison. His cruel rapacious face
could be seen half hidden in some pit of shadow in the gloomy
corridors. He would watch the prisoners who passed, stamp-
ing their faces and figures upon his mind for later use. He
was said to receive more blood money in the course of a year
than any dozen constables in London.

It was Kneller whom I imagined always at my shoulder as
I made my way along the quays and docks of Wapping, on
the search for some ship bound for America. The luck which
had held all the way from Port Jackson to Snapeness seemed
to desert me now. With England still at peace, half-starved
men haunted the river in hundreds, thousands, looking for

berths as seamen. Day after day I went up one side of the river and down the other, visiting every ship bound for America; and the result was always the same: no seamen wanted.

And so I was driven by hunger to my old occupation of lumper, unloading cargo from East and West Indiamen for the most part.

At this time, the Thames from the Upper Pool by London Bridge, downstream past the Horse Ferry to the Mooring Chains at Deptford, was a nest of water thieves on both banks. The police were helpless against them for the reason that they had no such close-knit organization as did the river thieves. There were hierarchies of the latter, from the Light and Heavy Horsemen, as they were called, down to the Mud Larks at the bottom. The lumpers were the Heavy Horsemen who broke out cargo. Coopers, rat catchers, and boatmen comprised the Light Horsemen.

When a ship was ready to discharge cargo, the watermen were ready with their boats and lay close by in the darkness. The lumpers broke out the tiers of casks in the hold. The coopers pretended to repair the heads of the casks, having first removed as much of their contents as they could manage to steal without detection. All worked with feverish energy, filling their black-strap bags and passing them along to the waiting lightermen and their assistants. Sugar, coffee, tea, spices, tobacco — everything portable went into the bags. They also had bladders furnished with nozzles, and these were filled with wine or spirits by means of a pump called a jigger, and tubes calculated to reach casks in any position. In addition to the black-strap bags, the plunderers wore an under-dress known as a "jemmy," with capacious pockets before and behind, and long narrow pouches attached to their legs beneath their wide trousers. In the case of a ship having a rogue of a first mate or purser, the thieves would pay as high as fifty pounds for the privilege of unloading that particular vessel.

They could well afford to, for the take in a single night, in an unguarded ship, often amounted to from three to five hundred pounds.

In my sorry plight I must confess that I was tempted to join these rascals, for I might easily have robbed enough in a week to buy me a first-class passage to America. I did not, however, and the result was that the others became suspicious of me. I had worked only a fortnight when I was discharged by the man who had hired me, and, word having been passed round that I might well be a spy in the pay of shipowners, no other boss would have me. Down to penury I went once more, earning a few pence per day as a porter and crossing sweeper.

My home at this time was a "Lodginghouse for Travelers" on a woefully miscalled Love Lane, in Wapping. Here I paid tuppence a night for the privilege of sleeping on a straw paillasse infested with the vigorous, sleepless descendants of countless generations of bugs and lice. There was one long narrow room lighted by the doorway and two unglazed windows in the same wall. It had accommodation for a hundred or more outcasts, and at the inner end was a fireplace where we were permitted to prepare our bits of food, in case we had them. Here were wretches in every category of wretchedness: boys and girls who lived by beggary, theft, and prostitution; Irish street peddlers, chimney sweeps, barrow women, porters and crossing cleaners like myself, ballad singers, blind beggars, real and fictitious — the homeless of both sexes and all ages, many of them here to-day and gone to-morrow. The very food we ate was stolen, for the place was visited, morning and evening, by young roughs known as "finders," who carried bags suspended from their necks, and sold at one-third the market price fish stolen from Billingsgate Market, chines and shins of beef, tripe, vegetables hooked from costermongers' carts, and, of course, gin, the one necessity of these folk.

At night, pigging it in our common room, I saw sights I have no desire to describe, and heard conversations that might have jarred the complacency of many a London citizen.

I slept in this place for three months; then something happened that drove me to the refuge of the streets. It was an evening late in August. I had had a good day at parcel carrying and returned to the doss house with a full belly for the first time in a week; but I was very weary and went early to my so-called bed. I was awakened sometime after midnight by the proprietor of the place shaking me by the shoulder.

"Up wi' ye, Cully!" he said, in a low voice. "P'lice is here! I'm obliged to shake 'em all out."

There was one lighted candle on the table near the centre of the room. As I got drowsily to my feet, I remember thinking: —

> How far that little candle throws his beams!
> So shines a good deed in a naughty world.

Then a chill of apprehension swept over me. What was it the man said? Police? I peered through the gloom toward the far end of the room, and there I could make out four men, police sergeants without a doubt. At the same moment I felt, rather than saw, that one, carrying a lantern, was Kneller.

The place was packed with lodgers that night, and the landlord was slow in arousing so many. He was helped by the others, save Kneller, who stood where he was, swinging his bull's-eye light with a kind of blood-chilling jauntiness, as a saunterer, at peace with the world, might swing his cane while strolling in the park. With despair in my heart I ranged myself with the others; we stood in a single line in the aisle that ran down the middle of the room between the rows of beds. The police were, I knew, in search of someone they had reason to believe had taken refuge here. The lodgers waited in a tense sullen silence as the constable with the lantern, accompanied by two others, started down the long line, flashing the light into the face of every man he passed, and holding it there as he scrutinized his features. In the deep gloom the concentrated light from the bull's-eye brought each face sharply out, so that it seemed to be detached from any body. The man was Kneller; I knew that before he had moved five paces in my direction. One of the constables guarded the door at the far end of the room. Quickly and quietly I buttoned my jacket, preparing to make a dash for it. Not a dozen lodgers remained between Kneller and myself. He moved slowly, and I could see the delight he took in the awe and terror he inspired: this was one of the secondary rewards of his position as an arm of the law.

Of a sudden he seized the man before him by the collar, and jerked him out of the line.

"By God, here he is!" he exclaimed.

"No, no, sir!" cried the wretched victim. "I've done nothing, sir! Indeed I haven't!"

The voice and the words were those of a man of considerable refinement, which seemed to add to Kneller's pleasure.

"No, no, sir! Indeed I haven't!" he mocked. "What d'ye call yerself?" he added, harshly.

"Robert Martin, sir. I'm a clerk . . ."

"Oh . . . Robert Martin, is it?" said Kneller, in the same tone of savage mockery. "Well, well! Will ye hearken to that, now!"

With that he gave the man so violent a shove that he fell at the feet of the attending constables. These yanked him up, drew his arms behind his back, and locked a pair of handcuffs on his wrists; then, without another glance at the rest of us, as though we were so much dirt under his feet, — and glad I was that he so regarded us, — he marched out, the others following with the victim between them.

That was my last night in the rat warren of Love Lane. The week that followed was a desperate time. At the end of it I moved across the river with all my possessions in a small bundle. I had a pair of razors my mother had given me before I left Canada, and the clothing bought in Capetown, which I spared to put on, for the thought of having it gave me comfort. I was dressed in a seaman's jacket and a pair of Osnaburg trousers I had bought at second hand months before. I walked to that true home of misery, Lock's Fields, — of misery, but, for the most part, of honest misery. The inhabitants of this forlorn suburb were decent folk — weavers and other artisans fallen upon evil days, but who had not lost that most precious of attributes, self-respect. The relief of being amongst people of this kind once more is past my power to tell. I had not one penny when I came, yet I was taken into the home — and a true home it was, for all the poverty, clean and neatly kept — of a weaver obliged to live on the pitiful wages of two days' work per week. His boys, of twelve and thirteen, earned more than their father as parcel carriers and linkboys, turning their hands to whatever offered in the way of employment. Their mother had the wholesomeness, the courage, the love for order and cleanliness, of Nellie Garth, and both she and her husband were determined not to be ploughed under by Fate. This little family welcomed me, penniless, as though I had been an honoured guest, but I was soon able to contribute my share to the small earnings that kept a roof over their heads.

My debt to this cheerful, unconquerable family is beyond computation. They lived on the very brink of disaster, yet, somehow, managed to avoid being swept over it. They gave me a renewed belief in human kindness, in human dignity. Their name was Holt.

A curious thing in life is that, when a man seems to be at the end of his rope, the meeting with others in the same situation who refuse to accept defeat will inspire the first with the same courage, and, often, bring a sudden upward trend in his fortunes. Such an influence the Holt family had upon my own fortunes, and when I remember what came of it, what I owe to this heroic family, I am overcome with gratitude too deep for words.

I resolved to have one more try at a seaman's berth in some American ship; therefore, one morning when I had dressed in my decent clothing once more, I set out to make the rounds of the shipping on the Wapping side of the river. I carried with me my only possession, the razors my mother had given me. Failing to get a berth, I planned to attempt bribing some third mate or boatswain to let me stow away. I walked hopefully and confidently, my chin up and my shoulders squared. I felt like Hugh Tallant for the first time in months. And I found a berth on the very first ship I boarded.

It was the American brig *Sterling,* from Portland, Maine, unloading deals by Wapping New Stairs. She was to sail for home in about three weeks' time, and her captain and his mates belonged to the Holt category of human beings.

The captain looked me over with shrewd kindly eyes, whilst he questioned me briefly about my seamanship. Then he said, "All right, young fellow; you're hired. Come back this day fortnight and ye can sign on."

If ever a man has walked on air, it was Hugh Tallant as he hurried toward London Bridge to return as quickly as possible to his friends the Holts.

I was just by the Custom House, below Tower Hill, when I spied a solidly built, elderly gentleman carrying a walking stick, with a young woman at his side, strolling in the same direction as myself, and not thirty paces in front. My heart all but stopped beating. I halted in my tracks for an instant, then ran forward. The man was Mr. Fleming, and the girl, Sally Munro.

I ask permission to pass briefly over the events of the next few hours, for how could I describe them? Even now, after the lapse of more than forty years, my pen trembles in my hand at the recollection of the moment when I stood before the Custom House with Sally in my arms, unconscious that there were any but ourselves in the crowded, busy street. Mr. Fleming stood by, vigorously blowing his nose with a handkerchief the size of a napkin, as though he took joy in the exercise of his lungs, and still greater satisfaction in the trumpetlike blasts he could produce with such ease.

Presently he said: "Hugh, I shouldn't wonder but you've visited the Tower Gardens?"

"I have, sir, often," I replied.

"Many a tragic event has taken place on Tower Hill," said Mr. Fleming, "and, no doubt, many happy ones. My guess is that the happiest ever is due to come now." With that he walked off, but turned to call back: "Dinner's at five, but, damme, it can wait till midnight if necessary!"

I doubt whether, in the venerable history of London, two people have ever been so happy as were Sally and I as we strolled up to Tower Gardens and seated ourselves on a bench screened from view of passers-by; and, screened or not, it would have made no difference, for we had no consciousness of others there besides ourselves.

I had been pardoned — freely and unconditionally; this was the first news Sally gave me as we sat, with hands clasped, looking down over the river. And now I will put into a few words what needed hours to say. I struggled for a good quarter of an hour trying to convince myself, with Sally's help, that I was, indeed, free, with no need to cast furtive glances over my shoulder, no need to fear the future. Sally then informed me that my mother had died before the departure of the First Fleet, without learning of the ten thousand pounds' compensation granted us at about that time. Presently we spoke of ourselves, beginning with the day when the captain of the American brig, having waited for twenty-four hours off Botany Bay, would consent to wait no longer for the boat, despite Sally's prayers and entreaties. He believed, what Sally herself deeply feared, that we had been caught in attempting to leave the harbour.

Upon arriving in Boston, Sally had sailed for Quebec, where she stopped with her aunt. Once there, she had written to Mr. Fleming, at Digby, Nova Scotia, acquainting him only with the fact that she had a matter of great importance to communicate. She received a reply from his nephew informing her that Mr. Fleming had returned to London, and giving Sally his address. After six weeks in her aunt's home, she had sailed for London, where she found Fleming living in Queen Anne Square. He had long believed me dead, but upon learning the true state of affairs he immediately set about the task of trying to obtain me a pardon. The record of the Tallant family during the American War, and my own part in it, worked strongly in my favour. Mr. Fleming was able to enlist the influence of Sir Joseph Banks, President of the Royal Society, and other influential Londoners, with the result that the pardon was granted. Sally's plan was to carry it herself to New South Wales, and on this same morning she had gone with Mr. Fleming to inquire about the next ships for Port Jackson. They had learned that two supply ships were expected to sail in either January or February.

*   *   *   *   *

Sally and I were married in mid-September, and went for a fortnight to a forever memorable inn at Eastbourne, near Beachy Head. The coast was lonely and beautiful in the early autumn, and we had one week of all but perfect weather, although had it been English weather at its worst, I should have called it perfect. In a hired coach with a pair of spirited horses, we explored the country on either side of Eastbourne, to Dover and back to Hastings. It was our first sight of the battlefield where William defeated Harold, but I fear we thought little of one or the other at the moment. We made long excursions on foot, and spent hours on the great promontory of Beachy Head, watching the ships pass back and forth through the Strait of Dover. The time was so filled with happiness that, if I chanced to be alone for ten minutes, I found myself doubting its reality, and I would hasten back to Sally to be reassured. And Sally, God bless her! had no trouble whatever in convincing me that she was anything but a wraith.

We settled into Mr. Fleming's small Georgian house as though we belonged there, and he assured us we did. During the weeks that followed we laid plans for the future. I had no desire to return to Maryland, even though I should be permitted to. That incomparable region held too many happy memories for me, overlaid with too many sad ones. We talked of Canada, New England, the Western Reserve, even the West Indies, as a possible home, but at last we half decided upon England. Mr. Fleming loved England only a little less than Maryland, and he had long since made his decision to remain there for life. He urged us so strongly to follow his example that we found our interest awakening at the prospect, the more so because he recommended with such enthusiasm a small estate near Halstead, in the Colne Valley, which he himself had been sorely tempted to buy.

The end of it was that Sally and I set out to look at the place in Mr. Fleming's chariot, with his man, Peters, on the box. The next morning we turned west, following the Colne Valley to Halstead through a countryside so beautiful in the golden autumn mists that we loved it on sight. The house was all that Mr. Fleming had claimed for it, and having examined it from attic to basement, we spent the rest of the day in walking over the estate, convinced that nothing we might find elsewhere, within our means, could equal this retired, enchanted place. There were seven hundred acres with the Colne running through them, and four tenants upon the land whose forbears had lived there for generations. The place was to be had for eight thousand pounds.

Sally and I were so taken with it that we were tempted to arrange for the purchase then and there; but we were both practical people, not given to making such an important decision on the spur of the moment. We spent the night at the Halstead Inn, where we discussed the matter until past midnight. The following morning we informed the bailiff that he would have our decision in a month's time.

Our journey into Essex had a double purpose: to visit the Colne Valley estate and to go on from there to Snapeness, to see Dan Goodwin and Nellie Garth, if she were still there. Goodwin's village lay some forty miles beyond Halstead. We drove at a leisurely pace by way of Colchester to Ipswich, where we spent the night. Snapeness village was not an easy place to reach. At Woodbridge we crossed the Deben, and turned toward the coast on a lonely road, scarcely more than a cart track that led to the hamlet of Shottisham. There we were obliged to leave Peters with the carriage and proceed on foot, along a path bordering the wide marshlands.

We quickened our pace when the Goodwin cottage came in sight, and at that moment we spied Tommy Goodwin coming toward us with a dip net over his shoulder. The lad stopped short, staring at us for all he was worth; then he turned in his tracks and sped toward the cottage, shouting, "Dad! Miss Sally and Hugh! Miss Sally and Hugh!"

Next moment Goodwin himself appeared, his ruddy face beaming with pleasure. Nellie Garth was right behind him. She hastened forward and folded Sally in a huge embrace.

"Well met, Hugh! Well met!" said Goodwin, wringing my hand. "But how's this, now? God bless me! I can't rightly believe my own eyes! Come into the house and set ye down!"

There, in all truth, was a happy meeting. Old Mrs. Goodwin was there, and Dan's brother, Howard, just such a rugged, broad-shouldered fellow as Dan himself, but some years younger. We talked the morning through and it seemed as if we had only begun to tell one another all that we had to tell. But the happiest news, to Sally and me, was that Dan and Nellie had been married only a fortnight earlier. Tom Oakley and I had often spoken of this possibility during the voyage home in the *Amstel*. We both wished it with all our hearts, but had not dared hint of it to Dan; and whatever he and Nellie may have thought, they kept their own counsel.

Toward midafternoon Sally and I were compelled to return to Shottisham. Dan and Nellie walked with us halfway, and it was then Dan told us of his plans for the future. He and Nellie and Young Tom were soon to sail from Bristol for America.

"We've talked it over this way and that way," said Dan, "and now we've settled down to goin', with the passage money laid out and all."

"Dan," said I, "you couldn't make a better move. Where are you bound?"

"For Boston, in New England. Ye've told me that seamen, fishermen, boatbuilders, and the like, don't come amiss there."

"Amiss!" said I. "Rest easy, Dan. You'll find work from the day you land, and have your own boatyard, or fishing business, — what you please in that line, — before you've been in the country two years. There never was such a place as New England for a stirring, thriving fellow like yourself."

"Hugh," said Nellie, "d'ye recollect the talks we had about America when ye was stoppin' with me at Wood End? Ye got me fair in the notion of goin' there, though I little thought, then, 'twould ever come to pass."

"I've a snug little capital to start with," said Goodwin. "My uncle here bought my lugger." He smiled as he added: "And I ain't done so bad at my old trade since comin' home. I been twice to Holland and once to France."

"Nellie, you've had no word of your old friend, Mrs. Windle?" Sally asked.

Garth shook her head.

"I'd a mind to write her, but I don't dare risk it, Sally, that's the plain truth. There never was a better friend and neighbour than Sarah Windle, but if I was to write, she'd get that stirred up and excited she might let out a word without meanin' to. No, I wouldn't dare risk it, though I'd give the world and all to see her."

We had Shottisham in sight when we halted to say our farewells. We lingered for another half hour, delaying the moment as long as possible as the sunlight mellowed toward evening. Presently Dan stepped forward quickly and gripped my hand, whilst Nellie took Sally in her arms and kissed her on both cheeks.

"Night promises fair," said Goodwin, gruffly, and with that he and Nellie turned and strode away homeward without a glance behind.

*   *   *   *   *

A fortnight passed, and neither Sally nor I had made up our minds about the Colne Valley estate. There was not one objection to be set against its desirability as a home; in fact, most of our discussions were concerned with pointing out to each other its undoubted merits. We were convinced that we might search the whole of England without finding another place that so completely met our requirements. For all that, no word was sent to the agent in Halstead.

I became more and more restless and uneasy as I considered the prospect of spending my life in the tame, long-settled English countryside, but I concealed the fact from Sally — at least, I thought I did. She went quietly about our affairs as though assuming that we would soon make our decision, but she never pressed me toward it.

One day when Mr. Fleming had gone to his club to enjoy a rubber of whist, I came into the library in a more than glum frame of mind. The newspaper was lying on the table. I took it up casually, and stretched out in an easy chair to glance through it. On the front page, in the lower left-hand corner, my eye was arrested by the following announcement: —

FREE SETTLERS FOR NEW SOUTH WALES

His Majesty's Secretary for Home Affairs has announced that Government will show special consideration to countrymen possessed of capital amounting to five hundred pounds or more, who signify their desire to emigrate to New South Wales. Grants of land will be accorded them at a nominal price per acre, to be paid over a long term of years; and, under certain conditions, convicts will be assigned to them as labourers. It is felt that great opportunities await experienced and industrious settlers, and that there is good land and to spare for as many as may wish to emigrate. Such settlers, with their families and household goods, will be transported free of charge, whenever space can be found on the transports or store-ships.

The brief autumn afternoon was almost over. A drizzling rain fell steadily outside. The newspaper dropped to my knees and I stared at the fire. In the mind's eye I saw Sydney Harbour rippling under the bright Australian sun; the hazy ridges of the Blue Mountains, distant and mysterious, shutting in no man knew what rich valleys and limitless green plains. I seemed to feel the warm westerly breeze on my face, scented with the aroma of untrodden forests.

The door opened, and Sally came into the room. She sat on a low stool behind me, and I handed her the newspaper.

"There's an interesting announcement on the first page," I remarked.

Sally glanced at me as she took the paper, and quickly found the announcement. I could not see her eyes as she read, but I knew that they were dancing along the lines. She put the paper aside.

"Hugh, do you mean it?" she asked.

"Do I mean what?"

"That you would like to return to New South Wales?"

"Would you?"

"Yes," she replied, quietly, without a moment's hesitation. "I've wanted to speak before now, but . . . tell me, truly: you wish to go?"

"Sally, there's nothing in the world I'd rather do than accept the Government offer."

"Then we shall," she said, her eyes shining. "I could never be happy in England. I've known it from the moment we visited the Colne Valley place. It's beautiful — everything it should be for . . . for Englishmen. But not for us. In my case, I suppose it's my father's fault. I was brought up on the edge of the wilderness. I've been trying to pretend for your sake, but it's useless."

"For my sake! And I've been pretending for yours!"

"Listen!" Sally went on eagerly, taking my hand and holding it in both of hers. "We could do this: we could ask for land in that fine country you and Tom Oakley discovered. Hugh, it would be perfect for us! It's strange; when I think of New South Wales, and hardly a day passes that I do not, I forget the dark side. I remember only the glorious lonely land far beyond the settlement."

"There is no dark side, save in Sydney."

"I know. . . . Sometimes I think I'm bewitched. I long for the bright sunlight, the clean air, the smell of the gum trees, above all, the loneliness of the great wide land."

We were off, then. Forgetful of everything but the prospect before us, we talked the evening through, and half the night as well, after Mr. Fleming's return.

His final comment, when we separated, was: "Hugh, if I may be permitted to say so, you're a pair of young fools." His eyes twinkled as he added: "But there's no cure for it. It runs in the blood of all Americans — mine too. B'gad, I wish I were thirty years younger. There'd be three in the party!"

XXIII

"TO BE HUNG ON MONDAY"

THE autumn months passed quickly, and Sally and I were well forward with our preparations for return to New South Wales. We had learned that two supply ships were to sail early in the coming year, with accommodation for a few free settlers. Others beside ourselves were planning to take advantage of Government's offer to establish themselves in the colony, but we were certain that there would be none amongst them in our strange situation. We spent many an hour in making lists of everything needful to set ourselves up in the wilderness: tools and utensils of every kind, furniture, clothing, arms and ammunition — all the thousand and one things that must be taken to a colony at the far ends of the earth. I could half believe that the events of my life, from the time of my first arrival in England, had never happened; that I had never been a convict, and was preparing to go to the new colony as one of the American Loyalists, under the plan abandoned so long ago.

It may appear strange that Sally and I should have had any desire to return to a land where we had suffered so many hardships and privations, where the inhabitants were chiefly convicts, and where the future could offer us little save the hard crude conditions of pioneer life. As for the latter objection, it was not one to us. We came of adventuring pioneering stock, and the passion for unsettled country was in our bones and blood. But more than this, New South Wales had first brought us together, and we felt that our destiny was linked with that of the great unknown continent. Our longing to return was based on something beyond reason: it was of the nature of a deep compulsion. We never doubted that so vast a country contained land far richer than any as yet discovered. Never, during these months of preparation, did we regret our decision. On the contrary, we became more and more impatient for the day of departure to come.

One winter evening when we had returned late from the city, we found Mr. Fleming in the drawing-room at Queen Anne Square, with a copy of the *Morning Chronicle* on his knees. We had learned only that day that the transports for New South Wales were lying in the Thames at Deptford. We spoke of this to Mr. Fleming, with an eagerness that might better have been concealed; so I thought when I noted the air of concern with which he listened to our news. When Sally went up to dress for dinner, I made my apologies to this old friend who stood in the place of a father to both of us.

"You must forgive us, sir," I said. "We are nothing like so happy as we may appear to be, but this, I confess, is only on your account. If you were to come with us we would have nothing left to wish for."

"Nonsense, Hugh. Why shouldn't you be happy? I shall miss you sorely, in all truth, but it's not that I'm thinking of at the moment."

"What is it, sir? You've had no bad news?"

He hesitated, regarding me with deep concern.

"Yes . . . sad news indeed for you. My first thought was to say nothing about it, but I fear you'll have to know. You would certainly learn of it for yourself."

"Well, sir?"

"Hugh, your friend Tom Oakley has been caught. Evidently he returned to his old life again. He's in Newgate prison at this moment, under sentence of death."

I stared blankly at him, unable to say one word, as he

took up the newspaper and pointed out the following paragraph: —

Among the four men to be hung at Newgate, on Monday next, is the highwayman, Tom Oakley, who was condemned to death at the Old Bailey in January, 1787, for the robbery on the Bath Road of Mr. Reginald Baxter. His sentence at that time was commuted to transportation for life, and he was among the convicts sent out to New South Wales in the First Fleet Expedition, in the Spring of that same year. Six weeks ago, in a daring single-handed attempt to rob the Night Mail to Dover, a man who gave his name as Tom Ashe was caught and, later, arraigned under that name at the Old Bailey Sessions House. It was proved beyond question that he is none other than the convict Oakley, transported in 1787, and when his identity had been sworn to by no fewer than six witnesses, it was admitted by the prisoner himself. How this man was able to return to England is a mystery he refuses to explain. He will, probably, carry with him to the scaffold the secret of his escape from a penal colony at the far ends of the earth.

I read the paragraph over and over again, in such a state of numbed horror and unbelief that I could not, at first, grasp its significance. Sally came down a few moments later and I blurted out the news without stopping to consider how cruel a blow it would be. Tom had less than two days of life remaining to him. That the date of hanging had been set was proof that he and the three men with him had nothing to hope for.

"You must go to him, Hugh," Sally was saying. "If ever he has needed a friend at his side it is now."

"But how can I?" I asked, miserably. "Here am I, a free man, with life before me . . ."

"You know Tom better than that," Sally broke in. "If you stood in his place and he in yours, would you not want to see him?"

"I know I should."

"Then don't waste a minute, but go."

"To-night? I shouldn't be permitted to see him at this hour."

"Then send him word that you will come to-morrow. Send it at once."

"That's the best of advice, Hugh," said Mr. Fleming. "It's a strange situation, God knows, but delicacy of feeling has no place here. If your friend should think it best not to see you, he can let you know . . ."

"But he won't, Mr. Fleming," Sally put in. "I know he won't!"

"Then send him a note. Peters can take it and stay for an answer."

Never was a message penned with a heavier heart. It was necessary to tell Tom of my pardon, else he would never consent to see me. And if I were to go without warning, he would look at me stony-eyed, without a sign of recognition, thinking I had come at the risk of my life.

Peters returned two hours later. I could hear Tom's voice in the words that blurred before my eyes as I read them.

DEAR HUGH:

The old Newgate smell is as rich as ever. If you can suffer it for the sake of an old friend, you'll render a service to

Yours,

TOM OAKLEY

*   *   *   *   *

Sunday at Newgate. Of all the days of the week in that forbidding place, I had reason to remember it best. It was then that friends and relatives of the felons awaiting trial or transportation came to spend a few hours in their company. It was then that the idle and the curious of the fashionable world treated themselves to the thrill of a visit to that vast hive of misery — above all, on the Sunday before a hanging, when they could attend a last service for the condemned in the prison chapel, and see and speak with the wretches who had before them but one more day of life. Thieves, pickpockets, receivers of stolen goods, and other members of London's underworld entered the place with brazen temerity to confer with confederates in the toils of the Law. They would bring with them food from the cookshops, tobacco, ale, spirits, and spend the day with their cronies in feasting, drinking, and card playing, for little was forbidden in Newgate to those with the money to pay for license and privilege. And one would see there women of the streets, and ladies of leisure of a higher category in the profession. These latter, elegantly dressed and enjoying the stir they created, would parade the gloomy wards and courts as, on weekdays, they frequented Vauxhall, or Ranelagh, and the lobbies of the theatres. From the hour when visitors were first admitted, throughout the day, the prison would be thronged with folk of all ages, all classes and conditions; and over and about them, clinging to their persons like an invisible, unescapable spirit of evil, was the horrible prison smell.

I was at the main gate an hour before entrance time. The customary Sunday throng was already gathering; these early arrivals were, chiefly, the only folk who could be said to have legitimate reasons for a visit to Newgate — the sons, fathers, wives, and mothers of prisoners within, bringing with them what small comforts their scanty means allowed. Many were the very embodiments of want and misery, and they waited, with the forlorn patience of the desperately poor, the pleasure of Newgate's lords and masters.

I recalled the December evening, five years earlier almost to the day, when Oakley, Nellie Garth, and I had stood before that gate; and again I was seized by the confusion of mind one experiences upon waking from troubled and chaotic dreams, or after a long period of wasting fever, when reality seems, rather, to be unreality, and familiar objects torture the memory in the attempt to place them in the right relationship to past events. I had passed through such varied experiences in so brief a span of time and over so vast a portion of the earth's surface that I could scarcely bring home to myself the fact that I was, indeed, the man concerned in them. Vivid pictures crossed my mind, giving way with the swiftness of thought to others. I saw the smoking ruins of our old Maryland home as I had seen it three days after it had been sacked and burned by a war-maddened mob. I saw my sad, brave-hearted mother standing on the deck of the British troopship on the morning we sailed from New York for Nova Scotia, with two hundred other Loyalist refugees. I saw Nellie Garth, Tom Oakley, and myself at the prisoners' bar on the winter afternoon when we had been sentenced in the Old Bailey Sessions House, and Sally standing by the gangway in the *Charlotte*, turning her head quickly at the moment when the body of her father was committed to the sea, five hundred leagues past Capetown. I saw the convict, Emmet Jurd, hanging from the limb of a tree at Botany Bay on the very day of our arrival there, his body seeming to cast a measureless shadow across the land, as it slowly swayed and turned in the light of the westering sun. I saw our little band of eight, in Goodwin's boat, pulling with desperate haste toward the American brig, and seven of us standing by Bella Goodwin's lonely grave on the Cape York Peninsula.

These and many other pictures flashed across my mind as I walked slowly to the end of the street and turned to come back, and the grimmest of them all was there before me, in its reality: Newgate Street itself, flanked on one side by the prison, on the other by dingy three- and four-story buildings — shops, dwellings, decayed-looking ordinaries and public houses. To-morrow, at this same hour, every window in those houses would be filled with heads, and the street packed from end to end by a vast throng all gazing in one direction, toward the black-draped scaffold erected before the Debtors' Door.

I was aroused by a light touch on the arm and turned to find an old woman at my side. She might have been seventy, but looked to be an active little person. Her face was shaded by a bonnet and she wore a faded green shawl over her shoulders, fastened with a brooch. I caught the gleam of spectacles from within the shadow of the bonnet.

"Please, sir," she said, in gentle, quavering voice. "Can you tell me the hour? Has it gone nine yet?"

"It's getting on for nine," I replied, reaching for my watch. Then I stopped short. I had consulted my watch not a quarter of an hour earlier, but now I had no watch to consult. For a moment I could not believe it was gone. I carried it always in the same pocket of my waistcoat and knew I could have placed it in no other; nevertheless I made a startled search through all, even to the side pockets of my breeches. And no watch was to be found. Mine was a splendid timepiece, the work of Mr. J. Harrison, one of the best watchmakers in London; but far beyond this, it was Sally's wedding gift.

"Why . . . it's gone!" I exclaimed. Then I made a second frantic dive into my inside coat pocket. "And my wallet's gone, too! I've . . . I've been robbed!"

"Oh, sir, don't tell me that!" the old woman exclaimed, in a horrified voice. "You're certain you brought it with you?"

"Yes, I know I did," I replied, as I continued to search my pockets with both hands.

"Dear me, dear me!" She regarded me with an air of the most woeful concern. "Was it a valuable watch, sir?"

I was so horror-stricken at the realization that I had lost, not only my watch, but my pardon as well — it was in my wallet — that I scarcely heard her question, but I managed to reply: "It was a wedding gift from my wife. I wouldn't have taken a thousand pounds for it."

Of a sudden, with an all but incredible change of voice and manner, she perked her head to one side. "If ye prize it at that rate, would ye give a pint of ale to buy it home?"

she asked. It was Ned Inching, and I would never have recognized him save for the voice.

"Shhh! Step round the corner with me, Tallant. Damn my eyes if ye don't need a bodyguard when ye walk out! Follow me, now, and say naught."

He led me through a narrow lane and down a flight of steps at the end into a dingy public house. There was no one in the place save the man behind the bar. A silent knowing salutation passed between the two as Ned preceded me to a table in the corner. When we had seated ourselves, he leaned back, his arms folded, with the air of a mistress at a dame's school preparing to scold a naughty boy. Then his shoulders shook with the dry little cackle I so well remembered.

"You double-dyed rogue!" I exclaimed, so overjoyed and astonished that I could do little more than stare at him. The barman brought the ale, giving Ned a quizzical glance as he set down the pint pots, and the latter, with a nod of his head, sent him away about his business.

Ned removed his spectacles and polished the glasses with a corner of his shawl.

"Tallant," he said, ruefully, "I've not lifted so handsome a timepiece since we came home, and it had to be yours! I had it and the wallet stowed safe in my petticoat pocket afore I saw yer face. Rogue, is it? Who's the rogue but yerself, makin' an honest woman o' me against my wish?" He glanced cautiously toward the man at the bar, before he added, in a lowered voice: "Hark ye! Have ye no more thought o' yer neck than to show yerself in Newgate Street in the broad light o' day? Ye've changed — I allow that — but not enough to make ye safe. Far from it."

"You know why I came?"

"It's no hard matter to guess. Ye heard Tom Oakley's took."

"I'm going to see him."

"What! No, by God! Old Woman that I am, I'll hold ye away by main force!"

"Wait," I said. "You all but murdered me by heart failure just now, and here's the reason why." With that, I took my pardon from my wallet and passed it to him. His eyes widened as he opened and read it.

"God's truth! Was ever a bird so easy picked, so crop-stuffed with luck!" he said, wonderingly. "In the crowd yonder by the gate there's a good dozen in my line o' trade. Any one of 'em could ha' cleaned ye out, though not so quick and neat as myself. Where'd the precious paper ha' been then?"

For a moment I forgot the numbness of my heart as I pressed Inching for news. He had long since regained the self-respect he believed he had lost forever in being once nabbed by the police and transported. He was convinced, now, it never could happen again, and told me he had "done famous" since I had last seen him. Nick's nephew Timothy Sabb, was now his fence, though the place of business had been moved to a new locality since Sabb presided over it. As for Nick himself, he was prospering in Rotterdam. Inching had kept in close touch with him through the nephew.

Then he spoke of Tom, and for all his attempt to assume a hard, indifferent manner, I could see how sincerely he grieved for him. He took pride in the fact that Tom had returned to his old life on the road.

"And mind ye! 'Twas only by the cursed luck o' Satan he was took. I got that straight from them that know. There was four Navy officers took the Dover mail that night, after Tom had been tipped off as to who'd be in it. They done for him."

"You've not seen him?" I asked.

"Me? How'd I see him?"

"Ned, you could walk into Newgate with me as safe as going to church."

"So I could, but I'm not such a fool as to chance it. No, no! But wish him a stout heart for me, lad, though there's no need for that. He'll step onto the drop like he was walking to his breakfast."

I was more than a little concerned about entering the gaol, but Inching gave me some reassurance there.

"I doubt there'll be any to know ye. Four years in Newgate's a long time for keepers and the like. The blessed gaol fever cleans 'em out like the rats they be."

Presently he drained his pint pot and rose.

"I'll not keep ye. Stay here for half a tick till I'm in the street."

"Wait, Ned! Tell me where I can find you. We must be sure to meet again."

He gave me the ghost of a smile as he adjusted his spectacles once more and shook out the voluminous folds of his petticoats.

"Look to yourself if we do!" he said. "Damn my eyes! As handsome a watch as that and I had to fork it over! Are ye sure ye've got it now?"

"Never fear. I'll not lose it again."

"Then close it in yer fist, with the fist in yer pocket. And put the wallet inside yer shirt with yer arm tight against it. Damn my eyes if ye should be trusted out alone, but I'll hold ye in sight till ye pass the gate."

It was well past nine as I approached the entrance, and the press of the early visitors had been relieved. I joined the line moving slowly forward; then the horrible breath of Newgate closed round me once more. As I approached the wicket in the door leading to the inner gloom, I seemed to hear Oakley's voice, saying, as he had on the winter night so long ago: "Draw it in and be done with it, for it will never be done with you."

The face of the keeper at the wicket was strange to me.

"Who for?" he asked.

"Tom Oakley, alias Tom Ashe," I replied.

The man seemed to paw me over with his glance, then the door swung ajar and I was through. I knew what money could accomplish in Newgate and I was not sparing in my use of it here. The effect was magical.

"This way, please Your Honour! Thank 'ee and hearty, Your Honour! . . . You, Joe! Look sharp! Show the gentleman to Mr. Oakley."

Of the turnkeys on duty I was deeply relieved to see not one I knew. The man who led me along the maze of corridors with their black sweating walls was a cadaverous, pockmarked fellow with a brisk, knowing manner. I asked him how long he had been in service here.

"Eight months, Yer Honour. I was in Fleet gaol, afore."

"You like it better here?"

"That I do, sir! The pickin's in Newgate is 'andsome alongside the Fleet. I take as 'igh as two quid 'ere, of a Sunday."

"You're not afraid of the gaol fever?"

"Me? Not likely! They ain't nothin' can kill me. That's w'y I was shifted from the Fleet."

We turned into a long passageway closed at the end by a heavily barred door with another turnkey sitting by it. I slipped two half crowns into the hand of the man who had brought me and, with a surprised "Bless Yer Honour's nobility!" he left me with the other by the door.

"I'm for Mr. Tom Oakley," I said to this man, speaking in a low voice, "but don't announce me yet. I'll look on from here for a moment."

"As ye wish, master. He's just at the end of 's breakfast. There's two merry hearts, sir! They'll never die dunghill."

Through the grating I looked into a small, stone-paved, stone-walled court with a vaulted ceiling. It was backed by a row of doors with a barred window in each, leading to the cells for the condemned. A table spread with the remains of what appeared to be a sumptuous meal stood in the court, and there sat Tom Oakley with one companion, their legs in irons, though I was not aware of them at first glance. The gloom here was almost that of night, but the light of two candles brought into sharp relief the faces of the two men. Oakley was dressed at the top of his bent, and a striking figure he made in those surroundings, against the wall, like a curtain of gloom, behind him. He wore a handsome sky-blue coat and breeches, white silk stockings, and black shoes with silver buckles. His hair had been carefully dressed and the snowy stock at his throat set off his ruddy complexion that showed, in the candlelight at least, no trace of prison pallor.

The man seated opposite was a formidable-looking fellow, a full head taller than Oakley, and with the physique of a Thames bargeman. His newly shaven chin and cheeks gleamed with a bluish light, and he held a fork upright in a fist that looked heavy enough to have felled an ox. Two shabbily dressed fellows sat near the breakfasters and I guessed their errand at once. They were Grub Street hacks, in the employ of some publisher of Newgate annals, whose business it was to furnish the public, on execution days, with the life histories and so-called dying confessions of doomed felons. One had a drawing board on his knees and was making a sketch in profile of Oakley.

"Hold that for thirty seconds more and I'm through, sir," he was saying.

"Look sharp," said Tom, "and mind ye make no daub of me!"

"Never fear, Mr. Oakley. I've caught you to the life if I do say it. . . . There, sir," he added, a moment later, holding the sketch at arm's length. "Will that do?"

The blue-jowled man came round, with a clanking of leg irons, to stand behind Oakley's chair.

"By God, Tom! 'Tis yer very image!" he exclaimed. He turned to the artist with a ferocious scowl. "Why couldn't ye have done as well by me?"

"I'll try again, Mr. Thorne, if ye'll be pleased to sit," the other replied, in a frightened voice.

"What, Dirk Thorne! Would ye be prettified?" said Oakley, looking up at him with a grin. "Ye'd best be proud of such a mug. The nursemaids will weep for me, but, damme, ye'll be giving the half of London nightmares for a fortnight! I warrant ye sell ten to one against me to-morrow."

"So I will," said Thorne. He turned to the artist, still scowling but with a mollified air. "Away with it, for I'll sit no more. Fork out the quids, ye shrimps, and tell yer masters we'll have the stories here the first thing to-morrow. I'll have mine read afore they stretch me."

"Never fear, sir. They'll be at the printing all day and half the night. The lads will be hawking 'em in the crowds by daylight."

"Are they talkin' of us outside?" asked Thorne. "Does it look to be a big day?"

"That it does, sir," said one of the newsmen. "Every window across the way has been sold out long since. The best places have fetched as high as three guineas. If there's one there'll be twenty thousand in the streets moving this way, by six o'clock."

"Good, by God! We'll give 'em a show, eh, Tom?"

"Will we not, Dirk! Will we not!" said Tom. "Hi, you at the door! Send in the waiter to clear away here, and if the newspapers have come, tell him to fetch 'em at once."

I nodded to the turnkey; he unlocked the heavy door, pushed it slightly ajar, and clanged it shut after me. "Visitor for Mr. Oakley," he called.

XXIV

THE HANGING CHAPEL

SHADING his eyes with his hand, Tom peered in my direction; a moment later he had me by the shoulders as though trying to convince himself that I stood before him in the flesh. There was such a lump in my throat that I dared not trust myself to speak, at first.

He searched my face with an anxious glance. "Hugh, it's no lie? You're clear — your own man?"

I nodded, and he seized my hand in both of his.

"Lad! I couldn't rightly tell ye the comfort I take, knowin' that!" He turned to his companion. "Dirk Thorne, I'd make ye known to . . . but it's no matter for the name. He's my friend, the best I've got in the world."

"That's enough for me," said Thorne as he shook my hand. "In that case, ye'll have a word or two to say to each other, I shouldn't wonder?"

"That we have, and none so much time to say 'em in."

"Never ye mind for me," said Thorne. "Step into the cell, why don't ye?"

"So we will; 'tis a good notion. If I'm asked for, Dirk, say my agent's come and I'm makin' my will."

The cell was just such a cage as Tom and I had once occupied together in Newgate, except that this was for one occupant. It was furnished with a cot bed, a table, and two chairs.

"We're livin' like a pair of nabobs, Thorne and me," said Oakley, with a grim smile. "Food, ale, spirits, tobacco —

there's naught denied us save the right to walk out, and that comes to-morrow. . . . God bless ye, Hugh! Is it yerself and all? Sit ye down and talk fast, for there's the world and more I want to hear. But this comes first: have ye any word of Nellie or Dan Goodwin?"

I told him of the visit I'd made to Snapeness, of the marriage of Dan and Nellie and of their plans for leaving England. "They've sailed long since. They'll be in America as we speak of them," I added.

"Good go with 'em!" said Tom, heartily. "Ye've relieved me no end on Nellie's account. There's been many a night, Hugh, I couldn't sleep for thinking of her. If ever she'd been caught, she'd ha' been for it, certain sure. Nothing could have saved her. And now . . . by the Lord! She's safe! . . . Poor Bella! I'll put no slight on the dead. Many's the kindness the pair of us has to thank Bella Goodwin for; but I'm bound to say this: Dan's got the wife he merits at last."

"That he has," I replied, "and what better fortune could we wish for Nellie?"

"It couldn't ha' come better. . . . Hugh, if ever ye have word of 'em again, and I warrant ye will, soon or late, say naught o' this Newgate finish. Tell 'em I was well and hearty when ye last saw me, and that'll be no lie neither. I'll cast no shadow from here over the hearts of such friends as they be."

He sat leaning forward in his chair, elbows on his knees, staring at the shackles on his feet; then he glanced up with a faint smile.

"I can hear ye thinkin' it," he said. "Ye make the walls ring with it. . . . 'Tom! Tom! Why, in God's name! What-ever did ye go back to it for?' . . . Lad, we've better to speak of than what's past mending, but I owe ye a word, and 'tis all that's needed . . . rhino. I couldn't stick the want of it. I couldn't abide the layin'-up of the sixpences like I said I would. Slow and sure and safe it might ha' been, but it wasn't my way. There's no cure for the old disease, easy come, easy go: that's the sum of it in a breath, and . . . well, here ye find me. Will that do, for a lame reason?"

The old merry look came into his eyes as he leaned back in his chair. "That's done," he said. "Now we can talk, and ye'll not grudge me the right to set the tune, as ye might call it. D'ye recollect the bright cool morning, just after we'd settled in at Blackwattle Cove, when yerself and Goodwin and me . . ."

And then Tom and I were abroad again, and pictures of old happy days when, in search of game, we tramped together along the shores of the lonely bays and coves of Port Jackson came into mind with such vividness that we could all but forget present time and place and circumstance. Never has an hour of life seemed so precious, so woefully brief.

"And the six black swans in the little glassy cove," he was saying. "How many times I've thought of that day! It belongs in our good books. Ye mind how we both raised our pieces as the birds flew off, and then spared to shoot? 'Twas like as if we'd been told not to."

He turned his head quickly as the great bell above the prison chapel began to ring. One thinks of the music of Sabbath bells, but here was no music; only a cold grey flood of sound as heart-chilling as the wards and courts and corridors through which it came, echoing from the vaulted ceilings, thrown back from wall to wall, as though it, too, were imprisoned here without hope of escape into the pure sweet air of day. All the prison rang with the mournful clangor; it seemed to grow in volume, rising in a sullen viewless tide until, finding no outlet, it stood motionless, dead, like water in the bowels of the Earth, filling every ward and cell and crack and cranny in Newgate gaol. Then came silence.

Oakley gave me a strange look.

"Ye remember old Gill, the Chaplain's flunkey?" he asked. "Wouldn't ye know it could be none but him at the bellrope? And, man, does he love to ring for a hanging chapel! . . .

What did ye give the keeper at the gate when ye come in?"

"Five guineas."

"Five guineas! Hugh, are ye made o' the stuff? But it's all gain for me. They'd never have let ye see me like this afore chapel, without ye'd sweetened 'em to it."

"You're compelled to go?" I asked.

"To chapel? Would ye have me miss it? Be damned to ye! 'Tis part of the finish, and I'm no wind-broken crock to lag now. No, no! I'll make a good end, and the hanging chapel belongs to it."

At this moment the turnkey who had brought me here appeared at the barred window in the cell door.

"Mr. Oakley! The gentleman must come along now!"

"Aye, directly. Will ye come back, Hugh, after service?"

"You wish me to?"

"What d'ye expect me to say to that? 'No?' But there'll be this about it: no more privacy. We'll be locked in the cells, the four of us, seein' company like the animals in the Tower Gardens."

"I'll come, for all that."

"Mr. Oakley! There ain't but twenty minutes to chapel!" said the turnkey.

"Then why d'ye stand there, ye cod-piece? Show my friend out!"

I was on the point of leaving when we heard a burst of harsh triumphant laughter from Tom's companion, Dick Thorne.

"Tom! Tom!" he called. "Come out here!"

Oakley and I went out together, and there stood Thorne, jingling four gold sovereigns in his huge hand, under the nose of a sheep-shanked fellow who was regarding him with an air of blank dismay.

"A bite! A bite, by God!" cried Thorne, laughing fit to burst. "The body-snatcher here has give me four gold quid for me carcase, and I'm to be hung in chains!"

"Ye've no right to cheat me," said the man, dismally. "Ye said I was to fetch the body from the gallows as soon as it was cut down."

"So I did, ye rat, and I still say it. Come fetch it and see if ye get it! I tell ye, I'm to be hung in chains arter they stretch me here."

"Then ye'd best give me back the sovereigns, else I'll report ye to the Master Keeper," said the man, who was a purveyor of corpses to Surgeon's Hall. It was a not uncommon practice for condemned felons, without friends, and who wished to do so, to sell their bodies in advance, for dissection.

"Report me, will ye?" said Thorne, laughing still more. "By God, ye liver-coloured louse, ye scare the lights out o' me! I reckon I'll get punished right bad if ye do!"

I was compelled to leave before the conclusion of this scene, but as I followed the turnkey out of the place I could still hear Thorne's roaring laugh echoing through the corridors.

The turnkey hastened on before me. "Beggin' pardon, sir," he said, "but I'm obliged to fetch ye along sharp. Ye was let stay to the last minute. There'd be the devil and all to pay if the Governor knowed. Will ye go to service?"

"Yes," I replied.

"Then I'll take ye back along another road, and there'll be none the wiser as to where ye've been. This way, sir."

I had believed that my own earlier experience of Newgate had given me a pretty clear picture of the place, but now as I followed my guide through labyrinth after labyrinth of crooked passages, up and down short flights of footworn steps, I was completely lost. We passed through narrow corridors where two could not walk abreast, with others branching off in what appeared to be blind alleys leading to courts so wrapped in gloom that we heard and felt, rather than saw, their wretched inmates. We halted at heavily barred doors, and at each of them sat a turnkey, his shadow huge on the floor or wall, in the dim light of a spermaceti lamp or a candle sputtering in a small lantern. Each of them appeared to have taken root in the dampness and dirt of his niche, like some horrible fungus growth. They would peer or scowl into the face of my guide, then unlock and push the door barely ajar as though grudging us passage. When one of them said, "Wot o'clock is it, Joe?" the sound of his voice came with a startling effect because of its human quality and the impression it gave of one who appeared to take all this misery, including his own, as customary and commonplace.

A thousand years of misery. My heart sickened as I passed over this plot of unhallowed ground hidden from sun and air for so many centuries; where the accumulated sufferings of thousands upon thousands of human beings had left, or seemed to have left, more than the mere memory of it behind them. The first Newgate prison was almost as ancient as the Tower of London, and far older than the Bastille. And for all the vicissitudes of Time, for all the chances and changes, — the Great Fire of London, in 1666, had nearly destroyed it, and it was gutted again at the time of the Gordon Riots, — it still gave the sombre impression of being coeval with the Spirit of Evil; of a monument built, not in the dawn, but in the night of human history, to commemorate forever man's inhumanity to man.

Presently I recognized our surroundings: we were in the corridor passing the Females' Common Side Court, and I had a view of it through the gate — the same gate which Nellie Garth had kept to her back on the night when she had given the convict, Moll Cudlip, such a trouncing. And where, I wondered, would Cudlip be now? Retaken, perhaps, long since, but I thought it more likely that she would still be at large, with the tribe of blacks. She was no squeamish person in the matter of company. I could easily imagine her as a sort of tribal chieftainess, her face and body decorated with weird designs in ochre and white clay, leading raiding parties by night to the outlying gardens of the Port Jackson settlement. As we passed along the court, I heard the same hideous uproar from within and saw two females who might have been Moll Cudlip's own kin. Their mops of hair hung in their eyes, their faces streamed with blood, and they were clawing and scratching at one another in a circle of yelling spectators.

The turnkey halted at the juncture of two passageways where, on one side, a door stood open, looking into what appeared to be a kind of taproom for turnkeys, wardsmen, and the like.

"I'll leave ye now, Yer Honour," he said, "for there's no more gates to pass. Take the passage to the right, bear straight on, and ye'll come out in the court under the chapel."

The hall by the main Newgate entrance, below the stairs leading to the prison chapel, was now so thronged with visitors that there was scarcely room to stir in it. Some were already making their way up the staircase; others stood in groups, conversing with as much animation as if they stood in the lobby of a theatre during the quarter of an hour before the opening of the play. Here was the cream, so-called, of Newgate's Sunday crowd: young rakes handsomely dressed, with their mistresses as gay as butterflies in their splendid toilettes; old rakes ogling them, but giving more particular attention to pretty women who came unescorted; dowagers of a certain kind in full paint and powder, who prided themselves on nothing more than their knowledge of the pedigrees and exploits of famous criminals, particularly those who followed the genteel profession of highwayman. They were far from being singular in this interest and knowledge. Indeed, folk of both sexes, notable in the political and social world of London, were frequenters of Newgate. Strangely enough, not a few would pay golden guineas for the respectful regard of the more daring and notorious among condemned man: it appeared to add to their self-esteem. And the condemned not only benefited during their last hours by these handsome bribes, but were flattered in their turn by the condescending notice of "the great."

Presently the Master Keeper, directly under the Governor of Newgate in authority, followed by several turnkeys, appeared.

"Room, gentlemen! By your leave!" he called. "Be pleased to make way!" And a wide lane was opened through the crowd to the foot of the chapel staircase. It was not unusual for the High Sheriff of London to add solemnity to these New-gate services, and he now appeared in the passage leading from the Governor's apartments, escorted by the Governor and followed by other lesser city dignitaries in their ceremonial robes. They proceeded slowly through the crowd and up the staircase to the seats set aside for them in the chapel. The hum of conversation increased as they passed. Two men standing directly behind me were talking in low voices.

"There — you see her?" said one. "The pretty wench in the blue gown and bonnet standing by the pillar."

The other gave an admiring whistle, under his breath.

"What a stunning little creature!"

"Beauty in the Courts of Grief, eh? Mourning for her doomed lover."

"What! Her husband's among those to be stretched?"

"Yes. At least, she's said to be his wife."

"Who is she?"

"Mrs. Tom Oakley, no less. Gad, how sorrow becomes her!"

And at the same moment I myself caught sight of Phoebe, standing in the forefront of the crowd on the opposite side of the opened lane. I stared hard, scarcely believing my eyes, but Phoebe it was, as dainty and appealing as she had been when I first saw her, at Portsmouth gaol; looking not a day older, and as virginal as a young Madonna. She had a tiny black-bordered kerchief in her small gloved hand and touched it quickly to her eyes as she gazed before her, unaware, it would seem, of the wide interest and sympathy she attracted.

Then she caught sight of me, gave the least perceptible start, and at once averted her glance.

Before I could recover from my astonishment at finding her there, the great bell gave four measured, sonorous clangs, and as the sound died away a voice was heard from a window or balcony somewhere above the crowd. The person was hidden, but I recognized the voice at once: that of old Gill, the Chaplain's assistant — a cold, impersonal monotone, as lifeless, as pitiless as the grey walls that sent it echoing and reverberating over the heads of the hushed throng: —

"You prisoners that are within, who, for sin and wickedness, after the many mercies shown you, are now appointed to die: give ear and understand that to-morrow morning the great bell shall toll for you in the form and manner of a passing-bell, as it is wont to be tolled for those who are at the point of death, to the end that all godly people, hearing the bell, and knowing it is for you going to your death, may be stirred heartily to pray to God to bestow His Grace and Mercy upon you whilst you yet live.

"I beseech you, for Jesus Christ, His Sake, to keep this coming night in watching and prayer for the salvation of your souls whilst there is yet time and place for mercy; as knowing that to-morrow at this same hour you must appear before the Judgment Seat of your Creator, there to give an account of all things done in this life, and to suffer eternal torments for your sins committed against Him, unless upon your dolorous and unfeigned repentance you find mercy through the merits, death, and passion of your Mediator and Advocate, Jesus Christ, who sits at the right hand of God to make intercession for as many of you as turn penitently to Him.

"Lord have mercy upon you!

"Christ have mercy upon you!"

The four doomed men, preceded and followed by guards, appeared from the corridor at the rear of the hall, bearing the emblematic coffin completely draped in black. Their shackles clanked dismally as they moved slowly through the staring throng. Oakley and his companion, Dirk Thorne, were in front. Tom, his head held high, looked straight before him, and there was a calm steady light in his eyes. Thorne glared to right and left, as though defying anyone to meet his glance. I already knew something of Thorne's history. He was a celebrated pugilist of formidable strength, turned footpad and housebreaker, and was widely known in the South of England. He had served various prison terms in county gaols; once before he had been condemned to death at Bedford assizes, and made a daring and spectacular escape the week before he was to be hung. Thereafter he had disappeared, but was caught again after a robbery on Hounslow Heath, where he had killed his victim with a blow of his bare first. He was first to be hung at Newgate, and his body was then to be rehung in chains on a gibbet at the scene of the robbery.

The two other condemned men were a counterfeiter and a forger. The first was a tall, stoop-shouldered man in middle life, dressed in a shabby suit of black broadcloth. His eyes were deep-set in cavernous hollows; he had a high-bridged nose and a sensitive, well-shaped mouth. The transparent pallor of his face gave him the appearance of a scholar and recluse. He kept his glance on Oakley's back and seemed quite unconscious of his surroundings.

The forger looked the very embodiment of despair and terror. No offense in the English criminal code was more pitilessly dealt with than his — there was never the least gleam of hope for either a condemned counterfeiter or a forger. As I looked at this wretched man I remembered another forger who had been condemned at the Old Bailey at the time when Oakley, Garth, and I were tried, and the words of the magistrate who passed sentence upon him came back to me. He was a terrorizing "hanging judge," and I have never forgotten the gleam of ferocious humour that came into his eyes as he said: ". . . Hanged by the neck until you are dead. And may you find the mercy Above, if there you are to go, which a right and proper regard for the sanctity of the paper currency of this Realm forbids you to hope for here."

I lost sight of Phoebe in the crowd mounting the staircase, but when I reached the gallery in the rear of the chapel she was already seated in the pew reserved for the relatives of condemned prisoners, in the gallery to the left. There was but one other occupant of the pew, a frail, shabbily dressed woman with snow-white hair, who, I learned, was the mother of the forger. A striking contrast the two mourners made: one so old and bowed and wrinkled, herself near the end of her journey; the other so virginal in appearance, so appealing in her youthful beauty. In this same gallery were seated the felons, capitally convicted, who had been respited and were waiting transportation for life to New South Wales.

On the opposite side of the chapel was the gallery for notable visitors who had come with special cards of admittance. In the pew next the gallery rail sat the sheriffs, wearing their gold chains, with two tall footmen, in state liveries, standing behind them. Below, and between the galleries, was the mass of the prison population. The pew for the doomed men was in the centre of the chapel. It was a large docklike structure painted black, visible to all in the place. The Chaplain's desk and pulpit were just in front of this pew and within a couple of yards of it. The emblematic, black-draped coffin rested on trestles, also painted black, in the little space between the condemned felons' pew and the pulpit.

The four doomed men were kept outside until the chapel was filled. During this time all glances were directed toward Phoebe and the solitary mourner with her; then a deep hush fell over the congregation as the door opened and Oakley, Dirk Thorne, and their two companions were marshaled to their seats. Guards stood to the right and left and behind the pew, facing the pulpit.

The Chaplain sat at his desk with old Gill, his assistant, below him. The Chaplain was the same incumbent who had served in Newgate in my time. He was a heavy-jowled, wall-eyed man whose fiery complexion indicated his devotion to the bottle rather than to his office as prison ordinary. Old Gill was precisely as I remembered him, pallid of complexion, with the same piercing black eyes and resonant, lifeless voice. He rose to announce the hymn, the "Lamentation of a Sinner," which carried me back in an instant to a hanging chapel I had attended shortly before leaving the prison for Botany Bay, when fourteen men and three women sat in the pews for the condemned, forced to listen to the words of that most melancholy hymn. On this present occasion not more than a dozen voices joined in the singing which added to the mournful chilling effect. Then the Chaplain rose.

"Let us pray . . . especially for those now awaiting the awful execution of the Law."

A sense of mingled horror and repulsion seized me, but I seemed forced to attend to both the prayer and the sermon which followed, as though I myself were seated beside Tom Oakley and about to share his dreadful fate. The voice of the Chaplain had in it a quality of softness, but it was a pitiless softness; he seemed to be either indifferent to, or unconscious of, the effect of his words.

"From Leviticus . . . the fifth chapter and the seventeenth verse: —

" 'And if a soul sin, and commit any of these things which are forbidden to be done by the commandments of the Lord; though he wist it not, yet is he guilty, and shall bear his iniquity!' "

From this text he drew cold comfort indeed for the four men on the brink of Eternity. The gist of the sermon was that, if a soul sin unknowingly and must yet bear his iniquity, how much deeper is the guilt of those souls who sin wittingly; with what bitter lamentations must they acknowledge their sins; with what woeful appeals for mercy must they turn toward the awful Seat of God's Judgment. There was neither compassion nor fire in voice and manner as he spoke. He seemed to be a mere passionless mouthpiece, both for the vengeful God of Israel and for equally vengeful Society — human Society, as represented by the great, the pitiless, and the powerful of the Realm.

Of the prisoners, Oakley alone appeared to attend. He sat with one arm resting lightly along the back of the pew, and gazed at the Chaplain, or the oaken canopy above the pulpit, with an air of bland respectful interest. He might have been a country squire, who, mindful of his duties, had come to church to set an example to his lesser neighbours. Dirk Thorne, ignoring the Chaplain, turned in his seat to regard the congregation, nodding and winking, and waving his hand to felons he knew. The forger sat with his head bowed. The counterfeiter stared at the coffin as though fascinated, unable to avert his gaze.

Directly the service was concluded, the felons of the congregation crowded out the door in a disorderly rout, impatient to be with their friends and cronies. The visitors gathered in the chapel court, to witness the return of the condemned to their cells, and, as soon as they had passed, thronged after them, for at this time they were given access to the small court to view the men who were then locked in their cells.

Then I caught sight of Phoebe once more and made my way to where she stood, seemingly unconscious of the stares and whispered comments of those about her. She gave me a wan smile.

"Oh, I hoped you would come to me, Hugh," she said, in a low voice. "Will you take me outside? I feel as though I were going to faint."

She took my arm, and quickly revived in the fresh air. We walked through Newgate Street to a quiet little tavern at the St. Paul's end of Cheapside.

"I used to come here with my father," she said, as we entered the place. She ordered a brandy-and-water which she sipped daintily, as though unaccustomed to drinking spirits.

"Hugh, how did you dare to enter the prison? I was so afraid for you when I saw you there."

I explained briefly what had happened since our return to England: my meeting with Sally, the granting of my pardon, our marriage, and our plan for return to New South Wales. Phoebe sat with her elbows propped on the table, her chin in her hands, regarding me with the air of grave, innocent appeal which so became her. Her eyes were bright with tears as she listened.

"I am so happy for you," she said. "And you will see Mama and Papa again, and my dear little son! You will never know, Hugh, how I have grieved for him. When will I ever see him again!"

Well as I knew Phoebe, or thought I knew her, she looked so woebegone that the old feeling of bafflement and uncertainty with respect to her real character returned to me. There was the fact of her planned and deliberate abandonment of Tom and their little son — no explanations or excuses could make it appear less ugly than it was. Nevertheless, one wanted to forgive it; to believe it had been an act of impulse, bitterly repented.

How small a thing may come between a generous impulse of the heart and the sober judgment of the head. Phoebe made no effort to restrain her tears, and I would have been far more deeply moved by her grief save for the tiny black-bordered handkerchief which she held to her eyes. I had no doubt whatever that she had bought it for the occasion of the chapel service: she was in mourning for her husband even before he was dead. It was an appeal for sympathy and pity on behalf of the beautiful young wife so soon to be a widow. But she had not expected to display it before anyone familiar with her history. Without appearing to, I observed her sudden startled awareness, and the silence rang with her unspoken, "Good heavens! I hope he hasn't noticed!" When I looked up again, the handkerchief had disappeared.

"Have you seen him, Hugh?" she asked.

I told her of my meeting with Tom before the service.

"He spoke of me?"

I shook my head.

"I can understand that. He wouldn't want you to know. He would think that . . . that, perhaps, you felt bitterly toward me for . . . for leaving him. But I loved him, Hugh! Indeed, indeed I did, and I always shall! And when I met him at Marlborough . . ."

She broke off and regarded me appealingly, yet with an expression of quick keen appraisal behind the glance.

"At Marlborough? How was that?" I asked.

"It was the strangest thing. I had been in Calcutta, with Doris. She wanted me to go there with her and . . . and I couldn't well refuse my only sister. We stayed six months, then Doris thought we should return to London. India has a horrid climate. We sailed in a ship bound for Bristol.

"At Bristol we took coach for London, and stopped for supper at the King George, in Marlborough. . . . Hugh, I had just stepped down from the coach when I saw him! Tom was head hostler there.

"It was meant to be — there is no other way of explaining it; we were meant for each other. Never for one little minute had I ceased to love him. You remember when we met in that hideous gaol in Portsmouth? I knew from that first day that I could never love anyone but Tom. And when I knew that he loved me as deeply and truly as ever . . ."

"You stayed in Marlborough?"

"Yes. . . . I shouldn't say it of my only sister, but Doris has a cold heart, Hugh. She called me a little fool for wanting to return to Tom. She was determined that I should go on with her to London. . . . But I didn't.

"Tom took lodgings for us near the inn. We were very happy. There was only one thing . . . he was bound we should live on his wages. I had three hundred pounds that . . . that Doris had given me, and he wouldn't touch a penny of it, not even to send for little Hugh. That's what we planned — to write Papa to send Hughie home when there should be a safe opportunity. But Tom was bound to wait until he could earn the money himself.

"We just managed on his wages. At last he thought he should look for a better position. London was home to me, of course, but I wouldn't have wanted to go there unless Tom had been so set upon it. He thought he would be safer in London than in the country."

She went on to tell me what had happened then, though I could easily have guessed the rest of it.

"I didn't know, Hugh," she said, miserably. "He told me he'd found a very good position as night hostler at the Angel in the Strand. He was making a great deal of money, but I never dreamed the truth of it, that he had taken to the road again. Then he was caught, and . . . that's all there is to tell."

"Where are you staying, Phoebe?" I asked.

"With Doris. She's seen Tom. She's come with me every Sunday since he was taken, but she wouldn't to-day. Are you going to see him again?"

"For a little while. I promised I would, after the service."

"Then I'll wait here. You'll not speak of meeting me?"

"Not if you prefer I shouldn't."

"That will be best, I think. . . . Go, then, Hugh. You can pass this way when you come out."

*   *   *   *   *

Upon returning to the prison, I found the court adjoining the cells for the condemned crowded with visitors. The four men were now locked in, each in his separate cell. I saw the old mother of the forger standing by his wicket, and the son with his face, deathly pale, pressed close against the bars. He had thrust out his hand, and his mother held it in both of hers, unconscious of the stares of the onlookers. My heart bled for the sweet-faced old woman who seemed far past any comfort that tears might bring. The counterfeiter was hidden in his cell, while the idlers gathered at his door peered through the barred opening in an attempt to catch sight of him in the gloom.

But the throng was before the cells of Oakley and Thorne. Each stood at his window, and Thorne at least was thoroughly enjoying the attention he attracted. Handsomely dressed women were passing him oranges, papers of tobacco, and other gifts. His harsh laugh rang out from moment to moment, as though he had not a care in the world.

"Afeered? Me, Lady?" I heard him say. "Damn my blood! Never in the world! Get ye a good place up against the scaffold to-morrow and ye'll see Dirk Thorne kick off his boots when the drop falls."

Tom stood at his window, lightly clasping the bars with both hands. This was his day even more than Thorne's: he was gay and condescending in manner, like a prince holding court, and seemed wholly at ease as he conversed with the handsomely dressed men and women who crowded close to his wicket, eager to be noticed by him. I had opportunity only for a brief word. The moment he caught sight of me his expression changed on the instant.

"It's no use, lad," he said, in a low voice. "We're on show. They've come to see the performing bears, and, by God, I'll carry it through!"

"I'd best go, then?"

"Aye, but . . . could ye be with me the morn?"

"Would it be permitted?"

"I've told 'em ye're my uncle's son. Sweeten the head turnkey and it's done." He gave me a keen smiling glance. "Can ye abide it, Hugh? It's past all reason to ask, but . . ."

"I'll come," I said.

XXV

NEWGATE STREET

IT was late afternoon when I returned to Queen Anne Square. After supper, when Sally had gone to bed, I sat for another hour with Mr. Fleming, in the library. There was the night to be gotten through somehow, and I could not hope for the oblivion of sleep; neither could I read, or talk, or sit with folded hands, staring at vacancy. Presently I changed into my meanest clothes, taking care, this time, to leave my watch and wallet at home. I put a five-pound note into a safe pocket, to be given the head keeper at Newgate, and set out to walk the streets.

The sky was overcast and a thin mist blurred the lights of the occasional street lamps. The clocks were striking nine as I crossed Oxford Street into New Bond Street, following it as far as Piccadilly where I turned east, paying little further heed to direction, concerned only to walk and to keep from thinking of Tom. Many a night I had tramped the streets of London in this fashion when I had no home to go to and the raw wintry air forced one to keep in motion. I went on and on through the maze of crooked streets in the central part of the city, and at last found myself in Wapping, in the same wretched quarter I had known so well in the past. By chance I passed the end of the very court, off Love Lane, where I had slept in the tup'enny doss house on the night when the place was searched by Kneller, the police sergeant. As I peered into the narrow pit of blackness, hemmed in with miserable tumble-down houses, the old hunted feeling so com-

mon to me then returned to send me hastening back toward
the better part of the city.

In spite of myself, it seemed, I was drawn toward St. Paul's,
though well knowing how near it stood to Newgate prison.
It was now past midnight, but many people were in the streets,
all moving in one direction. For the most part, they were the
dregs of humanity, drawn to a hanging as flies to carrion;
nevertheless, I saw many respectable-looking townspeople
amongst them, no less concerned to secure good places from
which to view the execution.

At this time, 1791, Newgate was the place of execution
for all London and its environs. The old procession to Tyburn,
dating back to the sixteenth century, had been abandoned in
1784 in favour of the Newgate hangings, in the hope that the
throngs of spectators might be more orderly because less
numerous, and free from the vast accession of drunken riotous
folk who invariably followed the Tyburn processions through
the heart of London from the prison to the gallows. It was
no less a person than the great Doctor Samuel Johnson who
frowned upon this change designed to improve public morals.

"Sir," he said to Boswell, when the procession to Tyburn
had been discontinued, "executions are intended to draw
spectators. If they do not draw spectators they do not answer
their purpose. The old method was most satisfactory to all
persons: the public was gratified by a procession, and the
criminal supported by it. Why is all this to be swept away?"

I far from approve of Doctor Johnson's sentiments in this
matter, but he need not have feared for a falling-off in public
interest. Newgate hangings lacked nothing to satisfy the
ferocious curiosity of the mob. The only change wrought by
the change of place was a fiercer struggle for good positions
from which to view the hangings, because of the compara-
tively restricted area of Newgate Street.

I followed the crowds as though pushed forward by the
same general impulse, but I had no mind to spend the rest of

the night before the prison. I knew I should have to come early, in order to be at the gate at the time of opening, but not so early as this. And yet the street was steadily filling even at this hour; there must have been five thousand people already present. Workmen were erecting the gallows by the light of flaring torches which cast weird shadows along the front of this most grim and gloomy of public buildings. Most of these early comers were gathered here and a loud buzz of conversation filled the air. Vendors of gin were everywhere, pushing their handcarts briskly through the crowd.

"Here y'are, gents! A kick in the guts for tuppence! Prime Geneva 'ere, tuppence a slug!"

They did a thriving trade; and there were piemen with their baskets, barrow women in their frowsty shawls and bonnets, selling fried fish, tripe, pigs' knuckles, and other refreshments. A troupe of street tumblers had an interested crowd around their strip of carpet laid on the paving-stone and lighted by torches. Ballad singers and professional beggars were out in force. Among the latter was a horrible slattern of a woman seated on the narrow curbing with two small children beside her. Despite the wintry air all three were half naked, and the children, a boy and a girl, neither of them over seven years, had great sores, artificially engendered, on their starved little bodies, designed to arouse the pity of passers-by.

Then I spied four never-to-be-forgotten people whom I had often seen in Newgate in the past: an itinerant parson whose pulpit was the streets and gaols of London, and three women who made up his choir. He was dressed in black, which brought out the deathly pallor of his long cadaverous face. His one theme was damnation and the horrors of hell. The grim-visaged women were like the three Fates, though when they sang, they resembled, rather, the Furies. This band, too, had its audience. When I came up, the man was in the midst of his terrifying sermon, preaching with a ferocious eloquence that held his listeners spellbound. "My friends" rang through his words, but it was as though Satan himself were thus addressing them while licking his chops at thought of the tortures he had in store for them at the end of their earthly existence.

At the conclusion of his remarks leaflets were passed out through the crowd containing the words of two hymns: "Hell," and "The Death of a Sinner." He then struck a tuning fork and led his choir in the latter hymn: —

> My thoughts on awful subjects roll:
> Damnation and the dead.
> What horrors seize the guilty soul
> Upon a dying bed!
>
> Lingering upon these mortal shores
> She makes a long delay,
> Till like a flood, with dreadful force,
> Death sweeps the wretch away.
>
> Then lost and shrieking she descends
> Down to the fiery coast
> Amongst abominable fiends,
> Herself a frightful ghost.
>
> There tortured sinners writhe and cry
> In everlasting chains.
> They may not, cannot, shall not die,
> And wait for fiercer pains.
>
> Not all their anguish and their blood
> For their old guilt atones;
> Nor the compassion of a God
> Shall hearken to their groans.

One of the women had a piercing, blood-freezing voice and, as the others sang, she furnished an obligato of awful shrieks and groans, as though she were the damned soul of the hymn descending to eternal torments.

I left Newgate Street — only a little less horrible than the promised hell of the song — and resumed my wandering, crossing the Thames by Blackfriars Bridge, against a stream of pedestrians bound for the prison from the Surrey side. I walked as far as that most poverty-stricken of suburbs, Lock's Fields, with its scattered hovels and vacant lots filled with accumulations of rubbish. I passed the Holt family's house, but at that hour they were asleep. I doubted my resolution to return; then Tom's face would rise before me, and I knew that I must, whatever the cost; but I went on, delaying the evil moment as long as possible. At last, to my astonishment, I was aware that the sky was paling in the east. I hastened back toward the city, but it was full daylight before I recrossed the river.

I was engulfed, almost at once, by a great, slow-moving tide of humanity so dense that I saw at once I could make little progress through it, so I made a wide detour to come in from the north by Aldersgate Street. Here the crowd was nearly as great, but I pushed and wormed my way forward, bitterly reproaching myself for so misjudging the time needed for reaching the prison. Tom would be waiting for me, looking more and more anxiously for me as the minutes sped past. What would he think if I were to fail him?

It was nine o'clock before I so much as reached the east end of Newgate Street, and there my heart misgave me. How could I make my way through the packed and struggling mob? Nevertheless, I inched along, determined, somehow, to reach the gates; but I was a good hour in advancing fifty paces, and then only at the cost of curses and imprecations of those I crowded and pushed aside. I was glad of my fourteen stone and my six feet four of height; I could easily overlook the crowds and make my way in the right direction. Small boys squirmed with the agility of terriers amongst the trouser legs and petticoats, clutching their parcels of broadsides under their arms. Their shrill voices rose high above the din.

"Life stories of the felons, 'ere!" . . . "Dyin' confession of the footpad and murderer, Dirk Thorne!" . . . "Life 'istory and last words of the famous highwayman, Tom Oakley, escaped from Botany Bay." . . . "Read all about 'em for sixpence!"

The roofs of the houses opposite the prison were filled with people, and all the windows below. A stand had been erected directly opposite the scaffold for spectators willing to pay high prices for reserved seats, and it was now packed to overflowing. At last I managed to reach a spot directly in front of the scaffold and not ten paces away from it. The main gate of the prison was only a little distance beyond, but I could go no further. I could neither advance nor retreat, and was obliged to stand where I was, so tightly wedged that I could scarcely turn my body.

A fence had been erected below the scaffold, providing a narrow space on three sides where a double file of soldiers, with fixed bayonets, stood. Presently the great bell began to toll and the tumult died away. The bell was rung for a full five minutes. As the brazen clangour ceased, the door opening on the causeway leading from the prison to the scaffold was swung back. The Chaplain and Gill his assistant, in their black robes, emerged first, followed by the four doomed men. Behind them came the hangman and his assistant and six guards. Gill stepped to the edge of the scaffold, and looked out in silence over the sea of faces; then I heard his resonant, heart-chilling voice for the last time: —

"*All good people, pray heartily unto God for these poor sinners going to their death, for whom this great bell doth toll.*"

He then turned to face the doomed men.

"*You that are condemned to die, who now stand at the brink of Eternity, repent with lamentable tears. In this last moment of your earthly existence, ask mercy of the Lord for the salvation of your souls.*

"*Lord have mercy upon you!*
Christ have mercy upon you!
Lord have mercy upon you!
Christ have mercy upon you!"

Against my will I raised my head for a brief glance toward the gallows. Tom stood erect and firm, without a trace or tremor of fear apparent in his attitude. Swaying against those so closely pressed against me, I turned my back upon the scene, but I could do no more than this. I was forced to stand in my tracks during an eternity of five minutes. Then it was over.

But a more awful thing was to follow. Newgate Street has witnessed many a grim and horrible scene, but never, surely, has the toll of its victims been so appalling as on this lamentable day.

I kept my back turned upon the scaffold, but I knew when the end had come by the sudden deep murmur of voices rising from thousands of throats. But still no one could stir from where he stood; indeed, many had no wish to move, but remained staring at the gallows. Half an hour passed, and by that time the hangman's agents had, somehow, managed to worm their way into this sea of humanity with bags containing bits of the ropes used in hanging the four men. The selling of these ropes was a perquisite of the executioner and his assistant. I could plainly hear the voices of the peddlers: "A shilling for an inch of the very rope!" "Who'll buy? A shilling for an inch of the rope that hung Tom Oakley!" "This way, gents! Take 'em while they last!" "A genuine bit of Dirk Thorne's halter, only a bob!"

It may appear strange that anyone should be eager to buy so gruesome a memento. The fact remains that many began thrusting and pushing against the crowd in an effort to reach the vendors.

Not far from where I stood was a pieman holding his basket on his head because of the want of room to carry it on his arm. In the surging of the crowd, the basket was knocked from the man's head and the contents spilled upon the shoulders of those around him. There was a wild scramble for the pies, and the man attempted to kneel to recover those that had fallen to the pavement.

Before he could even attempt to rise, those nearest stumbled over him, and fell and were trampled to death on the instant. Women screamed with terror; others fell and were trampled in their turn. Panic now became general, but in so huge a crowd, those at a distance were ignorant of what was happening. Men, women, and children were borne down to perish under the feet of the others, helpless to hold back the surging mob. It was worst for the children and the women, particularly those of low stature. Men nearest them tried desperately to hold them up, but the awful gathered force of this sea of humanity could not be withstood. Men were swept under with the women they tried to save. Among the rest was a woman with an infant in her arms. She stood not a dozen paces from me, and as she fell she thrust the child into the arms of the man next to her. He, needing all his strength for the preservation of his own life, threw it from him to another, and the child passed from hand to hand over the heads of the crowd until I was able to catch and hold it. I tried to stand fast, but I was carried this way and that, with the rest. In this convulsive struggle for life people fought fiercely with one another, and the weakest went under. Not one of those who fell ever rose again.

A more dreadful scene could not be imagined, and it was made more terrible because those at a distance could not know what was taking place and added to the slaughter by pushing forward to watch the taking down of the gallows and the removal of the bodies of the hanged men. Not until an hour had passed was the awful pressure of the mob lessened by those at the extremities of the street going homeward. As the crowd thinned, the city marshals and a number of constables were able partially to clear the place. The catastrophe exceeded the worst forebodings: nearly one hundred dead and dying lay on the pavement, and shoes, hats, petticoats, and other fragments of apparel were strewn everywhere.

I remained in the midst of this scene of horror and despair, holding the child that had been passed to me. She was an infant of about two years, and her poor undernourished little body, covered with a thin dirty frock, told me the kind of home she came from. She lay fast asleep in my arms as I waited, not knowing what to do next. I had had a glimpse of the mother as she fell, and I hoped that the father or some other relative might have survived. The gallows was now being taken down, and I had before me the grim task of claiming and removing Tom's body. This Phoebe had asked me to do. The body was to be carried to a burying ground at Swan's Fields, on the northern outskirts of London, and I was to meet Phoebe there.

Presently I saw a man, his hat gone, coat gone, and his shirt all but torn from his body, pushing his way frantically through the lessening throng in my direction. He gave a little broken cry when he saw his child in my arms. It was the father, and whatever desire I may have felt to heap the sternest and most bitter of reproaches upon his head for bringing his wife and infant daughter to such a place vanished as he took the child from my arms. He was half out of his senses, and tears streamed down his cheeks as he held his little daughter close to his breast.

A street urchin, not above four feet tall, who must have been through all that horror, stood staring at the father for a moment. He had a sharp, hard little face, and looked as though nothing could daunt him. His coat and trousers were five sizes too large for him. They were nothing but shreds and patches, but he had managed to preserve, under the coat, his bundle of broadsides. Of a sudden he was all business again and darted through the crowd, shouting: "Life 'istries and dyin' confessions of the felons! Last words of the famous 'ighwayman, Tom Oakley! Read all abaht it, 'ere!"

EPILOGUE

WE were sitting in the library at Queen Anne Square — Sally and I — with that feeling of content common to all voyagers to far places when, after weeks of preparation, they find themselves ready to the last detail. Everything but our cabin luggage was already stowed safely aboard the *Princess Royal,* the supply ship which was to carry us, and other free settlers, to New South Wales. Sally was weary, after the long ordeal of packing; nevertheless, she was bound that we should go over our lists once more to be certain that we had missed nothing.

"The *Princess Royal,*" said Sally. "It has a grand sound, Hugh, for a Botany Bay store-ship."

"But what of that queen of ships, the *Charlotte?*" I asked. "And we had the *Prince of Wales* as well, on the first voyage."

"I know. . . . Only one week to wait! Can you believe it? . . . Hugh, I'm going upstairs to rest an hour or two."

I stretched out in one of Mr. Fleming's deep leather chairs and looked out across the square, letting my thoughts stray where they would through the past and into the future. Half an hour later I saw Mr. Fleming's carriage approaching the drive. He came in, presently.

"Well, Hugh — everything in order?"

"Everything, sir, thanks to Sally."

"Where is she?"

"Lying down, upstairs."

"I've just seen Mr. Carleton, of the Home Office," Mr. Fleming remarked. "It seems that you two are doing the Colony a greater service than you suspect."

"How is that, sir?"

"You both know the country well. Now you are going out as settlers with some thousands of pounds to invest. . . .

Can you see what this means? The newspapers have been
filled with letters from disgruntled officers in New South
Wales who declare that the country is a desert, unfit for
settlement. Your action gives them the lie and will encourage
others to emigrate. They're in urgent need of free settlers
with capital and an understanding of farming, if the Colony's
to go ahead. . . . I'd quite a talk with Carleton."

Mr. Fleming paused, and glanced at me. "He showed me
an excerpt from one of the latest of Governor Phillip's despatches. The disappearance of the Government fishing boat
was mentioned, and a list of those thought to have escaped
in her."

"Good Lord!"

"Phillip believed that some arrangement for escape had
been made with the captain of the American brig. . . . Have
you ever felt, Hugh — what shall I say — a little hesitation
about meeting Phillip once more?"

I laughed. "Indeed I have! You put it most delicately.
After all, I was one of those who stole his boat. I've said nothing to you, sir, but I'm more than concerned about the matter. My hope is that, in view of my pardon, and my family's
services in the American War, he may be willing to overlook
my share in the theft of the boat."

"And so he will," said Fleming. "Carleton has written to
Governor Phillip. Rest assured, the boat will be forgotten."

"I'm greatly relieved to know it, sir."

I had a number of last errands to perform. Though I
omitted to speak of it to Sally, one was to see Ned Inching
again if he could be found. The only place where I could hope
to get news of him was at the pawnshop of Sabb's nephew.
Ned had told me that the shop was now on Vine Street, St.
Giles. Shortly after our midday dinner — "breakfast," as
Mr. Fleming called it — I set out on foot for Vine Street,
scarcely a twenty-minute walk from Queen Anne Square.

The weather was mild for February — more like spring

than midwinter, with the sun shining brightly and the grass fresh and green in the square. I sauntered cityward through the busy streets, thinking of Ned, wondering what disguise he might have adopted for the day. That of a threadbare curate, perhaps, or a respectable small tradesman; or he might be posing as the gentle, timid old woman who had taken my watch. I could even picture him as a neatly attired old gentleman, presumably on his way to his favourite coffeehouse for a rubber of whist. Ned might have given lessons to Proteus himself.

I wondered where he lived. Did he have lodgings like other men? Inching enjoyed companionship and good cheer, but his one passion was for the practice of his art. He considered most pickpockets as bunglers compared with himself, but he spoke with reverence of the old master, long since dead, under whom he had served his apprenticeship.

Vine Street was a mean thoroughfare, bordered by poor shops and ordinaries. I halted before a door with a sign swinging above it: "Timothy Sabb — Pawnbroker."

A bell rang in a back room as I opened the door. There was a dusty counter, and shelves behind it where the stock was displayed: cheap clocks, watches, and snuffboxes; wigs, hats, and the like. Hanging in an open wardrobe were various articles of clothing — the small, varied possessions of the poor. All this was the blind behind which the real business of the firm was carried on.

The door to the back room opened and Timothy Sabb peered cautiously out.

"Yes, sir?" he said.

"Do you remember me, Mr. Sabb?" I asked. "I once met you in a certain ship called the *Charlotte*, in Portsmouth Harbour."

He examined me more nearly.

"Why, damn my eyes! You're . . . you're . . . I can't call your name, sir, but . . ."

"Tallant's the name. I'm an old friend of your uncle Nick."

"So ye are, sir! So ye are! Damn my eyes! I recollect ye now!"

For a man whom I had met but once he seemed strangely pleased to see me. I could not account for the warmth of his welcome. When I asked for news of Inching, he shook his head.

"I couldn't tell ye where he is. There's none knows that save Ned hisself. But he's in and out o' my shop a matter o' once or twice a week. He's a clever one, is Ned! The best customer I got." He came as near to a beaming smile as was possible for Timothy Sabb as he added, "I know the whole of it, Mr. Tallant. Uncle Nick's told me. Have ye had word from him?"

"No. . . . I hope all's well with him?"

"Better than well," said the nephew, rubbing his hands. "How's this for a queer thing? There's a gent from Holland settin' in my back room this minute. Come in, sir! Come in! He'll be pleased to give ye all the news of Uncle Nick."

I was ushered into a good-sized room, comfortably furnished, and a proper background for the portly old gentleman seated in a leather chair by a window, giving on a walled court at the back of the house. He was well-dressed; his grizzle major wig would have adorned an alderman's pate; his fat calves were encased in white silk stockings, and a great beard, streaked with grey, all but concealed the broad expanse of chest and belly.

Timothy Sabb closed the door behind us.

"Mr. Tallant," he said, "I'll have ye know Mynheer van Schouten. He's a goldsmith from Rotterdam."

My heart gave a leap as the goldsmith struggled up from his chair.

"The devil he is!" said I, stepping forward to grasp his hand. "Nick, you fat rascal! Which hole, now, for the belly-gauge?"

"God's truth!" Nick exclaimed. "Did ye know me as easy as that? . . . Nevvy, I'm for to-morrow night's packet back to Rotterdam! Damme if I step out o' the house again till I step into a hackney coach for the docks!"

"Never fear, Nick," said I. "I'd never have known you save for the way you got out of the chair. It reminded me of how you used to struggle up from the foot of a gum tree at Sydney Cove when you spied a marine officer coming, to convince him you'd cleared an acre of forest since morning."

"Ye mean it?" said Nick. "Ye wouldn't ha' known me, else?"

"Never in the world."

"There, I'll rest easy," said Nick, lowering himself with a comfortable sigh into his chair once more. "It's the last hole, lad, for the belly-gauge. Nevvy, ye'd best mind the shop, for I've a deal to say to this seven-foot rogue, and don't wish to be disturbed."

I spent two hours with Sabb. He knew, of course, of Oakley's hanging, and we passed quickly over that. He told me he was prospering in Holland.

"Aye, we're doin' famous betwixt us, Nevvy and me. But Hugh, Rotterdam ain't Lunnon. . . . Hearken to that! *There's* music!"

We heard faintly the sounds of horses' hoofs on the cobblestones, the rattle of cart wheels, the cracking of whips, the cries of the hawkers, "Small coals! Small coals!" and a dozen others beside, against the rumbling undertones of the great city's life.

"I miss it," said Nick. "I miss it sore. Rotterdam ain't nothin' against Lunnon."

"Then why not come back?" I asked.

"Ye ask me that! I ain't such a fool. But I won't say I'll not run over, whiles, for a smell of it."

"Nick, you've kept your promise, of course, to deal in no Holland goods?"

He gave me a reproachful grin.

"Be damned to ye, Tallant! In my line o' trade, ye can't be forever askin' questions as to what comes in. But if I was to be brought a watch with the name Dykstra engraved in the lid, I'd see it got back to where it belonged. Aye, and I'd send with it six pair of the finest English razors could be had by fair means or foul, with a han'some gold case lined with velvet to put 'em in, and a snuffbox His Majesty himself wouldn't be ashamed to carry; and on top o' that, I'd have a model made in solid silver of the ship *Amstel,* set on a mountin' of ebony inlaid with ivory. . . . And that minds me," he added, before I could reply, "I got a bit of a keepsake here, for as fine a young lady as ever drew breath."

He stepped into an adjoining room and returned with a small case of morocco leather. Opening it, he showed me a magnificent brooch, set with small, perfectly cut diamonds. On the gold of the under side *Sarah Munro Tallant* was engraved.

" 'Twas Ned Inching told me ye was married," he said. "He was in here a two-three days back." His eyes twinkled. "Tell Miss Sally 'twas honest come by. Damme if I didn't go out to buy it meself, from a goldsmith on Cockspur Street!"

*   *   *   *   *

I had gone by hackney coach to the Shadwell Dock to carry one last box to the *Princess Royal,* which was to unmoor and drop down the river the following night. Sally and I were to leave with Mr. Fleming at dawn and drive to Sheerness, where he was to take leave of us. When I had seen the box safely stowed with our many others in the 'tween-decks, I drove back through the city as far as Hyde Park, and there got down for a last walk through the park before returning to Queen Anne Square.

It was midafternoon, and the air still mild and warm. The trees were leafless; the grass was green and the waters in the little lake sparkled in the sunshine. Many people were abroad, taking the good of so pleasant a day for out of doors. I seated myself on a bench to watch them pass.

Presently I observed a little chariot, very smartly turned out, approaching down the drive. The coachman drew up some fifty yards distant; the footman sprang down, opened the door, lowered the steps, and the occupants of the coach, two young ladies beautifully dressed, got down to walk, while the coach preceded them. At first I turned only a casual glance in that direction, but as the young ladies drew near I recognized them, and got hastily to my feet. I was recognized at the same moment by Phoebe and Doris Thynne.

Phoebe halted, with a little gasp, then came quickly forward holding out both hands. She was in full mourning, and a bewitching costume it was, with herself to set it off. Her thick corn-coloured hair appeared in little curls and tendrils at the edge of the jaunty bonnet. There was the finest of filmy lace at her throat and the cuffs of her sleeves.

"Hugh!" she exclaimed. "How fortunate! . . . You remember my sister, Doris?"

"Indeed I do," I replied.

"This is delightful, Mr. Tallant," said Doris, in her lovely contralto voice. "Phoebe and I were speaking of you only this morning. . . . So you're truly going back to New South Wales!"

"Yes. We're to go aboard at Sheerness."

"We were aboard the *Princess Royal* yesterday," said Doris. "We are sending out a *great* many things to poor Mama and Papa."

"They will be deeply appreciated, no doubt of that," said I.

Phoebe glanced up, her blue eyes misty with tears.

"I am sending toys and schoolbooks for little Hugh," she said. "We have heard from Mama and Papa. Hugh is very well and happy, Mama says. Papa is to teach him. I am so glad for that."

"How *can* you go back, Mr. Tallant?" Doris asked, with

a slight convulsive shiver of her fine shoulders. "Does your wife really wish to go?"

"It was she who proposed it."

Doris examined my face curiously, and there was a hard glitter in her dark eyes.

"Only fancy! Going to that dreadful place when you might remain in London!"

"It's not so dreadful as you think, Doris," said Phoebe. Her lids drooped and she glanced down at the toe of the little slipper peeping from beneath her gown. Then she looked up at me once more with that innocent, appealing look I knew so well.

"Hugh, will you tell Papa and Mama how much we miss them?"

"I will indeed."

"And will you say . . ."

"Yes?"

"Will you say that . . . that I am very well, now, and that I am living with . . . that I am living quite near Doris? I neglected to speak of that in my letters."

"I shall be happy to," I replied.

Doris drew out a tiny watch, scarcely as large as a shilling-piece, from a hidden pocket at her waist.

"We really must make haste, Phoebe!" she exclaimed. "It's nearly four o'clock!" She held out her hand, with a little mocking smile. "Good-bye, Mr. Tallant. It's been so nice, seeing you once more. I hope you have a *very* pleasant voyage."

I seated myself on the bench and watched the two sisters moving along the drive to where the chariot waited. They chatted as they walked, seemingly unconscious of the many heads that turned to look after them. They stepped into their carriage, the footman sprang to his seat, and a moment later they were lost to view.

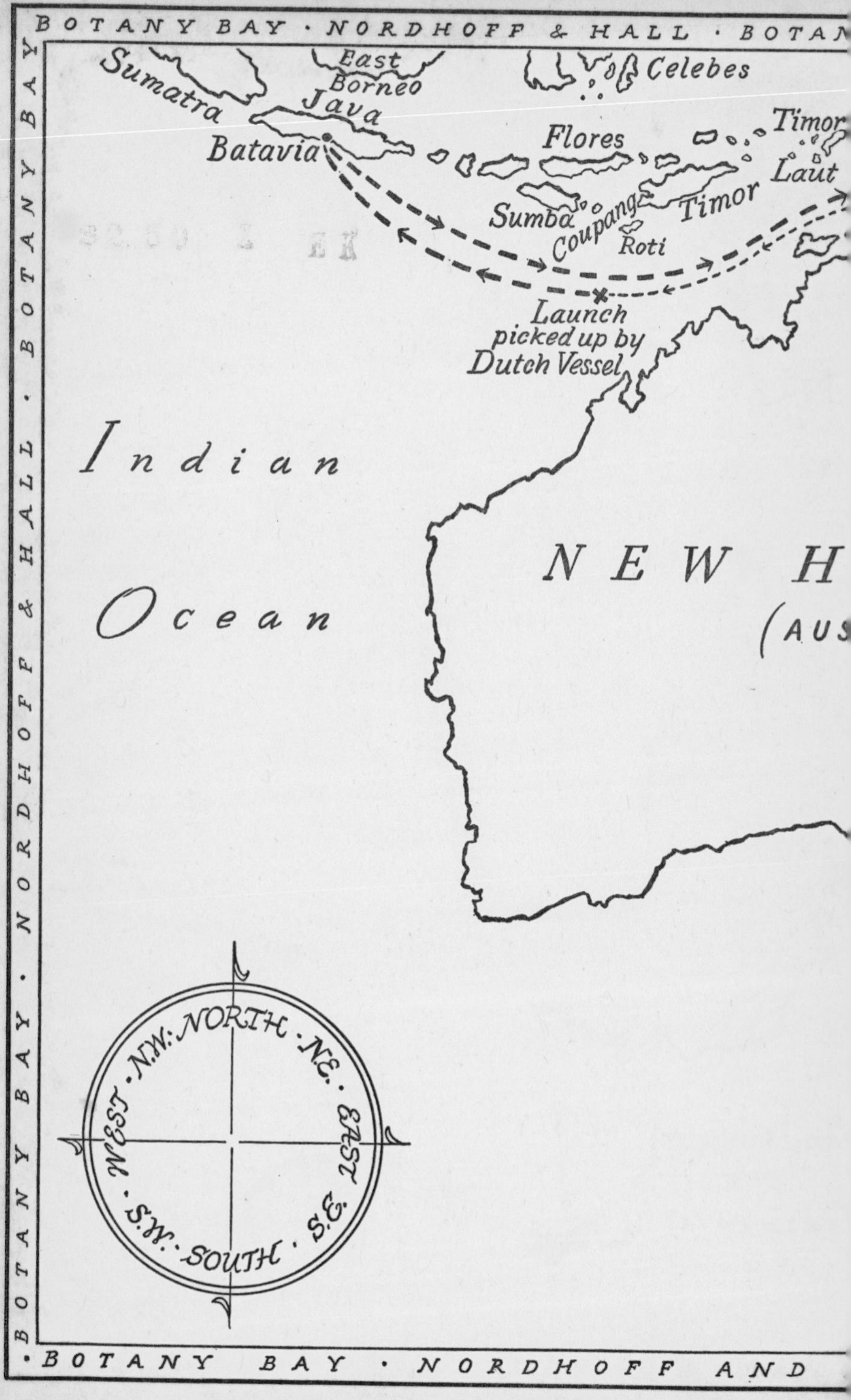